Redemption Road

By

Michael J. Griffin

To Pat —
with best wishes.
Thanks for reading!

authorHOUSE™

1663 LIBERTY DRIVE, SUITE 200
BLOOMINGTON, INDIANA 47403
(800) 839-8640
WWW.AUTHORHOUSE.COM

First published by AuthorHouse 12/03/04

ISBN: 1-4184-8603-5 (sc)
ISBN: 1-4184-8602-7 (dj)

Library of Congress Control Number: 2004095475

Printed in the United States of America
Bloomington, Indiana

This book is printed on acid-free paper.

Acknowledgements:

I would like to thank several people who helped me during the writing of this book. To my "critics" Cathy Berg, Art Berke, Ann Bowman, Paul Luther, Heather Melikian and Dean Schroeder, thanks so much for your insights and advice in helping me make this story better. To my proofreader extraordinaire, Trudy Watkins, thanks for finding the missing commas and other grammatical discrepancies. To my wife, Janet, whose unflappable faith in me was much more than any man deserves, I offer my love and gratitude. To my children Heather, Shannon, Shane, Tara, Nathan, Patrick and Eric, thank you for your comments and suggestions, as well as your love and support.

"*Evil is unspectacular and always human*
And shares our bed and eats at our table"
W. H. Auden

1

In the summer of 1942, on a night torrid with the breath of the devil, Grady Hagen lost his soul. He shed it as if it were afire and left it lying in the amber splash of a streetlight, trampled by the terrible thing he had done. Now, with death gathering like storm clouds on the horizon, it was time to go get it back.

He stood in his bedroom in the house in which he had lived for three decades. Fractured light poured in through the partially drawn blinds. It splayed a pattern of gold and black stripes across his chest and arms like some kind of translucent snake coiling around him. He examined the handfuls of clothing he held in his knotted fingers, underwear in his right, five balls of socks in his left, as if weighing them. Socks. Underwear. How many pairs? Probably wouldn't need any of them, he thought. His old man's feet, encased in a pair of Hush Puppies, squeaked on the carpet as he shuffled across the room and set down the clothing next to an open suitcase on the bed. A bed on which he had slept for so many years, and one on which – if he got the punishment he deserved, if freedom was stripped from his bones as it should be – he would never sleep again.

It wasn't that someone had finally found him out, tracked him down over all the miles and all the years and showed up at his door with a badge and a warrant. Much too much time had gone by for that to happen. In fact what he had done, what he had taken part in, while not exactly legal, was simply the way things were in that place in those days. And, as far as most of the participants were concerned – even the victims – once it was over, it was over and you just got on with your life. Grady Hagen had walked away from it with the other guys who unleashed adrenaline-charged laughs and clapped the dirt off their hands and went back to their homes as simple as that. But he never did laugh it away, couldn't dust the filth of it off his skin, and it seeped into his blood and then melted into his marrow where, every now and again when real life subsided, it would sear a hole in his consciousness. But he never did a thing about it, until now.

Although stewing for ages in his memory, Grady Hagen's decision to go back to Arbutus, Mississippi to face the consequences of his actions during a sizzling, frantic August night a long, long time ago, had come as subtly as a mouse in the dark. He could never have done it while his wife, Rachel, was alive, simply because he could never reveal to her this onerous truth that spread like a stain inside him. Goodness, what would she think if she had known this about him? What would that have done to their life together which she had mapped out in Berlin, he discovered later, in the heady fever of fear and smoke and destruction, and then orchestrated like a swirling, joyous symphony that didn't stop playing for more than five decades? She could have forgiven almost any sin, but this would have been so beyond her ability to comprehend that it would have struck like a hammer, shattering their relationship, or at least denting and reshaping it into an ugly thing with sharp angles and torn rivets. And he, being a coward, could not – would not – risk that. So he held it close, in a dark space. His one sinister secret.

It would float to the surface of his consciousness at its own discretion, chirping at him for no apparent reason while he was mowing the lawn, or operating the lathe at the mill, or having a beer in the thick nicotine air of the tavern, or holding Rachel's hand while jumping the waist high waves of Lake Michigan. It would come now and again at quiet times like when he was dozing off to sleep – and at noisy times like when he was watching the White Sox, and Little Luis Aparicio was standing on first base, shadowed by big, ugly Moose Skowron of the Yankees, and the fans in Comiskey Park would begin the chant, "Go, go, go."

So, yes, coward that he was, he could be accused now of refusing to deal with it until she was gone, but the implication that he somehow waited for her to die, that he ever conceived of her death, was hideous and despicable. He always thought he would die first; that he would rot into the universe without redemption and then march straight into the maw of hell carrying that sin slung over his shoulder like a filthy jacket. But, God go figure, he was still standing, blood still pounding relentlessly through him, and she was gone.

She did it without even telling him, died right here in their living room, in her chair, the one with the wooden arm rests and the curved top; this woman who was so much better than he in every single way, who somehow drew purer breath and spoke kinder words and whose restless mind was electric with ideas and curiosity and knowledge. She died even though she had not finished her life. A load of laundry thumped in the dryer, a tea kettle whistled on the stove. She had written a short shopping list for him and peeled off just the right amount of money to pay for everything on it so that he wouldn't go and grab bags of cookies and cartons of ice cream simply because he hadn't tasted that flavor yet. Certainly she had planned to cook these things on the list, hadn't she? She had put a magnet on the blood drive post card and affixed it to the refrigerator to remind herself of the bloodmobile's appearance at the Lutheran church in a few days. When Grady came home, bag of groceries in hand, and found her, she had a magazine on her lap, open to the middle of a story about osteoporosis, and Grady wondered where her eyes had stopped. Had she learned what she wanted to learn before death snuck into the house, seeping through the crack under the door, all gray smoke and gnarled fingers, and struck her from behind? So much she hadn't finished, he remembers crying incredulously, leaning sideways on the couch with his feet still on the floor while paramedics in white shirts clicked shut their cases and covered her on a gurney. But of all the things that she hadn't finished, the most important of all was loving him. How could she be finished loving him?

A wretched excuse of a man unworthy of what she gave.

Oh, gol'dangit.

She had stayed even after her death, for most of a year. Grady could hear her humming very softly at night to, he was sure, lullaby him to sleep. Sometimes lights would be on that he knew he had turned off. Every now and again her perfume would waft in unexpectedly, and he knew she, or her spirit, or whatever, had at that moment passed close to him, making a breeze out of her wonderful aroma. Other times, the television would turn on by itself when he was in the kitchen, or his watch would be somewhere he would never leave it lying, like beneath their wedding picture, a browning ragged-edged shot of two kids, one in a uniform, his body still held together with bandages, the other luminescent in a flowing dress, yellow in his memory but simply white through the cast of sepia that lay over the image.

Oh, she had stayed all right, even though skeptics would certainly say that because everything in this house had been chosen and placed with her hands, she was always present. And Grady, had he told anyone what he experienced after her death, would have nodded and said yes, you're probably right. But of course he had told no one these ghost tales. Sarah, their only child – and why was that, why weren't there others? – was much too protective of him and, being a doctor, would treat his notions of Rachel's presence as early onset Alzheimer's which would cause undue hysteria throughout the family.

Just because he believed what he saw.

But then one day the sounds from the walls, the light coming through the kitchen window, the sizzle of the air all changed, and a soft stillness settled in the house, rendering it emptier somehow. It was as if she had made sure he was all right once and for all before completing her departure, as if that was the least she could do after dying in the snap of two fingers while he was gone only for a gol'danged half hour to the store.

And, funny thing, it took that long for him to be all right, to get used to sleeping in the center of the bed.

Except for this thing, this thing he'd kept even from her that he now had to deal with once and for all.

So, rattling around in a suit much too large for his frame, the thin gizzard of his neck not even touching the collar of his shirt, he busied about his bedroom planning an escape. No one except Grady Hagen himself knew his plan. Not his neighbors with whom he had traded so many tools and so much sugar and milk and glue and whatever that it was impossible to know to whom anything had ever belonged. Not Sarah who would, of course, be hysterical and have him locked in some kind of assisted living facility like a child. Not even his grandson Charlie who, right this minute, was on his way here and was unknowingly already a conspirator in this scheme. The boy came almost every Sunday during the summer, and the two of them would hang out all afternoon. Although Grady never could figure out why a twenty-two year old would want to blow off the better part of the day with an old man, he nonetheless got the sense that the kid didn't mind at all. Sometimes Charlie would bring his girlfriend – or fiancé to be precise – a girl he'd met in college, kind of clingy and needy in Grady's estimation, but to each his own, he supposed. Grady kind of hoped she wouldn't be along this day, because it was going to be tough enough to convince the boy to drive him fifteen miles to the bus stop up in Garrison Harbor. Once upon a time he and Rachel lived there in the gloaming of effluent that poured from the smokestacks of the steel mill, on a picture perfect street with big maple trees where kids could lay down their bikes in their front yards, go to sleep and wake up to find them still there in the morning. Where the local butcher and barber knew your name and what cut you liked best. Where the mailman was welcomed with a glass of ice water on a hot day. Then the neighborhood changed, like one can in a seismic world of shifting boundaries and evolving geography, and once the first home was sold to a black family, the others fell quickly, the sellers insisting it had nothing to do with race. Property values, you see. My God, you can't wait until your property value goes down the drain. You have to take care of yourself. It's fiscal responsibility. One of the neighbors said that it's like someone spilled ink on a tablecloth and it seeped into the threads and spread further into the fabric, ruining it. But Rachel, being who she was, was one of the last holdouts. The more old neighbors left, the more pies she baked for the new ones. She had smelled the stench of hatred in another place and time, and no matter how you dressed it up or what you called it, it was what it was, and she'd be damned to succumb to it herself. Grady went along. After all, who was he to resist? But then the gangs showed up. And the car disappeared. And a woman was raped under the streetlight on their corner. And a man was shot in the alley behind their house. And a man claiming to be a meter reader pulled a knife on Rachel and forced his way into the house as she ran screaming out the back door.

Until then. And they sold the home and took a bath on the transaction like everyone had promised, and moved out to this place in a small town surrounded by farms where things were more like they once had been. In Garrison Harbor, though, Grady could have walked six blocks to the bus station. Or taken a cab. Here you took yourself wherever you needed to go.

That's why he needed Charlie.

Grady sat down on his bed with the burnt gold spread that was fit tight as concrete. He counted what he had placed there, three stacks of perfectly folded clothes, the underwear here, the shirts there, and the slacks in between, and several pairs of socks folded into baseball sized packages. To the left was his good luck Lucky Strike tin box that he had carried across the frozen tundra of Europe more than fifty years ago. It was lying open with the holy medal coiled inside, the one that Betsy Sue McDonough had given him, the medal that was going to protect him, even him, a Baptist, she had promised. And it did, by God, go figure.

He lifted the medal from the box and let the chain weave between his fingers. The medal, the miraculous medal, was tarnished now, the silver flecked away by time, leaving black splotches all over its face. Engraved on it was the Blessed Mother, a serpent strangling beneath her feet. How ironic that this medal with the image of a woman would be a link to the two women in his life he had loved. How funny, too, that it had provided to Rachel the first words she had ever spoken to him as he lay in a metal bed in a makeshift army hospital in Germany with the summer wind blowing in through white sheets that had been hung across the chewed out wall where the Russian shells had hit. He had been out, buried in a dark well, clawing his way to a pin dot of light high above, where he found her waiting for him, hair shining copper, eyes wide and as dark as ink. And she said to him as she tucked the bandages that spiraled over his torso, "I traipse all over the Russian zone looking for a priest for you, and you decide to live. That's what I call gratitude."

Then he laughed again, as he had that day, at the thought of a Jewish girl looking for a Catholic priest for a wounded Baptist boy all because of this medal.

The combat medals were there, too, the European African Middle Eastern Ribbon, two Battle Stars, the Good Conduct Ribbon, his Purple Heart. His awards for going through it over there. Shining up at him as if they made him some kind of hero. Because he had thrown himself into storms of bullets and shaking earth and was lucky enough to be one foot to the right or left of the guy who caught it in the forehead with a bullet you could hear whizzing past like a bee? Weren't the guys in the ground as courageous, shit, even more courageous than he was? He, who wasn't, for God's sake, brave at all but scared to pissing every time a pop was heard until it numbed the mind and you didn't really give a shit anymore. Didn't really give a shit.

He squeezed the medal one more time, folded the chain around it and placed it with the other things. Next to the tin were the photos of him and Rachel and little Sarah and then big Sarah married to Dan Garrett and then little Charlie Garrett who had come along two years later. And a picture tinged yellow with age now and crinkled at the corners and splotched with sweat, his Momma on the front porch with a little baby that used to be him in her arms. It was one of the only ones he had that didn't include his old man, the piece of human shit bastard, and that's why he kept it and carried it through Europe and up here to the mills in Northwest Indiana, up to the dreaded north where the streets teemed with Yankees and Negroes, a place as foreign as Persia as far as Momma was concerned.

Then he took the Bible, a weatherworn thing, once his mother's. It hadn't been opened in decades, certainly not by him, or at least he couldn't remember ever doing it. He held it in both hands now and glanced up at the ceiling to see if Rachel was looking at him at this moment from up there wherever, knowing she would be crossing her arms and gently shaking her head to see him with a Bible in his hand.

The Bible, and whatever truth might be in it, was going to fit right there on top, and in it he would tuck the picture card, the one no one, not even Rachel had ever seen. He pushed himself up and the bedspread sprang into shape and immediately erased the imprints of his hands. A reflexive grunt came out as he steadied himself. He was a bundle of loose sticks now, and the glue that had held together the bones and the once ripe sinew that had let him glide under a fly ball, snatch it out of the sky and whip it back in a whistling arc, had dried out and lost their grip so that you couldn't distinguish his creaking from the groan of the floorboards beneath his feet. But what else would you expect from a body that had been battered, abused, ripped open, reconnoitered, sewn back up, even shot? Now he was a conglomeration of joints ground out like cigarette butts, of stringy muscles that wrapped around the bone like electrician's tape, and of who-knows-what old man's disease that might be percolating malevolently in the dark corridors of his viscera. A little squeaking of the connections should not have surprised anyone. God in heaven, it was a miracle he could move at all, and even more amazing that for all the wreckage, he still got around pretty well once he got marshaled and moving in the same direction.

But now, in this moment of his life, he was reaching as deep as he could for the strength for one last task. All he needed was just a bit more electricity crackling in his nerves and for his muscles and bones to hold together for a few more miles and then, God, take what was left.

He looked at his watch. Charlie would be here in a few minutes, and there was one more thing he needed. The most important of all. He had to hurry.

In the hallway now, opening the door to a closet, Grady extracted a three-step ladder. He centered it under the ceiling trap door and climbed to its top step. Wedging his fingers around the white knob on the edge of the door, he pulled down. The steps unfolded with a clatter, loosening dust and residue that floated onto his head and shoulders. Grabbing the handrail, he put one foot up and used all his strength to mount the wobbly stairs. He worked his way upward and thrust himself into that musty, hot, familiar old-smelling air that sat in a huge bubble under the rafters of his home. At the top of the steps was another long string and he held shakily onto the rail with one hand as he reached up and pulled it gently, praying that the damned light bulb which hadn't been lit or changed in maybe five years would ignite, which it did with a noticeable click, spraying amber light over the stuff, the piles of stuff, the debris from Graden Hagen's life. Boxes were stacked akimbo and leaned against the inside of the roof like drunks on a street corner. One was short and fat with "Christmas/Chanukah" written in Rachel's perfect penmanship, another with "Sarah's School Mementos," another taller one that said "keepsake clothes" and an intriguing one with "who knows?" on it. Plus piles of others behind those, plastic garbage bags knotted at the top and old suitcases, some lying open. Out of the corner of his eye he caught something in motion and turned quickly enough to see a mouse scurrying to safety behind some of the boxes.

"Yeah, you better hide, you little prick," he growled. "I see you again I'll stomp hell out of you." He didn't like mice much. Came from his days using the outhouse in Mississippi.

Grady navigated between the boxes. So many things, so much life gone by, in the fury and flurry of noise and colors and words and thoughts and emotions. So many things so important, useless now, evaporated into space. Eighty years. Good Lord Almighty. Grady Hagen could rake through the debris of those eighty years and, perhaps, find enough remnants to fill two, three, maybe five at the most. So what happened to everything else? What happened to eighty years of steak dinners and car rides, and pieces machined in the steel mill, mortgage payments, doctor appointments, family picnics, bumps, bruises, thoughts and ideas and dreams? He lost all of them. All except one. It was the reason he was in the attic at all.

The picture card. He knew right where to find it because he had hidden it centuries ago by wedging it under an angle where a roof truss connected to a supporting beam, at the very end, far from where anyone would ever dream to look. So he held one hand above him to steady his steps and struggled to the end of the attic across the planks he had laid on the ceiling joists and reached high into the dark corner through silky cobwebs. His fingers trundled over the wood like a giant spider until they found the tattered edges of the picture. He gently slipped his thumb beneath a corner and wiggled the card free.

He took it, without looking at it, pulling it closely to his chest in case Charlie came in, and retraced his steps through the attic and down the rickety stairs.

He returned to the bed, sat down, placed the tin on his lap and took the post card away from his chest. It shook in his fingers as he held it to the light. More than a half century ago in the battle that would be called "the Bulge" his hands were white from blood frozen to a standstill in the veins, and everything he touched, his cartridges, his cigarettes, the Zippo lighter, shook just like this. Now the crooked fingers were frozen by time and covered in transparent parchment skin that leaked blue through the pores. But the shaking wasn't from any of that, not from time, nor pain, nor injury, but rather from the image on the card. In his fantasies he imagined that he would go to retrieve the card and it would not be there, or perhaps the image would have somehow changed to, say, a fishing boat from a Florida resort, and everything that had happened would have been just a dream. But of course that wasn't going to happen, and what had always been there was still there.

Like it had done so many times before, the photo cried out to him, and he tilted it into the shimmering threads of sunlight that slanted in through the drawn blinds and illuminated tiny bits of dust that floated off the card, each speck a memory, each memory a feeling. He bit his lip as he gazed at it.

From the clouds of an umber patina emerged an amoeba of people, gathered together in the center of a town he knew very well. Spilling out the door of the jailhouse and onto the street, old men and young men and women and children smiled, celebrated, and grinned at the camera with eyes white with evil delight. Posed like a baseball team that just won the big game. A gnarled tree crawled up the right margin of the picture, arthritic in its twists and bends. One huge branch extended out over the sea of faces, and from it hung a black man, his clothes hanging in ribbons as if they had been shredded by the teeth of some hideous beast. His legs were exposed almost to his knees and pockmarked with splotches of black that could have been blood. His head was tilted to one side so that his face was away from the camera lens. His feet were bound, and a piece of rope dangled loosely from his right arm.

In the foreground of the photo, almost dead center of the scene, were two young men. One was holding the wrist of the other, lifting his arm like a referee announcing the winner of a boxing match. Grady's eyes bore through the decades between then and now and locked onto the silent and still gaze of the boy whose arm was being lofted. Eyes to eyes. His own eyes to his own eyes. Oh, if that boy could gaze across the sea of time that wafted between them! If he could see this old man staring at him so far in the future, the same way the old man could look into the past. But it was a one-way mirror, wasn't it? And the young Grady Hagen in the hideous postcard had no way of knowing or sensing the pall of melancholy and shame that would follow him like a shadow from that moment until now.

Glory lord above, Grady thought, what sort of time and sensibility could make men act in this way and then - and then - take pictures like this and make them into post cards and sell them as souvenirs? Of course, at the time it didn't seem out of the ordinary at all.

He could have destroyed the post card a hundred times over, but he kept it because he knew that someday he would go back to it, go back to that boy who had been there that night and shake him silly until his teeth rattled in his head to get him to stop, to turn, to suck up from the depths of his guts enough courage to do what he was going to do now. He had seen himself doing it many times, walking into the Sheriff's office down there in Arbutus and dropping the photo card on the desk. Only in Grady's mind, the man behind the desk in the khaki colored policeman's shirt with fleshy gaps between the straining buttons and sweat splotches spreading like the tide from the armpits was old Chief Cecil LaGrone who was long dead now, and the boy dropping the card was a scared shitless seventeen-year-old.

He picked up the worn black Bible, and inserted the post card on the designated page as if, somehow, the words on the paper could erase the terrible image. Before closing the book he walked his fingers over the ancient lines of the psalm: "Oh, loving and kind God, have mercy. Have pity on me and take away the awful stain of my transgression. Oh, wash me, cleanse me from this guilt. Let me be pure again."

He closed the cover, placed it neatly into the tin and clicked the lid back on firmly. Then he ratcheted himself upright and moved to the window and opened the blinds that had been closed to conceal his furtive activities. Immediately a flood of white light overpowered the room and washed over him. He looked out at the summer day and noticed the bright red roses scratching against the glass in the breeze. Rachel's roses. She had planted them, by God, herself, on her knees in the mud a thousand autumns ago, a pair of worn out work gloves from the mill running half way up her delicate arm, a swath of earth cut into her forehead where she had wiped the sweat. And from that day, every year since, without coaxing or cajoling, these flowers would explode on the thorny vines, red and fragrant and as big as softballs. After all, that was what she did – bring life. She was an agent of life, a purveyor of life, and every person or flower or puppy who knew her lived better in her atmosphere.

"I suppose you want to know what's going on here, don't you?" Grady said, squinting into the waves of light rolling through the window. "It's just about the only thing I never told you - of the things about me that mattered, I mean." Then he remembered again that she was gone, and he stopped himself and rubbed the back of his head, embarrassed by his own foolishness. Old man, decrepit and addled, talking to himself. But the few words that had escaped had opened a flood gate, igniting in his mind scenes and thoughts and sounds and smells that he had not encountered for many, many years, though they were always somewhere behind him, panting to keep up as he raced through his life. The very act of packing and the thought of the miles ahead had his mind thrumming in counter rhythm to his heart, all agitated with memories. It was like they were in there, in his head, on so many scraps of paper, words and pictures, and a wind was blowing and rustling them up until one blew into his line of sight and he caught a glimpse of it and it was as real for that fraction of a second as if he was back there again. Then it blew away and another would flutter by.

What he truly desired, what would have made all upon which he was about to embark so much easier, was to be able to tell someone his story. It was lying in his gut and needed to be vomited, if only to make him feel better. Not because he thought he could explain it so well that it would somehow exonerate him from his sins, but just so that the listener might in some way understand that he was not, at the core, evil. That what he had done was pulled into his marrow from the land where he lived just as a tree pulls water through its roots.

And if he could tell his story, if he could get over his shame and spit out the words, he knew where to start.

2

Arbutus, Mississippi – June, 1935

Grady Hagen stood alone, swallowed up in his own anger and misery, surrounded by cattails that jittered in a whispered morning breeze. The sun had climbed only partway up the wall of the horizon, spilling nectar across Boone's Pond, but the promise of its rage was already being spoken, and Grady could feel the heat sucking sweat from his pores as he flung his fishing line again and again at the patch of fronds and lilies across the way. "Gol'dangit," he spat every time it got tangled. "Sumbitch. Piece of shit."

On real days, in normal times, this was one of Grady's favorite places, aside, of course from the baseball field. Here with his pants rolled up, shoes on the bank, warm brown water dancing on his calves, he could be alone, away from the people and things that drove him nuts. But today his arm where his old man had grabbed him and threw him against the wall was so sore that every thrust of the bamboo pole sent a lightning shock from his biceps to his fingertips. But this pain was nothing compared to the agony inside that echoed with every beat of his heart, and less than nothing compared to what Momma had gotten again last night when the asshole came stumbling home and fell onto the table where she had set out his dinner and knocked the food onto the floor, then blamed her and started to beat on her like he liked to do.

The summer sky in Mississippi in July sounds like bacon sizzling from the instinctual symphony of chirps and whistles and trills and

13

belches of the insects in the weeds and the frogs on the banks. And, by God, wasn't it hot enough to cook bacon just by holding it up on the end of a stick? But today these sounds were joined with another refrain. "Gol'dangit. Sumbitch. Gimme back that, you piece of shit." All because of the old man, who, Grady had decided once and for all, he was going to kill.

The question was how to do it? Bo Hagen was a big man with shoulders that rolled up 'pert near to his ears so it looked like his head was just screwed into the middle of his chest. His arms were like the quivers on a horse and his hands were swollen to the size of a pig's head. Probably from toting lumber all day at Fletcher Moody's mill, loading armfuls of two-bys like they was kindling. Funny thing was, for all the mass and bluster of his upper torso, what attached Bo to the ground were two chicken legs no bigger 'round than a shovel handle and all knobby and hairless. Graden Hagen, on the other hand, was only ten years old and weighed nothing, at least in his old man's hands.

The pole whistled over Grady's right ear and the payload on the end of the line flew to the thicket of stuff, getting hung up on top of some tails. "Damnation! Come on, get out of there you bastard," he cried, jiggling the line to free it. He reached out and pulled the line toward himself. By God, the worm was still there stuck on the hook as sure as anything. Cissy Moody – Clarissa was her real name, but she made it clear with her hands on her hips that everyone should call her Cissy – had invented a new way to put the worm on the hook so it wouldn't come off. And she was a gol'durned girl, too!

Originally, Grady's plan was to grow up and play in the major leagues and take Momma out of here and leave the old man to stew in his own moonshine or drown in his own piss, whichever came first. But that was still a few years off, and after last night, Grady had decided he couldn't wait that long. But it would have to be discreet. He couldn't just grab the shotgun and blow the old man's guts right out through a colander of holes in his back. Down here in Mississippi, beating on your wife and kid didn't warrant that kind of response, particularly when they probably deserved it anyway.

This time the hook and sinker found a hole in the water and plopped easily, gently wafting to the bottom. "Now we got it," Grady said, waiting for that big old bass to come strolling by, or maybe even a granddaddy catfish big as a possum.

Maybe if the old man passed out, Grady thought, he could jam a piece of meat down his throat and then make it look like he choked to death. Yes! That would work. But what would Momma do? Frankly, even she pissed him off sometimes. She would take the beating as if she deserved it and then help her husband to bed when he passed out and pull off his boots before putting a cold rag on her own swelling eye or lip. Then she would get up in the morning and make breakfast for him like nothing happened.

The line stood as still as a picture in the water and Grady grew impatient. He pulled it out again and tossed it farther, toward another shady clump of cattails and weeds. He felt a tug and pulled to set the hook, but again it had gotten tangled. "Damn fish know where to hide, sumbitch," he growled.

It was getting late, and he knew Billie Rae Tolleston, Jr. whose daddy owned the hardware store and who knew everything there was to know about everything would be rounding up the other boys for some baseball, those that wasn't in the fields. Thank God his dad didn't have crops to bring in every year, particularly cotton, which was a pain in the ass to pick which was why mostly niggers and Mexicans and hillbillies did that work. And Billie Rae would make sure, somehow, that Grady was on his team, even if the big kids showed up because Grady was already better than anyone in the neighborhood. For an instant Grady thought that maybe Billie Rae could be enlisted to help him put the old man down, but that concept was soon dismissed with a snort. Billie Rae was scared to death of old Bo Hagen.

Cissy, on the other hand, now here was an ally with enough piss in her to take him down by herself, if need be, especially considering what he done to Momma.

He tossed the line again, arcing the bamboo pole over his shoulder expertly between two cattails, and the hook, line and sinker landed with a definitive plop and disappeared in that shadowy spot where he knew, just knew, his fish was taking it easy and looking for breakfast. Immediately he felt the hook tangle and he cursed again and pulled on the line, but this time it wouldn't come free. He jerked it again. Above the water not a single strand of pond vegetation moved and the hook remained lodged in the invisible world beneath the water. "Sumbitch," he said, yanking again, this time until the bamboo pole bent like a bow. "Sumbitch, gol'dangit," he screamed and changed hands to get more leverage. Once again the line wouldn't budge. Shit. He couldn't afford to lose another hook and sinker. In these days scraping together the few pennies it took to buy one wasn't easy. So, he dropped the pole on the bank, pulled his pants a little higher and waded into the pond. A gentle, slippery ooze caressed his feet. He grabbed at a strand of cattail to steady himself as he slid deeper into the water. Then in a rush of sudden speed that caught him entirely unprepared, the ground fell out from beneath him and the sun disappeared. A torrent of water rushed into his mouth, cutting through his throat, and he flailed at the shimmer of light above him, reaching for it so he could just - just get one more breath.

Miraculously his head broke through and he unleashed a fountain of muddy water, coughing, spewing, and then just as quickly, something pulled at him again and he was going down at an unstoppable speed. Instinctively he closed his mouth and held his breath just as the water folded over his head.

He then realized he was caught. His foot was twisted in a snare of weeds that seemed to attack, wrapping, strangling his ankle, pulling him down. His cheeks puffed with air, his eyes bulged as he bent at the waist and tried to free his foot. His lungs screamed for oxygen and burned with a fire that raged all the way to the top of his head. But the more he clawed at the tentacles wrapping his leg the more others seemed to join in this conspiracy, as if this pond had suddenly come alive and decided to take revenge and mustered all its resources to come fly to this spot. He yanked and pulled and scratched, but he was losing it, he was going. He felt his strength sapping away from him.

Then everything stopped and darkness took over.

Almost instantly – or was it years later? – he felt himself flying. He could see the sky above, the sun bouncing. His insides shook violently and he puked water onto the ground that, for some inexplicable reason, was whirring past his eyes. Desperately he fought to make sense of where he was and what was happening, but his mind could not assemble a coherent thought. Then suddenly he heard voices.

"Oh my God, oh my God, my sweet Jesus, my sweet Jesus." It was a woman's voice, and it seemed to be coming closer. Sumbitch, Grady thought to himself. He raised his head and looked up. A silhouette came into his line of vision. The shape of a woman, that much he could tell. She seemed to glow from behind in spraying jewels of sunlight. Maybe he was in heaven and this was an angel or whatever, but why was he still bouncing and puking and gasping if he was already there where the preacher had told him the streets were paved with gold and there was no more pain or suffering? As he thought this he began to slide downward and instinctively put out his hands which crashed into solid ground. This ain't heaven, he thought, the ground is too damn hard.

"Rudy, what you do? What you do to this boy?" the woman's voice exclaimed again as Grady hit the dirt and rolled onto his back which sent him into another spasm.

"Nuttin' Momma. He was drowin' in the pond and I pulled him out," a boy's voice answered.

Grady shook his head as a pair of gentle hands rolled him onto his side. He was still spitting and coughing. "Lie there, boy, on your side and get it all out, get it all out," the woman said, patting him on the back. Things began to clear for him and he realized first that he wasn't dead as he expectorated a last dollop of swamp water and then reflexively belched. "That's a boy," the lady encouraged, stroking his forehead.

"Rudy, run to the house and get me something to wipe this boy's face. I got a clean rag drying 'bove the stove," she said, placing a hand on Grady's back and helping him to a sitting position. "You come, sit up now. Take it easy."

It was then that the scene focused in Grady's eyes and he was facing a woman, a colored woman. A little girl hid behind her pale blue skirt, kneading it into a ball in her tiny hands. Grady instinctively jumped backwards, his ass scraping the ground below him.

"Be careful, boy, don't worry," the lady stammered. The little girl buried her face in the skirt.

Grady squinted against the sun and cocked his head to get a better look at her. She was definitely a Negro lady, but young, somewhere between his momma's age and the girls in high school. As these thoughts subsided, he realized he was reaching up and stroking her face. Her skin was the color of tea and was perfectly smooth, and she was, well, as far as Negroes go, almost beautiful. He pulled his hand back. She grabbed it in her own which were rough, cracked, calloused and incredibly strong. "C'mon, I'll help you up if you wants to get up." She turned to the little girl. "Charlotta, please let go your momma's skirt so's she can help up this poor boy." Charlotta dug deeper into the fabric and closed her eyes.

Grady staggered to his feet like a newborn colt. "What? Who are you?"

"You're that Hagen boy, ain't you?" she asked, picking strands off his shirt. "I'm Mizz Principia Montcrief. And this is my baby Charlotta who is scared t'death of most everyone."

Montcrief. Of course, the colored family with the boy and the little girl who lived on the other side of Clayton's field. But that was a good quarter mile, maybe a half mile, from Boone's Pond and clear around the southern end. "What, how did I get here?"

Just then Rudy Montcrief burst from the house and flew down the steps in two quick strides and handed his momma a thin cotton towel. She took it and immediately began to wipe mud from Grady's face. "Here, let's clean you up," she said.

Grady jerked backward from the towel. "Uh, no, no, that's okay," he answered, realizing that he was actually letting Negroes touch him and minister to him and he had barely ever spoken to one, let alone actually felt their skin against his. It just wasn't right.

Principia kneaded the towel in her hand and took a step backward as if she could read his thoughts. She spoke softly, "My boy, Rudy, brung you here. Said you was drownin' in the pond."

Grady looked at Rudy Montcrief. He had seen him around before. On the periphery of life in Arbutus. Most of the Negroes stayed there outside the invisible lines as they were supposed to, coming into town for supplies and whatnot, but not getting in the way. Hard to believe he was Principia's son. Didn't look but a few years younger than her.

Rudy was standing there, his head turned so as not to make eye contact, and Grady could see that his chest was still heaving from the exertion of carrying him so far. The boy was two or three years older than him, but already looked like a man, 'pert near six feet tall with a man's arms and a man's chest. He didn't look real. It was almost as if he was transparent and you could see right through to the muscles cascading beneath his dark skin in perfect symmetry, like waves on the sea. He was more like one of those statues from Rome or whatever, Greece, that Grady had seen in the encyclopedia. Like that one statue of the guy with his little dick hanging out. Only black. Just a Mississippi nigger, that's all.

But at least he knew his place. His head was staring down at his feet, daring not to look up at Grady.

Grady's head swiveled from Rudy to Principia, who was leaning away from him at a severe angle, cowering backwards, ringing her own hands with her towel. "Drowning? What's he talking about? I wasn't drowning," he grunted, turning and walking away.

3

Charlie roared around the corner, arm hanging over the door of the bright red Mustang convertible, baseball cap on backwards, shades just right, boom box stereo bouncing the engine against its bolts. The small brick bungalows nestled behind huge maples and oaks, straight as soldiers in formation, were a blur, and the sudden thundering sound and burst of red on the landscape seemed to shake the leaves and make the stop signs shiver. The last turn put him in sight of Pappy's brown brick house with the matching garage at its side. He could see little Mrs. Caminiti puttering in her flower bed next door, and as he squealed into the driveway, she got up off her knees and looked at him, shaking her head in disdain or disbelief or bemusement at the color and noise that had suddenly entered her world. She stood there, hands dripping dirt, and put a finger to her mouth.

"Charlie, you come in here like a tornado!" she exclaimed as he shut down the engine just in time to let the words cut through the echoing din.

"Sorry, Mrs. C!" he greeted her, lifting a leg over the door and leaping out in a single smooth move.

"I used to be able to do that," Mrs. Caminiti said, shaking her hips, "when I was young and wild."

Charlie smiled and winked at her. "You're still young and wild, Mrs. C. You can't fool me."

"Where you taking your grandpa today?"

Charlie shrugged. "Aw, who knows? Maybe to the beach."

"Don't forget the ice cream."

"Believe me, he won't let me forget the ice cream," Charlie said, waving and backing toward the front door.

She shook a spade at him. "Watch him. He's up to something."

Charlie stopped. She was sweet on Pap, he was certain. "Like what?"

"Something's going on in his wrinkled old head. He's been bringing stuff back to everyone in the neighborhood, stuff he thinks he borrowed, like he's planning on . . ." she stopped, a sudden sadness in her eyes.

"Planning on?"

She forced a smile. "He's a crazy old coot. Who knows what he's thinking?" She turned and knelt down, driving the spade into the dirt.

Crazy old coot, indeed. What a character. Didn't weigh more than 160 pounds soaking wet, slathered over a six foot two inch frame, but he ruled like Goliath. Wanted things his way, not in a mean way, but just the way he wanted them. And he'd let you know with a pierce from his cobalt blue eyes that would run through you like a laser beam. Didn't have to say much. Just nail you to the floor with those eyes that fired out from the gaunt face that had grown even more sallow and distant since Nonnie Rachel had died, poor old guy. He was, perhaps, Charlie's best friend. A lot of what he learned in life was from his grandfather because Dad was too busy building his law practice and Mom, being a doctor, was always out fixing someone.

Pappy taught him how to fish. Taught him gin rummy and chess. Showed him how to grip and release a baseball so that it curved right at the perfect spot. And even with his skinny old arms, Pappy could still break one off that spun like a car on ice. So, coming on Sundays was cool because Charlie could spring Pappy out for a few hours and the two of them could hop into the Mustang his parents had given him for earning a Phi Beta Kappa key, and drive with the top down, and go and get ice cream and then maybe head out to the dunes and shuffle along the beach with their hands in their pockets and no socks on their feet and talk.

This was the first free and clear summer Charlie had since he was a little kid. Even though both parents crammed a lot of cash into their bank accounts every other Friday or whatever, they expected him to pay a portion of his own way, to understand the value of money and hard work and blah, blah, blah. So, while they could have shoveled some jack to the bursar and taken care of everything without breaking sweat, they made him work every summer, the usual fare – flipping burgers, waiting tables, even building houses which was actually kind of fun. But this summer was all his because he had pleased both of them to no end by applying to medical school.

Pleased them to no end, yeah, even though medical school was never anything he had ever considered, not that he had considered much at all. Shit, he never even played doctor when he was a kid. Didn't give a flying fuck about his mom's little doctor kit, or her office, or the hospital where she routinely, he guessed, saved lives and made pain go away, which sounded and seemed cool, he supposed, but never rang a single one of his chimes. Actually there had been a silent competition for his soul between Mom and Dad, something never spoken but something always hovering in the air in the family room and over the kitchen table, giving off some kind of subtle scent. Dad worked the lawyer angle now and again, using his fork to point as the juice dripped down onto his shirt. Mom would come home and shake herself out of her coat saying how great it was to see old man "what-the-fuck" up and around. When Charlie made his decision, he made them both sit down in the living room on the couch next to the fireplace and made it clear how hard the choice was. When he said med school, Dad stood up and clapped his hands, and then shook Charlie's and patted him on the back like he wasn't a teensy weensy bit hurt, but you could still sense it on him. Mom hugged him and didn't say too much, didn't gloat, but she was pissing-her-pants happy.

Charlie, the guy over whom all this attention was fussed, didn't give either option more than one minute's thought, truth be told. With a dual major in chemistry and business administration, plus a straight A average top to bottom, he could have gone either way and had the med school or law school of his choice licking his face like a puppy. Law school had its plusses, only three years. But it seemed like the only way to make a killing in law was by trading in people's misery. And who in the goddamn hell needed more lawyers anyway? Med school was longer, probably harder, but maybe a tiny bit more fun, and, hey, most of your patients didn't die. Right? Either way, it was just a job, and he was growing up and needed some kind of job, he supposed, and one was as good as the other. So, he did what he'd always done in every aspect of his life – live up to Mom and Dad's high expectations and do what they wanted because it was easier than arguing and, quite frankly, he could pull it off without too much sweat. Then he negotiated a free summer and spent it hanging out and trying to figure how to get out of the whole med school thing altogether and do what he really wanted to do which was far below anything his overachieving parents had ever considered. If that was possible.

Now he was trundling up the sidewalk, all his parts flowing like they do when you're twenty-two. A few steps from the porch he jumped at the vibration against his thigh. He reached down and pulled the cell phone off his belt. He turned the display away from the bright sunlight. "Shit," he whispered, reading the name on the display. He pushed the green receive button and put the phone to his ear.

"Hey, Reenie," he said.

"Hi, baby. Where are you?" his fiancée Lorene asked.

"I'm at my granddad's house. Same place I go every Sunday."

"Yeah, I know." She took a deep breath. "You didn't want me to come this time?"

Holy crap. "Sure, I wanted you to come, it's just . . ."

"What? What is it?"

"Uh, I'm getting a little worried about you and him. The way he looks at you. And you; I think you're getting a crush on him. I don't want to lose you to him, know what I mean?"

"How long will you be?"

"That was a joke, Lorene. You could at least chuckle."

"It wasn't that funny."

Charlie bit his lower lip. "A couple of hours is all."

"Are you coming over after that?"

Charlie removed his baseball cap and pushed his hair back as he replaced it. "Yeah, probably."

"You don't sound too enthused," Lorene snapped.

"Jesus, Reenie, it's my grandpa I'm visiting, not some hooker."

"I just don't see why you have to go over there all the time rather than be with me."

Good Lord. "Once a week, Reenie. That's all." He was on the porch stoop now. "Hey, I gotta go. I'll call you when we're done."

"Promise?"

"Yeah. Gotta go."

"I love you."

"Yeah, love you, too," Charlie said, disengaging the call.

"That your fiancé on the phone there?" Mrs. Caminiti said, wiping her forehead with her sleeve. "She's a pretty girl."

"I told you, Mrs. C, if you were only twenty years younger," Charlie smiled as he clipped the phone back onto his belt.

"Charlie!" she blushed. "When is the big day?"

"Oh, not set yet, what with med school and stuff. Maybe next year."

Mrs. Caminiti shook her spade at him again. "Fiddlesticks, young man. Don't you use medical school as an excuse. Plenty of med students are married."

"Sure, Mrs. C." he replied hopping the step on Pappy's porch. He knocked on the door and opened it in the same motion. "Road trip!" he bellowed. "Anybody wanna go pick up some chicks?"

"That you, boy?" Grady answered in that voice that still had about a teaspoon of southern accent in it.

"Yeah, Pappy, just me."

"Come on back here in my bedroom, give me a hand."

Charlie strode through the living room toward the partially closed bedroom door. It swung open suddenly, throwing into the hallway shafts of light that made Charlie recoil and shield his eyes. He stood in the threshold, squinting to regain his visual equilibrium. "We going or what?" he asked, eyes opening and closing against the butterscotch waves of sunlight that poured in through the bedroom windows.

Grady waved his grandson into the room with a plume of socks in one hand and a stack of shirts in the other. "Just finishing up here," he said, getting to the bed in two strides and sitting down on the stiff bedspread that responded with an emphatic sigh. He shaped and placed the last of his clothes into an open suitcase, pressed the lid down and clicked the clasps.

Charlie surveyed the activity of his grandfather. "What's all this?"

Grady scratched the back of his neck and said, "Little change of plans. Probably should have told you. I'm going on a little vacation."

"What do you mean?"

"I mean I'm going on a little vacation. What? Do I have to say it in French to get through your college educated mind?"

Charlie laughed. "Just like that? You're going on a vacation?"

"Yup." Grady dusted the top of the suitcase and picked it up.

"Where?"

"Back home."

Charlie wasn't sure what he was talking about. Maybe Chicago where he and Nonnie Rachel had lived when they first got married. "You mean Chicago?"

"Not that home. Arbutus."

"Arbutus?"

"Yeah, I told you about Arbutus. In Mississippi."

"Where you grew up."

"Right," the old man grunted, struggling again to his feet. He listed to one side under the weight of the suitcase.

"Why?"

"Why not? Haven't been there since the end of the war, but then just long enough to turn around and skedaddle up here. I thought now was as good a time as any to see how much the old place has changed. All I need you to do is get me to the bus station up Garrison Harbor way and let me get on the bus and don't go calling your momma or daddy and getting them all stirred up until I'm gone," Grady admonished, shaking his index finger.

"So, Mom doesn't know about this."

"Hell, no," Grady answered. "You think I'm nuts? She'd have a conniption. She thinks I'm too old and feeble for anything." He set the suitcase down and took a few deep breaths.

"You are kind of old and feeble," Charlie joshed, putting up his dukes and rolling them like a drunken boxer.

Grady Hagen's eyes opened wide, flashing bright blue. He rolled up a sleeve on his shirt and flexed his right arm. "Here, here boy. I'll show you old and feeble. Feel this muscle and tell me you think I'm old and feeble. Old and feeble my ass."

Charlie playfully pushed him away. "Momma's right about one thing, you're ornery as an alley cat, but are you sure you can handle this?"

Grady rubbed his temple and seemed to be trying to catch his breath. Then he lifted the suitcase again and turned to the boy. "You know, boy, I am an old fart that's been blowing in the wind a long, long time, and at some point I'm gonna become so decrepit and addled, your momma and daddy are gonna throw me into the old folks Hilton where I'll be doing crossword puzzles and eating pre-chewed food and watching the skin shrivel up on my house mates." He took the boy's forearm in his hand. "Before that happens, I want to live a little. Reminisce. Right now I can still do this, can still get around." He shifted the suitcase to his other hand. "So, let's go," he said.

"By yourself?" Charlie shook his head. "I don't know."

"Sure. Why not? You think I'm gonna get lost and wander into a pond or something?"

This was vintage grandpa. Another eccentric, wild idea. Charlie had to reorganize his thoughts, figure it out. "Wait, wait, Pappy. Come on, sit down," he said, taking the suitcase. The old man crinkled onto the bed. Charlie dropped the suitcase onto the floor and sat beside him. "How long are you going to be down there?"

"Maybe a week or two, that's all. I called my cousin Truman who lives in my old house and he said hell yes, come on down." He stopped and coughed into his fist.

Then the idea came to him. Charlie slapped a hand on his thigh and stood up. "Hey. Cool. Vacation. What the hell?"

"All right. Let's go," Grady said, clapping his hands.

"We're off to see the wizard," Charlie answered, sweeping his hat off his head and running his fingers through his hair. Then he muttered, "Mom will kill me, you know that." He put his hat back on.

"Just tell her I made you do it."

Charlie raised an eyebrow. "And she will buy that, you think? Mom? Doctor Mom?" A thousand thoughts swirled like gnats inside the walls of Charlie's brain, and he tried to pluck one or two from the swarm. Finally, he looked at the old man and put his hand on his shoulder, and then took the suitcase from the floor. "Okay, let's go," he said.

Grady moved through the doorway. "We're burning daylight."

"First we gotta stop at my house," Charlie answered as he moved to the door. "So, I can load some clothes into a gym bag for myself."

"For what? Where are you going?"

Charlie slid through the door and faced the old man. "To Arbutus, Mississippi."

"You mean both of us?" Grady exhaled.

"Why the hell not?"

"Nope."

"What do you mean, 'nope'?"

"Nope means no."

"Well, then, I hope you got good shoes, because the bus station is a long way up the road." Charlie answered, swinging the suitcase and making his way down the hallway. "And this thing will weigh about six hundred pounds by the time you get there."

"Shit," Grady spat.

"Shit nothing. You wanna go, I'm going with you."

"You're gonna drive all the way to Mississippi?"

"Yup."

"Take me home?"

"That's the idea." Charlie swept past him.

"That's not a good idea," Grady sighed.

"Why's that?"

"It's just – don't you have class or something?"

"Not for two weeks."

The old man rubbed his cheeks, momentarily distorting his features. Charlie wondered what was wrong with him.

"I just never figured you having to go all that way," Grady said. "It ain't your situation."

"Situation? I thought it was a vacation."

Grady deflated and shook his head. "It is."

"Look, I've been sitting around here all summer with nothing to do. This could be fun. Plus, I've never even been to Mississippi. Might be educational. Meet Uncle Thurman."

"Cousin Truman," Grady corrected, shuffling forward, his feet barely lifting from the carpet.

"Yeah, him," Charlie said. He was now in the living room, walking backwards toward the front door with the suitcase handle in both hands.

Grady stepped forward and shook his head. "This isn't right."

"C'mon, Pap, it'll be fun." Charlie answered, kicking the door open with his foot. "Do you know where you're going?"

"Do I know where I'm going? Hell no," Grady whispered.

4

"Do you know where you're going?" Grady shouted through the darkness. As usual, Cissy led the way on her rusty old bike, slowing every few hundred yards and then riding in circles to wait for them to catch up. She was, in many respects, the bravest of them all, undaunted by her gender or size. She wasn't afraid to do something like this – sneak out in the middle of the night and ride through the pitch for an adventure.

Grady rode the handlebars of Billie Rae's bike down the decimated road, wobbling frantically to and fro and taking every hole in the path all the way to his teeth, just to see the forbidden city which was really just a few weary buildings buried in the hollow seven miles outside of Arbutus, away from the revenuers. Cissy had talked the two boys into following Bo Hagen on one of his nightly jaunts just to see what it was like, to get a sense of the allure that made him go and get full of the hate and rage he brought home.

And, by God, she found the secret place; rode up to it as if she had been there a thousand times.

The three kids had stayed outside the plume of blue and red and green and yellow lights that boiled out from the buildings, far enough back in the shadows and darkness so as not to be seen. But close enough to make out what was happening behind the streaked glass, bodies colliding to music and shouting and laughter spilling out onto the dirt parking lot every time the doors opened. People having an

29

amazing good time with arms and legs going every which way despite what Parson Kincaid warned about the sin of it all, this drinking and carousing. The kids could see women throwing back their heads in laughter and coughing out cigarette smoke in blossoms of blue. Imagine that, women smoking cigarettes and drinking and dancing.

Occasionally the buildings would cough out a person or two in a cloud of blue smoke, just that quick.

"Listen to that music. What is that music?" Grady whispered to Billy Rae.

"That there is jazz music," Billy Rae who knew everything, replied instantaneously. "It's basically invented by colored folk up north in Chicago and places like that."

"Chicago?"

"Yeah, my daddy went up there once for a hardware convention and told me they had buildings bigger than the tallest trees in our woods with electric elevators that took you up and down and made your stomach tickle."

"Like a Ferris wheel, I bet," Cissy interjected. "I'm gonna live in Chicago some day. Find me a rich man to marry and he'll take me there."

"And listen to nigger music?" Billie Rae laughed.

Cissy slapped him on the shoulder. "I don't like that word!"

Grady's eyes widened. "Buildings taller than our trees?"

Billy Rae nodded. "Yeah, and my daddy told me that niggers and white people might be in the same restaurant and that the coloreds, some of them, wore suits and dress-up hats like church clothes in the middle of the week."

"Stop saying 'niggers,' Billie Rae," Cissy cried.

"Why? Do you prefer 'coon'?" Billie Rae teased her and both boys laughed.

Cissy folded her arms and raised her chin. "You should call them 'colored' or 'Negro'."

"Shut up, lookee there!" Grady said pointing to the building.

The front door opened and two people staggered out, holding one another up and ambling from side to side like a huge spider. The woman was amazingly beautiful, even to eleven-year-old boys who knew very little of these sorts of things. She wore a bright yellow dress with red roses splashed all over it and flung her left arm over the man's shoulder as she laughed and hiccupped and tried to stay on her feet. The top buttons of her dress were undone and the boys could see the bright white of her slip. The man was at least a foot taller, holding her up, so that at times her feet seemed to dangle in the air. His white shirt caught the colored lights coming through the windows, but there was no mistaking the huge splotches of sweat under the armpits. He wore a hat, pushed back on his head, revealing eyes that were wet and bright. In his left hand a cigarette dangled casually. So, locked together like that, legs, four of them, going one direction or another, the man and woman bounced between the cars in the parking lot, finally coming to one. He let her go and she seemed about to fall, but caught herself on the front fender as he opened the back door and reached for her hand. He pulled her close to him and suddenly his mouth was on hers, her arms pulling at his neck and his hands wandering over her, touching her, squeezing her, yanking and pulling at her clothes. She fell into the back seat of the car, her dress now up over her knees and her two white legs flew apart as the man fell between them. There was a violence to it, actually, the frantic way he reached under her dress and grabbed and pulled until something finally gave way and slid down her legs and he tossed it over her head into the backseat of the car. Then he in an instant had unbuckled his pants, pulling them to his ankles. He seemed to pull back and then hesitate for a second, and her legs, bare now and gleaming alabaster against the black car, arched upward. The man, much gentler now than he had been only a second ago, slid her dress farther upward and moved in again.

"Billy Rae! Billy Rae! What they doing?" Grady asked, in gasps of breath.

By now the man's bare rear end was bouncing like a bad hop grounder.

Billy Rae Tolleston's eyes were wide and white and glistening with pure glee. "Why, I do believe they're doing it."

"Doing what?"

"It!"

"What's it?" Grady asked, nudging his friend.

"It! They're doing sex."

"Sex?"

"Yeah, what's that?" Cissy asked.

"The man there is putting his thing inside the woman."

"His thing?" Cissy cried.

Billie Rae pointed at his crotch. "His tinkler," he said.

"Inside her?" Cissy's eyes were wide. She looked down at her own pants and smoothed the fabric. "How does it get in there?"

"Like, remember when old Clayton's mongrel got stuck together with that beagle?" Billie Rae answered.

Grady suddenly understood. "Holy shit," he said. "My momma says that how dogs make babies."

"Don't say that word, neither," Cissy admonished.

Billie Rae Tolleston put both hands over his own mouth and bent his head between his legs to squeeze the roar of laughter that had built up in him into a few phups of loose air. "You dumb shit," he stammered. "That's how everybody makes babies."

Cissy, again, "Don't say that word!"

"My Momma and Daddy never done nothing like that," Grady cried.

"Then you musta come from the moon or someplace," Billie Rae answered.

"Eeew, I ain't never letting no man lay on me like that," Cissy squealed.

"Bet you do," Billie Rae said. "And it'll probably be Grady!" he pointed and began to laugh at both of them.

Cissy Moody stood tall and shoved him back on his ass with both her hands. "Liar!" she cried.

"It'll prolly be you, Billie Rae," Grady laughed.

"I'll knock you down, too, Grady," Cissy fumed.

The man straightened up and backed away from the car. He turned in the direction of the kids, and they ducked farther back into the darkness. As the woman sat on the edge of the car seat and refastened her clasps and buttons, the man shook his pants as he hitched them up, as if ridding them of dirt. Then he fastened them, lit a cigarette that seemed to explode in a surreal blue ghost about his head, and handed it to the lady. He stopped and stared in the direction of the kids and chuckled before reaching out and helping the woman to her feet.

5

They were on the highway, Indiana flowing past as if it had been poured from a carafe. Grady sat with his arms folded, head turned away. He watched the miasma of swirling colors that gradually took shape as the passing corn fields undulated to the horizon. The top was down on the Mustang, creating a vortex into which frantic air rushed. Road sounds engulfed the car in white noise that Grady pulled over himself like a blanket. A welcomed hindrance to conversation. Kept him from having to speak or explain. He hadn't figured on this; that the boy would want to drive him all the way to Arbutus, and thus had conjured no argument against it. In fact, in some ways it was better. No strangers sitting next to him. No fumes from a toilet. But in the end it was worse. Charlie couldn't know why Arbutus beckoned now; couldn't discover the task Grady must complete.

But they would all find out eventually, wouldn't they? All of them. Charlie. Sarah and Dan. How could they not?

Gol'dang.

But Grady Hagen wasn't about to second guess himself now. He wasn't turning back, that was for sure. No, no possibility of that taking place, not now that he had leapt off the diving board. He was going to hit the water one way or the other.

Miles later the sky began to grumble and foam, so Charlie pulled onto the shoulder of Interstate 65 and put the car in park. "Looks like it might rain," he said, flipping a switch that raised the convertible roof into place.

The abrupt change of tempo pulled Grady out of his thoughts, and he sat straighter in the seat and smoothed his clothes. Then he ran his fingers through his disheveled hair, attempting to cajole it into place. "Smells like it, too," he said. "Mind if I get out and stretch a second or two?"

"Hey, no problem, take your time."

Grady stood up slowly and pulled his hands behind his back. His muscles creaked and his joints popped, but it felt good. He turned his gaze across a field to what must have been some kind of harvester that rumbled through its own cloud of dust, chewing up stalks and spitting the debris into what looked like some kind of railroad car, out there in the middle of the crops. Then he lumbered across a swale of grass toward the field where the remaining stalks stood like soldiers.

He walked between the rows, engulfed in tall waves. It was as if they were applauding, these leaves in the wind. He stood and sucked in the sweet aroma of summer and fingered a leaf whose colors had begun to melt from green to gold at this, the end of the season. When he was a kid, they played in a field like this. Hide and seek. Maze. Maze in the maize, he chuckled to himself, just now making the pun.

"You lost or something?" a voice came from behind him, and Grady leapt back, dropping the leaf that had rested in his palm.

He knew the voice.

"Who? Who is it?" he whispered.

"You goddamned know," the voice answered. Grady's eyes followed the sound and he scanned the pickets of corn looking for . . .

There. A half dozen rows away. His old man. Bo Hagen. Still young, jaunty with his wide-brimmed hat pushed back on his head. His hawk nose still looked as if it had been shoved into the center of his face, crinkling up his eyes into two pinholes. A cigarette hung by a thread from his lower lip, making blue flowers as he spoke. The bastard. Gol'dang.

"What are you doing here?" Grady asked.

"Question is what are you doing here?" Bo clasped the cigarette in his teeth and made it wag up and down. "Headin' back home, are you?"

"Yeah. What's it to you?"

He pulled the ciggy from his mouth and tapped off an ash. "Why you doin' this? What do y'all think you're gonna get out of it?"

Grady squinted into the evaporating sun, tilting his head to get Bo into focus from behind the stalks. "You're dead."

"Uh, yeah. But just 'cause someone's dead hasn't stopped you from talkin' to them, has it? Maybe you're going crazy, and I ain't here t'all. Ever think of that?"

"One way or the other, tell me what you want."

"I'm here because you need to answer my question, if not for me, then for yourself," Bo Hagen said, fading, disappearing into the dust that wafted between the corn. "After all, who else you gonna talk to?"

"I guess nobody."

"So, like I said, why you doing this now?"

"I don't know. Maybe clear my conscience is all."

Bo stuck the shrinking butt back in his mouth and lifted the flap on the pocket of his shirt and took out a pack of Camels. He extended the pack to Grady who shook his head. "No thanks, I quit," he said.

"Yeah, me too," Bo replied. "Right after I killed myself." He shook a cigarette free, took the stub from his lips and used it to light the end of the new smoke. "Hope it wasn't too late." He flipped the remnant butt onto the ground and stepped on it. It let out a final gasp of breath from beneath his boot heel. "So, tell me what y'all are planning to do."

"Just going to go to the police station and turn myself in."

"Turn yourself in?" He squinted as a ghost of smoke swirled around his head. "What you think's gonna happen then?"

"I guess they'll deal with me, whatever police are there."

"What do you want them to do, send you to jail for the rest of your life?"

"I don't really know."

"Beat the hell out of you?"

"I don't think so."

Bo Hagen, young and fluid, not like Grady who ached just standing, shook his head. "You really ain't given this much thought now, have you?"

"I guess not."

"So, why do it?" Bo had moved now, to the other side of him, farther away. Grady followed the voice.

"Why does it matter to you?" Grady said, shoving his hands into his pockets.

"Well, now if you remember right, I was there, too, as was a whole passel of other townsfolk. Y'all are just gonna dig them and me up right outta the ground, and disgrace our family name."

"Disgrace our name? I thought that was your domain."

"Why don't you just forget this whole cockamamie bullshit plan, buster brown shoes, and turn y'all's ass around and go home," his father answered, fading in and out of the rustling stalks. "Leave us to be."

"I ain't turnin' 'round," Grady insisted, his words slipping on a muddy slope and sliding into his old accent.

"Y'all a hurtful man. You gonna do nothin' but hurt people. Your family. Your friends. Ain't gonna do no good for nobody or nothin'. Just to make you feel better."

"What's it to you?"

"You gonna tell the kid over there?" Bo asked, pinching the cigarette between thumb and forefinger and pointing toward the highway. "Or are you gonna surprise him when you get there?"

"Leave me alone, goddamnit," Grady cried, his voice pinched now, like someone letting air out of a balloon.

"That's what I thought," Bo growled. "You were always weak, like your mother."

"Go back to hell, you bastard."

"I'll see you there soon enough."

"You're a hateful sonofabitch," Grady shouted.

"Pappy!" Charlie called.

Grady spun around. His heart chewed on his ribcage, frantic for escape. God. Don't let Charlie see.

"Pappy! You talking to someone in there?" Charlie asked, the voice coming closer.

Grady pushed his way through the corn. "Man can't take a leak?" he said, emerging. He stretched his arms over his head, then horizontally, yawning all the time. "Damn, the bones are noisy. Never used to hear from them." Then he looked back, checking to make sure his hallucination had been sucked back into the atmosphere.

"Thought I heard you talking to someone," Charlie answered, moving to the driver's door. He took off his sunglasses and clipped them to the visor. Then, with one foot on the floor of the car he arched his head. "What's that smell?" he said, sniffing the air.

"What?" Grady said, looking back over his shoulder at the cornfield.

"Smells like you were smoking in there, Pap."

Grady's breath got caught in his gullet. Had the kid somehow been pulled into his insanity? He looked back at where Bo had been standing. No one was there. No one had ever been there, of course. All that had been there was a picture painted by the misfiring synapses of an old man's brain going soft in its own ooze. That, and the corn dancing rhythmically in the breeze. Then again, maybe they were real. Maybe when you're falling apart and getting ready to cross over, the ghosts come and nudge you along so's you don't get frightened.

But why would it be that monster to show up? Hadn't Bo Hagen's corrupted perspective of life been, in fact, the genesis of the evil that Grady – beginning now – was trying to expunge from his veins?

6

Grady Hagen made the biggest noise he knew how to make, whistling like his daddy taught him in a piercing scream of air that shot thin as a string from between his lips, all to scare out the shit rats who lived beneath the outhouse so that he could sit in peace. The whistle was really something for an eleven-year-old boy; in fact there wasn't anyone his age who could even come close, although, God knows, he tried to teach them. Best he could get out of any of them was a mousy, squeaky fart sound from Puddin' Pitcock's dime thin lips. Made Grady king, though, this ability, like he was taller and older and in all ways otherwise superior to the other guys. But at night with Momma in bed and Daddy gone and all kinds of creatures skulking and chattering, Grady was reduced back to his real age, and that meant being scared of things he couldn't see. Most notably it was the rats. Why on God's earth they would actually live under the outhouse and scratch through the shit and piss in the hole for food like this swamp of crap was some sort of lush garden, Grady could not understand. Too lazy, probably, to go out and get real food the way all the other rodents did. Too lazy to go and search out acorns like the squirrels and take them into their nests or dig under the fence like rabbits to get to the cabbage patch. Lazy friggin' rats they was, and they were likely waiting to come right up the sides and nibble on him to see what he tasted like with their poisonous razor teeth.

38

Of course, he tried to talk himself out of it, out of having to go. He laid atop the sheets of his bed, his skin sticking to them in the airless, tepid night, and tried to persuade his churning, storming bowels that they didn't really have to, but of course, the more he thought, the worse it got, and then he was up and heading outside, whistling to scatter the rats and whatever, whoever, so he could sit down and get done, his heart going like a band.

On his bare feet the dewy grass felt cool and refreshing. Above him was spread a sky the color of grapes and punched full of holes as if a twelve gauge had been fired again and again into it. It was, he had to admit, something to see, the night, the way it filled up every crack and crevice of the world as if it had been poured from a bowl. And, of course, the darkness delighted those who lived in it and the air was crackling with sound. Grady wondered what in their lives could necessitate so much talk -- chirping and whistling all night long; negotiating, arguing, seducing, making music? He wondered, did they have names? Each of them, every invisible cricket and bird and worm and ugly toad and silent snake and even the shit rats under the outhouse? Was there a Bobby or John or Phyllis or Karen out there in the bug world? Or did they have names no one could pronounce?

This is what Grady Hagen thought of as he made his way to the outhouse – that there probably wasn't a whole lot of difference between the bugs and reptiles and the people of the night.

Finally, he was there, and he grabbed the rope handle on the door and pulled it, making the hinges and spring squeal. As soon as he ducked inside, a spider web wrapped around his face, and he jumped back, frantically swatting at it with his hands. Damn spiders. Or was it a cob web? He wasn't really sure what a cob was or why they made webs, but he knew that he could go into the outhouse and tear down the silky scrims and go back even an hour or two later and they would be back up as if the spiders or the cobs or whatever would not let him win, would not let him scare them out even though he was bigger and stronger and smarter. No matter how many times they were torn down, they would simply start over. They would live, by God, damn the giant.

In a second he was sitting, his feet on the floor. Once not too long ago, they wouldn't reach that far down. The violet night poured in through the cracks in the planking. Something skittered beneath him. He banged his heel on the side of the stool. Just get done, get out, get back to bed, he told himself.

Then he heard the noise, the steady gentle clumping of hooves, the swish and snap of branches and bushes. Daddy. On the back of Cree, his tawny mare, no doubt. Question was, what condition would the old man be in? Drunk and ready to fight? All full of mean and ignited by the fuel he took right out of the bottle? Grady decided to play it safe, stay hunkered down and not draw attention to himself. If the old man came forward and needed his seat, well ok, Grady would just come out and not make nothing out of his being there. Just as likely, the old man would take Cree into the barn and piss outside the door before going in and toweling her down, because, even if he was too drunk to stand up, too mad to keep his fists off of Momma's head, he still took care of that mare who he loved like probably nothing else in the world. So, Grady leaned forward and closed one eye to peer through the widest crack in the door.

Cree's head, bobbing with every gentle step, emerged first from the path in the woods. Then came the rest of the horse with daddy tall and steady in the saddle, not listing like a ship. He was extraordinarily bright in the moonlight, a huge white ghost in a flowing robe that hung over both sides of the saddle, gathering at the stirrups. Grady knew the outfit, had been scared to death by it in Momma's cedar chest, the triangular hood folded with two eye holes staring up at him like a corpse. Now this same hood was draped behind the saddle horn. Grady had never seen daddy wear the outfit, though, didn't know really what it was for.

Daddy got to the barn and dismounted, his feet firm on the ground. He walked forward and Cree wearily followed him as he pulled opened the door. No need to tug the reigns for her. She knew exactly where to go. Grady heard the sizzle of a match being struck, and an amber glow poured out the barn window. He finished, pushed the door open with his foot, climbed down and rubbed his hands on the moist grass to clean up a little. Then he went to the barn.

Daddy and Cree were enveloped in a circle of orange light. She was glistening, her eyes closed as if she were already going to sleep. The light from the kerosene lamp was feeble, though, and the rest of the barn, the tools on the walls, the piles of hay, were sucked into the darkness. Daddy removed Cree's saddle and flung it over a railing, his white robe swishing against her as he did this. He then unfastened her bridle, leaning close to her. "Cree, such a good, good girl. Y'all plumb tired, I betcha," he said in a soft voice, kissing the horse on the nose. "Sorry to keep you up so late, baby, but you can rest till noon tomorrow, how's that sound?" And then, without turning or looking, he said, "Come on in, Grady, you can help me wipe her down."

Grady, who had been watching tentatively just outside the barn door, stepped forward. "How did you know I was out here?" he asked.

Bo Hagen had grabbed a towel from a rusty nail and began to wipe Cree's back with soft circular swoops. "Heard you whistle," he said. "Heard it two hundred yards up the path. Could have heard it two miles up the road. Don't know no other kid can whistle like that. Knew it had to be you, making the spooks and goblins scared."

Grady moved out of the shadows and into the light. He could smell kerosene on his dad, a sour odor that made him reflexively turn his head away. He pulled a second towel off the post and began to help wipe down the horse.

Bo spoke again, "Y'all always gotta make sure she's cooled down before you put her to bed. Y'all don't, and she could catch pneumonia and die on you just like that. All because you was lazy or dumb."

Grady was gently rotating the cotton towel across her withers and they responded by rippling beneath his hands. "Daddy, are you in the Cooley Klops Klan?" Grady tried to get his tongue around the words.

Bo Hagen stopped for a second and wiped his own hands in the towel. "Well, now, son, why do you ask that?"

"Because you're in that robe."

"How do you know what this robe means?"

"Billie Rae told me."

"That Billie Rae knows everything, doesn't he?" Bo Hagen chuckled. "We're called the Ku Klux Klan."

"What does that mean, Klu Klux Klan?"

"Ku," Bo corrected him. "Ku Klux Klan, and it means circle in Latin or Greek or something. And the robe is like a uniform."

"Like for the Confederate army?"

"Well, not exactly, but I guess you could say we're kind of an army," Bo chuckled and walked around the horse, tousling his son's hair as he went by.

"Why do you wear that," Grady asked pointing to the hood, which Bo had draped over the stall railing. "So people won't know who you are?"

"Not at all, son. The Bible tells a man not to draw attention to yourself when you do good works. We wear these hoods as a sign of humility, so that only Jesus Christ, our Lord and Savior, knows."

"Were you out doing good works tonight, Daddy?" Grady asked.

Bo closed the stall gate and walked back into the light. "Absolutely. We had a meeting to talk about some things that just have to get done around here."

"Why do you smell like that?"

Bo laughed again, lifting a corner of his robe to his nose and smelling it. "I just got so used to it, I didn't even know I stunk," he said. "But I guess I do." He reached to the hem of the robe and pulled it up and over his head. Then he laid it over the stall railing. "That's from burning the cross. We do that to symbolize the light of Jesus in the world."

"Billie Rae says you kill niggers. Did you kill one tonight?"

Bo stopped and turned to his son. "Kill niggers? Is that what he said?"

"Yep. Says the Klu – the Ku – Klux Klan hates niggers and kills them."

"Well, your pal Billie Rae don't know everything, I guess. You think I hate niggers just because they're black?"

Grady shrugged. "Don't know."

"Y'all know that boy Toby who works down at the lumber yard with me? You know, cleaning up and stuff? Y'all ever hear me say anything bad about him?"

"No, sir."

"That's 'cause he's a good colored boy who ain't shiftless and lazy and who shows the proper respect to his superiors and the white man in general. Which is why Fletcher Moody hired him in the first place. He don't say nothing to us, don't look us in the eye. Just goes about doing his work and don't make trouble. Long as coloreds understand

42

that that's how we expect them to act, then ain't gonna be no trouble whatsoever. We're Christian men, boy. We don't kill for no reason."

"Then what does the Ku Klux Klan do in their uniforms and stuff?" Grady asked, snapping some moisture off a towel and then going back to work on Cree's hindquarters.

"All we're trying to do is keep the races apart like God Almighty and Jesus Christ intended in the Bible, and once in a while you see some uppity Negro talking to a white woman or not showing the proper respect to a white man and whatnot, and then you gotta teach him and all the niggers a lesson. They see what happens when you transgress against the white race, and they ain't going to be so eager to pull any shenanigans. But going out and rabble rousing against a colored man just for the sake of rabble rousing isn't what the Klan is there for. You understand what I mean?"

"I think so."

"You're what, seven years old now, right?" Bo asked.

"Eight."

"Well, that's certainly old enough to learn a little something here, I would suspect." He stopped wiping Cree and came to the front of the horse. Then he leaned against the railing and began speaking. "After the war of northern aggression, here comes down from the North all these carpetbaggers and scalawags and profiteers with the notion of reconstructing the South but who actually set into motion what you got today which is ruining this country for the white people who civilized it."

"How are they ruining it?"

"What you have, son, is groups of people who want to do away with our way of life."

Grady stopped and turned to him. "Who?"

"You got your colored organizations who are supported by nigger-loving white people who want them voting, like they do up north. Now the problem is, they breed like animals, they do, and before you know it, you're going to have more niggers in a town than white people, and if they get to vote, you're gonna see nigger mayors and even state senators. You understand?"

Grady had stopped still, his breath escaping in short bursts. He nodded several times in a row, unable to find the words mixed up in his fear.

"You want darkies governing your state? Making laws?"

"No, sir, I sure don't."

"Me neither," Bo Hagen continued. Bo had moved to Cree's head and was massaging her gently behind the ears. "The problem with the coloreds is, they ain't got the native intelligence to deal with life the way us whites do. The know-it-alls from up North think they did the blacks a favor freeing the slaves, but look around. Do they look better off to you?"

"I don't think so."

"Dang right, son. In the slave days, the field niggers was happy and well fed. At night, my grandpappy told me, he could hear them singing songs and dancing. Now they don't know which way to turn."

"All 'cause of the northerners?"

"If that ain't enough, you got the Jews. They run the world. They own all the banks, control the money, and who could take us all down by not letting good white Christian men and women get to their money in the banks. And finally you got the Cath-lics, the papists, who say they worship Jesus Christ but who also believe the Pope is God hisself, and prayin' to all kinds of saints and the Virgin Mary instead of the one lord Jesus like the Bible says. They got one mission, and that's to make all of us just like them, kneeling and counting beads. That's who we're up against. That's our enemies. And they're enemies to America and our way of life."

By now Cree was dry and asleep on her feet. So Bo gently nudged her forward to the stall, slapping her gently on the rump. Grady hung the towels on the nails. Bo lifted the glass on the kerosene lamp and blew out the flame. Then the boy and his father were walking out of the barn. Bo put his hand on his son's shoulder. "You don't have to go telling Billie Rae or nobody about me being out tonight, okay?"

Grady climbed the steps to his front porch, his dad's big, bent fingers resting on his neck. "Okay," he said, but all he had on his mind were Negroes, Jews, and Catholics. He was going to have to think about that.

7

Grady set two bottles of cold water on the counter and reached into his back pocket for his wallet. What a world! Who would have ever thought you'd be paying a buck for a bottle of water, he grumbled to himself, as he peeled bills off the stack. "I'll also pay for the gas out there," he said, nodding past the Coca-Cola display and the racks of potato chips and candy to Charlie, who was simultaneously jiggling a nozzle in the gas receptacle with one hand and holding a cell phone up to his ear with the other. But the girl behind the counter, high school-aged, sort of cute, a cheerleader type, Grady thought, had already discovered Charlie Garrett at the fueling island and had unplugged herself from the peripheral reality beyond a few feet from him. She didn't move at all to respond to Grady, and he became fascinated watching her watch his grandson.

It didn't surprise him, really. Something came off Charlie Garrett, moved with him, invisible, yet obvious. It was wrapped up and articulated in nuance, the way he moved, like an eagle riding an eddy; the way his eyes seemed to almost reach out and engulf you when you spoke to him as if nothing – nothing in the world – was more important to him at that moment than what you had to say. He pulled a room into himself when he entered, like some benevolent black hole, sucking not only the hearts and minds of its inhabitants, but all the various components of its atmosphere. He was tall and lean, an athlete certainly, an all-state quarterback recruited by everyone from Notre Dame to Florida State, but who eschewed college athletics to pursue a double major in business and chemistry, and had pulled a perfect four-point-o through his undergrad studies.

He got all this, Grady thought, this mesmerizing charisma and awesome presence not from the Hagen side of the ledger, not from that menagerie of sharecroppers, laborers, illiterates and moonshiners. This was a gene pool so shallow and polluted it was a virtual miracle it produced species who walked upright. Rachel's family, name of Burns, on the other hand, was comprised of physicians, professors, sculptors, musicians, even an astronomer, some of whom lay in pieces in Eastern Europe, smoke from the chimneys to be sure, drifting in their heavens as their children and grandchildren and great-grandchildren, including one Charlie Garrett, filled up a new world.

Some had come, Grady supposed, from Charlie's daddy's side, too. Dan Garrett was a bright, tall, and good looking man who passed on his shocking blonde hair to his son.

This was Charlie Garrett's pedigree and if Grady had made an infinitesimal contribution to it, it would have to be the boy's athletic grace. Grady was once almost as tall as the boy, 'pert near six feet two inches, before the bones began to collapse on top of themselves, of course. And he had once possessed animal speed and quickness, an arm that unfurled and shot the ball as if from the barrel of a gun, wrists that could flick a baseball into the tenth row of cotton plants, far over the head of the centerfielder as easy as tapping an ash off a cigarette, it sometimes seemed. So easy, so long ago, too. Charlie had these things. At least some part of Grady had spun off the roulette wheel into Charlie's essence. But there was more there than mere grace.

What it was, quite simply, was power. Power, an intoxicating vapor wafting off him; a gift that everyone could see except, of course, Charlie himself. It was even something Grady had become so familiar with, that even he was caught off guard at times like these when an awestruck teenage girl was virtually transported out of her consciousness. Grady could have robbed the store right then, could have reached over and popped open the cash register and emptied it, and the girl probably wouldn't have blinked. So he let her stare and watched her face for invisible twitches that might indicate an emergence from the spell.

Charlie was still on the phone out there, in an obvious heated discussion, pacing back and forth now, his left hand flapping. Grady canted himself to get a better look at the clerk and her name tag. "Excuse me, uh, Tiff," he said. "Can I pay for his gas and these here two bottles?"

The girl named Tiff suddenly snapped back to consciousness, her eyes refilling with the reality surrounding her. She turned to Grady. "Is he yours? I mean, with you?" She turned away again and stared.

"That's my brother," Grady joked. "Younger brother."

Grady had become not oblivious to, but at least used to, the aura Charlie broadcast, just as the people in New York sleep through street sounds, or the people in Los Angeles never notice the weather. Occasionally, however, when something like this happened, when a perfect stranger was literally frozen in place, he was more bemused than surprised. He looked up at the girl named Tiff. "He's my younger brother," he joked again.

She glanced out the window again with a quick dart of her eye, and then turned back to face Grady. "You're not from around here, are you? Not new to town or anything like that?"

"Nope, just stopping to get gas and these here two bottles of water," Grady said, sliding the two plastic containers closer together on the counter.

Tiff punched up the numbers from the pump, her eyes going back and forth between the display and the pump. "That will be nineteen ninety-seven," she monotoned, still looking out the window from the corners of her eyes. Grady handed her a twenty. "Just throw the change in the little cup here," he said, taking the two bottles of water and walking away.

Outside, Charlie was flipping his phone closed and hooking it back on his belt. Grady came toward him and handed him a bottle.

A new voice suddenly entered the conversation, coming toward them. "Excuse me, sir, you forgot these," Tiff was saying as she ran toward the car holding out two Milky Way candy bars. Grady's eyes widened and he popped backward slightly. "Oh, my goodness," he said. "I must be having a senior moment," he smiled.

Tiff walked around the front of the car and handed both candy bars to Charlie. "Hi," she whispered, turning her eyes away.

Charlie looked up at his grandfather. "You bought two candy bars for us?"

47

"Yeah, he forgot to take them after he paid for them," Tiff said. Grady folded his arms and leaned on the trunk of the car. Candy bars, my patoot. It's a nice touch, though.

"My name is Tiffany," the girl said, extending her hand.

"Nice to meet you, Tiffany," Charlie replied.

Then silence awkwardly stumbled between them. Tiffany was looking at her sneakers, obviously grasping for some words. Finally she let out a stream of air and looked up. "Well, have a nice vacation," she said.

"Hey, wait a minute," Charlie said, leaning over the Mustang and picking up a camera bag from the floor. "Mind if I get a picture?"

The girl blushed, her hands folded in front of her. "Me?"

Charlie already had the camera out of the bag and up to his eye. "Yeah, stay just like that." He snapped several quick shots. Then he lowered the camera.

"Can I get one if they turn out all right? I don't take very good pictures," she stammered.

"Sure. Here, right down your name and address." He reached into the camera bag and took out a small spiral tablet and BIC pen. Tiffany wrote her name, address and phone number on the first page and handed it back to him.

"Thanks," Charlie said, smiling his totally unaffected, instinctive, ferocious, atom bomb of a smile at her, and Grady could see it sucking the air out of her lungs. "I got to go back," she said unconsciously raising her hand in a slight wave as she pivoted and ran to the store.

"You gotta take pictures of everything?" Grady asked.

"Jeezus, what the hell is the matter with you people? Is everybody in the world pissed at me?" Charlie grumbled.

"What do you mean?" Grady replied defensively, knowing exactly what Charlie was saying. For crying out loud, give the kid a break. It's bad enough to be all wrapped up in your own angst and to become totally uncommunicative and grumpy. But to give him crap about the camera? The camera was always there, like the baseball cap and sunglasses. Like the cargo shorts and tee shirt. Crazy damned kid with the camera and the dark room in the basement, shooting everything that moved.

"First mom, all over my shit for taking you. Then Lorene, all pissed off," Charlie groused, putting the camera back in the bag and setting it in the back seat. "Then you. You haven't said four words in three hours."

"Don't feel like talking," Grady murmured, moving toward the passenger door.

"Then screw it! I'll just turn around. Take you back home and everybody will be happy. Shit, I thought it might be fun."

Lord, Grady thought, it wasn't Charlie's fault. He took a deep breath. "Look, buddy, I'm sorry. It's just that I had a plan and you . . ."

"Yeah, I know, I fucked up your plan. I'm really sorry." He ripped open the door and leaned on the roof. "Get in, I'll take you home or to a bus station or whatever-the-hell you want."

The air had been sucked out of Grady and he felt himself falling apart inside. His grandson! His pal! "Charlie, come on. I'm sorry. I want you to go with me, to take me to Arbutus. I apologize for being such a . . ."

"The word you're looking for is 'asshole'."

"Yeah. Asshole. Now I'm a sorry asshole."

The young man looked away and shook his head. "Yeah, yeah. Okay." He twisted the cap off the water container and took a swallow.

This will get him, Grady thought before blurting, "Can I drive?"

Charlie turned and looked out through the open door. "What?"

"Can I drive?"

Charlie's eyebrows shot upward. "You? Drive?"

Grady smiled. "I am over 16, you know; still have a driver's license."

Charlie shrugged and slid out the door. "Sure, Pappy, what the heck?"

Grady hopped in and buckled his seat belt while Charlie moved into the passenger seat.

"Of course, the license expired some years ago," the old man said, flooring the accelerator and throwing a tornado of dust and gravel into the air behind the car.

Inside the car, the road noise was muffled. The silence begged to be broken. Talk to the kid, Hagen. "So, your mom's not too happy? What did she say?"

"She pretty much told me to turn my butt around and get you back," he said. Charlie took a long swallow again. "Said you're too old to be taking trips like this. Afraid you're gonna have a heart attack or some goddamn thing." Then he lifted his chin and chuckled, his eyes sparkling. "You're not, are you? If you do, I'm putting you in the trunk."

"And what did you say?"

"What would you want me to say?"

"Well, I hope you would say that I am a grown man. That I'm not an invalid. That I am capable of making decisions for myself, and that before I leave this earth I'd like to go back to my own home town for a little visit."

Charlie winked at his granddad and pointed with his index finger. "Bingo!"

"That's what you told her?"

"Pretty much."

"And she said ...?"

"She said to stay with you and get you back within a week," Charlie answered.

Shit! How to get rid of the kid when he had to do his business? Gol'danged plan was getting more complicated by the minute. Grady tried to be lighthearted. "Well, now, as a matter of fact, what I want is for you to just drop me off at my cousin Truman's and skedaddle back up home. I might stay two weeks, might stay a month. I can take the bus when I want to come back." There. That should work.

Charlie shrugged and took a pull on the water bottle. "Whatever. That might get Lorene off my case."

"What did she say?"

Charlie chuckled and turned his attention back to his grandfather. "Lorene? Like I said, she's pissed. She's always pissed whenever I do anything that she's not involved in."

"Sounds like true love to me," Grady deadpanned.

"She's a fabulous girl," Charlie said. "She's intelligent, fun to be with."

"You talking yourself – or me – into it?"

"What do you mean?"

"Just what I said," Grady replied. "Does she stop your heart for an instant when you see her?"

"I never gave it much thought," Charlie said.

"Well, boy, take it from an old man. It's got nothing to do with thinking."

Charlie turned in the seat and faced his grandfather. "Is that how it was with you and Nonnie Rachel?"

Now that was an interesting question, and too many different kinds of answers flooded Grady's thoughts. He had been exploded, blown to bits, by love once, but it wasn't Rachel who had done it. She had never set off his heart like that, though he loved her unequivocally, had been faithful to her in every way. She, in turn, had been unconditional and generous beyond measure with her love. They had come together in an uncertain time, fresh from a hideous montage of unspeakable horror they had both witnessed. He was still in the hospital in Berlin when she told him they were sending her home. She pressed a note into his hand with her address on it and leaned over and kissed him, whispering in his ear. "There's a darkness in you, Grady. I can be your light."

And so, he followed the note to Chicago. After all, he had given up his birthplace forever, he believed at the time, exhaling its air in an emphatic final gasp. When he arrived at Union Station he saw her waiting for him through the crowds, enveloped in a cloud of steam being expelled by the locomotives, and they were married in her synagogue a month later. Then the years melted together in a furious brew. And they were, by and large, happy years. Rachel had become, quite simply, his life. Everything he knew was known through her. She had nursed him without complaint through a heart attack and subsequent open heart surgery, and had only been sick for a second, just long enough to die of a brain aneurysm when he was gone.

Love? He had known it in its many forms, but what he had with Rachel was different than what he was talking about to Charlie. It was a soft love, something he could wear unbuttoned and loose without fear or concern. Perhaps it was better that way, too. Better than the combustible, incomprehensible force that had once wrenched his heart.

And quite naturally, these thoughts gravitated into pictures, and Grady was lost again in the past to a time before Rachel; taken by the winds of memory to the face of someone else. And why not? Wasn't she a part of this story, too?

8

Arbutus, Mississippi – August, 1941

The first time Grady Hagen saw her was through a cloud of red-brown dust churned up by his own shoes plus the full-of-piss stomping of the boys on the other team as they walked off the field all hang dog, kicking up the infield dirt as if that slab of geography was the cause of their sudden misery, when in fact it had been Grady himself whose bat had strung a ball like a length of clothesline into the rice field so far beyond the Red Man Chewing Tobacco sign that it might never be recovered. It was the regional championship game and the fancy boys had come down from Jackson in their matching uniforms, ready to run roughshod over the ragtag Arbutus team like they always did. But this year was different. And the Arbutus fans who contributed to the swirling storm of dust with their own whooping and hollering were now pouring onto the field as Grady looped around third base, the wet wool of his uniform clinging to his skin and expectorating that musty wet animal smell.

She burned through the cloud like the sun, streaming into Grady's line of sight between the flailing arms and bobbing heads that had engulfed him as he crossed home plate. Then her image would disappear, and he would twist through the maze of shoulders and hats and elbows to try to find her again. She was away from the crowd, standing by the water pump with several other girls whom Grady knew from school, girls – what? – a year, maybe two, behind him whom he knew by face if not by name. It wasn't odd at all to have girls standing there, whispering with cupped hands into each others' ears while their eyes and the attitude of their heads were turned toward Grady. He was, after all, the king of Arbutus, and this was just part of the weather, as far as he was concerned. Got so he could block them out when they walked behind him in the hall at school, tongues skittering like mice on a wooden floor.

But there was someone new this time, and Grady wasn't about to ignore her. She was golden; not just her hair which she wore longer than any of the other girls, but also her skin which was a white of a different hue and texture, softer somehow, radiant. But what got him, what made him squirm through the celebrating masses, were her eyes that, even from this distance, maybe a hundred feet or so, he could see focusing on him. They were almost amber, and endlessly deep. He had never seen anything like them, like her, before, and he knew at that second that he had to hear her voice, had to go to her, even though everything about her said stay back, for this was a place that he had no business visiting. This was someone you certainly could watch and dream about, but approaching her, and then perhaps touching her were like grabbing a star so white with heat you would disintegrate.

But Grady Hagen, hero of Arbutus, ignored the screaming of his instincts and muscled through the crowd. Just as he was breaking free, a man he didn't recognize came up from Grady's left side. His gabardine suit pants were awash with red-brown dust, his shoes engulfed in it. His suit coat was draped in the crook of his arm. His white shirt was yellowed with sweat and grime, and his tie hung askew about half way down his suspenders. His boater was tilted forward, partially obscuring his eyes, and everything about him said Yankee to Grady Hagen. Nonetheless, the boy stopped when he understood that the man was trying to get his attention.

"Nice game, Grady," the man said, approaching and extending a hand. "My name is Chet Zane. I'm a scout for the White Sox."

Grady shook his hand. "The Chicago White Sox?" he asked, turning his head and scanning the disseminating crowd for her, whoever she was.

"That's right, son, and I have to say, I'm impressed with what I saw out there today," Zane said, reaching into his pocket and taking out a bag of tobacco. His stubby fingers pinched some and he popped it in his mouth. Then he offered the bag to Grady. "Gotta tell you, didn't come down here to watch you at all. Came to scout that Pinkerton kid from Jackson."

"He's a pretty good pitcher," Grady replied, taking some tobacco and stuffing it under his front lip. He unlocked from Zane's gaze and glanced far beyond him. Where was she? Where did she go?

"Yeah, he's all right, but you didn't seem to have too much trouble with him," Zane replied. "Four for four and not a cheap hit in the bunch."

"Well, I had to think more than usual," Grady came back now.

"Whatcha mean?"

"Usually, I just go up and swing, but with him I had to guess what he might be throwing from watching him pitch to the other guys," Grady said, wondering if the scout knew what he meant. Wondering, too, who the girl was. "So, you come to see him, but you're talking to me." He was walking again, caught in the riptide of the crowd and the moment.

"No law says I can only see one boy when I'm watching, and I seen you and I like what I see." Zane creased the bag shut and stuffed it in his back pocket. "You ever think about playing in the big leagues?"

"Never knew if I was good enough," Grady replied. His eyes were now focused on the horizon of the crowd. Sumbitch. She was gone.

"Well, now, boy, I don't know if you're good enough neither, but you might be. How old you now?"

"I'm, uh, sixteen."

"Sixteen! Dad'gum it. All them other boys, Pinkerton included, they're eighteen and you played over their heads."

Grady picked up most of the words, but still tried to look beyond the scout and into the crowd. "Why, thanks, sir."

"You almost done with high school?"

"I got one more year after this."

"One more year, huh? Tell you what, just for the fun of it, I'm gonna see if I can't get you down to Birmingham for a look see, maybe next spring or summer." Chet Zane reached into his shirt pocket and extracted a small writing pad and pencil. "You got a phone number I can call you?"

Shit. Bo Hagen wouldn't no more pay for a phone in the house than he would get up and fly. "I ain't got a phone, Mr. Zane. Wait!" Grady stood on his tiptoes and scanned the crowd. His eyes locked on Billie Rae Tolleston. "Billie Rae, what's your daddy's phone number at the store?" he shouted.

Billie Rae was stuffing bats into a canvas bag near the bench. He looked up, caught Grady and screamed back four numbers. Chet Zane jotted them down. Grady said, "Them is the numbers for my friend's daddy's hardware store right here in Arbutus. You call them and they can find me and I can call you back."

Then Zane flipped the page, wrote something else, tore off the paper and handed it to Grady. "This here is the number you call me back on. Reverse the charges," he said.

Grady took the paper, folded it and put it into the wet back pocket of his uniform. "Yeah, thanks," he said, turning away and then turning back to shake Chet Zane's hand again. It's a crazy gol'danged world when a major league scout gives you a phone number that might change your life and should have your heart leaping out of your chest. Instead, something else is burrowing through you, a face, an aura, a presence with a gravity so strong that everything else just fades and settles like the churned up dust of the baseball field.

"And if some other scout calls you or starts romancing you, you call me right now, y'hear?"

"Sure," Grady said, still sorting out bodies and faces.

"Okay," Chet Zane said, clapping Grady on the shoulder and walking away.

The crowd was fraying now, coming undone like a ball of yarn, spreading out over a broader vista that became increasingly more difficult for Grady's eyes to cover. He had lost her. Hell, maybe she hadn't really been there at all. Maybe she was just one of the freshman or sophomore girls who suddenly grew herself up a bit and the light was hitting her just so and Grady didn't recognize her. The hell with it.

"Who was that guy?" Billie Rae Tolleston's voice bit into Grady's consciousness.

His friend was next to him now, bag of bats clattering over his shoulder. Grady turned to Billie Rae. "Who? Him? Believe it or not, he's a scout for the Sox."

"No shit!" Billie Rae leapt up and down and pounded his pal on the back. "Goddamn man, you're going to beantown."

"White Sox," Grady answered.

"That's even better. Chicago! We're going to the big leagues!"

We? Billie Rae's uniform was still relatively white, not mottled with yellow like Grady's. Loading the bag and carrying it was the most action Billie Rae had seen all day. "Did you see them girls?" Grady asked.

Billie Rae's head swiveled. "What girls?"

"Ones were standing by the well pump."

"You mean Annie and Jane and them?"

"Yeah, and the blonde."

"Her? That's probably the new girl. Her old man's some kinda engineer or something for the army corps or whatever. Got something to do with TVA or something." Billie Rae re-jiggered the strap of the bag and the bats clattered again. "Some folks think he's a gov'ment agent of some kind, maybe a spy or something."

Grady pursed his lips and blew out an exasperated breath. Billie Rae jogged to stay abreast. He said, "She's got nice ones, though, huh?" He put his free hand a good foot in front of his chest.

Oddly enough, Grady hadn't really noticed her breasts, what with eyes the color of honey. "She live here now, or what?"

"Holy shit, you got a boner for her already," Billie Rae laughed, trying to keep up with the long, unencumbered strides of his friend. "Better be careful, she's a mackerel snapper, and a Yankee."

"What's that?" Grady said, craning his neck, over the crowd.

"Well now, son, a Yankee is a marauder from the North."

Grady punched Billie in the shoulder and knocked him a good six feet off stride. The bats smacked against each other and Billie Rae almost went down. "I know what a Yankee is, dumb ass. The other thing."

Billie Rae recomposed himself and was catching up again. "Mackerel snapper. Catholic."

"What does it mean, 'mackerel snapper'?"

"Fish eater. They don't eat meat on Friday. Think you'll go to hell. Not to mention they fuck like minks." They were almost to the gravel road now where Billie Rae had parked his daddy's truck.

What did it mean anyway, "fuck like minks?" If minks were continually fucking and making baby minks, Grady wondered, then why were mink coats so damned expensive? "Says who?"

Billie Rae grunted. "Common knowledge. They can do all the fornicating or drinking they want. All they gotta do is go confess to a priest and bingo, just like that, they're clean of sin." They had gotten to the pickup truck now, dirty gray blue with "Tolleston Hardware" painted on the door and across the side panels. He tossed the bag onto the truck bed. "Then they just go out and do it some more." He wiped his hands on his pants and moved to the driver's door. "Almost makes y'all wanna become Catholic, a church with so much forgiveness." Then he laughed.

Grady slid around the rear of the truck and stopped. She was there, right in front of him, burning a hole in the daylight. How did she get here? She must have just materialized. Everything around her was out of focus, bleeding off the edges of his peripheral vision.

"Hey, Grady," a voice, not hers, someone from the blurry fringes.

Grady took a breath, fighting to put things back together. Then he turned in the direction of the voice. It was a girl from school. "Annie, hi," he said, immediately going back to the center of his vision.

"How y'all doing?" Annie asked.

"We won," Grady said, shrugging, not taking his eyes away.

"Grady, this is my new friend," Annie said. "She just moved here from Ohio." Her voice lilted upward as if asking a question.

"Hi," Grady replied.

"Name of Betsy Sue McDonough," Annie answered.

"Hello," Grady said again.

Betsy Sue tilted her head and looked him over. Then she spoke, making a sound that was more music than words. "You aren't like the rest of them, are you?" she asked.

And that was how it began.

9

Pappy had driven until the sky swelled purple like a black eye, and they found a motel off the interstate. They wolfed down burgers and chili in the adjoining restaurant, and then the old man conked out with the television lights throwing the effluent of a baseball game – Cards and Reds – onto his bedspread. Charlie went outside and walked to the far end of the parking lot, every bit of a football field away from the two-story motel with the turquoise doors. The expressway hummed with cars close enough to spit at from the chain link fence on which he leaned. A can of beer dangled from his left hand; his right was tucked into the pocket of his baggy shorts. He set down the drink on a sawed off sapling stump and removed a meticulously engineered joint from his pocket. Downwind, he thought, should be safe. He pursed the cigarette in his lips, lit it and took a long pull. Bluish bullets of smoke stuttered from his nostrils as he coughed reflexively almost immediately. He wasn't a smoker; in fact, had never had the inclination to even try a tobacco cigarette. But this stuff, this was something else altogether now. He'd only started recently, what with Lorene on his case and med school looming. This stuff seemed to cool the blood in his veins, put a blanket on his mind that kept out the baying of his thoughts. It was religion, meditation, prayer, enlightenment, transcendentalism, made the music sound better, a clarifier, not to mention yahoo, zingba! And a million chuckles. But he was doing too much of it lately; he knew that. He was going to stop as soon as the world stopped beating on his mind.

As the cars and trucks screamed by, mingling their noise and fumes with the otherwise still darkness, the sweet juices from the doobie had begun to settle in Charlie's head. Just enough buzz – not too much – to sand down the edges of his mind. He exhaled again, then cut the sour taste with a long pull of beer.

If Pappy could see him now, what would he say? Probably not too much come to think of it. Likely he would come sauntering across the parking lot, a shadow in the purple lights, shoulders churning like two pistons the way they did, and come up and see him there and take the joint right out of his hand and then pull a toke that would untie his shoes. That's what he would do. Because he was cool. Pappy. Fucking Pappy. Charlie laughed out loud, spewing smoke from his nose and mouth like a backfiring Model T.

You didn't live to his age and see what Pappy's seen and do what he's done and then get shocked to discover your twenty-two year old grandson likes a doobie every now and then. Not this old man. Yeah, he may fool you at first glance with his slow drawl and the way he scratches his head when he talks, but every wrinkle on that guy's face was another folded page of history, another event, another experience, compiled into the pedagogy of this singular life. Every follicle held the DNA of thousands of days lived hard as a hammer on an anvil. Some stories he'd tell, but most he held inside, hidden under the skin.

And now, here were the two of them, on another planet, light years from home, where the people talked in syrupy drawls and the words fell out in splotches. A fuckin' road trip with Pappy! Who'd of thunk it this morning? Charlie had just the hell gotten up like always and laid around and then went to Pappy's and now here he was somewhere in space, it seemed, doing a joint in the parking lot of the Lazy Daze Motel with a curlicue neon sign out front half out of gas so that from a distance it read "zy ze tel." Just this past spring he and several buddies had loaded the Mustang and torn ass out of bleak, drizzly Indiana and into blinding light Florida where they bathed in beer, and rolled around with girls and partied until their heads were ready to explode, and got sunburned when their hangovers made them pass out on the beach. But this, Lordy, Lordy, was a whole lot different.

The cell phone in his cargo pocket trilled the "William Tell Overture." "Fuck," Charlie said, as he reached under the pocket flap and lifted the phone to his ear.

"Hey, Charlie."

"Lorene. Hi."

"Where are you?"

"Somewhere else, that's for sure."

"I tried calling you all day."

He had shut down the phone on purpose after the conversation in the gas station parking lot. Just didn't want the hassle. "Ah, well, you know the phones go in and out down here. I mean, it's not like we're in Chicago or anything."

"What's that noise in the background?"

"Trucks. I'm standing in the parking lot of a motel."

"When are you coming home?" she asked. "How long are you going to be there?"

"Hell, we're not 'there' yet," he answered, pinching the joint and taking another long drag. He stifled a cough.

"Are you smoking?" Her voice was angry, impatient. "Jesus Christ, are you fucking smoking? I hope you get busted!"

He didn't need this right now, just as he was getting mellow. He held his hand over the mouthpiece to exhale a bushel of smoke which rolled out like a thread. "Look, babe, you're breaking up on me . . ."

"I just want to know when you're fucking coming home."

Bullshit. He didn't have to explain everything. Jesus Christ. "I think I lost you. See you when I get back."

Silence on the other end.

Maybe he'd lost the connection.

No such luck. "Thanks for telling me."

"Look, Lorene, I tried to call you, but the phone was, you know, out of roaming area or something like that."

"It's not very considerate of you."

Oh, fuck. "Sorry, you're breaking up on me."

"I said, you're not very considerate. All you think of is you, you, you."

Get off my case. "Reenie, I can't understand you. You're breaking up on me," he lied, flipping the phone shut. Then he powered down. Sometimes you just want to be alone, you know.

By now Charlie had taken all the life out of the joint and drained the last few drops from the bottom of the can. He smashed the can between his hands, and spit away the tiny paper from the doobie. He took a deep breath of the diesel ripened air and began to walk.

He seemed to float across the parking lot to the door to the room. He was as quiet as possible opening it. Pappy laid there, rhythms coming from him short of a snore but louder than normal breathing. The room was totally black, darker than the parking lot. Charlie put out his hand to feel his way through as his eyes adjusted. His fingers found the edge of the bureau and he walked his hands one over the other as he moved toward the bathroom. Not easy, considering the spin in his brain. That's when his palm struck the corner of Pappy's suitcase which was open and on the top of the taller dresser, flipping it upwards. The contents, shit, so neat and perfectly arranged, poured out onto the floor.

"Fuck," he spat.

"Whatsamatter?" Pappy grumbled from beneath the covers.

"It's okay, Pap," Charlie replied, kneeling down and flopping his hands on the floor until they met up with something, a ball of socks, a folded shirt, a tin. By now the room was transforming from pitch to a murky violet and things started to take shape. Charlie knelt there, both hands full, and stared at the suitcase. Now to get things the way they were, that was the trick. He stood up and his foot struck something and kicked it farther under the bureau. He haphazardly set what he was holding into the suitcase and genuflected on the carpet, reaching under the bureau.

A book obviously, lying there, face down, open. He could tell by its feel that it was a Bible, the leathery grain cover, old and cracked on his fingertips. Pappy's? Pappy wasn't a Bible guy. He had married Nonnie Rachel who was Jewish, for crying out loud, even if she didn't do it all the time.

Charlie pulled the Bible free from the place it had fallen and sat down on the bed. Some of the thin pages had folded over and Charlie straightened them out. Then he saw something sticking out, the edge of something, catty-cornered toward the front. Wonder what it is? He opened to that page and took the thing out. A card, a postcard, it seemed. He turned it this way and that, trying to get it into the slice of bluish light that slanted in through the slit in the curtains. Probably a souvenir picture of the world's largest stuffed possum.

Jesus! He dropped the picture card as if it were on fire.

What the fuck was this?

Fuck. He exhaled loudly and picked it up.

Goddamn. Pappy had a thousand million stories, and now Charlie was gazing at a page of another one, a story he wasn't sure he wanted to hear, but one he instinctively understood – even through the buzz and giggle in his head – had something to do with this trip. Because the picture card was addressed to Pvt. Graden Hagen, c/o Camp Shelby, Looziana, and on the back of the post card, scrawled in someone's lousy penmanship were the words: *I see you got a front row seat. Dad.*

Charlie turned the card over and angled it this way and that, fighting for slivers of light coming through the blinds. Right there, in the center of the photo? Holy Jesus in heaven! It was him! It was his Pappy! Oh, there was no mistaking him. The face was the same, stretched smooth by youth, of course, but you didn't miss those eyes. No fucking way. Those were Pap's eyes looking right smack dab into that camera lens.

What in the name of Christ was he doing there?

10

Arbutus, Mississippi – October, 1941

It was as if God had spilled a treasure chest across the landscape. Autumn had risen to its peak and the woods were ablaze with gold. Grady Hagen was aflame as well. Life had reached a point of perfection for him. A mystic melody seemed to be playing in his heart, keeping him from sleep and igniting his senses. Everything was different now, smell, taste, sound. Even the air he breathed was surging with feeling. He had been helplessly, hopelessly, irreparably changed, shipwrecked by a benevolent storm known as Betsy Sue McDonough.

For three months since that day at the ballfield outside of town, every morning had begun with her consuming his mind from the moment his eyes opened. Not a day had passed that he did not see her. Between classes at school he couldn't wait to pass her in the hall and touch his fingers to hers if only for a second. The rest of the world, time, the vicissitudes of life, were obscured by her presence in the world, often much to the chagrin of Billie Rae Tolleston who only shook his head and said watch out she's using you. "You're king shit around here," he'd say, "and she wants to be queen."

Betsy Sue and Grady were together on this glorious day, being swallowed up by the forest. Grady had her hand in his, hers like a bird that he held gently, his large fingers wrapping all the way to her wrist. They had come to the creek, gurgling brown water, throwing off stars of sunlight that pierced the canopy of leaves above.

"Where are we going, Grady Hagen?" Betsy Sue asked, stopping at the bank. That's what she called him, both names at the same time. Gradyhagen.

"We're going across."

Betsy Sue gripped his hand tighter and lifted one leg. With her free hand she wiggled off her shoe. "You know, a philosopher once said you can't step into the same river twice."

"I don't get it," Grady said, steadying her.

"Sure you do. Think about it."

He had never met anyone like her, not because she was the first person from the north he had ever met, but because of the way she saw things, the way she made him see things. "I know, it's because the water is moving," he suddenly burst out.

"It's a metaphor for life."

"You can't go back in life," he said, proud to have figured it out.

"See, told you," she answered, shifting legs and pulling off the other shoe. "Let's go. Is it cold?"

And she feared nothing. Not water moccasins nor leeches that owned these muddy creeks. Not crayfish with their pinchers that rummaged the bottom. Not worms nor catfish nor crappie. She was up to her calves in swirling currents before Grady – Gradyhagen – could get his boots off. "It's warm," she said, her white teeth wide on her face. "Where we going, anyway?"

"We're going to a secret place that me and Billie Rae found when we were kids."

"Billie Rae and I," Betsy Sue corrected, reaching for Grady's hand and pulling him toward her in the stream.

"You talk like that because you're a Yankee."

"The way a man speaks reveals his intellect," she replied. "You talk like a hillbilly, people will think you're a hillbilly."

"I am a hillbilly," Grady said.

"No, you're not, Gradyhagen. I told you the first day I met you that you were different from all these other boys down here."

"How could you tell?"

They were across the stream by now, and Betsy Sue had moved ahead of him again, her bare feet rustling in the leaves. "I don't know. I just have feelings about people. You were born and raised here, but deep down inside you don't think you fit. Something right here," she poked a finger gently at Grady's heart.

This time he really didn't know what she was saying, but he strode quickly over to a fallen tree and leaned against it. "Better put your shoes back on," he said, "can't tell what might be under these leaves."

Betsy Sue's eyes widened in sudden recognition, and she ran to the tree trunk and jammed her foot into one shoe as fast as she could. Grady could only watch her. God of mercy how she glowed in this light, her amber eyes, her yellow hair melting into the shimmering ether as if she were painted for autumn by a hand in search of perfection.

She picked up the conversation where she had left off. "So, you have to think before you speak. People will think you are intelligent if you don't use slang and profanity, and if people think you are intelligent they will treat you differently and you will become intelligent," she said, fidgeting with the second shoe until it was just right. Then she put her foot on the ground and, satisfied, stepped away from the tree. "It's a self-fulfilling prophecy."

"What's that mean, 'self-fulfilling prophecy'?"

"It means you can predict your future if what you're going to do is everything that leads to it."

"So, I have to talk like a butler?"

Betsy Sue leaned her head back and laughed, a full, tinkling sound rippling from her throat. "You silly goose," she said, shoving him in the chest.

"Where'd y'all learn all this fancy talking and whatnot?" he asked as they trudged up the hill on that side of the ravine.

"Sister Bernadette, then Sister Magdalena" she answered.

"I didn't think you had any sisters. Where do they live?"

That laugh again, like a clarion. "You goof. Those are the sisters I had in grade school back in Toledo."

"They were sisters?"

"Yes, well, no, not sisters like that. Sisters like nuns. You know, with the black veils or whatever."

"Something Catholic, I guess?" Grady said. He was pulling her uphill now, the ground slippery and in motion. He reached for a hanging branch and steadied himself.

"You don't know about nuns?"

"Not really."

"You don't know much about Catholics at all, do you?"

Grady wasn't sure what to say. "Just that at your Sunday services your ministers don't do so much preaching and they stand with their backs to you and mumble in a foreign language."

"Who told you that?" Betsy Sue asked, pulling herself upward, her feet slipping.

"Billie Rae."

"Did he tell you…?" She stopped to catch her breath, then leaned closer to him.

Grady could feel the warmth of her coming from her mouth and he wanted to go into it, swallow it, let it poison him.

She held up one hand, "No, I can't tell you. We're sworn to secrecy."

Now she had his curiosity in her tender trap. "What? What?"

"Did Billie Rae tell you – no, there's no way he could know – about first born sons?"

"No. What?" This was intriguing.

"Well, you have to swear to secrecy," she said, placing a hand on Grady's heart.

"Okay," he said.

She leaned close to him and moved her mouth to his ear. "In the Catholic Church mommas and daddies have to do what God himself did and hand over their first born son to be sacrificed," she whispered.

"My God! Do they really?"

"Yes," she continued, "within a day after they're born. Then they have a sacrificial ceremony at the church." She made a stabbing motion.

Grady was stunned. Bo Hagen was right. This cult, these people who worshipped a pope and Mary instead of Jesus himself. "Is this really true?" he gasped.

Betsy Sue McDonough answered by placing the heels of both hands against his chest and shoving him. "Of course not, you fool. What do you think we are?" she cried.

But Grady wasn't really hearing her anymore. She had knocked him off orbit. Gravity, balance, vision had been suddenly disrupted and his feet pattered against the soft ground for stability. All that was keeping him from total destruction was the tree branch, and the tighter he gripped, the more slippery it felt until it grew shorter, shorter.

Nothing.

Everything collapsed. In a second he was unbridled and rolling down the hill. Leaves kicked up in cyclone swirls. His breath escaped in bass drum thumps. His hands windmilled out. Finally, he stopped, his foot sliding into a tree stump and reeling him in. He surveyed his bones, his skin, looking for pain. He was okay. Covered in golden leaves and sticks in his hair, but okay. What a ride. He looked up and Betsy Sue, framed in the white of the sky behind her, was clinging to the tree and laughing, choking, tears running down her face. "I told you before that if you spend your life listening to Billie Rae Tolleston, you're going to end up on your fanny," she said, sputtering out the words.

He ran up the hill to her. No soft mud, no slimy undergrowth was going to stop him now and she laughed in breathless gaps as he charged upward. Then he was to her, colliding but more like a cloud than a raging bull. He grabbed her by the waist and gently pulled her to the ground, and he rolled atop her and in an instant she had reached around his neck and their lips met. From all that had come before it, the panting and grasping and tackling, you would have thought it would be a hard kiss, but it was not. It was perfect and soft and so full of love that Grady felt his heart leave his body for an instant. They stayed that way, kissing, holding, saying nothing for several minutes.

Then Betsy Sue McDonough looked at him with liquid eyes and whispered. "Gradyhagen do you love me?"

Grady Hagen – Gradyhagen – had kissed many girls. Finding girls to kiss wasn't difficult when you were king of Arbutus. But kissing Betsy Sue here on this golden day was different than all the rest. He had never once told a woman, not even his mother, for the love of God in heaven, that he loved her. The thought had never occurred to him.

"Yeah," was all that came out.

Betsy Sue smiled. "I know," she whispered. Then she sat up. "Weren't you going to show me something?"

"Yeah," Grady said, standing and helping her to her feet.

Five minutes later, down a barely noticeable path that wound like a lizard through the trees, they came to an outcropping of bushes, thistle and ivy, tangled menacingly over a hump of rocks in the side of a hill. "See this here," Grady said, pointing at a smooth, blue, elliptical stone that jutted through the grass. "That's the bald man stone. That's what Cissy and me and Billie Rae called it, because it looks like the top of a bald head."

Betsy Sue looked at it. "I understand," she said, lacing the words with sarcasm – as if she couldn't figure out why a perfectly round stone would be called the "bald man stone."

"And it points right to it," Grady said, extending his arm toward a riot of vegetation.

"Wow," Betsy Sue replied, "weeds."

"These ain't," he caught himself, "aren't weeds, Miss McDonough. Come this way." He took her hand and they walked around to the side of the outgrowth. Grady crouched and pulled back a bush, revealing a gaping hole, like a wound, in the side of the hill.

"My gosh, what is it, a cave?" Betsy Sue said, following him into the darkness.

Inside now, it took a second for their eyes to adjust to the light. Grady felt his way against the left wall and found the lantern. He scraped a match against a flat of rock on the ground and lit the kerosene wick. The lantern threw off enough light to show the whole space.

Indeed, it was a cave, perhaps a hundred feet deep and twenty-five feet across at the middle, tapering down to a tunnel too small for a grown person to even crawl through. The walls were gray brown, full of sweat. It was obvious it had been occupied. A ring of stones held ashes and blackened sticks in the center of the widest part. Silly pictures of cowboys and Indians were drawn in crayons on the walls. Two blankets were folded in one corner. Square tins, sardine cans, were setting in the middle of the fire pit.

"Wow, look at this place," Betsy Sue said. "I've never been in a cave before." She was walking toward the far end.

Grady came up next to her and squatted down. He held the lantern into a black hole in the wall, only about a foot off the floor. "Come, look down here."

"Where does this go?" Betsy asked, kneeling down and peering into the darkness.

"It just drops down. See, Billie Rae and I tried to widen it once with our hammers," he said, running the lantern along the jagged edges of the hole, "so we could slide into the space, see what's in there." He pulled the lantern back. "But the rock's too hard."

"What do you suppose is in there?" Betsy Sue wondered, closing one eye and squinting into the dark hole. "Do you think there's treasure in there like in Huckleberry Finn?"

"Prolly just more cave. They say there's caves all the way up to Canada you could walk through if you know'd which direction you were going. But this one ain't too deep right here, 'cause Billie Rae and me, we threw stones in there and you could hear them hit pretty quick."

"How long have you known about this place?" Betsy Sue asked, grabbing the crook of Grady's arm and standing up again.

"Billie Rae and Cissy and me found this when we were maybe eight or nine years old and swore to one another to not tell anyone else about it," Grady said, sliding a hand across the smooth rock wall. "Took a blood oath, we did. Cut the ends of our thumbs with our pocket knives and streaked the walls right over here somewhere."

"Cissy, too? Cut her thumb?"

"Heck, yeah. She was tough as nails, that one. Still is."

"Did you ever? Tell someone I mean?"

"Yeah," Grady said, looking at her.

It took a second to register. "I'm the only one?"

Grady nodded.

Then Betsy Sue McDonough walked over to him, her hands behind her back, and kissed him again. "You make me feel special, Gradyhagen," she whispered in his ear.

Her breath, Jesus, the life coming from it, warm as it was, sent shivers through him and he took his head in her hands and kissed her back. In seconds they were on the ground, clawing, reaching, touching each other, electrified by their own youth and innocence and the dark and sinful mystery of it all. Grady's hands moved under her blouse just to touch, just to feel, the smoothness of the skin on her back which came up to his touch and poured over it like silk. His fingers found her navel, rolled around it as lightly as the steps of a fly. Betsy Sue released a whispered moan and arched her back up to him. Her skirt, by now, had been pushed up to her hips, and her legs had opened enough to press herself against him, against his raging hardness. And Grady pushed back and rocked with her in rhythm. His hand, no longer a part of his mind or body, had found her breast, had slid beneath the bra and sprung it loose. He had never felt. . .

And then she was pushing him away. "No, Grady, please, stop," she cried, pulling his hand from beneath her blouse and rolling out from under him.

It was like being thrown from Cree, his daddy's horse, taking the wind out of him and making the blood collapse throughout his body like rain. "Good lord, Betsy, I, did I do something?"

Betsy Sue had turned from him and was fidgeting her clothes back into their proper place. She raised one hand to him. "Don't, don't say anything, Grady. It's not you. It's got nothing to do with you. It just isn't right."

When they came out of the cave a few minutes later, the day had changed. The azure sky had grown angry, turned to gunmetal gray, and began dumping rain in sheets of shimmering silver. Grady dragged Betsy Sue through the forest, dodging raindrops, pausing under trees still thick with summer. By the time they made it to the road, the spew had turned into raging pellets of water. A truck was scurrying toward them, throwing fans of water off its tires, and Grady jumped into the road, waving his arms. The truck stopped and the passenger door opened. "Get y'all in here now, quick," Gap Browne shouted over the din.

Rain clattered on the roof of Gap's pick up like drumsticks on a snare. The tiny windshield wipers clicked in opposing rhythm to try to sweep a small crescent of clarity onto the glass. The blue smoke from Gap's unfiltered Camel mingled with the steam inside to further obscure vision. "Ain't never seen a day turn this quick," Gap said, as Betsy Sue slid in beside him, followed by Grady.

"Nope," Grady said.

"You kids been on a picnic?"

"Just taking a walk in the woods," Grady answered.

Gap seemed to chuckle without making a noise and took a drag on his cigarette. "Yeah, I know what you mean," he said.

71

They were less than a mile from town and arrived in a few minutes. By then the rain had begun to subside. "Right here?" Gap Browne asked, the truck stuttering up to the curb in front of Tolleston's Hardware Store.

"Thanks, Gap," Grady said.

"You kids be good now," the old farmer answered, threads of smoke streaming out of his nose.

"You ready?" Grady said to Betsy Sue, who had grown quiet since they left the cave. "We'll just run in and you can call your daddy. Billie Rae can get me home in his daddy's truck."

"That's fine," she replied.

Grady opened the door and slipped out, reaching back for her hand. She grabbed him, holding her other hand over her head as they ducked into the threshold of the hardware store. The passenger door thumped behind them and Gap's truck eased away, gears whining. The rain had transformed itself into a blanket of drizzle and their haste subsided. For some reason Grady scanned the street. Steam had begun to rise from the puddles. Doors had begun to open, disgorging people who had obviously been waiting out the storm. Several shopkeepers emerged with brooms, sweeping water from their thresholds.

Grady's eye caught, couldn't miss, Cissy Moody wrestling two bags of groceries out of Pillson's general store. His old friend. Cissy was, until Betsy Sue came to town, of course, the most beautiful girl Grady, or anyone else in Arbutus for that matter, he was sure, had ever seen. Somebody said once that she had Choctaw in her going back so far it didn't much matter to anyone anymore, which would explain the hair the color of a crow's wings, dark and shiny like no one else's. She was tight, that was the easiest way to describe her, her tiny body, perfectly shaped, always painted into a dress, but not in a dirty way. It was just the way clothes fit her. They clung to her supple shape, nestling into every nook and cranny. However innocent her intentions, the way she dressed, nonetheless, left little to the imagination, which was why, out of all the folks suddenly emerging from the barber shops and garages and grocery stores, she was the one who was most noticeable.

She was having problems with the grocery bags. A huge stalk of celery jutted out from the top of one and you could easily see the shape of cans pressed into the brown paper. She was trying to watch where she walked, but struggling to see between the two bags cradled in each arm. She wobbled from side to side on the sidewalk, doing her best to keep her balance on the slippery pavement. Grady thought of going to help her. She was, after all, not only one of his old friends, but also the daughter of his daddy's boss.

In the middle of that thought it happened. Her left foot lost the sidewalk, jutted out and slipped down the side of the curb. Everything went, groceries up and into the air, blowing out of the bags, cans and lettuce heads; Cissy Moody down, off the curb and into a puddle, elbow crashing into the brick pavement.

Instantly someone was there, his hands on her, leaning into her, taking her arm. It was Rudy Montcrief. Grady's instincts erupted within him. Rudy Montcrief, a colored man, with his hands on a white woman.

Betsy Sue pushed away from Grady and ran to them. "Come on," she said over her shoulder, "Aren't you going to help her?" Grady started running.

Cissy and Rudy were less than fifty yards away and Grady was there in a matter of seconds. Cissy was crying, holding her arm, her head lolling back and forth on, Jesus Christ, the colored man's shoulder. He was speaking to her gently. My God, this was a town where colored people stepped off the sidewalk and didn't make eye contact with white folks unless they were spoken to. And now, this.

Grady knelt down and began picking up the spilled contents of the brown bags that had now begun to dissolve in the rain. Betsy Sue disappeared into Pillson's store. His arms full of cans, stacked and uneasy, Grady got to his feet. Cissy was now sitting on the curb, doubled over. Rudy Montcrief was on one knee in front of her, his hand on her shoulder, his face only inches from hers.

Suddenly he was airborne, arms and legs akimbo, hurtling toward Grady who instinctively dropped the cans as he swept himself away from the flying boy.

"You goddamned nigger," a man was screaming. "You touch this woman?"

Rudy Montcrief connected with the brick pavement several yards away, splurging into a puddle, but landing not like a body that had been shocked into flight from behind, but almost like a bird, spraying

73

water in front of his outstretched hands and springing instantly to his feet in a single movement. He stood, his head back, and wiped the water from his clothes.

The screaming man – Grady recognized him now as Steve Pruitt from the assessor's office – stormed toward the colored boy, waving a finger. "You can die; you can die for this, boy!"

"It's okay," Cissy croaked from behind. "He works for my daddy. I know him."

Pruitt, veins throbbing on his temples, moved toward Montcrief. "What I oughta do right here. . ."

"He was only trying to help me," Cissy said again, her voice breaking.

By now a small crowd had gathered on the scene. Betsy Sue came out of Pillson's with two new, dry bags and people began picking up things and dropping them in.

Pruitt continued to rant, which brought several other men into a circle that began merging toward Rudy. Their hands were making fists, squeezing their knuckles white. Grady Hagen only watched, the tension of the moment tingling through his wet skin. Rudy Montcrief wasn't cowering, wasn't backing away. He merely stood, his spine as straight and firm as a tree trunk. The same way he had stood so many years ago when he had pulled Grady from Boone's pond.

"You think we're going to let you animals touch our women?" Pruitt growled, only to be cut off mid-sentence.

"Get back, get back, get away from that man," a shrill voice reverberated. Irene Finestra, umbrella flailing was parting the crowd like a rabid Moses. She whacked Steve Pruitt across the chest. "Stand over there! What's the matter with you?"

Irene was all of five feet tall, the librarian of Arbutus, but Grady couldn't believe how she quieted the crowd as she splashed through the puddles and positioned herself, umbrella poised, between the crowd and Rudy Montcrief. "My goodness gracious, you boys don't know what happened here, didn't see it," she said, waving the tip of the umbrella shaft at them. "I saw it all, and this young man was only helping Miss Moody when she slipped and fell."

"She's right," Cissy cried again, this time loud enough to stop everyone. She got to her feet, leaning on Betsy Sue. "That boy was only trying to help me. Leave him alone."

Pruitt pointed past the man. "Nigger graveyard," he said. "Nigger graveyard, right out there."

"Shame on you, Steven Pruitt," Irene admonished. "Where did you learn such language?"

Pruitt stared at her as silence descended on the crowd with the mist. Just then Chief Cecil LaGrone shoved his way through the still burgeoning gathering. "What's going on here?" he asked.

"We've abandoned all sense of civilization and humanity," Irene Finestra said. She had gone over to Rudy Montcrief and was trying to dry his shirt with her sleeve.

"This jigaboo had his hands on this white woman," Steve Pruitt seethed. "Don't matter he was trying to help her or not."

Chief LaGrone waved his hands at the crowd. "Out, out, go home, y'all, back to work. Go, go now," he shouted.

As the crowd dispersed, Steve Pruitt pointed a finger at Rudy Montcrief. "You watch it, boy," he said.

Grady walked over to Cissy and picked up the few pieces that still lay on the ground. "You okay?"

Cissy was watching Rudy walk away, his head down. "The people in this town are animals," she whispered.

"C'mon, I'll walk you home," Betsy Sue said.

Grady dropped the dry goods into the bag, then shoved his hands into his pockets and started breathing again. The day had held in its crucible so much beauty, only to spill it out at the end.

11

The ball came off the bat an eye blink before the sound of leather on wood. But Grady had been moving before either of these things had occurred, seeing the pitch, sensing the speed of the bat and knowing, just knowing, where the ball would go if the batter connected. He was in center field, the place he had been assembled by the gods to play, he believed. Gave him the acres he needed to let loose with his long legs. Everyone said you could put a birdbath in left and a bucket in right and as long as Grady Hagen was in center the other team was only slightly more likely to get a hit.

Now the ball came in a frantic arc, seams chewing at the air like the teeth of a saw, and Grady turned so that he could be where it fell.

But he couldn't move.

His legs were frozen in place. He tried lifting one foot and it was welded to the ground. "Gol'dangit," he shouted, the ball whooshing away. His arms, both of them, were pinned to his sides and he screamed, head back, mouth open, choking on the winds. And then . . .

Light.

Grady sprang upright in his bed. Where was he? Lord. His room? Not his room. It was cave dark in here. Thin sunlight hung like a piece of gauze across the center, blowing in from the crack between the curtains. The walls, coming into focus now, were textured, like the surface of the moon. A cheap painting, a bullfighter, over a dresser. It was the motel room, in the place with the burned out sign by the expressway. Charlie was entangled in the sheets on the bed next to his, one foot hanging out. And just as quick as that, as quick as it took a dream to morph into a nightmare and then to dissolve away, Grady was awake and aware and back in this world. He rubbed his eyes, waiting for the rest of his body to get the news.

You get at least five bodies in your lifetime, he thought, and he was on the last one. The first is your baby body which, of course, you don't remember. Second comes the kid confection, all loosey goosey and growing out of itself. Then you hit your prime from your teenage years until, say, your late twenties or so when everything is juicy and strong and you're pretty sure you'll live forever. The sinking body is next, where all the muscles droop and your paunch pushes against the button on your trousers and the hair starts to disembark your head. Finally you get this, the body Grady Hagen was trying to muster at this moment. Holy smoke, it's hard, he thought as he swung a leg from beneath the covers. His skin was getting assaulted by the cool expectorate of the air conditioner, rippling pimples up his entire torso. An involuntary noise, a grunt or *firp* of air, escaped from somewhere as if he had stepped on a squeeze box. Used to wake up and my dick was hard and my legs were loose, he thought. Now it's the other way around.

Charlie stirred. "You okay, Pappy?" he said, sitting up, opening one eye.

"Just trying to get my ass to agree with my bones, that's all," Grady answered, moving to a cadence of snap and crackle as he struggled to the bathroom.

Charlie moaned and rolled back over. "We gotta get up already?"

"We're almost home," Grady said.

The bathroom light came on in a sizzle, turning the room yellow. Grady Hagen pulled the tee shirt up and over his head and looked at the face that came out of it. It was on old man's face, but it seemed to be moving on him, morphing from this thin, gaunt, skeletal visage to that of a teenager in a wool cap, a bulge of chew in his cheek, then back to a dashing fellow with wavy black hair and a huge smile. It was as if there were layers of ancient skin only partially concealing a montage of images underneath. But as different as they were, each had the same eyes, the same clanging mechanisms behind them. Each was there as full and real as the others. Grady closed his eyes tightly, mesmerized by the crackling of colors that exploded in the darkness he had caused.

Michael J. Griffin

When he opened them, only the old man was looking back at him. Then, for the first time in many, many years, he noticed the scar. Not the neat and clean one that ran straight as a string down his sternum like beads of solder, but the one beneath his right nipple, about the size of a quarter, but splattered like a bug on a windshield and the color of butter.

This he had gotten a long, long time ago, in April of '45 when the war was, for all intents and purposes, done and they were just cleaning up the last few pieces, and they all couldn't quite reconcile the reality that they had survived and were going to live and go home.

There was a flash of light and Grady snapped back to the present. The dew and mist of the memory night drained away, and he was again in the middle of yellow light.

"You used to tell me you were attacked by a dinosaur."

"Huh? What?" he asked turning around to the voice behind him, suddenly realizing that Charlie had taken yet another shot of him.

"That scar there you've got your fingers on," Charlie said from the open doorway of the tiny bathroom. "You always told me when I was a kid that you got that from fighting dinosaurs."

Grady moved his hand away and chuckled. "You betcha. Tyrannosaurus Rex did it to me, but I got him!" He made a fist.

"I didn't believe you then, but I'm starting to now," Charlie said.

Grady looked at the camera. "You gotta take a picture of me even when I'm butt naked in the gol'dang bathroom?"

Charlie chuckled. "Just habit, I guess." He pointed at the mirror. "I forgot about the scar on your back. Was that from a dinosaur, too?"

If you only knew, Grady thought. But what was the use? He never discussed the war with anyone, and his lovely grandson certainly didn't need the gory details. On the other hand, maybe he would be amazed at what the doctors in the blown out hospital in Germany told Grady when he came to, six days later: that somehow the bullet had entered his body directly in line with a major artery (they had a fancy Latin name for it, but Grady didn't remember it), and exited directly behind the artery; that it had somehow made a left turn and scooted around the artery altogether. Had it hit the thing, blood would have spurted out so fast, they said, he would have been dead in minutes. Said it was a miracle. Missing the artery like that.

Of course it was, Grady thought to himself then and millions of times afterwards. Betsy Sue had called the silver pendant a "miraculous medal," and it did exactly what it was supposed to. What kind of an ungrateful moron would consider questioning the simple truth of it?

12

Arbutus, Mississippi – 1941

The screen door sprang back like a rattler's jaws, only inches from Grady's ass, as he knifed into the house like a zephyr. His arms were caked in a fine spread of infield dirt that meandered down the front of his shirt and onto his pants. He tossed the flat leather mitt into a wicker basket, just inside the door, and didn't break stride through the living and dining rooms and into the kitchen, where he virtually skidded to a stop at what was awaiting him there.

Bo Hagen, home in the middle of the day, in the middle of the week, was holding the wrist of his left hand as his right dangled over a glass bowl on the edge of the table. Momma was wiping a moving thread of blood from it, and pinched a needle between her other thumb and forefinger. Grady could see a large blue contusion framing a narrow cut.

"What happened?" he asked, not really caring. As far as he was concerned, Bo Hagen could have his whole arm chewed off by a bear and it wouldn't make him sorry a bit. Grady was moving to the icebox. "We got any milk?"

"Got a splinter the size of a sapling run clear to the bone," Bo answered. "Got the most of it out, now your momma's picking out the small pieces," He jumped, shaking his hand. "Goddamnit, Rhea. Be easy."

"Please don't blaspheme in my home," Rhea snapped, grabbing Bo's wrist and guiding him back into his seat.

"It ain't blaspheming when it comes out without no thought," Bo replied.

"How'd it happen?" Grady asked. He moved a chunk of ice and extracted a bottle of milk. He leaned his head all the way back and took a long, hard swallow.

"That jig, Rudy," Bo replied. "Don't know the difference between push and pull." He winced again. "Typical dumb nigger."

"Must we?" Momma sighed.

"Must we what?"

"Talk like that. I'm sure it was an accident. He's just a boy, not much older than your own here. You act like all Negroes is stupid or something."

"Chee-rist, woman, what world do you live in?"

"I'm saying that there are plenty of very intelligent Negro people, school teachers, some of them, and businessmen. They're not all animals, like you think," she answered, dropping his hand into the water.

Had to agree with Momma, Grady thought.

"Show me an intelligent colored person and I'll show you someone 'been encouraged by white blood in their veins," Bo answered. "They mostly come from the slave owners who mated with the women and had little ones who was half white, in the blood, anyway."

That made sense, too, Grady considered. He took another pull on the milk bottle and set it back in the ice box.

"Please!" Rhea Hagen said, lifting the hand from the bowl and then leaning back in with the needle. "You don't know that every intelligent Negro has white blood. No one can know that, and it just ain't fair or right to make such a generalization."

She was right. How could he know?

"Let me tell you some true history, woman. And the boy, too. You ever hear of, or see, one scrap of intelligence ever come out of Africa culture? African literature, I mean books and stuff? Any scientific discoveries come out of the Dark Continent in the last million years? Heck, no," he exclaimed. Then he winced as Rhea pushed the needle under a fragment of wood. "Two thousand years ago, the Greeks and Romans built cathedrals and those Parthenon things, and even had running water and sewers, and the Africans are still living in trees and shitting in their own yards. Don't tell me they're human like us."

Now that he mentioned it, it made sense.

"Maybe they just didn't have the same opportunities," Momma replied.

That was a good point.

Bo Hagen plowed on. "All we got today that's worth a hoot and a holler is from the brain, the mind, of the white man. Electricity. Radios. Medicine. The telephone."

"We ain't got a telephone," Grady interjected.

"If we did it would be one invented by a white man," Bo Hagen answered. "Why? It's nature, pure and simple. Inferior species. Ain't their fault 'tall. Which is why I'll go up to Rudy tomorrow and tell him I ain't mad or nothin' at him. I ain't gonna whip him or nothing." Then he laughed.

"The poor boy is just trying to earn money to help his poor widowed momma," Rhea explained, using her fingernails to pull a small speck of wood from the cut.

"Oh, more than that, from what I hear," Bo answered. "That boy thinks he gonna be a doctor someday; gonna go to college. Imagine that! A nigger doctor!"

"He wouldn't be the first," Rhea said. "There's a colored doctor up in Memphis with all the full credentials, from what I hear."

Bo turned his chair, scraping it against the wooden floor, to square himself with Grady. In doing so, he pulled his arm away from Rhea. "By the way," he began to say.

"Hold still or I ain't never gonna get this cleaned out," she snarled, grabbing his forearm and re-centering it.

"Like I started to say, you better talk to your girlfriend," Bo said, not taking his eyes off Grady.

"My girlfriend?"

"Cissy."

"She ain't my girlfriend."

"Is she a girl?"

"Yeah."

"Is she your friend?"

"Yeah." Grady hesitated before getting the point. "Yeah, okay, okay. Talk to her about what?"

"She's always comin' out to the yard and walking right up to that Rudy and sashaying around him and flirtin' with him."

"Oh, my," Rhea whispered. "That isn't right."

"What's wrong with that'?" Grady asked.

"Number one, he's supposed to be workin', and she don't make that too easy, being all cleaned up and smellin' nice and whatnot. She gets too close to him, and pretty soon you got yourself some trouble," Bo replied. "Now, I'll give the boy credit, he knows his place and tries to get away from her, but she follows him like a puppy. It ain't natural what she's doin'."

"Why don't you just tell Fletcher what's happening?" Rhea said, taking the towel and wiping down the arm. "I think I got it all; now for some iodine."

"I ain't saying nothin' to my boss about his daughter flirtin' with a nigger. It ain't my place."

"It ain't my place neither to tell Cissy what she can and can't do," Grady interjected. "She's a grown up girl."

Bo made a spitting sound. "All grown up? What she don't understand is that she's playing with fire right there in her hands. Coloreds ain't like white men. Once they get the agitation for a woman, you ain't gonna stop them without a gun. Especially with white women. They got no control. They become animals." He winced and pulled his arm back as Rhea poured iodine into the cut. "Damn!" he growled.

Rhea laughed. "Like anything could ever stop you when you got the 'agitation'." She slapped him playfully on the shoulder with the towel. Then she turned to Grady. "Just tell Cissy nice to act like a lady and be careful, Grady."

13

The restaurant bled wood, knotty pine crawling the walls, beams across the ceiling, more wood beyond that, giving the whole room an orange patina. Pappy rubbed his hands together when the waitress laid down a large plate of biscuits and gravy. June was her name; she had made that perfectly clear when she took their orders, without taking her eyes off Charlie for even a second, even though she was old enough to be his, well, way older sister, at least. Charlie was already into his pancakes when she put one hand on her hip, threaded a curl of hair in a finger on the other and leaned toward the young man. "Y'all boys want anything else? Anything?"

Charlie, of course, oblivious to throbbing signals she was sending, just mumbled, "Fine, thanks," and leaned over his plate as he shoveled a huge forkful of dripping food into his mouth.

"We're quite all right for the time bein', June," Grady said, his accent coming back as if the air or something had stirred it right up and out of him.

June departed and Charlie pointed at Grady's plate which was oozing a white cream all the way to the edges. "Your arteries been way too open lately or something?"

Grady looked up. "What do you mean?"

"Blood just blasting through them unfettered?"

"Oh, you mean this?" Grady replied, pointing at the food. "I haven't had authentic biscuits and gravy for many, many years. What? You think one plate of this is going to kill me?"

84

"I doubt that very seriously. I just never considered gravy a breakfast food."

"Knew a guy down home used to drink it for lunch," Grady said, taking a huge bite.

"I hope I get to meet him," Charlie replied. Then he chewed for several seconds, looked over his shoulder at nothing in particular, it seemed, and turned back to his grandfather. "Saw last night you had a Bible with you."

Grady stopped, fork in midair. "Only way you coulda seen that is by going through my stuff."

"I came in from having a beer in the parking lot and it was so dark and I didn't want to wake you up, so when I was walking through the room I accidentally knocked your suitcase off the dresser."

"So, does it make any difference if I have a Bible with me?"

Charlie seemed to ponder the question a bit too long. "Not really. I just always thought you were sorta Jewish like Nonnie Rachel and Mom."

"Nope."

"Anything?"

"What?"

"Anything? A religion or anything?" Charlie queried, now playing with his food.

"What is this? The Spanish Inquisition?" Grady growled.

"No! Jeez, I'm just curious, just making conversation."

"I never gave it much thought."

"Oh, well, okay."

Grady chewed for several seconds then swallowed. "The older you get the less you believe, I suppose. At this stage of my life you could say I don't believe in anything, but I sure consider the possibility of everything."

"What do you mean?"

"I mean, who are we to know what's going on out there? If anything? A lot of people think they know, and every one of them has a different thing. Sanctifying grace, séances, spirit guides, beatitudes, reincarnation. Which works better, baptism or bar mitzvah? You got your Passover, karma, nirvana, the immaculate conception, meditation, Shiva, Jesus, loaves and fishes, Allah, Jehovah, original sin, heaven – which is it?

Some? All? I suppose any of them is possible." He took another bite of food and continued while he chewed. "Transubstantiation and transcendental meditation, why not? If there is a God do you think he'd sit there in one place where only some kind of people could find him? Or does it make more logical sense that you could just as easy find him in a gothic cathedral or a teepee or a revival tent or with your feet in a river?"

"Jeez, for a guy who hasn't given it much thought, that was a lot of thinking," Charlie said.

Grady sighed, took a sip of coffee and answered. "At my age, you start thinking like that."

"At your age?"

"I'm pretty sure I'm not going to live forever. And chances are, it isn't long in the future."

Charlie leaned back in his chair and stared past Grady, lost in a thought. "Are you scared of it?"

"I don't know."

"What do you think happens?"

"Now that's the big question, isn't it?" He ran a wedge of biscuit through the gravy and lifted it. "I guess we find out sooner or later," he said, popping the bite into his mouth.

"Mom says that each of us is inconsumable energy gathered in one place for a very short time but connected to all the other energy in the universe, like a huge lake fed by many streams, and when we die we are propelled into the universe."

"Sounds like her."

"Do you think there's a heaven?"

"It would be nice."

"How about hell?"

"There certainly are people who belong there," Grady replied.

Charlie continued to stare past him. "Maybe it's 'click' lights out. Nothing. Maybe there is no God, no afterlife, none of those things."

Grady interjected. "Or maybe we come back. Who knows? Just don't seem right that God would only give us one little chance on a tightrope and then throw shit at us to see if we can keep our balance."

"I find it hard to believe there's a God up there pulling the strings on us."

Grady picked something out of his teeth with a toothpick. "Sometimes I'm sure that's true, and sometimes I just wonder," his voice trailed off. He stopped chewing, set down the pick, lifted the paper napkin from his lap and wiped his mouth.

"So, you're saying that maybe there is a God out there, somewhere?"

Grady folded the napkin and placed it on the plate. "Let's just say, I wouldn't be surprised."

Charlie cleared his throat. The next words came out meekly. "Is that why you carry a Bible?"

"I don't gol'dang carry a Bible, I just happen to have one with me at this moment. Is there something wrong with that?"

"It's just that the Bible," Charlie paused.

"The Bible what?"

Charlie dropped his fork and pushed his plate away. "Ah, nothing. You answered my question."

Something was eating the kid now. "What?" Grady asked, picking up the fork again.

Charlie hesitated. "Nothing. We just never talked about religion before, I guess. I was just curious."

Then it hit Grady between the eyes. Shit! The Bible! Holy Christ. The card is in the Bible. Did he see it? Maybe not. Then again, maybe. Gol'dangit. Grady didn't know what to say. He looked Charlie up and down, searching for a hint in the boy's eyes or in the way he was slouching in the seat like he always did. Looking for a "tell" like in a poker game. The kid was staring out the window and fidgeting with his fork. What was going on in his mind? This was bad, very bad.

He should have just stuck the card in the lining of the suitcase and left the Bible home. What good did it, or the religions it represented, ever do him anyway?

14

Well, he had certainly screwed that up. The whole conversation. Didn't have balls enough to just come right out and say what the fuck is this picture card and what does it have to do with you? Then again, grandsons don't confront grandfathers. The protocol of their relationship precluded that, didn't it? What right did he have to speculate on the old man's past, let alone ask about it?

For the first time since embarking on this sojourn, Charlie thought maybe this wasn't such a good idea. He was walking to the Mustang; Pap was still in the gift shop of the cheap hotel. As he tossed the suitcase into the trunk, he noticed it, even this close to the highway where exhaust fumes and effluent from the fast food restaurants perfumed the air with colliding smells. A sea change of some sort in the sky, in the atmosphere. A beckoning perhaps. Like a storm coming. Was it a voice telling him that he was somewhere else now, and portending that this journey was about to change his life in profound ways? Ways he could not imagine, but sensed nonetheless, rippling in the air like whispers?

It made him queasy. Not sick exactly, just locked, smothered to sluggishness by an empty aching that blew through him like the wind. No, it wasn't such a great idea, coming all this way. He should have let the old man get on a fucking bus and come down here and do whatever. It wasn't just that people were royally pissed at him. Lorene, shit, who would have rung his cell phone until it melted on his belt if he hadn't shut it down; Mom who said she didn't need this crap right now, what with six surgeries lined up over the next few days. Bad enough these two. But it was Pappy who had him most puzzled; the way a pall of melancholy had settled on the old man like ice on a pond. And the way he just went blank now and then; just got to staring? Obviously his gaze went far beyond the landscape that swirled by, and resided in a deep and private place unbounded by time, unfettered by chronology.

And now, the picture. This hideous, unbelievable picture, this nightmare with Pap right there in the front row! What did that have to do with this journey?

Oh, for chrissakes, it was the whole goddamned reason for the fucking journey, wasn't it?

It gnawed at Charlie's guts that he really didn't know much about his grandfather. The old man's past had never meant anything before. There was no reason to wonder what he was like as a kid, a young man, who his parents were, what they did for a living. Arbutus, Mississippi was simply a name of a place and nothing else. There were no pictures of it that Charlie had ever seen, no words spoken about it by Pappy or Mom or anyone. And, of course, for chrissakes, it was all part of the old guy, and Charlie felt – what? – guilty for not ever being curious. Then again, the old man didn't make it very easy. He volunteered nothing about his life, afforded no glimpses of the forces and incidents that shaped him. Sure, Pappy might talk your ears off about baseball or fishing. He'd set your politics straight in a heartbeat. He'd philosophize about life and death. But anything about his past, anything at all, even a glimpse, was like scratching away carefully at the silt on an archeological site, searching for clues beneath, finding bits of bone and shards of debris that required assembly to make any sense.

Charlie saw in his grandfather a longing, a gaping hole, a forensic goldmine of explanations of how the old man's life had evolved him into who he was, but the boy wasn't allowed to go into it. Was he?

Now Charlie was beginning to maybe understand why, and the thought of it made him shiver, even in the heat.

Grady's voice brought him back. "We ready? Or not?"

"You want to drive some more, Pappy?" Charlie asked mechanically, unlocking the door of the Mustang.

"You go ahead, son," came the reply. Grady slid into the passenger seat and pulled the seat belt across his chest. When Charlie was similarly situated, Grady reached into the pocket of his suit coat and removed a cassette tape. "Your machine here play this kind of gizmo?" he asked.

"Sure, right there," Charlie pointed at the slot in the dashboard. "What you got?"

"Just something I found in the gift shop in there. You don't mind if we listen to this, do you?"

"It's not something really weird, is it?"

"Nope," Grady replied sliding the tape into place. A soft melody wafted out and then a trembling voice.

"Willie Nelson," Charlie said.

"He's a good old boy," Grady answered.

"Hoagy Carmichael," Charlie said, nodding to the rhythm. "Stardust."

"How'd you know?" Grady asked, his eyebrows rising. "I thought all you knew was hippity hop and rap."

"Took a course in college. Music appreciation."

"Is that a fact? Didn't know that."

"It's a nice song."

"My old friend had a hardware store, well his daddy did, and in the summer they'd put the old Victrola out on the street and play 78s." Grady laughed wistfully. "You probably don't even know what a 78 is. Anyway, it was a way to sell Victrolas, I guess. You had to crank up the turntable to get it to spin. I'd come by and crank the old thing back up if it was stopped. I'd take off whatever record was playing and reach down into the compartment and pull out 'Stardust'. Play this song over and over," he leaned his head back and closed his eyes. "Play this song."

It began to rain. Big clumps of it smattering the windshield of the car. Grady began singing along in a soft, raspy voice.

15

Hatred came and settled on Arbutus like hoarfrost, gray and heavy, reflected in the crackling eyes of the citizens. It had emerged on a Sunday in the static cadence escaping the radio, words and emotions that seemed to spread out like a net and drag everyone to the sets where they sat and listened for hours on end. Grady had never heard of Pearl Harbor before that day, had barely paid attention to what had been happening in Japan and Europe. Love and baseball had filled him up to bursting, it seemed, leaving no room for anything else. But the next day it was obvious that the world – the entire damned world – had changed. It manifested itself first in a soapy scrawl on the window of Tolleston's Hardware that Billie Rae Tolleston, Sr. discovered. Someone had used a paint brush to make a twisting symbol and write the words, "Kraut go home." The same message had been deposited on Bauer's drug store window as well. Tolleston, Sr. came and fetched the boys before school.

"What's that mean, that mark? It looks like some kind of emblem," Grady said, dipping his sponge in the bucket of warm soapy water that steamed in the cool morning air.

Billie Rae, Jr. grunted. "That's a swastika. Symbol of Hitler's boys."

"Why they paint it on your window?"

"Some wise ass who thinks all Germans are Nazis, I guess."

91

"You're German?" Grady asked. He had never really thought about it.

"I'm a goddamned sumbitch fucking American," Billie Rae answered, soapy water streaming down his arm.

"My dad says we're all probably gonna get sucked into this thing, all the boys our age, soon as we get out of school."

"All because that crazy bastard couldn't content himself with just killing the Jews. He had to go invade Poland and bomb England."

"Who?"

Billie Rae threw his sponge into the bucket. "Jesus, you're as dumb as a stump sometimes. Hitler, you lame brain."

Grady wrung out his sponge and watched the foamy water trickle through a crack in the sidewalk and spread out into the crevices of the brick street. "You think you and me are gonna have to go, too?"

Billie Rae snorted. "Me and you and any other boy who can stand up and walk straight. You'll see 'em lining up today to enlist, can't wait to get their slick new uniforms and a free gun and a helmet." He pulled his sponge out and began scrubbing the window in huge circles. "Soon as I'm finished with school in May, I'm going in."

"You are?" Grady asked.

"Hell, yes. I don't want to miss this one. It's going to be a doozie."

"Oh, my goodness, what happened here?" a voice from behind startled them. Grady recognized it instantly and turned to face Betsy Sue.

"Hi," he said, taking her in with his eyes.

"Some sick pervert with a bent sense of humor thinks my old man's a Nazi," Billie Rae answered.

"That's terrible," Betsy Sue said, hugging her books to her chest. Then she turned to Grady. "Meet me after school?" she cooed, barely above a whisper, taking his finger.

"Sure," he replied, beginning to count the minutes.

Five hours later they were climbing the hill toward the cave. It had become their secret place where they could be alone and talk and then go at each other with all the exploding hormones and instincts that naturally pulsed through their veins – always coming close, but never fully arriving at the tree with the forbidden fruit. And Grady would have to roll away from her and sit himself up against the cave wall and breathe himself back to a normal, un-agitated state. Still, he wouldn't dream of not coming here with her where the world stayed away and only the two of them existed.

"It's kind of cold today, isn't it?" he asked, putting his arm around her and pulling her close.

"It's not that bad," she said, breaking away and pulling him toward the cave. At the entrance, she pulled back and let him enter. "You first," she said, looking around.

Grady pulled back the thicket that concealed the opening and squeezed in, finding the lantern and lighting it. Then he came back to get her, gently leading her in by the hand.

Immediately she turned to him, cupped his face in her hands and kissed him, hard and almost angrily, forcing open his mouth until their tongues met in what, by now, had become a familiar dance. She pulled away a few inches. "Gradyhagen, do you love me?"

"I don't know how to say it in words that even come close," he stammered, but before he could finish his sentence, she was kissing him again.

He pulled her close and felt her chest heaving against him, her warm, sweet breath in his ear. Their lips met again, but this time it was different, deeper, darker, more consuming, like the cave itself. Gently, he lowered her to the blanket on the floor. The rest just happened, exploded in a frenzy of maneuvering, unbuttoning, pulling, and moaning. They were both naked from the waist up, her soft and sweet breasts against his chest. He looked at them, nipples as soft and red and fragrant as rose petals. Gently kissed them; couldn't believe what was happening.

Her eyes were closed, her mouth open as she seemed to drink from him with an insatiable thirst. Then his hands, his uncontrollable hands, detached from his mind, were at the elastic of her skirt and it was sliding down.

And this time she did not stop him.

Something, some force outside both of them, had taken over. His pants were down now, too, around his ankles, and he was being sucked into a vortex of mystery and incomprehension. There was resistance, a tearing, Betsy Sue's fingernails digging into his back. Was she in pain? What was this?

And then he was engulfed, enfolded, enraptured, and totally lost. The world had dissolved around him, come crashing down on him like a storm. He was no longer in it nor a part of it nor connected to it, but a wisp of smoke or cloud adrift on a storm. He was finished, it seemed before he had really begun, depleted with what must have been a scream from deep in his heart, and they lay there, Betsy Sue with her head buried in his chest, soft tears dripping onto his skin.

If Billie Rae could only see him now, he thought. Of course he would be royally pissed that Grady had broken the solemn blood oath and revealed the whereabouts of the cave; but if he could see them now in each other's arms, boy, would that get his goat but good. Look at this, pal, you always saying she's out of my league. Saying she's only using me. Look at me now.

16

The Mustang was almost alone on the road, floating over a ribbon of bubbling asphalt that slunk thinly past empty fields and clapboard towns. Now and again a truck would come by, huffing and swooshing inches past them, causing the car to rock.

Nothing had been said for some time. Charlie just moved the Mustang forward like a needle through fabric, passing under railroad trestles and then up and over bridges, and then between the folds of the hills. Here and there, houses popped up like mushrooms, just suddenly there – along the highway with no stores or gas stations to knit them together, ash colored against the harsh green fields. Dirty wooden things, leaning, paint flaking off, with front porches adorned with stuffed chairs propped up on blocks and expunging wads of stuffing. Dead and decaying cars graced the front yards, kids crawling on them. And heat. Heat, wet and relentless, seeping in through the vents, straining the car's air conditioning system.

Grady suddenly came away from the window and raised his hand. "Stop, stop, turn in right here, my good Lord," he breathlessly exclaimed.

"Here?" Charlie asked.

"Turn, turn, right in here."

They were on the outskirts of a town; all the telltale portents were there; railroad tracks with arms, speed limit signs to thirty, a cemetery. Charlie slowed down and turned into a yellow clay parking lot, kicking up clouds of dust. Gravel cracked beneath his wheels. About a hundred yards ahead sat a large cinder block building flanked by the skeletal bracing of bleachers. A ballpark. The car came to a stop, and Grady was out and sliding through the gate of a chain link backstop before Charlie could put it in park and shut down the engine.

Grady didn't say a word, just ambled over the pitcher's mound, through the clay infield and stopped where – if a game was on – second base would be anchored to the earth. He spread both arms wide and closed his eyes, inhaling deeply.

"Pappy, you all right?" Charlie called from the other side of the fence.

But, of course, Grady wasn't all right, not exactly. He had been swallowed whole by the place and was tumbling through it.

This ballpark, the very place where he had made history in Arbutus, about a half mile outside of town on the county road, was different, of course, than it had been sixty years before. But what wasn't? The bleachers that had once tilted on splintering black wood were now made of aluminum. The old barn-sided shed behind the backstop at home plate had been replaced by the tall cinder block building that was obviously a concession stand and announcer's box. There was a brand spankin' new scoreboard in centerfield with a big red round Coca-Cola sign on one end. The chain link fence that surrounded the outfield wasn't even there when Grady had ripped that homer against the Jackson team, not to mention all the advertising signs on it. The *Arbutus Daily Democrat*, Dr. Pepper, Farley's Store for Men, Bauer's Drugs, Winn Dixie, Central Mississippi Bank, Panzer's Excavating, Edmunson Brothers Funeral Home, Carley Insurance, Eileen's Fabric Shoppe.

Tolleston's Hardware.

I'll be damned, Grady thought. Do I want that or not? Do I want to see him, if he's still alive, if he's there at all? Grady shook out of those thoughts and took another deep breath, and the mingled and mixed aromas enlivened all his senses.

"Smell that?" Grady shouted over his shoulder. "We're home."

They say the sense of smell is the strongest trigger of memory. Grady had read that somewhere once, and the theory sure seemed to hold up in this instance. It was the scent of the South, and it sent rivers of memories pulsing through him. A sweetness, a pureness, that was picked up by the wind from the cotton fields with their gnarled gray bushes bent over from the weight of the snowy white blossoms and the rice fields from across the Arkansas line, from the lumber mills and that pungent smell of ripped pine, and even, he supposed, from the Gulf of Mexico, far away for sure, but not too far for the currents to reach down and grab a handful of salty air and pull it up here to sprinkle over the land.

The land that still had a hold on him, God only knew why.

And what was happening to him now was a flooding of his nostrils that ignited dormant fuses in his brain, firing off pictures. It was a smell he hadn't experienced in sixty some odd years. Lord almighty, think about it, more than half a century, and yet it all came back, every single event of his young life, in a blur of feelings and imagery.

The air echoed with the heartbeats of all the souls of his past, and what dwelled there was mostly sadness.

"Pappy, you still here?" It was Charlie's voice, far away, now closer.

Grady shook out of his reverie and the world rushed back to him. He was standing now in centerfield. In grass heavenly green and soft. He had floated out there, he was sure, on the eddy of his emotions.

"I thought I lost you there for a second," Charlie said. "I spoke to you and you didn't say anything. I thought you had a stroke." Then he patted the camera he was holding. "Got some good shots, though. Think I'll call them 'Old Man in a Trance'."

Grady looked at his glorious grandson and smiled. "I guess I was just taking a little trip, that's all."

"Brings back a lot of memories, this ballpark?" Charlie said.

"You could say that."

"This is where you played, huh?"

Grady smiled. "Do you know what I would give to just one more time stand out here and watch a ball coming to me; go after it like a lion?" He pounded his right hand into his left, then raised them both and looked up into the clouds.

And then, hurtling through time and space, came the ball, soaring like a bird in the crystal blue sky.

17

Arbutus, Mississippi – October, 1941

. . . came the ball, soaring like a bird in the crystal blue sky, and Grady Hagen, lean and fluid, seemed to rise up to snatch it, and in the same motion hurl it back from where it came, on a blistering line, straight and strong. The ball struck the clay infield, spewing dust into the air and careening into the catcher's mitt, a full ten feet in front of the foolish runner who had dared Grady's arm. And while the rest of the team leapt and celebrated, Grady tossed his mitt to Billie Rae and slid through the crowd to find her. Betsy Sue also came to him and took his hand. They then walked into the glorious day toward their secret place.

The sounds came out, shredded by the branches of the bushes and cut to small pieces by the rocks, but unmistakable, and surprising, because the cave had always been stoic in its silence and tranquil in its anonymity. They had laid claim to it and its darkness, wrapped themselves in the solitude it afforded them. Here they were shielded from the world and they could taste each other and touch each other and love each other in the frantic way that young people do, knowing that they were hidden from the rest of the world and its judgment.

Betsy Sue heard the noises first from a hundred feet away and pulled Grady back. "What's that?" she whispered, curling into him.

"What?"

"Sssshhh. Listen."

Grady leaned forward. Good Lord, something coming from the cave, his cave, their cave now, the place they came. A steady, thumping sound. "What the heck?"

Betsy Sue was backing away, back toward the woods but still facing the cave, pulling him with her. "What is it Gradyhagen?" she cried. "Some kind of animal?"

Grady listened. Animal? A bear maybe? There were bears here, he'd heard, but he'd never seen one.

"Let's get out of here, Gradyhagen," Betsy Sue said, letting go of his hand and turning her back to the cave.

Grady raised his hand to slow her down, taking a few tentative steps closer. Two sounds, different kinds, coming out. One a soft grunting, steady. Hunh, hunh, hunh. The other almost a whispered whimpering, like air coming out of a bicycle tire. Eeeh, eeeh, eeeh. Playing off one another, it seemed, in some kind of bizarre cadence. Together they clattered, making a whole noise, but not the sound of pain or distress.

What kind of animal makes a sound like that?

Betsy Sue had come back to him now, and was pulling on the crook of his arm. "Grady, come on. It could be dangerous. You don't know what's in there."

The sounds, faster now. "Hunh, hunh, hunh."

"Grady, we can't go in there. Let's go home."

"Hunh, hunh, hunh."

"Gradyhagen, don't be a fool."

Something about the noises. Something not right.

"Hunh, hunh, hunh."

"Eeeh, eeeh, eeeh."

Something, Jesus, not animal at all.

"Please take me home."

Then a change. "Eeeh, eeeh, eeeh, oh, oh, oh."

Words. Bears don't make words. Grady stepped toward the cave and then stopped, changed his mind. He turned and went back toward Betsy Sue who had, by now, gone to the edge of the woods. "Get behind the tree," he said, moving in front of her as she did.

"Oh, oh, oh God, oh."

And then the noises stopped.

"What? Why? What is it?" Betsy Sue whispered.

"Not no animal, that's for sure," Grady said, crouching behind the fatter part of the trunk. "Just sit tight for a few minutes."

A few moments later the bushes in front of the cave stirred, then bent. Betsy Sue buried herself in Grady's back. He could feel her shaking.

"Is it going to kill us?" she cried.

"No, it ain't gonna kill nobody," Grady said, confident now, expecting none other than Billie Rae Tolleston, Jr. to be the thing rattling the bushes like that. Probably in there, the little bastard, with Marilyn Smith, breaking the blood oath.

But when the bushes parted and someone emerged, the sight sent Grady Hagen backwards and took the breath out of his lungs.

Rudy Montcrief, furtive, obviously frightened, looking every which way with his twitching Negro head, staring right at the tree where Grady and Betsy Sue crouched, but obviously not seeing them.

"Isn't that that colored boy?" Betsy Sue started to say, before Grady put his finger to her lips.

Rudy had emerged fully now from the cave and walked back and forth around the front of it, putting his hands on the boulders and peering over the back side of the indentation for several seconds. Again, he turned and looked into the woods, still thick with brown leaves. Finally satisfied, he skipped back to the opening and reached into the thicket.

And helped Cissy Moody out of the cave.

Goddamn. Jesus. That colored guy is, for chrissakes, holding Cissy's fucking hand!

"Is that?" Betsy Sue said in a voice as soft as a butterfly wing in motion.

"Damn nigger," Grady said.

"Don't use that word," Betsy Sue said, punching him in the arm. "Not either of them."

They were walking away from the cave entrance now, Cissy Moody and Rudy Montcrief, and when they had gotten clear of the thicket and into the open space between the cave and the woods, they stopped.

Damn Cissy broke the code and brought a stranger into the cave! Of course, look who's talking. But how long had they been coming here?

Even though they were only two hundred feet away, Grady could hear them speaking, but it was impossible to make out their words. Then Cissy leaned up to the much taller Negro, put both arms around his neck and kissed him.

"Jesus," Grady spat.

"Eeew," Betsy Sue said, screwing up her face.

"I thought you Yankees loved niggers," Grady replied, turning toward her.

"Yeah, but not for kissing," Betsy Sue answered.

Then Rudy moved away from Cissy, his hand running down her arm until only their fingers touched as he went one way and she the other.

This is just against nature, for chrissakes, Grady steamed. How can someone like Cissy Moody who is the daughter of one of the wealthiest men in Arbutus, cavort with an animal?

Cissy stood and watched Rudy for a minute or more, her arms folded. Then she straightened her skirt and checked the buttons on her blouse, turned and began walking gingerly across the clearing and directly toward Grady and Betsy Sue.

"Oh, shit," Grady said realizing there was no way to hide from her.

"Don't say that word," Betsy Sue said, pulling him away from the tree. "Let's act like we're just walking through the woods by accident."

Gotta tell somebody. Somebody has to know what he saw here. It was, for sure, going to be hell for Cissy, but, Jesus Lord, that's not his fault. As for the colored guy . . .

Cissy Moody was somewhere else, her eyes and mind, anyway, a melody coming off her like perfume. She was kicking the mounds of dry leaves as she walked. Maybe she won't see us, Grady thought, an instant before she caught sight of them and screamed.

"Oh! My goodness gracious," she gasped, patting her fluttering heart. "Y'all scared me to next Tuesday."

"Hey y'all Cissy," Grady mumbled. Betsy Sue had pulled herself close behind him, as if she were trying to hide.

Cissy was fighting the awkwardness of the moment, trying to stay calm. "Y'all just out for a walk in the woods now, are ya?"

"Yeah, yeah," Grady said. Good Christ, her words were coming out of a mouth that, moments before, had been pressed against a Negro's lips.

"Uh, you two getting to be a real item," Cissy said, reaching up and gently tugging on one of the buttons on Grady's shirt.

"Yeah, maybe." What they would do, of course, is probably hang the nigger if they found out. Not to mention disgracing Cissy clean out of Arbutus. And what about poor Fletcher Moody, her damn daddy, for chrissakes? How could he cotton to losing a daughter to a colored man?

"You, uh, been out here long, in the woods, I mean?" Cissy said, looking down at her feet which were still sweeping leaves.

"Not long," Betsy Sue immediately answered.

"Yeah, not too long," Grady added.

Cissy looked around at the massive maple and oak trees that trembled in the breeze. "Sure is pretty out here. I like the smell. The smell of the leaves." She glanced at Grady's face. "Y'all, uh, didn't see no one else out here, did you?"

"No," Betsy Sue said quick as a dart.

"Thought that on a day like today maybe somebody else would be taking a walk. Like y'all are. And me. Uh, just me."

Silence threaded itself between them uncomfortably. So many things, gol'dangit, that needed to be said like what the hell are you doing out here with him, Clarissa Moody, and don't you know what happens to people like you who go and up and violate the very laws of nature? And I suppose you expect me to say nothing, not a damn word to your father who is my old man's boss? Even though you and me, Cissy, been friends from school and growing up and all, for all our lives? Damn you, Cissy.

But instead, he took a breath. "Yeah, well, we're going to get going now," Grady said. Reaching behind himself and taking Betsy Sue's hand. "Y'all know how to get back all right?"

"Yeah, Grady," Cissy said. Then she took Grady's free hand in hers, holding it with her fingers and swinging it as she spoke. "I wish we still got to see one another more." She turned to Betsy Sue. "Me and Grady were good friends," she caught herself, "not like that, I mean. Just good buddies for a long time." She dropped his hand. "Y'all make a very cute couple," she said, turning and walking away. Then she stopped and faced them again. "Would 'preciate it if you don't tell no one you seen me out here. Okay?"

Grady didn't answer, but she had heard something in his silence, because she blew him a kiss and started running.

When Cissy was deep into the woods well past them and the scent she loved so much, Betsy Sue turned to Grady. "She knows we know."

Grady furrowed his brow. "How can you tell?"

"Trust me."

"I don't think so. She would have said something."

"She did. Just not with words."

"How can you say something without words?" Grady asked.

"You've got a lot to learn, boy," Betsy Sue answered.

"I suppose that's true."

"What now?" Betsy Sue asked. "What happens now?"

"Danged if I know," he answered, spitting and unconsciously wiping his mouth with his sleeve.

18

The world had stayed away from Arbutus, blocked out by the pouring of woods and hills. Even now, more than six decades after he'd shaken its dirt from his shoes, there was an intense familiarity to it, and Grady couldn't get enough of it as Charlie nudged the Mustang into the center of town. Charlie was speaking, but Grady wasn't listening. He was spinning in the seat, up on one knee, looking first through the windshield and then the window on his side, and then the windows on the other side of the car, and then to the back window as the tiny hamlet enveloped him.

"Is it always this hot down here?" the boy asked.

"Slow, slow down, Charlie," Grady said.

Just past the baseball field was Moody's lumber yard where Bo Hagen had worked. It now had a different name, Central Mississippi Lumber and Supplies, painted in red letters on a bright yellow background on the tall side of the open storage bin. A forklift scurried through the open lot with a stack of two-bys twanging at the ends and threatening to flop right off the forks.

"Don't see how you could stand this heat," Charlie grunted.

"Weren't any forklifts when my daddy humped lumber for Moody," Grady thought aloud in a soft voice. "Used to do it by hand. No wonder he was so angry."

"What'd you say?" Charlie asked, leaning toward him.

"Not too much farther, just over those tracks," Grady said, pointing out the front of the car. And then as quick as that, they were there.

Arbutus. Lord in heaven. The chisel that had shaped him, that had left on him indelible nicks and slices that no amount of travel or denial or time or experiences could hide. So much the same, yet so different. It was as if he had walked away from a chess game years ago and now come back to see, indeed, the same board, but with pieces moved from where he thought he'd left them.

"Is this it?" Charlie asked, sounding under whelmed.

The town hadn't grown at all. In fact, it seemed to have contracted upon itself. Two streets, Jefferson running north and south and Main, running east and west, formed perpendicular rows of two-story red brick storefronts which all faced out to a park, replete with a bronze statue of a proud Civil War veteran leaning on a rifle and seemingly looking down to the plaque on the base with the names of the fallen. And the stores, had they moved them around? Was the drug store always there, between the cleaners and the insurance agency? Seems it was the other way around. Now the bank was on the corner, feeding cars from a drive-thru window in the alley space that separated it from the grocery store. The brick roads had been paved over, sucking away much of the red cast that had once dominated the town. They were wider now, too, so that cars could angle in on both sides, as perhaps a dozen did at that very moment. And the trees. What had happened to the trees? Arbutus always seemed clutched in trees, but now you could see the tops of the buildings across the park. Most of the residents lived away from downtown, close to the farms they sharecropped, and the others lived in neat rows of clapboard houses behind the commercial buildings. Grady could see that those streets had lengthened, that new homes had been built, or maybe they were always there and he didn't remember. Maybe the picture he carried in his mind was wrong.

"Oookay," Charlie exhaled. "What now?"

"Pull in. Anywhere here," Grady answered. "Let's take a walk."

The opening of the car door threw heat at them, but Grady, nonetheless, hopped out and was up on the sidewalk in a second.

"Slow down, Pap," Charlie said. "Let me get my camera, if this hell heat doesn't melt my film."

The rhythmic thrum of air conditioners seemed to vibrate storefront windows, and Grady's image shimmered back at him as he slowly walked along, his hand touching the brick facades and wooden brocade of the doors. He stopped beneath a barber's pole, swirling like a candy cane, and looked through the glass door. Amberson's Barber Shop then, it was now called Smitty's, but to his eyes the name was all that had changed. The walls were mud yellow, festooned with calendars and cheap prints of landscapes. Red vinyl chairs, their numerous cracks and tears pinched together with duct tape, were lined up against the side wall and separated in threes by rickety wooden tables strewn with magazines. Two barber chairs, masterworks of rampaging steel and porcelain, had to be the same ones his very body had occupied once a month or so back then.

Two doors up a bell tinkled and three young girls emerged from a storefront, oblivious to anything but the moment in time and the infinitesimal spot in the world they occupied. They were eagerly unwrapping candy bars and leaning in to see what each other had bought. They were black, these girls. Grady had never been in this town when black people could go right into the drug store right there and walk up to the candy counter or the soda fountain and get whatever they wanted and be talked to in congenial terms and even be thanked for their purchase.

"What are you looking at, Pappy?" Charlie asked.

"So much the same, so different," he replied.

An old man rocked rhythmically, arms folded, in front of an antique store. He was wearing a long-sleeved white shirt accented by two red suspenders clipped onto faded khaki pants that billowed against his crossed leg. His eyes were partially obscured by shadows from his fedora. He glanced up at Grady and Charlie as they passed by. "Mornin' folks, how y'all doing?" he said, tipping his hat. "Fine day, fine day."

"It is, indeed," Grady replied. And it dawned on him that the last time he had walked down this street, everyone knew him. Probably, even, this old guy who was, now that Grady thought about it, most likely a few years younger than he. Just as he remembered how sixty years ago an old man sitting on a rocker in front of a store would have sprung up out of his seat and grabbed Grady Hagen by the arm and pumped his hand and slapped him on the back and talked to him about baseball until Grady, full of it up to the chin, would wriggle free with appropriate apologies for being in such a hurry. Just as he was believing that he was now as anonymous and meaningless as his life had turned out, something changed in the old man's eyes and they locked on Grady for what seemed like several minutes.

"You. I know you. Almighty-damn if I don't know you," the man said, creaking upward and out of the rocker, which responded by continuing to sway. He scratched his neck and circled Grady for several seconds, looking him up and down. Then he finally spoke again. "Ain't you Grady Hagen?"

Grady swallowed hard. What to say? Don't get into it right now. Just deny it and walk away. Probably not a good idea. He tried to strip the lines and creases off that old man's face and reciprocate the recognition being given him, but no matter what he did, he couldn't place the man.

"Well, ain't ya?" the codger insisted.

"As a matter of fact, yes, I am," Grady answered.

The old man took off his hat and slapped it against his thigh. "Gol-damn. I knew it, just knew it! Grady damn Hagen, wow!" He offered his hand, and when Grady took it, began to pump furiously. "I can't believe it."

"I'm sorry, I don't remem . . ."

"It's me, Grady! Lee. Lee Lee."

"Lee Lee?" Charlie asked.

"Oh, for cryin' out loud, of course!" Grady said. Lee Lee, perhaps the oddest named individual in Arbutus, was the batboy for the baseball team when Grady played. "Lee, how you been?"

"Oh, man, Grady Hagen," he answered, shaking his head. "Oh, man, I still tell people how – remember that time that boy from Tupelo, musta been in the semi-finals, big kid, looked like he was some kinda lumberjack or somethin', rips a liner that took off like a rocket, though we didn't even know what a rocket was in them days, whoosh, flyin' like fire into the hole in right center. That gol'durned baby was gonna clean off them bases. And then out of nowhere comes you, flying like an eagle, fifteen foot off the ground if you was an inch, laid out straight as a clothesline and I'll be damned if that ball didn't dive straight into your mitt like a puppy dog comin' home to its master." His eyes were wide as he told the story. He turned to Charlie. "And then this man right here slud 'cross the outfield grass, holding the mitt and ball up for the whole world to see. And for a good ten, fifteen seconds, you could hear a sparrow fart it was so silent. Then the crowd went nuts. Nuts! There was never nothin' like that before, and I tell you on my daddy's grave, ain't nobody seen nothin' like it since, including Willie Mays!"

"Lee Lee, you're going and exaggerating again," Grady said. "You were just a little kid in the dugout with eyes like saucers."

"I seen what I seen," Lee answered, his head swiveling between Grady and Charlie, finally stopping on the young man. "Who's this here? He a ballplayer, too?"

"Uh, this is my grandson Charlie."

Charlie reached up and shook the old man's hand. "Mr., uh, Lee, nice to meet you."

"Crazy, huh? The name, I mean," Lee replied, pumping Charlie's hand. "I guess it was the best my parents could do with the pressure on. Kind of hard to tell if someone is calling you by your first or last name, ain't it? You get used to it, though, eventually. I figure I will be in about two years." Then he bent back his head and roared.

"How about I get a picture of the star centerfielder and his bat boy?"

"You ain't from the *Enquirer* are you?"

"No, sir, just passing through," Charlie said.

"Whatcha'all want me to do?"

"Just stand there together. Look natural," Charlie replied, lifting the camera to his eye. The two old men stood shoulder-to-shoulder, hands clasped in front of themselves. When the photo was taken, Lee put his hat back on his head and shook Grady's hand again.

"Gol'durn good seeing you, Grady. You was my hero," he whispered.

"Lee, you take care of yourself," Grady said, letting go of the man's hand and turning.

Lee Lee had already spun himself away and waddled up the sidewalk, positioning himself in front of a lady who was coming toward him. He waved his hat as he spoke. "Martha, Martha, look yonder there. See him? That there is Grady Hagen."

Grady and Charlie continued down Jefferson Street until Grady could clearly see the spot at the far end of the park where once stood a gnarled, ancient oak tree. It was gone, replaced by a clump of evergreen shrubs that spilled across the grass. Grady wondered when it had disappeared, if it had been cut down for some reason, or struck by lightning, or succumbed to some oak tree disease, or perhaps died from shame.

"Hey Pappy, can we go in somewhere and cool off? How about a beer or something?" Charlie asked, removing his ever-present backwards baseball cap and wiping his brow with his forearm.

"No beer here," came the reply.

"What does that mean?"

"Dry county. No booze whatsoever."

"Jeez, it's fucking Iraq," Charlie grumbled. "How about a Coke?"

Grady's own shirt had started to congeal against his skin, and he cursed his weakness, decried his yearning for air conditioning, for comfort for his own shameful body. "Yeah, in a minute," he said. One more stop to make, one more thing to see, before he and Charlie could leave and head out to the old homestead. So, he moved forward, cutting diagonally across the park toward the store on the corner. Then he was standing directly across the street from Tolleston's Hardware. He paused and took it in.

The old store hadn't changed at all, it seemed. Oh, the fancy sign hanging above the door was something new, but it was no disguise for what was beneath it. The interior was still dingy brown, Grady could clearly see, colored by yellow lights on the ceiling. He took a breath and wedged sideways between two cars to get a closer look. As Grady mounted the sidewalk in front of the store, the door clattered open and a boy, ten years old or so, emerged, squinting into the sunlight. A bittersweet smell, a mixture of hot varnish and leather, rushed out with the kid and Grady drank it in. God almighty, he thought.

The boy removed a square box from a Tolleston Hardware bag and extracted a wad of tissue that enfolded a shining new white baseball. Then he tossed the refuse into a wire trashcan. Grady approached him.

"Got yourself a new ball there, huh?"

The boy looked at him and squinted. "Yup."

Grady put out an unfolded hand. "Can I?"

The boy tossed the ball, and Grady caught it. He pulled it to his nose and smelled it, then rolled his hands over it, caressing its seams, feeling the smooth silky leather. "There are only a few things in life that are perfect," he said to no one in particular. "Perfect in size, in shape; the way it fits in your hand."

"Can I have my ball back?" the kid interrupted.

Grady looked at the kid and continued. "You ever lay there in your bed and toss it to the ceiling?"

"Just so it grazes the ceiling!" the boy said.

"Exactly!"

"Don't let it hit the ceiling. It'll put a smudge on the paint and my daddy'll kill me."

"That's right. Just swoosh, just kiss the ceiling with it and let it fall back into your hand." Grady tossed the ball several times into the air, letting it land with a smack against his skin. He looked again at the kid. "How much you pay for this?"

"Six," came the reply.

Grady reached into his pocket and extracted a fold of bills held together with a rubber band. He peeled one off. "I'll give you twenty for it."

The boy's eyes bulged as he reached for the bill. "Are you kidding me?"

Grady snapped it back playfully. "Just one thing. This store here, who runs it now?"

"That there hardware store?" the kid drawled, "Same rascally old bastard what always run it. Old man Tolleston." He pulled the bill from Grady's fingers. "And I gotta go in and see him again. Then he breezed past, looking over his shoulder and saying, "You'd be going in there you better be ready to buy something or he'll throw your ass out."

Old man Tolleston's still alive? Grady's initial visceral reaction discombobulated him for an instant, until he snapped back to the obvious and realized that the kid was talking about Billie Rae.

"What was that all about?" Charlie asked.

Grady flipped the ball in the air and caught it. "Why not?"

"Why didn't you just go in and buy one?"

"We're not going in there," Grady replied.

"You got something against hardware stores?" Charlie asked, nodding toward the door.

"Nope," Grady said.

Charlie moved closer, his shoulder touching Grady's. "You just paid a kid twenty bucks for a baseball because you don't want to go into a store? What's the story?"

"Someone in there I don't need to see right now."

"You don't want to see someone? Who? Someone you used to know? An old friend?"

"Nope."

"C'mon. I'm sure he'd be surprised to see you."

"That would be an understatement."

"Was he a good friend of yours?"

"Yeah." Not just an old friend, but his best friend from as far back as Grady could remember. But even that had turned suddenly, tragically, irrevocably as the result of a single incident.

"I can't believe you'd come all the way down here and not want to see a good friend," Charlie said.

There was nothing in the world Grady would have enjoyed more than seeing his old friend again. Laughing once more with him. Remembering the foolish notions they had once shared. God, how that crazy know-it-all made him laugh, followed him like a puppy dog, instigated everything fun or funny that had happened to Grady. Certainly Billie Rae Tolleston, if things were only as they should have been, could fill him up with memories he had long ago forgotten. But some things never come back to you once you throw them away. Time and the wind erode and decay them until they crumble in your hands.

Grady stood and stared at the store, the hole in his heart opening. It was at this exact spot that the world as he knew it had begun to unravel. "Let's go," he said, turning his back on the store, and his memories, and walking toward the car.

19

Against the sheet-white summer sky, cackling with the sounds of tiny and invisible life scurrying and scratching within, sat the barn, or, more precisely, what was left of it. It had imploded, its exterior walls falling inward, causing the roof to slide to the left side where it leaned precariously against a vertical beam. Time and weather and decay had sucked all color from the boards, turning them a dingy gray as forlorn as the dirt that ate away at them. Gaps were formed where the boards had loosened or rotted and Grady could see the patterns of sunlight that projected through them into the interior darkness. Weeds encircled and engulfed and sprang from virtually every open crevice. A maple tree had bent itself to follow the sun before erupting through the ceiling joists. Birds emerged through thin openings and disappeared into them as well. The barn – his barn, the barn of the lovely and gentle Cree and Bo Hagen and the first car the old man had ever owned, and the milk cow they had purchased when Grady was little and ended up being the first animal he had ever seen butchered – was now gone, replaced by a pile of rotting timbers. Although it was teeming with life, it was on the whole silent, belying the benign violence of decay that raged within its depths. This was the first thing he and Charlie saw while winding up the long dirt path that led home.

Home. Now there was a strange word that Grady heard himself think and say so many times in the past few days. Home? It was odd that a place where he had lived for only seventeen years, less than one-fourth of his life, could somehow elevate its status to this height. It certainly wasn't the happiest place he had ever lived; God knew that. It was more than a box full of memories. In fact, he could count on one hand the details of life there that still stuck with him. Certainly the encompassing experience of living there, the mundane daily routines, the breathing in of the family air, the stuff that occupied existence, were always somewhere in his subconscious, and perhaps this explained his reluctance to resent the audacity of this memory calling itself home. In fact, the best home he had ever had was the one Rachel had made for them. There was obviously more here than he understood.

"Nice barn," Charlie joked, churning a cyclone of smoke behind as he cruised up the dirt road. "Must have really tiny cows to get in that front door."

The driveway turned ninety degrees in front of the rubble, around a grove of trees under which an old pickup truck was being slowly sucked into the ground, birds flying through its glassless windows. Then the house came into view. Grady reached out and brushed Charlie's arm. "Slow, slow down for a second," he said. "Good God almighty, look there."

The home had succumbed to many of the same elements that ravaged the old barn. One side of the porch had entirely collapsed, and huge weed trees had overtaken its place. A faded blue couch, its stuffing seeping through gaping holes, occupied what was left of the flat surface. The clapboard siding was unpainted, dark and naked, as if it had never seen color. The grass in the yard was a foot high, pockmarked with clumps of thistle weeds.

"Well, must be the yard boy's day off," Charlie said.

Scrunched up next to the house was an old Ford pickup, blue over white, with the rear light hanging out like the entrails of a gutted fish and a bumper rusted brown and dangling on one end. The back windshield sported a Confederate flag decal.

The front screen door squealed open and a man emerged, pulling what looked like a small silver luggage cart bearing a green cylinder. He stopped and held his hand up to shade his eyes. Truman Morse stood crookedly like a sapling after a storm. He looked as though all the air had been squeezed from his lower body to his head, the way a child would squeeze a thin balloon. He was dressed in overalls and a sleeveless t-shirt, baggy on the emaciated frame.

"That you, Graden?" he croaked.

The Mustang stopped at the edge of the tall grass and Grady was out in an instant. The old man on the porch waited with a hand out. "Hello, Truman. Long time, huh?" Grady said, taking the man's hand and shaking heartily. Grady noticed the slim plastic tubes running from the green canister up Truman's back and over his shoulder to the elastic that held in place the breathing apparatus placed in his nostrils.

"You ain't changed a lick," Truman said, patting Grady on the shoulder.

"That's a gol'danged lie."

"Yeah, in fact, you look like hell, but then again, I ain't exactly Cary Grant," Truman chortled.

"Who's your friend there," Grady asked, pointing to the canister.

"He's my seeing eye dog," Truman laughed. "Who's your friend there?" He pointed to Charlie.

"That's my grandson, Charlie. Charlie, meet your cousin Truman Morse. My momma's sister's son."

"Pleasure," Charlie said, ascending the porch and shaking the old man's hand.

"C'mon, c'mon inside," Truman said, pulling the screen door and ushering them in. "Good God almighty. We've got lots to catch up on."

"Charlie's gonna crash here for the night, if that's okay, and then head home tomorrow," Grady said, sliding past Truman and into the house.

"I am?" Charlie replied with a grunt. "Oh, yeah."

Grady stood in the living room and waited as his eyes adjusted to the darkness. Shades had been pulled to keep out the sun, but the reality of the space soon revealed itself. The first thought that came to his mind was how small the place was. Cramped and crimped and piled with furniture and knickknacks and stuffed with indescribable debris. It was obvious that Truman had invested no time nor money in upkeep. The wallpaper was brown with age and peeling off in several sections. Several stacks of newspapers, each as tall as a man, leaned against one another and the wall, like a group of drunks on a street corner. Mismatched furniture, some balancing on mortar encrusted bricks, sat to and fro, holding old clothes and rumpled hats. Heat radiated from the walls and ceiling and floor, interrupted only briefly in rhythmic intervals by a breeze produced by a large fan on a silver stand sweeping the room. "Is that the air conditioner?" Charlie asked.

"Born a Yankee, can't take the heat," Truman mused. "Still can't figure out how they whupped us."

"Whupped us?" Charlie whispered to Grady.

"Civil War. They aren't quite reconciled to it yet down here," Grady answered.

"You're shitting me?"

"C'mon, sit down here," Truman said, lifting a pile of newspapers off a couch. "We've got lots to talk about. How about some beers?"

Charlie sagged in the mushy couch as the two old men talked about things and used the names of people he'd never heard of. The only thing that kept him alive was the steady supply of cold beer. He rolled the icy can on his forehead and cheeks between sips. Cousin Truman was at least a thoughtful host in that respect, asking him to bring refills from the refrigerator. Seems the old fucker lost one lung and part of another to cancer, and the strain of getting up and walking the few steps to the kitchen, dragging Rover, the seeing-eye oxygen canister, was too much stress on what was left of his moving parts. This, of course, was fine with Charlie. Gave him a chance to stretch his legs and, hell, it was free beer.

When the evening came, Truman fired up an outside grill and cooked to perfection steaks and fresh corn on the cob, followed by heaps of homemade potato salad. Charlie had to admit to himself that it was a fabulous meal. The corn was unlike any he had ever tasted, erupting with flavor.

"That's 'cause it's fresh right out of the garden not store bought from a Mexican truck, or packed in plastic and sprayed with water and sold five days old," Truman explained. "Corn's got a shelf life of one hour, I figure. Get it in the fire by then and you got yourself a goddamn taste of heaven."

Bellies full, heads tingling, the three men retired to the living room, and cousin Truman slid across the hardwood floor with an old man's steps, his shoes making a shush-shush sound. He got to the corner of the room where several haphazard piles of folded clothes and old newspapers were stacked on an old cedar chest. With gnarled hands he made new stacks on top of stacks as he cleared the top of the chest. Then he called out to Charlie. "Come on, boy, grab this and drag it over to your Pappy." As Charlie stood up, Truman slid back to his rocker, sucking air now through a tube he held to his mouth. With his other hand he flipped open a pocket knife and handed it to Grady as Charlie dragged the heavy chest across the floor. "Use this to open it. I ain't got no idea where the key is," he drawled, taking another sip of air.

Grady wedged the knife blade into the gaping keyhole on one of the flap locks.

"What is it?" Charlie asked, flopping down beside his grandfather and disintegrating into the soft cushions of the old couch. His eyes were heavy now. Trouble sleeping tonight? Even if a poodle-sized rat from under the barn came up the stairs with a trombone, he'd sleep through it.

"Your grandpappy came back from the war in forty-five, a big hero and all, and didn't even stop for a cup of coffee. He stuffed a few things in his army bag and then went up to Chicago to seek his fortune," Truman explained. "Left behind this trunk of his very own things. I kept it here all locked up for when he came back to get it."

"Don't need no key," Grady said, giving the blade a twist and watching the snap spring open. When he did the same with the second clasp, he set down the pocket knife and held the trunk top with both hands, pausing. "Wonder what's in here?"

Charlie leaned forward to the edge of the couch. "C'mon, open it up, let's see."

"Whatcha waitin' for?" Truman wheezed.

Grady raised the lid. The ripe smell of cedar and antiquity wafted out. The trunk was loosely packed with neatly folded clothes and other paraphernalia. Atop everything was a yellowed envelope which Grady extracted first. Flecks of paper floated down and he opened it and pulled out a stack of old photographs. "Now, what's all this?"

"Let me see," Charlie said, leaning in again.

From behind a sepia cast peered a group of dirty baseball players, draped over one another with languid arms. A pile of bats was splayed like the spokes of a wheel in front of the team. In the center of the back row, encircled in the embrace of boys on both sides of him, was

116

a young reed of a guy, cap pushed back on his head with a smooth, smiling, yet unmistakable face.

"That's you there, Pappy!" Charlie said, pointing. "I can tell!"

"That's it, that's the team right there," Truman said, rocking faster, a smile on his face.

"I remember when this picture was taken," Grady whispered, "like it was yesterday. Remember standing there looking at the box camera." He pointed to the guy on his left. "That's Rufus Marquardt right there. Real good pitcher."

"He died somewhere 'round sixty-eight, sixty-nine, Grady," Truman said. "I remember 'cause it wasn't long after they shipped that Cavanaugh kid back from Vietnam."

Grady looked up and shook his head. "And this guy here on the other side of me is . . ."

"Why, that's Billie Rae Tolleston, of course," Truman interjected. "He's still in town, ornery as ever and still knows everything there is to know about everything."

"The guy who owns the hardware store," Charlie said.

"That's him. You oughta look him up, Grady," Truman said.

Grady seemed to shake off the suggestion when he flipped through the photos and stopped on another one. Charlie leaned in. "Holy shit, Pap, who's the babe?"

Every ounce of air seemed to escape Grady Hagen at the sight. He fell back in the couch and held the photo closer. Charlie reached up. "Can I see it?"

Grady held it for several more seconds before giving it to his grandson. Then, in an instant, whatever nostalgic melancholy that had ambushed him only a second ago had lost its grip and he sat up. "Was that your girlfriend?" Charlie asked.

"Yes, one of my high school girlfriends," Grady answered, leafing through more photos.

"Yeah, *the* one from what I understand," Truman chortled, immediately sticking the air dispenser back into his mouth.

"What was her name?"

Grady seemed locked into another photo now, and it took him several seconds to answer. "Uh, I think that's Betsy Sue McDonough, if I remember correctly."

"If you remember correctly!" Truman teased. "That there young thing was your granddaddy's very favorite girlfriend."

"Well," Grady stammered.

"You know, Pap, you're entitled to more than one girlfriend in your life. I'm sure Nonnie would understand," Charlie said. "For chrissakes, you were in high school."

Grady took the photo from his grandson and perused it. "Yes," he finally whispered, "that's her. That's Betsy Sue."

Charlie looked at her closely. Betsy Sue McDonough lit up the graying, frayed paper like a comet. She and Grady were leaning against the trunk of a bubble-shaped car. His arm was draped around her waist. She was resting one of her arms on his shoulder, her other hand was on his chest. Even though the clothes and the hair and the essence of her were far removed even from the eclectic styles of today, Charlie knew a beautiful woman when he saw one. "Do you remember when this was taken, too?"

Grady didn't look up from the snapshot. He spoke, but to someone not in the room, it seemed. "I remember it very well, in fact, this day, the way she smelled. So clearly I can feel her standing here against me as if it was yesterday." He looked up. "Does that answer your question?"

"Whew," Charlie exhaled. Maybe it was the remnants of the beer, then again maybe something profound had just happened to him. Charlie thought about Lorene back home and the dozens of other girlfriends he'd had and wondered if any of them could do to him what this photograph, this girl, had just done to his granddad; if the mere sight of one ten or twenty or sixty years from now would ignite a memory that literally took his breath away and sapped all the color from his cheeks. And the answer came without hesitation. No.

He placed the photo back onto the stack. "It wasn't long after this that she left," Grady sighed. He was silent for several moments, fingering the pile of photos. "You know, when you get to be an old man like me, it suddenly dawns on you that there is a last time for everything in the world. There is a last time that you catch a fly ball. There is a last time that you walk out of a house that you lived in. There is a last time that your little girl crawls on your lap and you hold her there." He was staring straight ahead, a jumble of thoughts going through his mind. "The last time you love somebody, hear her voice, and make love." Now he turned to Charlie and smiled.

Grady continued, "The problem is, when you do something for the last time, you're very seldom aware that it's the last time. Know what I mean? 'Cause if you did, you would savor the moment. You would hold on to it and squeeze it tight. Like when I had my heart attack. You know, they say that having a heart attack is like being shot, well, I've been through both and they're nothing alike. But I had the big heart attack and came out of the hospital and never smoked a cigarette again. If I had only known that whatever cigarette I smoked before I had that attack was my last one, I would have sat down and taken my time and enjoyed it, savored it. But I didn't. I don't even know when it was. But I'm pretty sure it was just another cigarette that I took down as fast as I could and flicked it away certain that there was another one in my pocket waiting. I took it for granted in exactly the same way that we all take everyday things for granted. And then they disappear."

"I remember my last cigarette," Truman interjected. "I could hardly breathe at all and I passed out and it landed in my lap and set my pants to a smolderin'." He laughed. "I woke up to a big old bonfire in my crotch. Fortunately, I had a can of Carlings Black Label to pour on it and put it out. Went to the hospital, and that's where I got my scuba tank."

"I can't remember the last time I took a leak," Charlie joked, pushing himself to his feet. "Where's the john?"

"It's outside. Take that there catalog with you," Truman deadpanned, pointing to sales flyer on the end table.

"Outside?" Charlie's eyes widened.

Then Truman and Grady started laughing. "No! Back of the house. You think we're a bunch of hillbillies down here or something'?" Truman roared, pointing.

"Yeah, well, if the shoe fits," Charlie muttered.

Grady ran his index finger down the cheek of Betsy Sue's image and cleared his throat. "Last times," he whispered, feeling a river of pain course through his chest, "some last times, you remember."

20

Arbutus, Mississippi – January 1942

The constant cool of the cave washed over them, but now, in the midst of winter, it was actually warmer than the spitting gray sky outside. Nonetheless, Betsy Sue seemed anxious to dress and she said nothing as she gathered her clothes and shakily pulled her sweater over her head. She would not look at him.

"Hey," Grady said, touching her shoulder.

"Don't!" She pulled away from him.

"Betsy Sue, what's wrong."

"Nothing."

"Something."

She turned on him, something coming out of her eyes. What was it? Hatred? Fear? Some parts of both? "I'm late," she snarled.

"Late for what? You going somewhere with your parents?"

She had begun to tremble and, even in the darkness, he could see the tears welling up in her eyes. "Late, you dumb hillbilly. Late!"

Grady scratched the back of his head and pursed his lips. "Should we get going then?"

"For my period!" she finally shouted, pounding him with both fists on the chest. "You're so confounded stupid sometimes."

Grady remembered Billie Rae Tolleston saying that the reason Laura Banning was crying one day in the hallway is because she was late for her period and that meant she was pregnant. Could Betsy Sue? "Damn," Grady exhaled, falling onto his back. "Damn."

"That's it? That's all you can squeeze out of that little pea head of yours?" Betsy Sue cried, wiping her cheek with an open palm. "Dang? Dang?"

He folded back into a sitting position and put his arm around her, trying to pull her closer. "Don't worry; I'll take care of you. We can get married."

Betsy Sue pushed him away and stood up, yanking on the hem of her skirt. "You fiddley dee. We can't get married," she cried. "That's the stupidest notion you ever had."

Grady pulled himself up. "Why not? Just tell me why not."

"I'm not supposed to be late. I'm not supposed to be pregnant. It's not supposed to happen."

Not supposed to happen.

And, of course, it didn't. Her period came a few days later, and she was elated. While his own relief was palpable, deep down inside he wondered what life would have been like if it hadn't.

But this thing seemed to change everything between them, and it became apparent almost immediately. What was it? Guilt? Fear? They had, certainly, crossed a border – been dragged across by forces neither of them could control, to tell the truth – that society and religion had forbidden them to cross, but one that biology had, and always would, crash through with impunity. They had sinned for certain, as both of their silly religions would shout to them. They could have created a child, and what would that mean for the rest of their lives? But hadn't they both been equally culpable? Equally to blame, if blame was the right word to use? Something delicate had been raised between them, like a soft scrim through which everything became murky if not invisible, all their feelings for each other, their moments, their memories.

So, as the days passed, Betsy Sue inched away, it seemed, like a dune in the wind, imperceptible to everyone except Grady. It was becoming difficult to meet her eyes, which seemed always preoccupied with something out the window or on the floor. The tender touch of their fingertips as they passed in the hallway had become almost perfunctory. After school she always seemed to have something else she had to do. But he dared not ask what was wrong. The implications of the answer were too frightening to comprehend.

Then she was gone. As simply and quickly as that. First, not in school, and when Grady asked her friends where she was, they just shrugged or looked away; said they didn't know. But Grady didn't believe them, even though he was too dumb to sense the seriousness, the finality of what was happening. Then Annie, Betsy Sue's best friend, came up to him and handed him a small package, wrapped in butcher paper. An envelope was taped to the top. He opened the letter first.

My dearest Grady,

I first must beg you to forgive me for the weak and cowardly way that I have handled this important endeavor. My heart is broken over what I am about to say, for myself and for what I must leave behind, but most importantly for you. I can only imagine that your pain is so much greater than mine because I could not find the courage to tell you to your face, which was the least I owed you after all that we went through together.

The tears had begun to stream down Grady's face, and he found that in the time it had taken to read those first few words, he had somehow transported himself to the park in the middle of town. He looked around to make sure no one was nearby and tried to stop his hands from trembling.

As you know, my father works for the government. He isn't a spy or anything like that, like Billie Rae always says, but the events of the past few weeks have resulted in him having to transfer back to Washington, D.C. immediately. Please believe me when I tell you that we didn't know for sure about this until a few days ago, which is no excuse for me not telling you in person. Grady, please believe me when I tell you that the love I felt for you was as real as love can be for people our age. Maybe someday I'll know if that's what real love is. All I know for sure now is that I'm going to have to find a way to make this feeling in my heart go away, and you must do the same. That's why I think that writing to each other is a mistake, as I will never be coming back to Arbutus.

I don't know what the future may hold, particularly not in these uncertain times. If, by chance, we ever meet again by some stroke of luck, who knows what might happen? I just don't think that waiting or even planning for that to happen is a good idea.

I will always remember you, Gradyhagen, even when I'm eighty years old.

Fondly,
Betsy Sue

P.S. In the box is a medal for you. It's called a miraculous medal. I know you don't believe in such things, but if you wear it, the Blessed Virgin will protect you. Please give it a try. It would mean a lot to me.

By now the tears had nearly blinded him and he furiously tore the letter into tiny bits and threw it against the wind where its remnants took wing and departed for eternity. Then he began to run, disbelieving what he had just read. His legs carried him without fatigue or pain through town and out to her house a mile or more away. From the long, winding, dry brown clay driveway he heard emptiness even before the house was in sight, heard it wafting around the bend at him as sure as the wind. It started softly, like a hiss, rolling, rolling, and when he turned the last kink in the road just past the grove of trees that obscured the structure, it hit him like a rumble of thunder.

The house had stopped breathing and sat like a corpse on the small hill. The car, her daddy's Ford, was not in the driveway. It seemed that the tracks from the tires in the soft earth had already grown over, as if no one had been here for months or even years. Grady stumbled up to the door and knocked, knowing that no one would answer. His hands began to tremble, and he slid off the stoop and straddled the evergreen bush under the window to cup his hands and peer inside. The house was, of course, totally empty, and he pushed off the window and fought for his balance as he pulled his leg from the entanglement of branches and leaves.

What now? What in the goddamned hell now? What does he do with his life? What force of will could conceivably stop what was boiling in him? A pain he wasn't even aware he could feel? Where could he find the strength to even keep breathing?

Grady Hagen, alone in front of an empty house, collapsed onto his knees, looked up to the heavens and screamed. A name. Over and over again.

"Betsy Sue!"

21

Grady was feeling the pain of her loss again, and the emotions slithered up his throat and welled in his eyes. He blinked away the tears and swallowed as he slid her picture back into the pile. He didn't know on that day long ago that he could, or would, ever love again, but of course, he did. But he would never love again the same way, because there is nothing like first love. Nothing ever again as pure, as unbridled, as reckless and free. And that's because you haven't yet learned the danger. All you see is the sheer, overwhelming thrill of it, the way it pours into every crevice of your body and soul, filling you up with feeling, even to the hairs on your arms. You don't see, or refuse to acknowledge, that this force has to have an opposite side, equal in force, one that can take the ground from under your feet and collapse you as if all your bones had been sucked out of your skin. And so you ride at full gallop, nostrils flaring, ears pinned back, going like hell, until you fall off, and everything inside you disintegrates into tiny fragments. Of course, you get over it, the pain. But some piece of it stays with you forever. It's as if you were in a terrible accident that shattered your leg and now you have a limp. It doesn't hurt anymore, and you hardly notice it, except once in a while. Like at this very moment as her photo disappeared back into the stack, Betsy Sue McDonough would come back to Grady Hagen thousands more times in his life, little pieces of her, keyhole glimpses of memories that pricked the skin like a short needle and then went away, and he would wonder for a second where she was and, more importantly, who she had become. Even though it didn't matter. Not really. Just wondering.

Charlie moseyed back into the room as Grady leaned into the trunk again and removed a flat wad of cracked brown leather. He turned it this way and that, displaying five fingers, almost welded together.

"What the hell is that? A hat? A dead animal?" Charlie asked, flopping onto the couch. "Is that a baseball mitt?"

"Good lord almighty," Grady whispered, stretching out the strap and inserting his hand in the weatherworn leather. He put it up to his nose and closed his eyes. "Look at this old thing."

"Is that really a mitt?" Charlie asked, leaning over and studying the glove.

Grady took it off and handed it to him. "Here, you try it on."

Charlie slipped his hand in and pounded it a few times, dust breaking away with every blow into the flat pocket. "Looks like somebody ran over it with a car," he chortled. "How the heck did you catch with this thing? Or did you just knock balls down so they wouldn't hit you in the face?"

"Goddamn, Graden, didn't you ever tell this boy you was the greatest ballplayer ever to come out of Arbutus then or now?" Truman grunted, pulling the air dispenser from his mouth.

Grady was now unfolding a thick yellow-gray woolen jersey with the word "Choctaws" embroidered on the front. "Oh, I told him a few things," he said. Then he shook the jersey. "Look at this."

"Oh, he told me about a thousand times. And today some old guy with two of the same names went on and on about the great Grady Hagen. I almost puked," Charlie teased.

"Musta been Lee Lee," Truman nodded.

"That's your jersey?" Charlie asked, taking it from Grady's hands. He fingered the heavy wool. "Choctaws," he said.

"Indian tribe," Grady replied.

Charlie unbuttoned the front and stuck his arm through one of the arm holes. His forearm emerged, practically strangled by the tight fit. "Must have sweat like a pig in this. It's so small, Pappy. Did it fit you?" He removed his arm. "Itchy as hell, too," he grumbled.

Grady was pulling a flattened cap from the trunk now. He punched it up with his fist and nestled it onto his head. "Hat still fits," he laughed, removing it and fingering it. Then he brought it to his nose and smelled it, inhaling the years and sweat that stained its brim.

126

"Your granddaddy never told you hows he could run down a fly ball and scoop it," Truman said, swinging his arm in an arc, "and I mean scoop it out of the air with one hand in that there mitt and shoot it like a rifle shot back to the catcher?" He took a long pull on the dispenser. "Won the league championship for Arbutus one year doing just that. Then racked a homer the next year."

Next out were the woolen pants and stockings. Grady laid them out and ran his hands over them. "These old things held up pretty good for all these years," he said.

Truman leaned forward. "That's 'cause of the cedar. See here," he reached in and pulled back some more piles and pointed to the interior lining of the trunk. "Keeps the pests out. Doesn't rot. 'Magic wood' my daddy used to call it. Expensive. Hard to come by."

Grady rummaged past some other miscellany and pulled out a small piece of orange paper with dark orange printing. He held it up to the light.

"What's that, Pap?" Charlie queried.

"Oh," Grady dragged out the word nonchalantly, "My goodness. Look there. That's my ticket stub to Birmingham, Alabama. Bus ticket." He handed it to the boy.

"Why did you go to Birmingham?"

"Tryout with the White Sox."

"Ah-ha! The famous White Sox tryout that you never explained."

"Never figured out why those idiots down there didn't take up this boy and turn him into the best centerfielder they ever had," Truman growled through the plastic hose end in his mouth. "Bunch of damn fools, they was."

"So, what did happen down there in Birmingham?" Charlie asked.

Grady pondered, shifted gears. "I found a quarter on the floor of the bus. Big money in those days. And we stopped on the way home at some town, not too small, in Alabama; for an hour layover. I walked to a diner and the guy sitting next to me got a plate of something," he made a mound shape with his hands. "Golden brown slices of something. I asked the waitress what that was and she said French fries. I asked her if they were any good, seein' as how they smelled mighty fine, but I was reluctant to try them because I'd never had

French food before. She laughed, leaning back with both hands on her hips. Thought I was the cat's meow with my bumpkin stupidity. She brought me a plate of 'em. Cost a nickel. And that was my first taste of French fries."

Truman laughed, rocking vigorously and slapping his thighs. "You never told that one before!"

"Just now remembered it," Grady grinned, shaking his head.

"You never had French fries?" Charlie was chuckling. "Man, you learn something every day." He leaned forward. "But what happened in the tryout with the White Sox?" he said. "You never did tell me. I mean, if you were so good."

"Busted arm. Kicked by a horse. That's what did him in," Truman sighed, shaking his head.

"Yeah, a horse," Grady whispered, looking across the room and down the hallway to the exact spot where the "horse" had kicked him.

"You tried out with a broken arm?"

"No, it just hadn't healed altogether," Grady took the ticket back. "And it just wasn't my luck, I suppose, to do much good when I went down Birmingham way." He set the stub on the table. "Bad luck. Maybe bad timing. That's what it was."

22

The smoke from their cigarettes had turned the inside of Billie Rae's daddy's truck as blue cloudy as a stormy horizon. Outside the open windows, a mild evening poured in, carrying with it the aroma of wet decay that had overtaken the leaves. They were tearing a hole in a country road, spitting dust and gravel. Billie Rae hung one limpid hand over the steering wheel and ratcheted through the gears with a flick of the lever on the steering column.

"Reach back behind the seat there," he said, cigarette bobbing in his pursed lips. "Got somethin'll make you forget that Catholic girl once and forever."

Grady tapped a spray of ashes out the window and put the cigarette back in his mouth, holding it with his teeth. "What is it? What's back here?" he said, climbing to one knee on the seat and leaning over. He moved some oily rags and tools out of the way, finally coming into contact with the bottle. He triumphantly pulled it out and held it up. "Could this be it?" he asked, the caramel liquid swirling as he shook the container.

"Compliments of Newt Tully's still," Billie Rae sang. "They say it's the purest, sweetest, hottest hooch in the southeast. Why don't we see for ourselves?"

"I thought old Tully was in jail for making this stuff," Grady mused.

"LaGrone arrests him once a year or so, just for show," Billie Rae snapped. "Now open that up and let's have some."

Grady pulled the cork from the bottle and handed it over to Billie Rae who pushed it back toward him. "No, you first. Be my guest."

Grady spit his cigarette out the window and took a swig. A rain of fire swept through him, taking the breath out of his lungs, filling his eyes with tears, and making his feet splay on the floor of the truck. "Jesus Christ," he sputtered.

"Told you it was good," Billie Rae said, grabbing the bottle and jamming it to his lips. His response to the burning whiskey was a muffled cough. "Sonofabitch," he said, handing the bottle back to Grady, who had lit another cigarette.

"Where the hell we going?" Grady said, taking another swig which rolled through him with a bit less resistance.

"Surprise, surprise," Billie Rae replied, his eyes narrowing. "Gonna make you forget that girl. Gonna make you a man." He grabbed the bottle from Grady and threw his head back, this time taking several swallows.

Something had gotten into Grady's head, a gauzy web that seemed to tangle up his thoughts. It was the moonshine, sure as hell, bouncing off his brain cells. Felt good, felt real good, and it was the first time he had felt that way since she – gol'dang bitch Betsy Sue – had pulled up and left without saying a word. Bitch. "Sounds good to me," he slurred, taking the bottle and pouring another stream down his throat. The booze had taken on a sweet, benevolent taste now. "Everything's gonna be all right."

Sometime later they had arrived in another town, a place Grady didn't recognize. Small place, even smaller than Arbutus, believe it or not. With a single street lamp out front of a gas station. Big Coca-Cola sign on the outside wall of the garage. They slowed down and Billie Rae nudged the car into the parking lot of the station, then kept going, following a loud gravel road up a slight hill. They came to a clearing dotted with a random scattering of cabins, ramshackle log siding, shredded shingles thrown haphazardly on the roofs. Only a couple exhaled light through the windows. Several cars, a few with their engines running, sat in the parking lot.

"Here we are," Billie Rae said.

"Where we are?" Grady replied, his voice a hundred miles away from his body.

Billie Rae had stopped the truck and thrown the gearshift lever straight up. "Come on," he said, opening the door with a squeak and hopping out.

Grady pushed his door away and slid down. His feet flew in opposite directions from one another and he had to catch himself on the looping fender of the truck to get his equilibrium. Shit. He'd never felt like this before, out of control of his arms and legs. He'd always been able to get them to do just what he wanted. Yet, instead of being frightened, he felt light, happy. The rhythmic pulsing of his temples was pleasant. Now, if he could just get across the parking lot and follow Billie Rae who had gotten a good hundred feet ahead of him and was dissolving into the ambient light of one of the cabins.

By the time Grady got to him, he was on the porch, talking to a man whose cigarette ebbed and flowed in the darkness. Billie Rae was snapping closed the open wallet in his left hand.

"Won't be long now, buddy," he said, shoving the wallet back into his rear pocket. "Follow me." He hopped off the porch step and moved across the lot toward one of the lighted cabins.

Grady turned and caught up in two strides. "What the hell's going on here?" he sputtered, his tongue thick.

"I'm buying you an early birthday present," Billie Rae replied. "You're the only guy in the history of the world who couldn't get a Catholic girl to put out, so I figured I'd make sure you didn't die a virgin." He bounced his eyebrows several times. "Besides, it'll make you feel one helluva lot better and maybe cheer you up. Frankly, you're starting to bore the shit out of me with all your boo-hoo-hoo crap."

"You mean?"

"Right behind that door," Billie Rae said, pointing. "Just gotta wait a few minutes." He got to the cabin and sat on the wooden steps. "Where's the hooch?"

Grady threw his thumb over his shoulder toward the truck. "Back there. You didn't tell me to bring it." Sumbitch, now he was waiting for Billie Rae to tell him what to do. His stomach seemed to gurgle. "You want me to go back and get it?"

"Naw, y'all gonna need it afterwards, anyway," Billie Rae said, bouncing on his tiptoes and heels. "Yep, it won't be long now."

"I don't know," Grady stammered.

"Y'all are gonna be a man and slide out of your fucking panties, get your pecker at attention and march in there and do it to her. Don't worry; it ain't like you gotta please her or nothin'. She's just a goddamned whore. Besides, you're gonna thank me for this."

Just then the door swung open. A triangle of light swept over them and Grady winced. A man came out, fiddling with his belt buckle. Grady stepped off the porch to make room for him to pass. He was a small man, rumpled and sweating, moving like a little boy. His head hung and was turned away as if he were making sure they wouldn't recognize him which, of course, they wouldn't, not out here in the damn boondocks in Christ-only-knows where and with Grady's head in turmoil.

"Okay big boy, y'all go get her," Billie Rae said, grabbing Grady's shirt sleeve and pulling him past and into the light.

Grady stumbled into the room and heard the door slam behind him. The room glowed softly, and he saw her waiting for him. She was sitting on the edge of the bed, wreathed in a garland of smoke that came through her nostrils in soft streams. She was dressed in a long shirt that hung to her knees and he could see her nakedness through it, soft gray lines. She was older than he, at least ten years. Small. Not unattractive. Her brown hair was pulled back tightly, forming a round cap on the back of her head.

"Hello there," she said, taking another draw on her cigarette and then turning into the yellow wash from the table lamp to stub it out in the ash tray. She repositioned herself on the edge of the bed. "Why, you're just a boy." Her breasts peeked through the opening in the shirt. "Is this your first time?"

"No." Why lie, Grady thought. He stood a little taller. Besides, she doesn't have to think he's a kid or nothing.

"Then come on, come here," she said, beckoning him forward. "I like a man with experience."

Grady hesitated. His head crackled and he wobbled. Holy Ghost, he thought. What now?

"Y'all a little nervous, are you?"

"Um, no," Grady insisted.

She pulled at her blouse, revealing a little more. "Come on, ain't gonna bite ya or nothing," she laughed.

"I know you won't bite me. I'm just working up to it. Don't worry."

Her demeanor suddenly changed. "Come on, bubba. Get outta them trousers. I haven't got all night." She reached out and grabbed his belt, pulling him close. She unfastened the buckle and inched his pants down his legs with one hand while exploring his stomach and moving down with the other.

Grady felt himself stiffening. Her fingers were wrapped around him, stroking him with a gentle expertise that made his knees buckle. Even the wicked Mississippi moonshine crackling in his brain couldn't dull the desire that welled up in him, an animal instinct as uncontrollable as breathing itself, it seemed.

The woman – he never would know her name – looked him up and down. "You're a pretty big boy, aren't you?" she asked, going faster now, fingers in exactly the right place at the right time, growing him, tightening him. "I'm gonna like you." She gently withdrew her hand and slipped the gossamer shirt over her head. Now she was completely naked, her legs opening as she leaned back.

In an instant, Grady was on her. "Oh," she said in an oddly surprising tone as he plunged in. He kept his head turned, his eyes clenched, and was finished quickly and pushing away. She didn't say anything, just reached for a tissue from the blue and white box on the nightstand under the light.

It was nothing, nothing like before. Too fast. Something unclean about it. No part of his body except that – that part – involved in the act. No kissing. No holding. It sapped something from him, some part of him that he felt he could never get back. A piece of his soul, maybe? Like the squirrelly little man who had come out the door before he went in, Grady was suddenly and unabashedly ashamed of himself.

He didn't remember pulling back on his pants, but was soon outside where Billie Rae jumped up from the step and flipped a cigarette into the night. "My man, my man," he said, slapping his friend on the shoulder. "How do y'all like them apples?"

"Yeah," Grady said, forcing a smile.

"You didn't dirty her up too much for me, did you? Didn't stretch her out?"

Grady looked down at his shoes, saw them quivering spastically from the knocking of his knees.

"Don't leave without me, you stallion," Billie Rae said, tugging on his own pants and disappearing into the cabin. "Yahoo!" he screamed as the door closed behind him.

Grady's head spun. His stomach was storming. He walked around the corner of the cabin and put his hands on his knees. He was eye level with the window and could see Billie Rae hopping on one foot to kick out of his pants. Grady leaned forward and threw up in the weeds, vomit sliding out of him in ropes of hot liquid.

From the day a long time ago when he, Cissy and Billie Rae saw the couple screwing in the car at the old juke joint – and he learned that's how babies are made – Grady still couldn't imagine his own mother and father finding even the few minutes of tenderness, of love, that it took for two people to complete such an intimate act. And as he stood there with his hands on his knees, spitting white fire from his mouth, he thought that this experience with the whore is probably how *he* must have come into the world: in an explosion of fury, of beastly lunging, of gritted teeth and held breath, of tightly squeezed whimpers of pain, and maybe even of vomit and tears.

As Grady stood and gathered himself, Billie Rae came out whistling and hitching his pants. They left the cabins a few minutes later, only driving for a few miles before pulling off to the side of the road where they finished the bottle and talked about everything until they both passed out.

Morning came in with a vengeance, all hot and pink and slicing like a knife through the windows of the truck. Grady's eyes exploded open, and he shot from the darkness into this blazing light. His head was erupting in sweat, beads emerging, bursting, running in streams down his cheeks. His shirt was plastered to his skin. His mouth was dry and swollen. He reeked of cigarettes and moonshine and the effluent of the whore he had been with a few hours before. He reached across and smacked Billie Rae on the shoulder.

"C'mon, asshole, get up, it's morning," Grady said. Billie Rae grumbled and then cut loose a trumpet fart that made even him sit upright.

"Goddamn, was that me?" he said. "That's the way to start the day, huh?"

"What time is it, anyway?" Grady mumbled, leaning out the window and spitting.

"Forgot to wind my watch," Billie Rae answered, holding up his naked wrist.

"Just get me home quick. My momma and daddy's gonna tan my ass."

"What? Y'all can't thank me for the piece of ass I bought you last night? It cost me two dollars, for chrissakes."

Grady shook his head, disgusted with himself, the world, Billie Rae Tolleston and life in general. "I'll mail you a thank you card tomorrow."

"That would be appropriate," Billie Rae answered, pushing the start button on the truck.

The truck bounded through the tracks and holes of the dirt road running through the woods and up to Grady's farm house, and every jolt made his teeth clatter and his head reverberate. He staggered as he got out of the truck, wondering what he was going to say, knowing she, at least, had been up all night stewing about him. On the other hand, he was seventeen, for chrissakes, a man now. Maybe they had gone to sleep just believing he would come home like he always did and not give them any reason to worry. Maybe he could still get away with it if it was early enough and they weren't up. Maybe. The house was quiet, after all. Not a sound came from it; not even a breath.

Grady's feet tingled as he came toward the porch. He stopped, crossed one leg over the other and pulled off his shoe. Then he reversed the action until he stood in the grass in his stocking feet. He then ascended the two steps and drifted across the porch. The door squeaked as he opened it, so he just opened it enough to wedge himself in. Still not a sound.

This might be okay.

Grady was tiptoeing across the living room when the scent gripped him. Cigarette smoke, clear and loud as a bell, wafting from the kitchen.

Shit. The old man. What if he had just gotten in, too? All boiling with liquor? Sonofabitch would be hell to deal with. Then again, maybe he would understand better than Momma. Hell, Grady could tell him, "Hey Pops, I'm late 'cause I was out all night with Billie Rae drinking moonshine and screwing whores. Ain't you proud of me now?"

Grady turned the corner, shoes in one hand, and stopped in his silent tracks. Sitting at the kitchen table, smoke circling her like the mist on a cold morning, was Momma. An ash tray erupted in front of her, a mound of mashed cigarette butts crumbled onto the table, each end rimmed in lipstick.

"Momma, why are you smoking?" Grady stammered. His mother didn't smoke. Did she? He'd never seen her smoke. Did he?

Rhea Hagen turned to face her son, and the sight clogged the words in his mouth. Her lip was distorted, swollen, and a gash brown with dried blood twisted grotesquely through the pink flesh. Her cheek was knobby and blue. Her neck was streaked with slashes. She dabbed a moist, bloodstained wash cloth on the wounds.

"Gol'dang, Momma," he said, dropping his shoes and going to her. Now his hands were shaking as he reached for her, wanting to hold her, but fearing he would hurt her more. "What happened?"

But he didn't need an answer. He knew.

"That goddamned sonofabitch," Grady shouted, turning away from her.

"Grady, baby, don't, don't," she said, reaching up to him. "It's okay, baby. It's okay."

Grady turned, his hands clenched at his side. "No, gol'dangit Momma, it's not all right." Tears pooled up in his eyes and he began shaking. Perhaps it was the moonshine still blasting through his veins; perhaps he had just been pushed enough, but Grady Hagen turned away from his mother and stomped toward the bedroom in which his father slept.

"Get up you bastard!" he screamed.

"Grady, no, no, please, no," Rhea cried, pushing away from the table and running to catch him.

Grady kicked open the door to the bedroom. Bo Hagen lay on the top of the bedspread in his white boxer shorts and a sleeveless tee shirt, his head back and his mouth open. "Get up you sonofabitch," the boy shouted, reaching down with both hands and grabbing his father.

Momma was in the room now, grabbing at him. "No, baby, don't, please," she said, pulling at his arm, her hands sliding down to his wrist. He shook her away.

Grady didn't stop. Now his fists were swarming like bees, landing against his father's ribcage. Bo Hagen twisted away from the barrage to the other side of the bed, his eyes wide, bewildered, but rapidly gaining consciousness. Grady charged after him, leaping up onto the mattress, swinging wildly.

"Oh, God, oh, God," Rhea cried, burying her face in her hands.

"You bastard," Grady said, closing in on his old man, who had steadied himself against a dresser.

"Get back, boy, I'm warning you," Bo growled. "You don't want no part of me."

But Grady kept coming, and that was his mistake.

Bo Hagen shot forward like a tiger, burying his head in his son's stomach, lifting him off his feet, and driving him across the bed. Airborne now, Grady saw the ceiling spin and then his insides exploded as he landed on his back on the floor, all breath expelled from his lungs. A lamp from a nightstand crashed next to his shoulder. He reached up, grabbing at anything, trying to stop the flurry of punches that were raining on him.

"Bo, Bo, stop!" Rhea cried, kneeling down and inserting herself between her raging husband and her son. Bo Hagen, veins swelling on his forehead, spittle foaming at the corners of his mouth, flicked her against the wall as if she were a doll.

Grady struggled for breath, and then felt his fingers digging into his father's face. They crawled forward, upward. If he could just find, yes, the eye! With all his strength, he dug his fingers into Bo's eyeball.

The man cried out in shock and fell backwards. Grady twisted from beneath him and rolled toward the door, but just as he did, Bo grabbed his right arm.

Everything changed at that instant. The fury, the blinding white hysteria, melted away, and everything seemed to float, as if they had all been suddenly submerged in water. All sound, texture, and feeling were muffled. Bo Hagen, his forearms bulging from years of slinging lumber, had Grady's wrist in a deathlike grip. The boy tried to pull free, but couldn't. The old man's face was afire, his eyes wide, a rake of blood dribbling down his cheek. He was screaming something.

Then it happened. Grady watched it, as if he was detached, a mile away. The arm in Bo Hagen's hand snapped in two, bending horribly backwards toward the elbow. The skin split and a bloody splinter of bone tore through. Grady felt no pain at first, just a white flash of light erupting in his brain.

23

Satiated and growing tired and getting used to the heat just now as the sun melted away over the horizon, Charlie looked for an opportunity to sneak away from these two old codgers to take a few tokes just to shine the edge off all the way.

He wandered to the back side of the dilapidated barn where no one could see him, and found a reasonably flat surface where the boards had broken away from the short concrete block wall. He sat down, fumbled through his pockets for a tightly rolled joint, took it between his fingers and pinched the ends. I'm gonna need this if I'm sleeping at Fred Sanford's tonight, he thought. Then he pulled out a Bic and lit up. The first hit went down like a cyclone, all the way to the ends of his toes.

Charlie surveyed the exquisite wreckage and rot of the fallen barn. What a panorama of chaos at rest! Boards and bricks and shingles lying helter skelter and creating tiny little caves and hiding places. Probably should get some shots of this wreckage and that old house there tomorrow when there's more light, he thought. The next drag made him sputter, but the good stuff in the smoke caught the flow of the four beers he had consumed in a heated frenzy and rode the current straight to his brain, arriving with a zing and pop.

So, he was heading out tomorrow, or so Pappy said. Well, that's not all bad, judging from what Charlie had seen of Arbutus so far. It was a pretty depressing place, actually, significantly unpainted and exuding a lethargy that ruffled the leaves in the trees. And the people. Lord almighty. So many seemed angular and disproportioned, with odd, lopsided gaits and faraway looks in their eyes. And no fewer than three guys he'd seen had strange protrusions, lumps, somewhere on their heads. One guy looked like he was hiding an egg under the skin of his forehead, the other at the back of his jaw, and the third on his left cheekbone. Like they were in the middle of some kind of morph from man to stone.

Acck!

He sneezed out a stream of smoke followed by a stuttering string of chuckles. It took him a few seconds to catch his breath. Shit, he was judging people. He'd never done that before. Then again, he had never seen people who could walk without lifting their feet. He started laughing again.

Pappy sure seemed in a hurry to get rid of him. That's okay. He wanted to go home. But he wanted to never go home at the same time. Figure that out. There was too much to deal with at home. He was tired of being Charlie Garrett, perfect kid. That was it. What his parents wanted, what they knew, was that it was now time for him to slide into that transition from perfect kid to perfect man, and he didn't want to motherfucking do it. Didn't fucking know if he could do it.

He took another drag and held the smoke in as long as he could. And now, here he was in this godforsaken hell hole, sitting on a pile of rotting lumber where rats the size of Dalmatians were probably looking at him like food. And Pappy says tomorrow get the fuck out of town, kid, leave me alone here. What's that all about? Why did Pap come all the way down here now? And why is he in such a hurry to be left alone? Alone in this godforsaken place?

Charlie exhaled, felt his head reeling.

It's pretty, though. Far away. That was it. And there was something to that. No other houses to be seen from here. Dense woods of boiling green. The sky tonight. The way it turned from flat white to this purple swirling color like grape ice cream.

Grape ice cream?

He took another pull on the joint.

"Who the fuck ever heard of grape ice cream?" he croaked.

He started to giggle, coughing at the same time, pushing tears down his cheeks and even out his nose.

He didn't want to be a fucking doctor. He didn't want to be a fucking lawyer either. What he wanted to be would disgrace his family.

Fuck them.

Well, not really. They were actually pretty cool.

Fuck him. He was the problem, not them.

But how was he going to tell them? How in the fucking world was he going to get out of this shit they wanted to throw him in?

He could always tell Pappy. Goddamn, he loved Pappy. Pappy was good, good to the soul. He never judged him. Never said a negative thing to him. He was the only person who fully and totally accepted him as he was. The only one still alive, anyway. Nonnie Rachel, too. She was great. Goddamn, she died without warning anyone or saying goodbye. He looked up to the sky. "You up there somewhere, Nonnie? I've got Pappy here with me in east bumfuck Egypt. He's up to something and it's no good."

What the hell was he up to? That was the question. This whole trip, yeah, it looked like a little traipse down memory lane, but something else was going on here, and every fiber in Charlie's mind realized it. This good-to-see-y'all crap with Truman – whom he'd never even heard of his whole life – what was that all about? I mean, wouldn't Pappy have at least fucking mentioned him at some time or another rather than all of a sudden one day jumping up from the orange striped couch in his living room and deciding, let's fucking go to see my goddamned cousin. How about the way Pap wouldn't go visit that old friend of his, yet here he was a million and a half fucking miles away from civilization, for what? To see the goddamned statue in the park? Something was wrong here.

"Something's wrong here, Nonnie," Charlie said to the clouds.

Not to mention the Bible and that post card. Yeah, really smooth the way he tried to get the old man to talk about that. That's what the fucking trip's all about. No doubt about that. And it couldn't be good; couldn't be good.

"What the hell is that noise?" he said, jumping suddenly from the concrete stoop and peering through the cracks in what was left of the barn siding. Nothing moved, only some tiny dust particles in the orange sunlight that still meandered through. He could see them clearly, these little animals and pieces of skin and dirt and wood and grass and bugs. So tiny.

This is pretty righteous stuff, he thought, holding the now diminished joint between two fingers and examining it. Wonder what its shelf life is off the Mexican truck? Longer than corn on the cob? Then he laughed and laughed and laughed some more.

He finished the joint and let the storm in his brain settle as much as it could so he wouldn't look like a stumbling stony. Darkness had settled in once and for all, bringing barely discernable relief from the heat. As he approached the house, knowing he was weaving on his own unsure noodle legs, thankful for the darkness, he heard the voices. An argument. He stopped and wiped his eyes. Maybe that would make him hear better.

"You are out of your goddamned mind, Grady," Truman was saying, his voice high pitched and quick. "You ain't doing y'all or that boy or anyone down here a damned bit of good. I'm telling you."

Pappy responded calmly, and Charlie could only make out some of the words. "My decision . . . what has to be . . . made up my mind . . . leave the boy here with you . . ."

"They're all dead or moved on," Truman shouted. "Why stir up trouble? Jesus Christ if I'da known you was comin' down here for that, I'd have had you stopped at the Mississippi border."

"I know you don't understand . . . we're family . . . don't interfere . . . just let . . . what I have to do."

"And that means I should let you hatch this half-baked piece-of-shit plan to fuck up your life and a whole passel of other folks?"

"I'm not . . . up anybody's . . . it's only on me."

Charlie retreated quickly to the car, leaned over and reached into the glove compartment. He then pulled out the cellphone and powered up. What if it didn't work out here in the hinterlands? Sometimes at night, though, it works, you know. "C'mon, baby," he said. "Just this once." The green glow of the display ripped through the darkness. Ten messages, all probably from Lorene. Lord above. The "No Service" warning flashed for a second, then disappeared. "Yes!" he said. "Fucking okay." He scrolled down his phone book and speed dialed the number. "Pappy, don't kill me," he said, lifting the phone to his ear.

24

Grady Hagen slouched through a wretchedly rainy spring and an early summer. That was the best way to explain it. Slouching. There hadn't been much to smile or laugh about with the coming of the new leaves. Even the sweet smell of wet grass and the resurgence of the crickets and frogs and other critters of the woods couldn't pull him out of himself. He yearned only to be alone. Strange how this would be his desire. In all the time he was with Betsy Sue, the concept of being by himself was not within his grasp. Every second was occupied by her presence. Now, he was so devastated by the hole she had created at his side that he sought to crawl into it, to seek solitude, if not solace, in it; a way to hold at bay the rest of the world for which he now held no interest.

He dug a hole in the clay with the toes of his right foot and swung the bat in a soft arc across the plate. Behind him, he could hear the thwack-thwack-thwack of balls hitting mitts as the other tryouts played catch outside the foul lines. In front of him, left arm resting on a cocked knee was a bonafide major league pitcher named Pete Weston, down here in Birmingham with the scrubs and prospects, rather than up in Chicago with the Sox, working through a sore ankle.

Grady had watched him carefully from the on deck circle, hurling the ball with a snap like a bullwhip and creating a dusty blur into the catcher's mitt. If Weston's ankle had ever been sprained, it certainly

143

didn't look like it now, spiraling into a hole beyond the mound as another ball invisibly whistled from his hand.

From the batter's box, Grady stared at him. Weston's eyes were tiny slits, partially obscured by the shadow from the bill of his hat. The horizon beyond the left field fence was a mountain range of bending and meandering steel buildings, cylindrically-shaped edifices wrapped in thick pipes, churning out their own storm clouds of egg smelling smoke, and smokestacks wreathed in a reddish mist, erupting like a row of soldiers from an angled roof. A steel mill, of course, larger and more impressive than anything Grady had ever seen. The entire complex was laced together by bridges and catwalks. The buildings seemed alive, chuffing and chugging and rumbling hard and fast and relentlessly to chew ore into steel which was to be shaped and hammered into weapons for the war.

Birmingham was monstrously different from anything Grady had ever seen, and he instinctively understood that it was only a glimpse of an unknown world that he wanted to taste and see and hear.

But first he had to prove to Chet Zane, White Sox scout, and the other coaches, that he belonged in the buses and on the trains that carried ball players to these exotic cities. Pete Weston was crouched and waiting to mess with that dream.

Grady swung the bat again easily. No pain. The arm that had been broken a few months earlier had expunged all its pain, but was still noticeably thinner than its counterpart. The surgeon in Jackson who had reassembled the bones assured him it would be good as new.

The old man had called Fletcher Moody right after the fight, and the three of them went up to the big city, Grady going in and out of an electric haze while Bo and Fletcher laughed at how stupid the boy had been to startle a horse from behind, even a horse as old and gentle as Cree.

Grady nodded at Weston and took his stance. Watch. Just get a reading on the first pitch.

Weston wound up and uncoiled in what seemed like slow motion, and then from his tangle of legs and elbows a ball came humming out and smacked into the catcher's mitt in an eye blink.

Gol'dang, Grady thought, stepping out of the box for an instant. Watch one more. Again, there was a whipping of arms and an explosion of motion that terminated in a puff of dust in the catcher's mitt.

"Gotta swing at something," the catcher grumbled.

But Grady had seen the pitch that time, had locked his eyes on the point within Weston's body from which the ball emerged. Got it, he thought, rolling his fingers on the bat handle. C'mon, Weston, give it to me. Bye-bye, Mr. Spaulding.

The ball came from exactly the spot Grady had anticipated, and it was no longer a blur. He could see it spin, could see the laces blurring in the air. Easy, he thought, driving the bat to meet it.

Thwap. The catcher's mitt. On the bat, nothing. He had totally missed the ball. But how? He had seen it all the way.

Another pitch, and again he was locked on it, and again the bat whooshed in the air. Pitch after pitch came at him, and even though he looped a few into short right field, the bat refused to move as his mind and his eye and his nerves and his brain commanded. Something was wrong here, very wrong. What was once so natural, so easy for him – whipping the bat like a piece of leather – had become tedious, difficult, as if swinging through water.

In a few minutes he was finished, the blood and breath of his body pooling around his ankles, it seemed. His eyes refused to look up, and they followed his feet as he walked off the field. "Don't sweat it, kid," the voice startled him and he looked up. Chet Zane was leaning against the side of the dugout, jotting something in his notebook. "Probably just nerves. Happens to a lot of kids out here. Haul your ass out to center and take some fly balls. Show off your cannon arm."

But this didn't work, either. Certainly he read each ball off the bat and glided to it like a cat. But the throw to the cutoff man died far short.

"Whatsamatter with you?" Chet Zane shouted as Grady jogged in. "Suddenly you throw like a girl. I seen you nail a guy from left centerfield three hundred feet away on the fly. Now you can't get it to the infield?"

Grady stuck out his right arm. "Broke my arm, compound fracture three months ago. It still ain't grown as big as the other one," he pleaded. "Look, lookee here." He held the two arms up side by side for Zane to see, but the scout just shook his head. Grady continued, "I just need a coupla months to build it up."

"Humph," the scout replied. "Then you shouldn'ta come. You make me look like a damn fool. Plus, you hurt yourself. You get labeled; it's a long row to hoe."

"Can I come back when . . .?"

But Chet Zane was walking away.

25

"Shit!" The word bounced off of Charlie's gullet and flew like a peach pit, without thought or reason, out of his mouth as he sat upright in bed. He fumbled for his watch on the nightstand, but he already sensed that he had blown it again. Something about the color and mood of the sunlight wending its way into the small bedroom told him that Pap had gotten the jump on him, and whatever crazy fucking idea about which he and Truman were arguing last night had been let loose to run like a deer. Charlie's head was like the old house, full of cobwebs and decay, jammed with stacks of thoughts and questions and exhausted from the beer the night before. His temples thumped to the bass drum beat of his heart and reverberated in dull pain. He flipped his feet to the floor and rubbed his eyes, yawning, standing, hooking his watch on his wrist, stepping into his baggy shorts, all in what seemed a single motion.

He bounded down the stairs like a dropped sack of potatoes, and slid into the kitchen. "Truman!" he shouted.

No answer.

Did the old man go with Pap?

Charlie made his way around the table and past the refrigerator. The room was empty, but a pot of coffee percolated on the stove, and the aroma swirled up and wrapped itself around his head. Then he noticed the folded piece of paper nestled between the sugar bowl and creamer on the table. He pulled it out and opened it. Ten twenty-dollar bills fell out.

Charlie —

Thanks for the ride. Made some coffee for you. Here's some money for gas. Have a safe trip home. See you soon. Love, Pap.

"Shit!" bounced out again, propelled by reflexes. Then Charlie realized he had left his cell phone on the charger upstairs. In a matter of seconds he was up and back down again, punching speed dial. As the line rang, he made his way onto the front porch. He could see Truman's pickup truck now, bounding over the gullied driveway, pieces and parts ricocheting. Amidst the settling clatter as the truck stopped, the old man tumbled out, pulling his canister cart and swaying as he walked toward the house.

"Truman! Where's Pap?" Charlie shouted.

A voice came through on the line. "Hello."

"Mom, thank God! Where are you guys?"

"Charlie! We're almost there. Thank God for GPS."

"I just dropped him off, stopped for a donut afterwards. That was, oh, 'bout," Truman pulled the chain that hung from a button on his overalls and extracted a pocket watch. The old man flipped it open, "'bout pert near an hour ago, now."

"Hold on, Mom," Charlie said into the phone. Then he looked up at Truman. "Why'd you just take him? Why didn't you wake me up?"

Truman shrugged. "He asked me to, you didn't."

"Charlie, your dad and I should be there in less than an hour. We've been driving all night. What's going on?" Mom said.

"You just, just took him? That's it? Where?" Charlie cried to Truman.

Truman scooted his old body toward the porch steps. "Just done what I was asked to do."

"Mom! Wait, please, one at a time. I'm trying to figure out what's going on," Charlie said, turning back to the cell phone. Then he pulled it away from his ear. Truman was only a few steps away now. "Where did he go?"

"Can't say," the old man said, shaking his head.

"Does that mean you don't know?"

"Charlie!" the voice rattled through the handset. "Tell us what is going on!"

Truman looked away. "Means I can't say."

"Why the fuck not?" Charlie's voice was high pitched now.

"Watch your language," his mother said through the cell phone.

Truman hooked both thumbs in his pants pockets. "Because he's a crazy old coot about to go insane once and for all, and if I coulda, I woulda brained him with a two-by-four, but he's my cousin. And he made me promise not to tell you."

"Tell you what? What's he talking about, Charlie?" came the voice from the phone.

"C'mon, Truman, goddamnit," Charlie shouted.

Truman exhaled and looked across the field, shaking his head. "He's going into a bee hive and he ain't comin' out without getting stung bad."

"Charlie! Charlie! Can you hear me? Answer me!"

The boy was bouncing like a tennis ball between two conversations. "Truman, you have to tell me, so we can help him, whatever the fuck is going on."

Truman blew out a loud breath. "I can't, boy. I give my word."

"Even though you know he's in some kind of trouble and maybe we can help him? Your word is more important than that?"

Truman's blue eyes widened and his nostrils flared. "Ain't nothing more important, boy, than a man's word, a man's honor," he grunted. "That's the problem with you kids today. No sense of honor or duty."

Charlie deflated. "Please help us," he whispered.

Truman pondered for several moments, his eyes wandering far. Then he freed one of his hands and held it out. "Gimme the phone."

"What? Why?"

"C'mon," the old man said, wiggling his fingers.

Charlie held the phone out. "I don't get it."

Truman's leathery, thin fingers coiled over the keypad. "He made me promise not to tell you. Didn't say nothing about whoever's on the phone."

26

On a white hot morning in August, a native son came home to bare his soul and seek punishment for his sins. Graden Hagen, born on just such a hazy day more than three-quarters of a century ago, teetering now on spindly legs, swam through the stifling heat and made his way up the steps of the police station.

The fear Grady had felt all night, the kinetic energy zipping through him during the darkness that kept him awake and staring at the ceiling of his room in his home, had been muscled aside by the rage and fury of adrenaline that now coursed through his fiber, and he walked strong through the door, shutting out the pounding heat behind him.

Like most everything else in Arbutus, the police station and jail had changed and, yet, were somehow unchanged at the same time. Certainly the décor was different, a mélange of bad colors and ideas from the mid-seventies. The floor was covered in a palsy of orange and green shag carpeting, worn thin from shuffling feet. Scuffed beige paneling lined the walls, and the counter on which he rested his hands – and the Bible – was laminated with a fake gray marble top that was nicked and chewed in random splotches until it looked like a map of the moon.

On the other hand, an eerie sameness permeated the environment. The space was still tight and struggled to hold air. Pairs of gray metal desks sat end to end three rows deep. The bars from the cells were still visible, as shadows were thrown on the wall of a hallway beyond a windowed door. A police radio popped and sizzled, filling the room with garbled language and numbers. A glass case with a neat row of shotguns and rifles dominated one wall.

Grady waited for the heavyset woman in the khaki shirt to finish a phone call. Even though he only heard half the conversation, it was obvious things were being said that were less than pleasing to the woman, whose face was reddening by the second.

"Ain't no way. Uh-huh. Well, that ain't my problem, it's y'all's. You just gonna have to work it out, honeychile," she said, holding one finger up to Grady.

"Bull-loney," she finally said, dropping the receiver into its cradle and expelling a whistle of air. "Fool," she spat and then turned to him. "Can I help y'all," she said, a smile coming to her face. That was the way it was down here. Southern hospitality. Couldn't help but be nice, no matter what.

"I'm here to see the chief of police," Grady said.

"Is he expecting you?"

"I don't think so, no."

"Well, right now he's out on the highway taking care of a crash." She looked at the watch on her wrist." "He shouldn't be long. Is this an emergency?"

Emergency? Cripes. It had taken more than six decades. Yet, as the moment of truth got closer, it became more urgent to Grady. "Sort of," he replied.

"I could get him on the radio," the deputy said. "May I tell him what this is about?"

"It's a personal matter."

Her eyes swept him up and down and she leaned over the counter and looked at his belt. Then she lowered herself back and said, "Yeah, well, then just have a seat over there for a short spell." She turned and moved back to her desk, picked up a stack of files and moved to a filing cabinet.

God of mercy this place is small, Grady thought, his eyes scanning the surroundings. So much smaller than he remembered. No wonder it was so easy for the crowd that night. What was there to stop a wave of humanity so embroiled with hatred? A few doors? A cell? Big fat old Cecil LaGrone, who didn't even have balls enough to bust up Tully's still, even though it poured smoke practically into his own house? This was hardly an impenetrable fortress. Grady glanced up at the large clock on the wall, then at the watch on his wrist. He turned the Bible over and over in his hands. Time crawled in front of him, stopping to laugh, to ridicule. It seemed to take two hours for fifteen minutes to slither by.

"Morning," a voice riled Grady from his thoughts. "I'm Chief Caleb Mitchell," the man said. "How can I help you?"

Grady stood up. Chief Mitchell was nothing like old LaGrone. He was a tall man, his shirt starched tight as skin, muscles pouring out the sleeves, a waist almost feminine in its delicacy. Not the stereotype that had resided – even – in Grady's mind for all those years. LaGrone, now, he was what a southern policeman was supposed to look like, fat and sweating and fighting with every breath to stay alive.

"I'm sorry, sir, what can I do for you?" Chief Mitchell asked again, a little louder.

Grady made a fist and put it up to his mouth. He coughed softly, then spoke. "My name is Graden Hagen. I was born here in twenty-five. Haven't been back since the end of the war, World War Two that is." He hesitated and pulled the Bible closer to himself.

At that moment the doors swung open, and a storm swept in. "Grady, don't say another word," it was big Dan Garrett's voice, dragging behind it Sarah and Charlie. "Chief, this man is my client and. . ."

Sarah was up to him now, shooting past Dan, "Daddy, good lord, what are you doing?" she cried, brushing his shirt, pushing his hair back. Then she kissed him on the cheek. "Oh, Daddy," she breathed.

"What's going on here, people?" Chief Mitchell asked.

"Frankly, I can't wait to find out," the heavyset woman said.

"Lord above, Sarah, why are you here?" Grady asked, then glanced at Charlie, who had retreated to a corner. It became clear. All the cell phone calls. Charlie had an idea what was going on! Grady stared at him and shook his head. "You," he whispered, then turned away.

Dan Garrett reached into the inside pocket of his suit coat and removed a gold case which he flipped open. He extracted his business card. "My name is Daniel Garrett, I represent Mr. Hagen here."

"No one represents me."

"Daddy, listen to Dan," Sarah pleaded.

"This isn't anyone's business but mine," Grady insisted.

"Chief, I need a few minutes with my client," Dan Garrett interjected.

Grady made a fist and laid it on the counter. "No few minutes, let's get this done."

"Daddy, Dan is a lawyer, he knows what he's doing," Sarah said.

The thought of Dan Garrett representing him in a case of this nature bemused Grady for an instant. Dan probably hadn't been in a criminal courtroom in thirty years. He was a corporate attorney, specializing in mergers and acquisitions and things of that nature. Now here he was, chest all puffed out like Perry Mason.

"I can handle this myself," Grady said.

"No! Daddy."

"Grady, please just give me a few . . ."

Hands were fluttering, words were crossing like sabers.

"Hold it!" Chief Mitchell shouted.

The noise stopped.

The Chief turned to Grady. "Mr. Hagen, please continue."

"Grady, don't say a word," Dan Garrett interjected.

Chief Mitchell put up a hand to silence the attorney. "Please, let's just get control. All I want to know is why he's here."

Grady, his hands shaking now, set the Bible on the counter and let it naturally fall open to where the card had been inserted. He took the photo out and handed it to Mitchell. The Chief's face seemed to deflate, change color.

Sarah leaned over the man's shoulder and looked. "What is it? My good lord!"

"That's what I saw, Momma," Charlie said from the corner.

It was obvious that the Chief recognized that the photo was taken not a block from his very office, which you could see, in fact, in the background. He studied the post card, turning it over in his hand to see what was on the back. Finally, he grimaced, dropped it back on the counter and slid it to Grady. The cop shook his head with his lips pursed. "I heard there were still some of these around, but I never saw one." He exhaled audibly. "Long time ago." He looked up at Grady. "Why are you showing it to me now?"

The old man reached out turned the card around, so that Mitchell could see the picture right side up. "I got this when I was at Camp

Shelby in basic training. My old man sent it to me, wanted to make sure I had a memento." He pointed to the two young men in the foreground of the shot. "See this young fella here," he said, tapping the face of the boy whose hand was being raised.

"Yeah," the policeman replied.

"That's me."

This caused the officer to pick up the card again and dance his eyes back and forth from it to the face of the old man in front of him.

Grady said, "I knew that boy we hanged that night. His name was Rudy Montcrief."

"My God, my God in heaven," Sarah stammered. She stepped back, away from the counter.

"Okay, that's enough," Dan Garrett said, sweeping the air with his large hand.

"No, gol'dangit!" Grady shouted, pounding a fist. "It's not enough! I came here for a reason and I'm going to see it through."

Chief Mitchell turned to Grady. "What is it you want me to do, Mr. Hagen?"

"Let me tell you the story, then you decide."

The cop turned to the others, his eyes stopping on each set of theirs. "Okay, but let's not do it out here. We got a nice little room; come this way." He walked to a swinging gate and opened it.

"No recording devices, this is officially off the record," Dan Garrett sputtered.

"Look Mr., uh," Chief Mitchell looked at the card in his hand, "Mr. Garrett. All I want to do is separate the meat from the chaff, as my gramma used to say as she got older." He chuckled at the malapropism. "Meat from the chaff," he whispered, shaking his head.

Grady stopped and turned to his daughter. "You shouldn't come in here. You shouldn't have to hear this."

"Oh, Daddy," she said, clutching his arm and walking him through the gate.

27

The room into which Chief Caleb Mitchell ushered them could barely possess this much humanity, and much clattering and jostling accompanied the skittering of chairs up to the scarred brown table splotched with cigarette burns. The room was framed in murky windows, the walls a faded pinkish-orange and devoid of any décor at all. No calendars or cheesy pictures. No wanted posters or wallpaper. No blackboard. Just streaky, dirty smudges.

Once everyone else was seated, Chief Mitchell opened the palms of his hands. "What say I get everybody something cold to drink? This room's pretty stuffy, you'll soon see, no matter the miracle of air conditioning. Sodas for everybody?"

Everyone nodded. "I'd prefer diet," Dan Garrett answered, "and Coke, if you have it, rather than Pepsi."

"Yeah, well, I'll see what I can do," Mitchell replied, turning and walking out the door.

Dan Garrett watched the door decompress and then looked up at Grady. "I don't like this one bit," he said. "Whatever's going on here, this is not the way to do it."

"Please, Dan," Grady said.

"Yes, please, Dan," Sarah echoed. Then she turned to her father. "Daddy, what's going on?"

Grady rubbed his temples with both hands. "Y'all aren't supposed to be here. I came to pay a debt, that's all, and none of you had to know anything about it."

"It's my fault," Charlie whispered.

"My goodness, Judas speaks," Grady replied, raising his eyebrows.

"I was scared, Pappy. I tried to bring it up at breakfast yesterday, me seeing that picture thing when I accidentally knocked over your suitcase."

Grady scrunched his eyes and rubbed them with his thumb and forefinger. "You weren't supposed to see it, son."

"It's not like I was snooping. It fell on the floor. Then I heard you talking last night to your cousin, and I got scared. So, I called Mom."

"And we couldn't fly Dan's plane because of the weather," Sarah said. "So we drove all night."

"I was hoping to just come here and . . ." Grady's voice trailed off, like a last breath.

"And deal with whatever it is this post card thing represents?" Sarah interjected.

The old man lifted his eyes and caught the gaze of his family, his family there in the room in a place he never wanted them to be. "I suppose you want to know if I had anything to do with what's on that post card?" Before anyone could answer, Grady continued. "I'd pay hell to deny it because I'm right there in the picture, right in the center of it."

Charlie couldn't inhale. "But did you? I mean did you, you . . .?"

"I suppose I could say to you that what happened in those days was just one of those things, that I got caught up in what was going on and was only a kid. Hell, I was only seventeen. Or maybe I could defend myself by telling you that you did those things because that was how you were accepted in your community, and no matter who you are you don't want to be an outcast or a coward." Grady sniffed once and subconsciously rubbed the back of his hand against his nose. "Or I point out that the whole damned town, including women and even some children, were there and everyone was screaming and out of control, and mad, holy lord they were mad. There was no stopping it. And then all these things, these motives or reasons or whatever you would call them, would somehow excuse me from it, saying I just went along with the tide." He leaned back in his seat and tilted his head. "Even then you wouldn't understand it, because I don't. All the explaining in the world doesn't forgive or excuse such a thing."

"Were you, like, in the Klan, or something like that?" Charlie asked, gripping the edge of the table until his knuckles turned white.

Grady's head sprang forward. "Now, to that I can honestly answer no."

The boy's grip softened. "Glad to hear that."

Grady turned to him. "You know, inside we don't change much throughout our lives. I'm not fundamentally different right here," he tapped on his heart with two fingers, "than I was when I was a little boy. 'Course you do lots of things and stuff happens to you, and you react in this way or that and, sometimes, maybe several times in your life, but not a lot, what you do is out of character. And you might even have a real gol'danged good reason for doing it, but you still know in your heart that it just isn't right. Then you try to push it out of your life, out of your mind, and it does go away for periods of time. But just because it disappears doesn't mean it didn't happen. Just because time went by, or because you forgot about it for a few months or years doesn't mean you're now forgiven. Because every now and again, bang, it comes back. And then a day comes in your life when you finally, inevitably, irrevocably realize what you knew the whole time: you better do something about it." He raised his chin and looked away.

"And so here we are," Sarah whispered.

"Bingo," Grady replied.

"My God," Sarah moaned. Then she stood up and began pacing the room, gnawing her thumbnail, like she used to do when she was a little girl. "How could you? How could this happen? What could you have been thinking?" she shouted.

Grady looked up at her. "You know, Sarah, you've known me all your life. But you haven't known me all mine. And there's a big difference there, because I was somebody for a lot of years before you were born. And part of what or who I was is somebody I'm not too proud of, to say the least. In fact, I'm disgusted and have been my whole life." He sighed, "But I'm finally facing up to it."

Sarah made some unintelligible noises that sounded only vaguely like words, took her thumbnail out of her mouth and shook her head.

Dan put his hand on the back of the chair in which she had been sitting. "Sit down, honey, please." She slumped into the chair.

Grady stared at the wall for several seconds. Without turning back, he quietly said, "So now you're going to get an opportunity to learn some things that you just might not like. You have to decide if you want to. I didn't want any of you here. Didn't want Charlie to come along. Never planned it. Didn't ask you to. But if you're here, I'm not going to bullshit you. I never have, never. And even if you hate me when it's all said and done – and I tell you, that would break my heart beyond measure – I would understand."

At that moment the door swung open and Chief Mitchell nuzzled in, holding five cans of soda pop against his shirt. "Here y'all go, now. Let's see, we got Dr. Pepper and 7 Up." He set the cans onto the table with a clatter. Then he turned to Dan. Sorry, Mr. Garrett, no diet."

"This will be fine," Garrett replied.

The cans were opened with a succession of clicks and hisses. The officer wedged his way between the occupied chairs to the other end of the table and the open seat there. He scooted the chair on the wooden floor and it screeched. Then he fell into it, set his can in front of him, popped the top and turned to Grady. "So, Mr. Hagen," he said, "welcome home."

Grady cleared his throat. Where to start? He hadn't really considered this. Just thought the photo would say it all and that would be that. How much did he need to know, this police chief with the easy manner and the light in his eyes? Because the story was much bigger and deeper and more complicated than the explosion of fury that ended Rudy Montcrief's life on the end of a rope. Grady closed his eyes, squeezing them with his fingers. Then he looked up and started to speak. The words collided, one against the other, like a braking freight train. And, of course, with each thought came a picture. "There was a girl, you see, named Cissy Moody," he began.

28

The Greyhound bus brought him back, belching blue diesel clouds
as it hissed and humphed away, and Grady was standing on the street
corner with his duffel bag. He had only been gone ten days, but it
might as well have been a lifetime. He felt like a stranger in his own
town, but the bus ride home had simmered in him a new determination
to somehow get that big league contract and go and show Chet Zane
what for and end up in Chicago; not just because playing baseball
was the only thing he was fit to do, but because Chicago would be a
billion times bigger and more rambunctious than even Birmingham.
Just what he wanted. Big. Exciting. A place with lights on all night
and movie theaters and music coming out onto the streets from bars.
If he could just get this chicken arm to heal full through.

Just as these thoughts crystallized in his mind, just as the pictures
took form in his imagination, Fletcher Moody's big Lincoln – you
couldn't miss it, it was the fanciest-assed car in town by about a million
– flew up the street past him, throwing a breeze in its wake, and came
to a crashing stop in front of the police station. Fletcher tumbled out,
nearly falling on the pavement, just catching himself with one hand.
The cigar in his mouth wobbled a few times and flew like a propeller
down to the street as he slipped. He kicked it under the car, then
slammed the door and stomped around to the other side. Wrenching
the passenger door open, he reached inside and dragged Cissy out by
the arm.

Grady stood frozen, the hysteria of the scene rolling over him like a tidal wave. Cissy fell against the side of the car, and the sight of her threw him backward. Her face was like a wretched piece of clay, a child's pathetic attempt at sculpture, all purple and distorted. One eye was completely swollen shut; the other had been pummeled into a tiny slit above a bulbous yellow knot. Her mouth was caked in brown blood. She was bent like a seahorse and could barely walk.

Grady dropped his duffel in the center of the street and sprinted to her. "What the – what happened, Mr. Moody?" he stammered, coming to Cissy and taking her under his arm. Immediately she buried her head in his shirt and began weeping.

"I'm so sorry, I'm so sorry," she whimpered.

"Goddamned sonofabitch nigger did this to my little girl!" Fletcher blubbered, skittering over the curb, clinging to her loose arm. His face was bright red, his eyes wide and frantic. "Goddamned sonofabitch."

"Why you bringing her here?" Grady cried. "Let's get her to the doctor."

"Gotta tell the chief," he sputtered, then pulled Cissy's wrist toward him as he shouted up to the doorway of the office. "LaGrone! LaGrone! Jesus Christ!"

Grady grabbed Moody's forearm and squeezed. "Let her go, Mr. Moody." When the man resisted, he twisted the arm. "Let her go," he said, breaking Moody's grip. For an instant he held on to Fletcher's arm and noticed something. The skin was scratched, fresh stripes, some still seeping tiny beads of blood. Grady's eyes ran down to the hands. Moody's knuckles were skinned, as if someone had taken a metal file and buffed them. Some of the sores had begun to scab over. Some were still white-pink and oozing clear liquid.

For a painful instant of terse understanding, the two men's eyes locked. Then Grady thrust the arm away. "You go to the sheriff. I'm taking her to the doc." He began to pull her away from her father.

Then the door to the police station swung open and Cecil LaGrone rumbled down the stairs, a cloth napkin still tucked into the front collar of his shirt. "What in the Sam Hill are y'all doing now?" He froze when he saw Cissy. "Holy smoke!" he exhaled.

"That's my little girl, goddamnit! That's my little girl!" Fletcher screamed, pointing at her. Tears were pouring down his face now.

"A nigger done this to her! A nigger! Do you believe it, Cecil? A nigger!"

"Shut up, Fletcher," LaGrone shouted, putting himself between Moody and Cissy, and pushing the man away. "Grady, take her, take her to the doc."

"That nigger's gonna die! That nigger's gonna die 'cause of what he did!" Fletcher Moody cried.

"Get hold of yourself, Fletcher," LaGrone said, grabbing the man by the shoulders and turning him around. "Now, who did this? What nigger?"

Grady didn't need to hear the answer, but it rang in his ears anyway.

"That Montcrief boy. Rudy, that's his name. Rudy Montcrief."

"No, No!" Cissy burrowed deeper into Grady's shirt, smearing it with blood and sweat and tears and mucus. She came and went, right there as he held her; in and out of consciousness. How many times had he seen her on the streets of Arbutus, and as much as they tried not to, their eyes would lock if only for a second and then turn away, away from an abominable thing they both knew? This was why she wouldn't look at him. Shame. Shame on you, Cissy Moody. Goddamnit for putting me in this position. As if it wasn't enough, having his guts ripped out by Betsy Sue; having his arm – and his dream – snapped in two by his old man. Her problems weren't his. Weren't his at all. And she couldn't, gol'dangit, even look him in the eye.

But he loved her, didn't he?

He whispered to her, pulling her tight, protecting her. "C'mon, Cissy. It'll be all right."

29

"It was a miracle Rudy Montcrief made it in at all, the way the town reacted when the news got out about how Cissy was all mangled and mauled up by a black man," Grady sighed, leaning back in the chair now, his head against the wall, eyes staring at the stark light on the ceiling. "In those days it didn't take long for word to get around."

"Same today," Caleb Mitchell said, taking a swig of Dr. Pepper. "But before you go on, let me ask a question." He slid forward in his chair, making another screeching noise on the floor. "You say old man Moody had scratches on his arm and hand."

"Yeah, all 'cross here," Grady said, tracing a path on his arm. "And the knuckles all busted up."

The Chief pursed his lips. "How you suppose he got those marks?"

Grady looked up at him and raised his eyebrows. "Two plus two equals four, even in Mississippi."

Mitchell continued. "So, you're saying maybe the black man didn't do it to her? It could have been the father, considering the wounds?"

"Of course, it was him."

"But why would her own father do that to her and blame it on a black man?"

"I'll get to that," Grady answered. "Suffice it to say that Cissy crossed a line into forbidden territory."

"I understand," the Chief replied.

Sarah arched her shoulders. "My God, it's horrible enough that a man was lynched. But for something he didn't do? Lynched out of pure

162

hatred by a bunch of, of animals," then she caught herself, obviously realizing that she had included her father in her generalization.

Grady expelled a mouthful of air and ran his hand through his hair. "It was a different time, baby," Grady said. "Full of different notions."

"I can't believe you would say that," she argued, "as if it were a valid excuse."

Grady rubbed his chin. "Well, I already explained that nothing here is an excuse. It's just the way it was. That was the rain that watered my fields," Grady whispered. Then he looked up. "My momma used to say that."

"What does that mean?" Charlie asked.

Grady eased himself forward and reached for the can of pop, took a swallow, and turned to his grandson. "It means, of course, that it was a different time and a different place, and the ideas and beliefs we grew up by are – were – different." He looked at Sarah. "You all came along to a different world. Your momma wouldn't let words through our door that were just part of the everyday vocabulary down here." He pointed to Charlie. "And he came into an even different world than you, with black people everywhere, where it doesn't mean anything to sit next to an African-American person in a movie or on a bus, or even have one in your house for dinner, as something more than a servant. Where Michael Jordan sells shoes, and Bill Cosby stars on television, and Vanilla Iced Tea rapper, or whatever his name is, comes out of my grandson's CD player at a million decibels. " He shook his head. "I didn't grow up on that planet. Down here when a white person walked on the sidewalk, the protocol was for black people to step off and let him pass."

"My God," Sarah hissed.

"It was the unwritten rules we lived by," Grady shrugged. "Terrible as they were, few people questioned them."

"People tell you something enough, you believe it," Chief Mitchell said.

"More than that. It just is what it is. It's in your bones, soaking in until this truth, no matter how untrue it might be, is a part of the air you breathe and the trees and the water. Something so profound and sacred that men were willing to die for it. Imagine that, dying for a notion so corrupt and wrong!" Grady sighed. "Then we're just supposed to get it out of ourselves. Well, it don't move too easily, no matter how hard we try."

Chief Mitchell collapsed his finger tent and dropped his hands onto the table. "So, they brought Rudy Montcrief in."

"Yeah," Grady answered. "And like I said, they 'pert near killed him before he ever got into the jail."

30

Arbutus, Mississippi – August 8, 1942

It was as though a live cable had broken loose and fallen onto the street and was writhing like a snake and spitting white hot electricity into the air. The people of Arbutus had been shaken out of their homes and now gathered in front of the steps of the police station. An incessant buzz emerged from the sinister mingling of people, heat, hatred and anger, plus the inability to comprehend that such a diseased concept could somehow pour into this town. Office doors, up and down the street, yawned wide, shelves of stuff and cash registers right there for the taking if there had been even one person more occupied with the notion of robbery than the lust for revenge. Any bumbling idiot thief could have walked in and leaned over a counter and reached into the cash drawer and taken what he wanted, if there was anyone with such a desire, which, of course, there wasn't. The painful irony was that these were fundamentally honest people, by and large, despite what was going on.

Both concrete banisters leading to the porch of the police station were festooned with men; angry males of all ages in white shirts with the sleeves rolled up, boaters or floppy hats keeping the cigar smoke low and in their eyes. Some sort of unofficial and unspecified pecking order placed these men at this point. Steve Pruitt, Bill Tolleston, Sr., Ben Bergey, president of the town council, Herb Finnegan, the general manager of the lumber yard, Carl Fleming who owned the gas station and livery stable, all men of some prominence in town. They comprised the vortex of the flowing crowd that poured like milk from a pitcher into the street and park, widening, widening, widening the further back it flowed. A cluster of people on Main unfurled a huge Confederate flag.

Grady had ridden with Dr. Max Randall and Cissy to the hospital across the county where a swarm of nurses – like seagulls in their white uniforms – surrounded her, lifted her to a gurney and took her through a large green door. Grady rode back to town with another local family who was bringing their son home after a tonsillectomy. It was supper time when he arrived back in Arbutus, and he immediately was sucked into the crowd.

Grady moved to the front. Even though he was still only a kid a few weeks past his seventeenth birthday, he was accorded a certain respect, and the crowd let him through. In a second, Billie Rae Tolleston, Jr. was swimming toward him.

"Did y'all hear what happened?" he asked, coming to Grady and shaking his arm.

"I just got back from the hospital. I went with Cissy and Doc Max." Grady stood on his tiptoes and looked back over the crowd. Out of the corner of his eye he caught a movement in the alley entrance on the side of the police station office. A phalanx of horses clomped toward the street, the white robes of the riders blazing in the sun. Grady craned his neck. Of course, he wouldn't recognize his old man under the hood. But he would know Cree. "Looks like everybody's here," he said. "Don't nobody want to miss this."

"Chief and Deputy Clem went out to get the boy. I pity the bastard when he gets here," Billie Rae squealed.

"Gol'dang," Grady whispered.

"How's Cissy?"

He turned his head away and spat. "She ain't gonna die."

"More'n can be said for that nigger, I bet," Billie Rae laughed.

Then there was a noise, from the far end of the park, a vibrating of voices that washed like a wave from the back of the crowd to the front, increasing in intensity and volume. Grady hopped up on the second step and looked out. Daddies held toddlers on their shoulders to watch as the police car crawled up Jefferson Street. The crowd, of course, slid off to the side to let the vehicle through, but immediately closed on it, peering in the windows with faces cupped in both hands.

"There he is!"

"I seen that rapist nigger."

"You gonna die, boy."

"Why'n the hell didn't you kill him right there, Chief?"

Fists pounded on the glass of the car, and Chief LaGrone rolled down the window as the crowd squeezed tighter. "Get the heck out of the way," he screamed, leaning into the siren that wailed like a bleating sheep.

"It's your last day, nigger," a man said, reaching into the open window and grabbing toward the back seat.

"Get the . . ." LaGrone said, pushing the arm away.

Finally the car pulled up to the front of the building. Cecil LaGrone angrily pushed the door open, dispersing bodies with the sweeping motion. He rolled out. "What in the Sam Hill has gotten into you people?" he screamed. The crowd was vibrating as a single reed now, pushing toward him. He shoved several men aside and ascended the steps. "I ain't taking this boy out of this car until y'all get a hold of yourselves." He raised both hands and lowered them. "Simmer down, simmer down, I tell ya!"

The line of horsemen, twelve in all, shotguns on their hips, wound slowly to the rear periphery of the crowd.

"Settle, settle," LaGrone shouted again, and gradually the energy subsided. Satisfied, he raised his hands again. "Okay, now, I 'preciate everyone's concern with what's going on here today. But let me make myself clear as ice to y'all. Y'all are gonna step back and let me take this boy into my jail, where we're gonna keep him," he thrust out his jaw for emphasis, "and guard him, and let the law deal with him as it may."

"Let us deal with the nigger," somebody cried, and the thunder started again.

"We ain't, we ain't. . ." LaGrone waited for the noise to subside. "Dang it, people, we don't do things that way in this town. We ain't Nazis or communists. We're God fearing Christian folk." The crowd sounds rolled away into the air and everything became still. "Thank you," LaGrone said. "Now, make me room up here," he continued, moving people off the steps, clearing a path. "Deputy Clem and me's gonna take this boy up these steps, and ain't nobody gonna do nothing to him. You understand?" he turned and looked directly at Steve Pruitt, who leaned on the banister at the top of the steps. Pruitt locked him in a stare for a second or two, then turned and got out of the way.

"Good. Now just stand back," LaGrone said, moving down the steps to the passenger side of the car. He rapped on the window. "Okay, Clem, come on out."

Deputy Clem opened the door and slid out of the front seat. Then he unlocked the back door of the car, reached in, and pulled Rudy Montcrief into the sunlight. The sight of the young black man, whose head was bowed over a sweat-stained white shirt and gray pants, ignited the crowd, which surged forward, closing like a fist. Clem and LaGrone literally picked up their prisoner and whisked him up the steps, where they disappeared behind the closing door.

Billie Rae looked over Grady's shoulder. "Good thing I didn't make a bet. I thought that boy'd be one dead monkey by now."

Grady Hagen's insides seemed to melt in the heat and fury of the moment. Goddamn you, Cissy Moody, he thought. Look what you did to this town.

Just then the door to the police station opened again and Cecil LaGrone emerged, pouring sweat in rivers down his shirt, his face tomato red and looking ready to explode. "Thank y'all for your restraint. Now go on home and back to work. It's supper time," he said, nodding once and heading back into the building.

"It's gonna be a long night for the Chief," Steve Pruitt said to no one in particular. Grady heard it and instinctively understood that this incident was far from over.

Nights that boil hot with a relentless insistence are always the most dangerous time. Because now, when the bones and body and mind crave repose and the sizzling fever of the darkness won't allow it, anger and frustration pour through the skin. Grady sensed it as he sat on the wooden stoop of Tolleston's Hardware, Billie Rae beside him, sipping a Coke from a bottle that disappeared in his large hand. The crowd had thinned somewhat, but there were still people on the street, clusters here and there, enveloped in clouds of cigarette smoke that wafted upward along with the murmurs. More than usual. More than right.

He leaned his head back as far as he could and let the last few drops from the green glass bottle dribble onto his tongue. Then he set the empty down on the sidewalk. "They don't put nearly enough in these tiny things," he said. "Night like tonight I could drink a gallon." He wiped his chin with the back of his hand.

"What do you suppose is gonna happen?" Billie Rae asked.

"Y'all the boy genius who knows everything," Grady answered. "What do you think?"

Billie Rae sucked on the end of his bottle, then blew into it, making a steamship sound. "Me? I can't see how the nigger makes it. Trial and whatnot takes too long. This town won't wait, not when you consider it's Cissy and all."

"I suppose you're right."

"Old man Moody's got too many people right here." Billie Rae patted his back pocket.

"Somehow I s'pect it don't matter who it was. Not with the nature of the thing. Could be any old girl, I bet. The town wouldn't put up with it," Grady guessed.

Billie Rae began flipping the empty Coke bottle end over end in his hand. "Well, you're prolly right, there, unless it was some ugly old slut like Margaret Salisbury," he laughed.

Grady shook his head and grunted. Then he grew pensive and said, not exactly to Billie Rae, maybe more to himself, "Even her, she couldn't get away with this."

"What do you mean? 'She couldn't get away with this?' Cissy didn't do nothing wrong."

Grady caught himself. "Yeah, that's not what I meant. It come out wrong." When, in fact, it was exactly what he meant, even if he hadn't meant to say it. There were prices to be paid for what Cissy and Montcrief had done in that cave, even if no one else knew anything about it. Old man Moody might have taken care of one-half the business himself. Grady hoped that Cissy being beaten up by the old man was punishment enough for her; that she wouldn't now be ostracized for even letting a colored near her. He prayed that somehow this was the end of it, but he knew that it wasn't. Cissy's punishment was far from over. She would be blamed for what happened to her, even if the lie Fletcher Moody created was believed as gospel. Too many people – Grady's own father for crying out loud – had seen and remarked about her flirting with Rudy at the lumber yard.

No, Cissy's punishment had only begun.

The colored boy's punishment, on the other hand, was another matter.

"Just the boys I'm looking for." The voice startled Grady. He hadn't felt, hadn't sensed, anyone approaching, and now Steve Pruitt was standing alongside him, coming out of the shadows like a cat. "Mr. Pruitt," he said, standing up, brushing off his pants. Billie Rae also came to his feet.

"Look boys, we need your help," Pruitt said, nodding toward the jail house. "Need all the big, strong boys we can get."

"What for?" Grady asked.

Pruitt walked around in front of them, the streetlight catching his cheekbones. The brim of his hat threw a shadow, however, that totally obscured his eyes. "Nice night, ain't it?" he said turning and looking over the trees that lined the park. "Little too hot, though, don't you think?"

"Real hot," Grady said.

"Yeah, real hot," Billie Rae agreed.

"Makin' people all agitated. Can you feel it?" Pruitt continued, slowly walking away, then turning back. "Kind of like it's the lord's way to stir up the blood, give us all the courage and intestinal fortitude we need to do what we must do, what's right to do, what is only fair and just." He stopped and folded his arms. "That colored boy in the jail house there is like an animal, like a bear. Strong beyond his size. And you get his kidneys secreting adrenaline and he's gonna be a load to bring down, not to mention dealing with interference from Clem and LaGrone."

Oh, Jesus, Grady thought.

"So, we're going to need a few strong men like y'all to help us," Pruitt said, unfolding his arms. "Key members of the circle. Doing justice."

"I'm in," Billie Rae said.

Pruitt turned his head, pushed his hat back, revealing two pin holes of light where his eyes would be, and looked at Grady. "You?" he said.

"Goddamn right," Billie Rae Tolleston answered for him, putting an arm over Grady's shoulder and jostling him. "We work together."

At that precise moment, two more men rounded the corner of Tolleston's store and approached Pruitt. Even while they were still in the darkness, Grady recognized them from their general shapes and the motion of their steps. Ben Bergey came into the light first, a vapor trail of cigarette smoke curling behind him. Carter Fleming, only about five feet five inches tall, carried a coiled rope in his hand. "This gonna do it?" he asked proffering the rope to Pruitt. His voice was shaking.

Pruitt fingered the rope. "Should be fine." He turned to the boys. "Now, let me tell you, the crowd is going to dictate a lot of what goes on here. Once they know what's happening, it's going to be chaos, pure chaos. But we gotta remember that everybody here has a job. I'll deal with LaGrone. All you boys need to do is hold that nigger still so we can tie him up, and then make sure we get him out. It couldn't be more easier."

It was as if an earthquake had struck Arbutus. All it took was the sight of Steve Pruitt marching down the center of Main Street, with a cobra of rope in his hands and his boot heels thundering on the brick pavement, to mobilize the tiny coagulations of people into a single body that surged toward the jailhouse from all directions.

The door exploded inward and Chief Cecil LaGrone froze in his chair, a pork chop bone in his hand, strings of meat hanging from his mouth. His eyes erupted from his head, and he stammered, juggling words between his mind and his mouth. Deputy Clem swiveled in his chair and sprang to his feet, windmilling toward the case of rifles on the wall.

"Stay down, Cecil. Stop right where you are, too, Clem," Steve Pruitt screamed. "You ain't gonna stop us."

"Gol'darn it, Steve, what the heck y'all doing?" LaGrone cried, dropping the bone onto his plate, where it landed with a ringing echo. "Lord almighty, don't do this, please don't do this," he pleaded, standing up, folding his hands.

"It's the right thing to do," Pruitt shouted, now to be heard over the hysteria of the crowd that swept into the room. He kicked open the swinging gate and moved quickly to LaGrone, pulling a ring of keys from his belt. "Which one is it, Cecil? Come on, make this easy for us."

By now bodies clotted the entrance. In every window burned the frantic, contorted face of a citizen of Arbutus. Screams reverberated, rattling the windows.

"Oh Jesus, oh God, oh God," LaGrone cried, tears streaming down his cheeks. But in a second he was pinned to his desk by the surging mass.

Pruitt pushed Grady and Billie Rae through the door and down the hallway leading to the tiny cells which, until this time, had primarily housed local drunks and the occasional moonshiner that LaGrone periodically used as an example to make it look like he cared. Grady steadied himself by walking his hand along the wall. His head vibrated with noise and pain and confusion. A screaming yellow cloud engulfed him. The walls seemed to be moving, the shadows of the bars separating and closing like the ridges on a squeeze box. He didn't hear the jangling of keys or the moan of the door, but he was suddenly in the cell with Rudy Montcrief, who had rolled himself tight into a corner, arms and legs tucked within his folded torso.

Billie Rae grabbed an arm first and tried to pull it free. "Jesus Christ, goddamnit," he screamed, then stopped pulling and began punching the man on the back and side of the head.

"Get in there, Grady," Pruitt shouted.

Grady moved forward and reached under Montcrief, grabbing both of his wrists. Strong, God he was strong, like Pruitt had said, like a cougar or a horse. Grady strained with all his might, the heel of his foot buried in Montcrief's hip.

"I can't do it! I can't do it!" Billie Rae said.

I can't do it either, Grady thought to himself, letting his arms go slack. What the hell is going on here? I have to get out of here. Jesus, get me out of here.

Just then Grady felt a rush of wind pass his ear, again and again, and he backed away and saw Ben Bergey beating Rudy on the head with a broken broom handle. Whap, whap, whap, until the victim reflexively broke his posture and reached his arms up to fend off the blows. This was when Billie Rae moved in and grabbed one arm, twisting it behind his back. Grady, by now, had fallen into the corner, his cheek pressing against the concrete wall.

"Tie his fucking hands," someone screamed, and a short piece of rope spiraled through the air. Ben Bergey dropped the broom handle and twisted Montcrief's other arm behind him. With a few quick flips of the rope, his hands were tied and several men were lifting him to his feet. Blood poured down his temple, blacker, even, than his skin. It puddled on his pants in greasy globs. Rudy looked up from beneath a furrowed brow and his eyes caught the eyes of Grady Hagen, who lay in the corner, hands hanging limply at his sides. A bubble of blood erupted and then seemed to burst in Rudy's nostril. For what seemed like an eternity, the two men – boys, really, their lives connected so peripherally, yet so, so permanently – just stared at each other and spoke a million words and feelings with only a glance.

At that moment the fight went out of Rudy Montcrief. Grady saw it die like the flame on a candle, blown out, leaving a whisper of smoke as it passed.

"You all right or what?" Steve Pruitt asked, reaching down to Grady. He took Pruitt's hand and slid to a standing position, his back against the concrete wall of the cell. He used the wall to brace himself as he staggered to his feet. "C'mon, get a hand on him," Pruitt said.

Grady shook loose from Pruitt's grip. "I'm done," the boy said, raising his hands and turning away.

They rustled the prisoner out the door and into a writhing gauntlet, where he was pummeled with spit and stones and fists flying from the clusters of people. One hand came free and he used it not to fight, but to keep the flying debris from striking his head. Grady followed behind, swept forward by the crowd, but detached from all of this, as if he had taken flight from his own body, his own being. Yet he still soldiered on, driven by something beyond his control.

They marched Rudy down Jefferson Street to the far corner of the park, where stood a gnarled oak tree, older than anyone in the town, more ancient than the brick streets, here before the whites or the Negroes, before one nail had ever been driven, but now destined for an ignominious fate. And Grady suddenly believed that if this living tree could, it would pull its roots from the depths and flee this horrendous duty being forced upon it. And yet, why could he not do the same, with feet unfettered and free? With a mind and a soul with the power to know what was right and what was wrong?

Steve Pruitt launched the rope upward in a perfect arc. It uncoiled over the branch and snapped into place. Three men beneath the tree took the flying end and pulled, lifting the knotted loop off the ground. The noose cast a huge shadow in the glow of a street lamp and it looked to Grady like the yawning entrance to hell.

Rudy stood, hunched over himself, a man on each arm holding him upright. His legs vibrated like saplings in a storm. The slice of rope that had once bound his arms dangled from his right wrist. Pruitt wrestled him to the top of something, maybe an apple crate, it was hard to tell. Grady stood frozen at the back of the crowd. They inserted Rudy's head into the noose, pulled it taut and kicked away the crate. The three men on the other end of the rope pulled in unison, and Montcrief rose above the crowd. He jerked violently, both hands reaching up, clawing at the rope around his throat. His legs splayed and vibrated, twisting this way and that, climbing an imaginary ladder. His hands flew at the rope like birds attacking.

The three men wrapped the rope several times around the tree trunk and surged forward to watch Rudy die.

The concept of hanging was to snap the neck and deliver instant death, but this wasn't what was happening here. This was a slow strangulation, and it took so long. Rudy Montcrief fought it with a fury, with all his strength, with both hands and both feet. But he couldn't beat it away. Finally he stopped, dropping his arms. He twitched, eventually only at the ends of his fingers, the spirit leaking out of him. Then he was horrifically still, and his body swung in a silent circle.

"Jesus, look at that," Billie Rae Tolleston said, coming to Grady who somehow now stood in the inside circle of the crowd surrounding the corpse.

A cheer rumbled over the crowd, spreading like a wave as people moved in for a closer peek at the victim.

"Hey, y'all, look up this way!" someone said.

Billie Rae grabbed Grady's arm and raised it above his head. A flash exploded in the darkness like a rush of heat lightning.

31

To Grady Hagen, everything had turned blinding white, and all sound and scent and depth and breadth had been stripped away. Like dying, he thought, or maybe those old films of ground zero during an atomic explosion. He had relinquished control of his own words as the story came pouring out. And then he was finished, a vessel emptied.

How long did it take for the white hot sheets to melt away? He didn't know. But the room was coming back to him now. He picked up bits and pieces. The pop cans were drained and expunging circular puddles on the wooden table where they had rested. The room had grown even smaller, it seemed, forcing the vapor from Grady's story out through the crack under the door. No one spoke. Of all the people he could have noticed first, it was Dan Garrett who came into focus, leaning back in his chair, his hands folded over his stomach, head back, eyes closed. Then the whole scene sizzled to life. Charlie was hunched forward, rocking the bottom rim of his pop can back and forth, staring through it. Sarah blew her nose softly in a tissue and wiped from her eyes tears that burned Grady like acid. Then his heart nearly stopped.

Behind her stood Rachel.

Christ almighty.

Then she was gone.

Chief Mitchell took a deep breath. "I don't really know what to say."

Dan uncoiled from his position and leaned forward causing the front legs of his chair to smack on the floor. "Very clearly, Chief, this incident was neither instigated by my client, nor by his own admission did he . . ."

The policeman raised his hand. "Please, sir. Not now," he sighed.

"He's right, Dan, not now," Sarah replied.

Grady closed his eyes and whispered. "Kil't old Cecil LaGrone, too, it did." He opened his eyes and looked up. "I heard he died in his bed a few weeks later. Massive heart attack, they said. But everyone knew what brought it on."

Chief Caleb Mitchell leaned toward Grady. "I know this was a difficult thing for you to tell me, especially with your family here." He paused and cleared his throat. "Now, what is it you want me to do?"

The question froze Grady on the spot. He had soaked up every last drop of courage to get this far, believing that from this point on it would be someone else's responsibility to determine what happens next. He had surrendered, damn it! "I just thought," he stammered, "Uh, you would know what to do."

Chief Mitchell scratched his temple. "Well, now, that there is a conundrum, if you know what I mean," he said. "Let me ask a few questions, just to clarify. Okay?"

"Sure," Grady said.

Dan Garrett started to say something, but caught himself and leaned back.

"According to what you described about that night, did you have any knowledge of, or part in, the planning of the lynching of Rudy Montcrief?"

"Other than what was just, you know, happening in the air and whatever, no. But in those days, it wasn't unusual for things to go in that direction, so I can't say I was surprised," Grady answered.

"But you did not know for certain, didn't help plan it, correct?"

"No, I didn't. I mean, yes, you're correct."

"And when you got in the cell and realized what was going on, you backed off. Is that right?"

"I think I knew what was going on before . . ."

Dan Garrett interrupted, "Grady, just answer yes or no."

"Yes. I didn't want to be a part . . ."

Chief Mitchell pursed his lips and nodded. "Good." He picked up his pencil and fiddled with it for several seconds, turning it end over end on the table. Finally he looked up. "Now, Mr. Hagen, I've listened to your story, to what you had to say. I don't do a heckuva lot of things well, but one little talent I think I have is hearing words where there are no words. Do you know what I mean?"

Grady nodded. "Yeah, I know exactly what you mean."

"You know, this town has changed a lot since you were here. Sure, there are still some guys who think dressing up in bed linens has a meaningful purpose, but they're few and far between. Now, I'm not saying that race isn't an issue in some people's minds, but by-and-large we've simmered it down. People come and go as they please. Blacks and whites play together on the teams and whatnot. It isn't perfect, by a long shot, but it's a far cry from that night when Rudy Montcrief was hanged." Mitchell leaned back and folded his arms. "Now, I'd heard of the incident, of course, bits and pieces. It's a horrible and unforgivable thing. But if what you told me is the way it happened – and I have no reason to disbelieve it – you were, at worst, an accessory to the event. One of several hundred. Even you admit that you actually backed off from the actual crime before it happened." He looked at Dan Garrett, "As I'm sure your lawyer would insist. And I doubt seriously that there is anyone left who would put you in the forefront of this event, even if someone ever could have."

"But I was still . . ." Grady stammered.

Chief Mitchell raised his hand. "Let me finish," he said. "I know what you're looking for, what you want, what you need to happen. And I can't give that to you. Even if I was moderately inclined to, say, arrest you for your part in this incident," he turned to Dan Garrett, "which I am not, it wouldn't take away what you want taken away. It would turn this community upside down, dredge up old pains and sorrows, cause all sorts of commotion, bring hate back out onto the streets, and, when all was said and done, you would still be burdened."

Grady cleared his throat and held his head in both hands. What was the feeling? Relief? Confusion? Had he done all he could and sacrificed himself before the law, only to be shown mercy? Or was there still more to do? He looked up. "You might be right," he whispered.

Chief Mitchell brightened a bit. "Where you stayin'?"

"My cousin's. Truman Morse. Lives in my old house. Do you know him?"

"Sure, I know old Truman. How's he doing? How's his breathing?"

"Pretty tough," Grady answered.

Mitchell shook his head and pursed his lips. "Old timers like that didn't know what cigarette smoking could do to them. Now you got school kids with all kinds of information coming out and standing right out there in the park smoking like locomotives. With all they know. It's a shame." He stood up and placed both hands on the table. "You enjoy your visit here in Arbutus, Mr. Hagen, and y'all. But this conversation today, it didn't happen. Take that any way you want to, but don't stir up a frenzy in my town. We may be the so-called new South, but you know as well as I do that some attitudes are covered with a very thin veneer. We don't want it scratched off, if you know what I mean."

Grady pushed his chair away from the table and stood up. "I appreciate your time," he reached across and shook Mitchell's hand.

Mitchell intensified his grip. "Just remember what I said." The natural congeniality that seems to seep into the pores of every southerner suddenly faded on the skin of the policeman. "You want to keep the peace down here, and that begins with me."

32

Outside, the heat coiling on them from the ground up, Dan Garrett spoke first. "Let's get in our cars and get out of here now, as fast as we can. I'd say we're pretty damned lucky to have dodged that bullet."

Grady was walking faster than the rest of them, his hands scrunched in his pockets. "Ever think someone would prefer not to dodge a bullet?"

"That's ludicrous," Dan replied.

"Well, not at all. Was a guy in the army with me named Garrison, similar to your name, I guess, now that I think about it." Grady walked as he talked. "Man was scared so badly by what we were up against, night after night, the shells coming in, shaking the earth, the endless waiting for the next one to hit. He'd piss his pants and then the stuff would freeze on the outside. Finally, one day, bright sunlight, the Germans are coming at us, into the woods, behind trees, bullets flying around like bees, and Garrison stands up, drops his rifle, spreads out his arms like Jesus and takes one right in the chest."

"You mean on purpose, Pappy?" Charlie asked.

"You gotta think that's what he was doing," Grady answered softly. "At least, that's what it sure looked like. But the point is, you see, sometimes living through any more of something may be harder than taking the bullet, literally or figuratively. Just depends on your constitution."

"I can't imagine," Charlie whispered.

"I agree with Dan, Daddy," Sarah said, clutching herself with both arms and then wiping downward. "Let's get out of here."

"I can't do that. I'm not done yet."

Sarah was frantic now and began chewing her knuckle again. "Oh, Daddy! Please, please go home."

"I am home, little girl," Grady said, pulling his hands from his pockets and removing a handkerchief. He handed it to her. "I have work to do." Then he turned and bounded into Bauer's Pharmacy. "I don't know about y'all, but I need a drink, and seeing as how this place is dry as lizard's hide, ice cream will have to do."

A few minutes later the four of them, a family, came out into the day, each with a cup of ice cream, except Dan Garrett, who insisted on a cone, despite Grady's warnings. "Let's walk a few blocks that-a-way," the old man said, pointing with his plastic spoon at a church spire knifing through the trees a few blocks off Jefferson Street. "Something you all should see up there."

"So, this is the famous Arbutus we've heard nothing about," Sarah said, walking shoulder-to-shoulder with her father. "Guess I know why, now."

"It's something I can't change. Nobody can change where they were born." Or where they die, he thought.

"Did Mom ever know?"

"That I was born here? Of course," he answered, though he knew what she was really asking.

"No, about this. All this!'"

"No."

"You couldn't tell her?"

Grady shook his head. "Why? What would that do? What good would it serve? Your mother's heart was as fine and generous as any God ever built, but this would have been too much for her to carry." He scraped the spoon against the edges of the cup and captured quick scoops of the rapidly deteriorating ice cream. "I couldn't do it to her. It would have made her need to stop loving me, and that would have been unbearable for both of us. Why inflict my pain on her?" He licked the spoon clean.

"So, you kept it all to yourself. That couldn't have been easy for you," Sarah said.

"I didn't deserve easy, never asked for it. You gotta understand, it was always only about me. It was my crime, my sin, my great cataclysm, perhaps my damnation. It was a wound incapable of healing, bleeding into my soul. Dragging someone innocent into it would have only made it worse."

"I can't believe Mom wouldn't have understood," Sarah said, touching him on the arm.

"Do you? Understand, I mean?" Grady said, stopping and facing her.

Sarah Hagen Garrett, M.D. sagged visibly, her color changing to chalky white. Her eyes brimmed with tears and her lip trembled. "Oh, Daddy, do you think I didn't watch you all my life? Didn't see, didn't know, what kind of man you were?"

"Please forgive me, baby," Grady said, opening his arms.

Sarah dropped her cup of ice cream and reached for him, hugging him tightly, burying her face in his shoulder. "Yes, Daddy, yes," she cried.

They held each other for several seconds, and Grady wiped the tears from his daughter's cheek and kissed her where his fingers had been. "You guys coming?" Grady said, turning to catch the attention of Charlie and his father. They were fifty yards or more behind. Dan Garrett had taken off his coat, slung it over his shoulder, and was wiping between his fingers with a handkerchief, as Charlie held his disintegrating ice cream cone between two fingers at arm's length.

"Just throw the damn thing in the trash," Dan grumbled. Charlie walked over to a rusting oil drum and tossed the remnant in.

"This has to be the hottest place on the planet," Dan groused, stopping to lick ice cream off his hand and sleeve.

Grady swirled his spoon in the puree remnants that had formed in the bottom of his cup. "I told him not to buy a cone. He never did pay any attention to me," he said to Sarah. "Always thought I was a crazy old hillbilly."

"Daddy, that's not fair."

"I think we have to go this way," Grady said, nodding and turning to his right.

They walked past the old church and turned down another street that led to an iron gate framing the entrance to a cemetery. "Here, here it is," Grady said, shooting ahead of the others. The aura and echoes of antiquity wove through the cemetery. Canopies from huge oaks virtually obscured the sky, allowing only a few jewels of sunlight to spill between their tight leaf formations onto the graves, as if the trees were cooks seasoning a broth. Tombstones festooned with lichens, and streaked with moss, leaned this way and that, throwing subtle shadows over the remains of Confederate soldiers and doctors and farmers and housewives and artists and dreamers and children, their names and dates worn to near extinction by the constant rubbing of time against the stones. Moldering with these bones were all the things that made each person unique, the lilt of a voice, the ideas and plans, the talents, the good deeds, the sins. And the thought silenced Grady and pulled him inward.

He pushed ahead, placing his right hand on his knee as he climbed a slight incline. He could see it now, the simple red granite tombstone, and was surprised that he remembered so easily where the grave had been placed. He stopped and looked down at his mother and father's resting place.

"Bo Hagen, 1902-1944. Rhea Wood Hagen, 1905-1944," Sarah read aloud. "They died the same year?"

"Yeah, car accident," Grady said. The old man killed her, just like Grady thought he would, but not with his fists. His head rampaging with liquor, he was driving home from Thanksgiving dinner at Uncle Truman, Sr. and Aunt Rose's, not ten miles down the road. On a dove gray day, dry brown leaves in the air. His foot was to the floorboard of the car he'd finally broken down and purchased when his beloved Cree died. There were too many curves in the road, too much loose gravel, too much discord in his nerve endings, too much wobble on the front wheels, and suddenly the car was going in two directions at once until it rolled and rose, going airborne before flipping over three times and imploding. Momma got spit out like a watermelon seed, and they found her sitting against a wooden fence, her legs folded, not a mark on her. Daddy stayed with the disintegrating automobile and mingled his viscera and nerve ganglia with the steering column and the fractured glass and steel.

"You never talked about them," Sarah said.

"No one ever asked," Grady replied, bending down on one knee and running his fingers through the grass.

"I don't know why, why I never asked. I guess they just seemed like someone so far gone, that we never really gave it much thought."

Grady canted his head and squinted as he looked up at her. "Well, they never lived in your world. But they did in mine, and much as I wished when they were gone that they would stay gone, they didn't." He tapped his temple. "Right here, all the time. Never gone. Their voices, the way Momma smelled of Cashmere Bouquet when she came out of the bath tub, the rosy fragrance of the hair slick Pop used to put on." He wiped a sleeve across his forehead. "Lots of pieces of them still in my mind. And now, so many years later, I'm glad. Glad to remember them."

"Faulkner said, 'The past is not dead. It's not even past,'" Sarah replied.

"Southern writers, they always get it right, don't they?" Grady said.

By this time Dan and Charlie had arrived. "Hon, do you have a Handi Wipe or something?" Dan asked, then stopped when he saw Grady at the grave. "Sorry," he whispered.

Sarah rummaged through her purse and produced a packet that she handed to her husband. "I knew I could count on you," he said, tearing open the serrated edge.

"That's my great grandparents," Charlie said, crouching next to Grady. "Right?"

"Yep," Grady replied, allowing loose dirt and blades of grass to trickle through his fingers.

"Bo Hagen. Bo – that was his name?" Charlie asked.

"Yep."

"Not short for anything, like Beauregard, I guess?"

"Nope. Just plain Bo. It's very Mississippi."

"What was he like?"

"Enigmatic. Tormented."

Sarah nudged closer. "Why do you think that was?"

Grady coughed, somewhat self-consciously, stood up, and brushed the dirt off his hands and pants. Then he half-chuckled. "I never thought to ask. Wish I knew. Might have made a difference."

"Maybe he didn't have a dream, or couldn't make it come true," Charlie replied.

183

Grady exhaled. "Couldn't afford to dream in those days."

"How about your mother? What was she like?" Sarah asked, then added softly, "My grandmother."

"I never heard her utter an unkind word to or about anyone." Grady closed his eyes and sighed. "That should explain it."

Dan Garrett finished wiping his hands and rolled up the sleeves of his shirt, then folded his suit coat over his arm. "What now, Grady?"

"Wish to hell I knew," the old man replied. He nodded to his mother's name. "She could tell me."

"I think I know what she might say," Charlie interjected.

Grady raised an eyebrow. "Go ahead."

"Well, I was thinking about what that policeman was saying back there," he jerked his head in the direction of the heart of the town. "I was just thinking that maybe the man," he stopped and caught a breath, "from that night, maybe he has family still."

Grady caught the rest of the idea before the words could come out of Charlie's mouth. How clear it suddenly became, like a stream rushing over and smoothing pebbles and rocks, stirring no mud or silt on its journey. "Damn, boy, that's it!"

"What's it?" Dan Garrett asked.

"You're right, Charlie," Sarah said.

"Right about what? What's going on?" Dan asked again.

"What Daddy needs is forgiveness," Sarah replied. "I understand that now, too. The only place he can get it is from those he's hurt."

"Bullshit!" Dan said. "I can't let that, the liability . . ."

Sarah continued, "At the very least he has to go to them and let them know that someone is sorry for what happened, whether they forgive him or not."

Dan growled, "And risk them *not* forgiving him and filing a civil suit? I don't think this is a good idea at all."

Grady started to speak, but Sarah raised her hand to silence him. "Daddy's going to find Rudy's family, Dan. It's as simple as that."

Dan expelled an exasperated sigh and reached into his suit coat pocket to extract his electronic palm device. "Okay, let's see here, I have negotiations at the end of next week; I could . . ."

At the same time, Sarah tore through her purse, removed her calendar and began flipping through the pages. "I have a hospital board meeting Tuesday night, I don't think the agenda is too critical."

"I could call some friends, see who might be down here who can help him," Dan continued.

"McKinney's surgery isn't until Friday; I could cancel my Wednesday appointments, move some of them to next week," Sarah calculated aloud.

"We don't need you." Charlie broke in.

Sarah and Dan froze in mid-sentence. "What?" they replied in unison.

"Pappy and I. We can handle this," Charlie said, expelling air and then straightening himself.

"Yeah, Charlie and I started this thing together," Grady said. "Let us finish it."

"Baloney," Dan bellowed. "The risk is too. . ."

Sarah raised a hand. "Wait." She turned to Grady and Charlie, who were now standing together. "You two? Handle this by yourselves? You think you can do it?"

The two men nodded.

"How long?"

"Give us a week," Grady said. "Fudge factor."

Sarah's eyes ping-ponged from her husband's, to her father's, to her son's, where they froze. "Okay," she said in a whisper. She pushed a stray hair off of Charlie's forehead and kissed him on the cheek. "But you have med school a few days after that. Don't forget."

33

That night the rains came, rippling across the roof of the old farmhouse, and Grady Hagen was a young boy again, curled under the covers of his bed, wrapped up in the gentle rhythm of the storm. A cool breeze rolled in through the window screen, causing the curtains to slap in time against the frame. How far he had traversed on this dusty road to his past, seeking redemption, only to be still unfulfilled on this night. Certainly, what he had feared – arrest and prosecution – was not going to occur, and, yet, there was no satisfaction in that fact. How much easier would it have been to turn the whole concept of punishment over to someone else? Do to me as you wish, he thought. But that was not going to be. The burden still weighed on him like stones in his pockets. He would have to become the architect of his own redemption, supplicating himself in front of those he so grievously hurt. It was difficult, but he knew in his heart it was right.

Before he went to sleep, he thought of something strange: the mouse in his attic back home in Indiana. Had that little bastard sensed the emptiness in the house and moseyed down a two-by-four behind the drywall to some sliver of an opening that would admit him to a whole gigantic world of fun and delights?

Gonna have to get that rodent. Gonna have to get him. Then darkness overtook him and he fell into a deep and dreamless sleep.

By morning a gray mist lay over the land, milky skies pawing at the wet ground. Grady had awakened a reluctant Charlie at dawn, and the two of them set off on foot across the field and into the woods just past where the barn used to be. It was the shortest route to Boone's

Pond and the place where – Grady had hoped against common sense – the little cabin perhaps still stood and, more impossibly, housed a Montcrief of some sort. Then again, you never knew. Wasn't Arbutus still a town essentially occupied by the same names and genetics that flowed backwards through its history? Weren't these the type of people who simply never left, who spent their lives here believing that this was how the world was? Wasn't everyone here absolutely convinced that what they felt and believed was certainly right, and that the rest of the world, if it wasn't yet wise to these truths, would discover them sooner or later?

If *they* didn't leave, maybe the Montcrief family never left.

It took only a few hundred yards of clawing through a jungle of briars and scrub oaks, however, for him to realize that this hardtack piece of land had been abandoned back to nature, which had reclaimed it with a vengeance, strangling it with twisting thorn apple trees and wild rose bushes. Even Boone's Pond, which once seemed deep and wide, was now clogged with islands of cattails and had shrunk to nothing more than a large puddle. The tiny cabin, which was disintegrating even back then, a million years ago, had been sucked back into the earth. Grady, his pants crawling with burrs, kicked at the grasses, hoping to uncover, perhaps, a timber or a block from the foundation. But the prairie foliage was thick and unyielding. It had digested this part of the past, and Grady felt a new sense of despair fall upon his shoulders like a yoke.

Until Charlie asked for a computer.

That was what brought them back to town and Grady to a park bench, not thirty feet from where the tree had once been. His grandson had gone into the library. "Give me a half hour on the internet," he'd said, "and I will find a Montcrief."

Grady sat in a shady spot. The rain had stopped hours ago, but tenacious drops still slipped one at a time from the branches above him. He had a plastic bottle of Coke, from which he would take a swallow then unconsciously retighten the lid. He spoke to Rachel who was sitting at the other end of the bench, though he was too humiliated to look up at her.

"So, you followed me down here," he said.

"Of course."

"I thought you were gone."

"I am. But I'm always here, too. That's the thing about death."

"You think I'm a fool?" Grady whispered, head down. He fidgeted with the bright yellow lid.

"All men are fools," Rachel replied, "women, too. That's what life does to you."

"Am I doing the right thing?"

"Well, now, you have to make that decision for yourself, don't you?"

How ridiculous was this, Grady suddenly thought to himself. It's bad enough to think you're hearing sounds or sensing someone's presence, but now he was talking to a ghost who, he knew if he looked up, would not even be there at all. Then again, he was getting used to it to the point where it didn't even seem weird anymore. This is what happens to old people, he guessed. The brain gets so dried up and addled that you start seeing things and then, worse, talking back to them. On the other hand, maybe the closer you get to a horizon, the more you see. "I suppose I already have, made that decision, that is."

"And was it so hard?"

"Figuring out the right thing to do? No. I had that put together a long, long time ago. Doing it, now that's a different story." He loosened the cap on the bottle and took a swig. The Coke was warming now, becoming more tingly, like jangled nerves.

"Well, that's pretty much the way it is in life," Rachel answered. "Figuring out the right thing to do is always pretty easy, pretty obvious. Having the courage to do it is the hard part."

Grady raised his head slightly. "Do you think I have courage?"

"Are you scared?"

"Yeah."

"Are you still going through with it?"

"Can't turn back now."

"Then I'd say you have courage." Her voice was soft, ethereal.

"Well, you would just say that."

"I would. But it doesn't mean it isn't true."

"Are you angry at me?" Grady whispered.

"Of course not."

"Disappointed to learn what kind of man I was?"

"Not at all. None of us gets through life without some sin. It's how we deal with our sins that defines us."

"I didn't think you believed in sin."

"Well, now, there you're wrong. It's pretty hard not to believe in sin. Just look around."

Grady nodded. "That makes sense."

"Everything makes a lot more sense when you're dead, honey."

"It does?" Grady exhaled. "I guess I understand, but are you in – what? – heaven or someplace like that?"

"I'm not really sure, but I guess you could call it heaven."

"Now that's something I know you didn't believe in."

Rachel laughed. "You're right about that. Imagine my surprise."

"Well, right now you must feel like your sitting in hell, because right over there is where it happened," Grady said nodding to the spot where the lynching tree once stood.

"Did you ever think maybe all of earth is hell and heaven at the same time?"

"Places like this, defiled by the ideology of hatred. Must be pure hell."

Rachel chuckled, her bluebird laugh that used to make his heart beat faster. "You think Mississippi has the market cornered on hatred? That the south is where the sinners are and everyplace and everybody else is exempt? You know better than that, Graden. Prejudice is everywhere you look, even in so-called civilized societies. I mean, remember the three forks?"

"My God," Grady whispered. "I forgot about that entirely."

"My father, my father, my father," Rachel sighed.

Forks. Three of them. A tiny little thing on the tablecloth at the top of his plate. A medium sized one next to the regular one. And two spoons; his face upside down in the concave contours. All blinding silver that matched the trim of the pure white china stacked before him, a large plate with a small one in the center. He would need to watch, because each utensil had its obvious purpose, and heaven forbid he pick up the wrong one and crumble like the cracker he was in the eyes, the cold and fixed eyes, of the two strangers who occupied the other end of the table. He was sitting next to Rachel, and her hand on his knee failed to transmit its intended comfort.

They were in the dining room of her father's home, high up, higher than Grady had ever been in a building. Outside the windows which wrapped around the room were the spires and cornices and severe angles of other buildings, forming a canyon that flowed to the shore of Lake Michigan which glistened azure against the sky.

A young girl, maybe fifteen, dressed in a starched black dress draped with a lace apron, silently removed the unused stack of plates in front of him. Callie was her name. She was from Ireland. He had spoken to her in the foyer when he awaited Rachel shortly after his arrival. She wouldn't say much at first. It just wasn't proper, he assumed, not in this stifling air pungent with an unspoken protocol that he dare not breach. But he was a country boy, after all, full of manners and courtesy, so when he removed his pack of cigarettes to light up, he offered her one which she eagerly accepted after surveying the scene to ensure no one was watching. Then she slipped it into the pocket on her apron. They spoke in whispers then for several minutes, until Rachel came.

Now at the breakfast table, Callie tossed him a soft smile as she set before him a new plate bearing three paper thin pink strips of something the sheen and consistency of rubber. How strange to take away two unused plates and replace them with yet another, Grady thought. And how strange, this food. He just looked at it.

"Lox," Rachel whispered to him, leaning close.

"Do I eat them with a key?" he asked. She pushed him on the shoulder with the heel of her hand. He watched Frederick Burns, her father, square-shouldered and unblinking, like a puppet, lift the smallest fork and a knife and begin to cut the lox.

"So, mmmm, Graden," Frederick said, an Eastern European accent on the words as thick as paint, "you are from where again? Was it Missouri?"

"Mississippi," Grady said, cutting a piece of fish and bracing himself as he lifted it to his mouth. Raw, rubber fish. At least in Mississippi we had the common decency to bread the stuff and fry it.

"Is that near Missouri?" Tante' Tonya asked. She was, indeed, Frederick's sister, and the resemblance ran through them like a shared electric current. They were built of the same square blocks, with straight backs, and an ashen gray patina that began at their hair and flowed into their skin.

"Tante' Tonya, the states are not arranged in alphabetical order," Rachel pointed out. Her aunt's eyes widened at the umbrage.

Grady broke in. "It's not like they're a thousand miles apart." He looked up at the old woman who did not return his gaze. He was trying too hard.

Frederick was using the tip of an oddly shaped knife to apply cream cheese to a bagel. "And you were, mmmm, a soldier?"

"Yes, sir."

"Where you met my daughter?" he pointed his knife at Rachel.

"That's right, in Berlin."

"It was not right for her to be there," Tante' Tonya broke in.

"Why not?" Rachel bristled, sitting straighter suddenly. "Was it up to everyone else to fight our war for us?" She dropped her fork on her plate. "I think not."

Frederick, undeterred with the sudden detour of the conversation, steered it back on his course. "And now you are, mmmm, here from Mississippi?" He took a bite and continued to speak, chomping between the words. "Do you plan to return home soon? Your home?"

Grady had, by now, gotten over the initial shock of the slimy texture of the smoked salmon and actually liked the taste. He swallowed. "I went back there; picked up a few odds and ends. I kind of like," he found himself glancing at Rachel, "uh, like it here in Chicago. I was thinking to find some work. Stay."

Frederick's head swung back and forth between Rachel and Grady. Enlightenment crept into his eyes, it seemed. "What work do you do?"

"Sir?"

"Are you a doctor? A lawyer? A, what do they say, Indian chef?"

"Chief," Rachel corrected.

Frederick glared at her, but continued. "A man is defined by his work. Work is purpose. Work is life. Have you been trained for a profession?"

"And have you been trained in rudeness?" Rachel asked.

Grady froze. Frederick stared at his daughter. Grady wondered what the old man would do. He knew what his father would have done if such insolence had come from his mouth. He would have been batted clean out of the chair with the back of a meaty hand.

"Grady is my friend, and he is a guest in your home. He should be treated as such," Rachel said.

Frederick blinked. Then he turned to Grady. "I apologize if I was in any way rude. It was not my intention."

"That's all right."

"Grady is thinking about finding a job in the steel mills in Indiana," Rachel said.

"Indiana?" Tante' Tonya shrieked.

"I heard they're starting to hire again," Grady interjected.

"It's only twenty miles from here, love," Rachel said to her aunt. "There is an electric train that runs from Randolph Street station. We can come and see you every Sunday. Or whenever you want."

"We? What? Who is we?" Frederick stammered. He removed a napkin from his lap and trembled as he dabbed his lips.

"Pa-Pa, Grady and I are going to get married," Rachel answered, her eyes glowing. She clutched Grady's arm and pulled him close.

Oh shit, he thought.

Frederick Burns pushed himself away from the table and stood. "He is not of our tribe," the old man said, throwing the napkin down and walking away.

"I didn't fare too well that day with your father, I guess," Grady chuckled. "But I don't suppose you would have done much better down here with mine."

Silence.

Looking at the ground below his feet, Grady suddenly noticed the waves of ants busy in the roots of the grass. It was as if they had suddenly appeared there, yet he knew they had, in fact, been there all the time; he just hadn't focused in their direction. Then he turned and glanced at the spot on the bench to which he had been speaking. It was, of course, empty. "You're gone now, aren't you?"

No answer came forth.

"And I'm crazier than a loon."

A motion picked up by the corner of his eye made Grady turn in the other direction. Across the expanse of park, through the trees, he saw him. He had come out of the door swinging a broom like a madman, and Grady recognized him instantly. Not because he looked the same, no, not at all. He was diminished now, bald but for a rim of salt over his ears, stooped over. But the essence that spun off him, as he swept the water off the sidewalk in front of his store, was the same as it had been sixty years ago; the little hitches and ticks and nuances that made you recognize someone without seeing his face, or even if his face had gone white and saggy. Billie Rae Tolleston, heir to his daddy's hardware store, decked out in light blue pants and a white shirt, the sleeves rolled up. He was slapping at the puddle, chasing it away as if it were a stray cat.

"Hey, Pappy!" It was Charlie's voice. Grady slid forward and turned to see his grandson rambling across the grass with a sheaf of papers in his hand. "I hit the jackpot!" the boy exulted.

Grady stood up. "What you got there, son?" He looked back over his shoulder. Billie Rae still whacked at the puddle, as if trying to kill it. Well, at least Grady had seen him. At least he discovered that he was still alive and seemingly as cantankerous as ever.

"I got a bunch of information, and then more." Charlie jogged the last few yards. "This was easier than I thought. Take a look."

Grady took the papers and glanced at them as Charlie continued speaking. "This has to be her, Charlotta Montcrief, born in . . . look right here, Arbutus, Mississippi in June – the eighth, to be exact – nineteen thirty."

"That's about right," Grady said. "She was a half dozen years younger than me." He glanced at the grainy photo on the printout. A very dignified woman in a black robe, her arms crossed. He held the picture closer and examined the face. There was nothing there he recognized. He shaded the photo with his hand. Nope. Wouldn't know her if she ran over him with a car. Of course, the last time he saw her was more than six decades earlier, and she was only a little thing then.

"This is quite a woman, here, Pap. Graduated cum laude from Grambling State University. Law degree from Tulane. Dean of School of Law at Eastern Indiana from seventy-two to eighty. She moved to Emory University in Atlanta, and then was appointed judge of the U.S. District Court by Reagan. Go figure. Married Anton Endicott in 1955. Had four kids. Endicott died in 2000. She lives in Atlanta now."

"How'd you get all this?"

"Technology. Ain't it something?"

"All from that computer thing?" Grady asked, turning to the next page.

"Yep. You can find almost anything on there if you know where to look."

"How do they fit all these pages and pictures in there?"

Charlie raised an eyebrow, as if to ask him if he really wanted to know, because, after all, the boy genius could probably explain it. Instead, Charlie mused, "Same way they get seven foot basketball players into a television set, I guess."

"Could you find me on there?" Grady asked.

Charlie snapped his fingers. "About this quick."

Grady snorted. "I guess you can find out almost anything about people nowadays. And if you can't, you just make it up."

"It's the age of communication, Pappy," Charlie replied.

Grady scratched the back of his head. "She's a judge, huh? Well, I guess it's only appropriate, if not for the irony."

"What do you mean?"

"I'm looking for judgment, aren't I? Where better to go than to a judge?"

"I see."

"Do we know where to find her?"

"Yep. Right there is her address," Charlie said, pointing at a line.

"Holy ghost," Grady sighed.

"Easier than going through sticker weeds, isn't it?"

Grady handed the papers back. "Looks like we're going to Atlanta. Wonder what's the best way to get there?"

"You didn't look at the last page," Charlie answered, sliding a paper from the bottom of the stack to the top. "Got the map, too. Problem is, you can't really get there from here. Bunch of backroads and towns just like this."

"Then we'd better get going," Grady said, looking at the opposite end of the bench on which he had been sitting. Tiny beads of water, like rhinestones on a wedding dress, adorned the newly painted white wood, except where he sat. There was a dry spot in the shape of a circle.

There was also one where Rachel had been sitting.

Grady looked at it and nodded. "I ain't crazy," he grumbled, walking toward the car.

"What did you say?" Charlie asked.

"Said I ain't crazy."

"You sure?" Charlie replied.

Grady glanced across the park. Billie Rae Tolleston was back in the store.

34

Charlie's problem – although defining it with that term was ludicrous – was that everything came too easy for him. He just flat out got it. Almost anything. Nothing was too hard to comprehend or execute. In the back of his mind, he remembered a teacher in kindergarten showing a drawing of a snake in the shape of an "s" and making the sound, and from that instant the rest of the alphabet just fell into place, and he could read. He saw numbers in his head like so many dots of light that, when added or subtracted, seemed to automatically regroup and change color in an instant, so that the answer was as simple as looking only at the blue spots. Higher math was just as easy. It took him a few minutes to memorize multiplication tables; he understood calculus the first time his high school teacher scrawled a formula on the board. Physically he was equally as precocious and proficient. He taught himself to ride a bike, staying up for a hundred feet the first time he tried, then staying up for good when he brushed himself off and got on again. His first at bat in Little League he hit a home run, on the first pitch. He'd occasionally play golf with his dad, even though he didn't particularly like the game, and beat the old man every match. Easy, everything easy.

Until now.

They were somewhere east of Arbutus, two hours out. Grady was casual against the passenger side door, but his fingers were drumming on the armrest.

"Pappy, you still here?" Charlie finally asked.

"Hmmm?" Grady said, coming away from the window.

"Can I talk to you?"

"Sure. What's on your mind?"

Charlie cleared his throat. "When you were a kid, what did you want to be?"

Grady arched an eyebrow. "You mean like when I grew up, or something?"

"Yeah."

He shrugged. "Still don't know."

"I thought you wanted to be a ballplayer."

Grady paused for several seconds. Finally he said, "That's what everybody, including me, thought was going to happen to me. But you gotta understand, there wasn't all those million dollar contracts floating around in those days. Ballplayer had to work at something in the off season, and most of 'em made as much, or more, in the winter jobs as they did on the field."

"So you had to have a back-up plan, huh?"

"Exactly."

"What was yours?"

"Didn't have one," Grady chuckled. "Didn't have an alternate plan, either, in case baseball didn't pan out." He turned toward the window and watched the landscape blur by. "Times were different than today. Dreams died quickly in the air. You just did whatever came next, without thinking much about it. You were just thankful to have a job, even if you dreaded going to it everyday." He turned back to Charlie. "Why do you ask?"

"I, uh, you know how I'm supposed to start medical school in a few weeks?"

"Sure."

"Well, I don't want to go."

Grady's eyes opened wide. "Well, now, how about that?"

"What should I do?"

"What do you want to do?"

Charlie snorted out a self-deprecating laugh. "You won't believe me if I told you."

"Why not?"

"Plus, you'll think I'm nuts and that I wasted four years of college and blah, blah, blah. The whole spiel." He stuck out his tongue and blew raspberries on the last words. "I'm a loser."

"Let me take a shot," Grady mused.

"Okay."

"You want to be a photographer."

"Yeah! How'd you figure that out?"

"Jeez, take a guess," Grady replied.

Charlie exhaled. "I don't know what to do; what to tell mom and dad. I don't even know if you can make a living, much of a living anyway, in photography. Not like being a doctor, I'm sure."

Grady scratched his chin. "Well, I think maybe you underestimate your momma and daddy. All they want is what's best for you, and seems to me, doing something that makes you happy certainly falls into that category."

Charlie leaned forward, wrapping both arms around the steering wheel. Pappy always seemed to know what to say, and the young man felt buoyed by the words. "You wanna know why?"

"Why what? You want to be a photographer? I suppose it was born in you. Hell, you've been taking pictures since you were a tike. Fascinated with all that stuff."

"Yeah, Pap, but there's more," Charlie enthused, lifting up from his seat and settling back down. "What gets me about photography is that I don't know – I can't figure out what makes a good picture."

"What are you talking about? You won awards in high school."

"Yeah, but that's just it. You see, you can take ten snaps of the same scene and only one of them, if any, turns out to be just absolutely perfect. Only one, maybe, catches not just the image of the moment, but the feeling, the smell, the essence. And I don't know why that is. Is it dumb luck? Is it something the subconscious sees? Everything else in my life, I've been able to figure out. This, this mystifies me, and that's why I love it so much."

"Well, listen to you! That's wonderful."

"It feels just so amazing to get a photo that pulls you into it, that makes you feel like you're right there," Charlie rattled. "If I could have the chance to do that everyday and have people see my photos and be as amazed as I am – wow, that would be something."

Grady chuckled. "You know, I can pull out all the clichés if you want me to right now. The grandpa's guide to the right words probably has a whole chapter on it." He changed the tone of his voice, as if reading rather than merely speaking. "You know, follow your heart, don't give up on your dream, all that stuff." He laughed again. "Hell, who knows if it will work out or not for you? I'd say you have a good chance, from what I've seen, but I'm no expert. All I know is that life zips by in a flash – no pun intended – and if you don't give it a shot – again, no pun intended – you'll kick yourself in the ass and continue to do so until it's old and wrinkled like mine."

"So, you think I should just . . ."

"Just tell your mom and dad that's what you want," Grady answered, his eyes twinkling. "I'd do it right after cocktails, though."

Charlie bounced in the seat again and laughed. "You're a crazy old coot, Pap, abso-fucking-lutely nuts."

"Nice talk," Grady chuckled.

"Sorry, I'm just a little revved up."

Grady opened the glove compartment and extracted the computer printouts from Arbutus. He riffled through them, finding the one he wanted. "Is your cell phone working?"

The phone had been plugged into the cigarette lighter for recharging. Charlie picked it up and looked at the display. "Yeah. You wanna use it?" He handed it over.

Grady took it and his palm engulfed the tiny device. "Just a little tiny thing, ain't it?"

"Just flip it open there," Charlie instructed.

"Where?"

"That little notch."

Grady flipped the phone open, revealing the keypad. "The keys are so small," he said.

"Who are you calling?"

"Charlotta. We can't just go up and knock on her door." He squinted at the keys as he punched in the telephone numbers. Then he put the phone up to his ear. "The mouthpiece is so far away. Will she be able to hear . . .?"

Charlie could hear the voice on the other end of the line, and for a second, Grady froze.

35

She was sitting on the front porch, her legs dangling from a wooden swing, when the car rolled up, and she immediately rose and came to the first step. Charlotta Montcrief Endicott glowed against the caramel sunset that slanted through the huge oak tree in her front yard. Even from a distance, Grady could see that, at more than seventy years of age, she was still stunningly beautiful. Her body was lithe, thin and fluid, seemingly coiled into her pale blue flowered dress. She held her head regally, chin up, eyes wide and bright. Everything about her broadcast an essence, a presence, of substance. The only thing that gave away any sense of nervousness, was the way her right hand leaked out of her folded arms to stroke her left biceps. As Charlie pulled the car to the curb, she descended to the second step.

Charlie looked at Grady. "Well, here we are. You sure about this?"

"I wasn't afraid of the police," Grady said softly. "Didn't give them a second thought." Now a bitter taste leaked into his mouth, metallic, hard. A taste he hadn't experienced since the war. Fear. "But this, this is something I hadn't expected." He exhaled and opened the car door.

Charlotta had come as far as she was going to. That was obvious. She looked the two men up and down.

"Mr. Hayden?" she asked.

"Um, Hagen, ma'am. H-a-g-e-n," Grady said as he arrived at the stoop. "Grady Hagen."

"Sorry. It sounded like Hayden to me on the phone."

"Phone was so small, my mouth was far from the . . ." he pantomimed the act of holding up a small phone.

"Who's the boy?" Charlotta asked, nodding at Charlie.

"This is my grandson. Charlie Garrett."

Charlie moved in front of his grandfather and extended a hand. He removed his cap with the other. "I am very pleased to meet you."

Charlotta's stony demeanor cracked for an instant. She smiled slightly and then resumed her stoic pose. Looking over Charlie's shoulder, she spoke again to Grady. "Nice boy," she said, letting go of the hand. "Respectful enough to take off his hat. Somebody brought him up right." Then she refolded her arms. "I get a phone call out of the blue, saying you wanted to come and talk to me about my brother Rudy, and that it was very important, and I, like a fool, agree. Now, Mr. Hagen, please tell me why I agreed to this, because I can find no earthly reason in my mind."

Fear. It inched up his throat again. He prayed that it wouldn't boil there, making his arms and his legs shake. He choked it down, feeling it burn to his gut. "Miss Mont, uh, Mrs. Endicott,"

"Look, call me Charlotta. That will be fine."

"I'm here because," Grady swallowed again and took a deep breath. What words to use now? He hadn't thought about it. Rachel, what should I say? What would you say? Then they tumbled out, totally disconnected from his thoughts. "Because I had to come."

"Sounds ominous."

"I, uh, just want to tell you something, and then I'll be on my way. Won't take but a few minutes."

Charlotta furrowed her brow, as if trying to figure out this strange old man. Then she relaxed her facial muscles and raised her chin again. "If I let you come into my home, you're not going to kill me, are you?" she asked, smiling slightly, cocking her head. Then she turned to Charlie. "He's not going to kill me, is he?"

"I'm sure he's not," Charlie answered.

I'm not so sure you won't want to kill me, Grady thought.

Charlotta motioned them in with a slight tilt of her head and led the way. "Sit down there," she said, pointing to a couch in the well-appointed and cozy living room. "Iced tea okay?" she asked over her shoulder as she glided into the kitchen.

"Thanks, that would be great," Grady answered.

The sounds of clinking ice and running water rolled out. "You know, in England they consider iced tea an abomination. Me, I live on the stuff in the summertime," Charlotta called from the distance. Then she was floating through the door with a tray containing a pitcher of tea and three glasses of ice. "I guess it's never summer over there, though, so they never got into the evil habit," she continued, setting down the tray and then pouring three glasses. She took her glass and sat down in a soft chair. "There's sugar and Equal if you need it."

"Thanks," Grady replied, picking up a glass and drinking it straight. Charlie was scooping sugar into his glass by the spoonful.

Charlotta was removing the brim of her glass from her lips. "Okay, here we are."

Grady leaned forward, elbows on his knees. "You know, ma'am . . ."

"Ma'am! I'm not a ma'am. Call me Charlotta, like I said, because I'm going to start calling you Grady whether you like it or not."

"Okay, Charlotta. The last time I saw you, you were hiding behind your momma's skirt, about this tall," Grady laughed, putting out his hand to demonstrate her height. "I was maybe ten, nine, something like that. Was down at Boone's Pond fishing. Do you remember Boone's Pond?"

"Sure do. Rudy and I used to pull crappies and cat out of there, and my momma would fry them up. A king's feast, we thought."

"I somehow fell into the pond and got tangled in all the stuff."

"It was impossible to swim in that pond even when we were so hot we couldn't stand it. All because of the tangles and then, of course, the cottonmouths," Charlotta interrupted, taking another sip of tea.

"Your brother Rudy, he pulled me out."

"Sounds like him."

"Do you remember that?"

Charlotta held the glass close to her face and pondered, he eyes alive with thought as she pored through her memory. "No, no, I really don't think I do."

"You were scared of me, I think."

"Well, Grady, you were a white boy in my yard. In those days that meant trouble."

Suddenly there was a loud knock on the front door that made Grady and Charlie both jump. They turned to see three black teenage boys standing on the porch, jersey shirts bagging over equally billowing cargo shorts, caps on backwards. "Ever'thing all right in there, Mizz Charlotta?" one of the boys asked, cupping his eyes and pressing his face against the screen door.

"Everything's fine, Donnell. You boys can go ahead," Charlotta said, without getting out of her chair.

"You sure, Mizz Charlotta?" the voice came back.

"Everything is okay, really, Donnell," she answered.

"Cool," Donnell answered and led the group away.

Charlotta turned back to Grady. "My posse," she laughed.

Charlie started chuckling, choking to keep his iced tea from spraying through his nostrils.

"They come check up on me whenever something odd happens in the neighborhood."

"Something odd? What happened that was odd?" Charlie asked.

Charlotta nodded toward the door. "That fancy Mustang parked out front. Plus, I called them after you called, asked them to stop by and make sure things were okay." She finished her glass of iced tea and set the empty down, refilling it from the pitcher. "Just for backup; you know what I mean?" She leaned forward, enthused now, eager to hear more. "Now, Grady, tell me more about you and my brother. Did you guys do things together? Play ball? Go fishing in old Boone's Pond? Tell me. This is exciting."

Oh, Jesus, Grady pondered. I could do it, tell her we fished and played ball and whatnot together, and she would be happy for the memories, and maybe that was what he should do. Just lie and make up stories about what great pals they were after Rudy had saved him, and how all the bullshit about race was washed out with the water of Boone's Pond. But he didn't come to lie. He came to put to death the lie he had been hiding his whole life. He took a deep breath. "No, we, uh, didn't. It wasn't like that," Grady whispered, staring now at the ice in his glass. He held the pose for several seconds. Silence overtook the room. The ticking of the clock on the mantel seemed to thunder, becoming increasingly more frantic. Even the crickets and the other night sounds that had provided a rhythmic backdrop as the sun set seemed to pause, waiting for Grady Hagen's next words. Finally he spoke, still not looking up. "I was there the night your brother died." He seemed to breathe out the words, rather than say them. His heart pounded, twice as fast as the ticking clock, and he could not say the words that were suddenly bollixed inside like a chain reaction crash on the freeway. He hadn't anticipated this. It was as if he was losing his grip on a window ledge, and he felt his hands slipping, slipping, slipping.

"I was there, and I helped," he blurted. "I helped kill your brother!"

There, he had forced the words out.

And then Grady Hagen disintegrated. Like the old barn in front of his homestead in Arbutus, the confluence of time and age and neglect and decay suddenly reached a precise moment in time where one piece slipped and then another and then another, until the whole structure imploded, expunging the grief like clouds of dust, and Grady let it pour out. "I was there, I was there, and what I did, I deserve to burn in hell, and I don't expect you to forgive me, but I want you to know how wrong it was, how wrong I was, how evil, how disgustingly evil." His head fell into his right hand and he sobbed, gasped and shook with pain. The iced tea in his left hand began to quake.

Charlie took the glass and set it down on the tray, and the old man covered his eyes and continued to weep. Charlie put his arms around his grandfather, laid his head on the knobby, throbbing back and held him tightly, choking back his own tears.

It took quite a while for the debris from his pain to float softly back to earth, but Grady finally came out of the wreckage, wiping his eyes with his handkerchief, sucking air in huge gulps.

All the while, Charlotta Montcrief Endicott sat frozen in her chair. Not a muscle moved on her face. Her glass of tea hovered in front of her, stiff in the grip of her fingers.

Grady put his hands on his knees and struggled to stand. Charlie helped him to his feet. "That's all," Grady said in a barely audible rasp. "That's all I came to say," he repeated, wiping his eyes again. "I just want you to know how very sorry, how very sorry I am. Just so you would know."

Charlie, who held Grady with both arms to keep him steady, looked at Charlotta and said, "My granddad's not an evil man. He's a good man. I've never known a better man." A diamond-shaped tear ran down the boy's cheek at precisely that moment, leaving a stream in its wake.

Grady continued. "I understand if you can't forgive me. It's too much to expect. But if it's in your heart," he said, straightening himself, "if it's in your heart, I would consider it a blessing." He took a quivering breath and steadied himself. "I had to come and tell you, you see. No matter what. It was all I could do." He expelled the air that was still left in him and muttered, "All I could do."

Charlotta raised an eyebrow, cleared her throat, stood up, and placed her empty glass back on the tray. "Wait," she said, disappearing back into the kitchen. After a bit of clattering dishes and slamming cabinet doors, she emerged, carrying a bottle of Jack Daniels and three tumblers. She breezed past the two men on the couch, speaking over her shoulder. "Come out here," she said, nudging the front screen door with her shoulder and holding it open. "Come on, come on," she repeated.

Grady and Charlie came after her. She thrust a glass into Charlie's hand. "You old enough?" she asked, poising the bottle over the glass.

"Uh, yeah, you bet," Charlie replied.

She filled the tumbler and motioned toward a wicker chair on the end of the porch. "Go sit over there." Then she turned back to Grady. "You come sit by me on the swing. Here, take this. You do imbibe, do you not?" She handed the glass to him.

"If I didn't, I would start right now," Grady said, taking it. Composure was slowly flowing back into his veins.

"Probably a good idea," Charlotta replied, filling his glass half way.

Grady immediately took a hard swallow. The Jack went down hot but smooth, flooding his raw nerves. Charlotta sat down on the swing, filled her own glass and then set the bottle on the rail of the porch. She patted the slats next to her. "Sit down here, Grady," she said gently.

Grady obeyed. An occasional spasm backfired in his chest from the crying. "I never cried like that before," he said. "Even when I was a kid."

"It's good for you," Charlotta said. "Cleans you out."

"Well, I'm not so sure."

She stared off into the dark purple sky for several seconds, then took a deep breath. "I love this time of night. Things just seem to settle in the dark, don't they?"

"It's very peaceful here," Grady replied.

"It's an amazing world we live in, when you think about it. All this nonsense about time and days and years. It can all come down to the size of a dime, when something like this happens."

"I don't know really what you mean," Grady said.

"You know, how you go through your life, day in and day out, and nothing too important happens. Then all of s sudden from out of the blue, boom, an explosion that changes everything," Charlotta took a swallow, wincing as it went down. "Whew, that stuff is something," she said, shaking her head. "Just think, four hours ago I'm in exactly one of those simple, typical days – doing this, doing that, when my phone rings and on the other end is a raspy old man saying he wants to come and talk to me about my brother; that he knew him in Arbutus. That was all he said. I had no idea it would end up like this. Momma, momma, I had no idea." She swirled the glass and took another swallow.

"I almost didn't come," Grady said. "Thought about turning back, but then that's what I had done all my life, you know? And it didn't serve me well."

"I know it took a lot of courage for you to come here and tell me this, Grady."

"It was the least . . ." he interjected.

"Let me finish," she said. "You know, in all my life I never heard what happened that night. Do you think you could tell me, or would it be too hard?" She turned and looked at him. Her face was soft and gentle and beautiful, but at the same time urgent. "It might be cathartic, you know. For both of us."

Grady took a long sip of the whiskey and a deep breath. "There was a lot of anger in our town in those days, anger over a lot of things . . ." he began.

Grady spun the story delicately, not embellishing, just giving enough information for Charlotta to understand what had happened.

When he was finished, his glass was empty and so was hers. She reached for the bottle and filled both up.

"Did you ever think about my brother after that?" she asked.

"Lots of times," Grady replied.

"No, I mean as a man, what kind of man he was, what he might have become?"

"I don't think I was capable of that."

"What you have to understand about the Montcriefs is that we weren't from the fields, didn't come from that place, that heritage," Charlotta said, fondling the glass with both hands and looking up at the stars. "Not that I think that accident of birth somehow makes us better. Plenty of good, fine people were chained to those cotton plants. My daddy's name was Eugene Montcrief and he was a colored Creole from Louisiana. A brilliant man, son of a free man, wanted to be a scientist. He studied on his own, then got a degree from the Tuskegee Normal and Industrial Institute. He met my momma in Alabama and married her a month later," she brightened at the memory, then slapped her knee. "Can you imagine the sparks that must have been flying between those two?"

"That happens. I know," Grady replied, staring at the swirls in his glass.

"Mother had no formal education to speak of, but had taught herself to read when she was a little girl after a preacher showed her the alphabet and how putting letters together could make sounds." She smiled as she spoke. "Daddy got a teaching job in an Arkansas high school, and then got consumption one cold winter and died in a few days. Devastated my mother and us, but I was just a little baby." She took a sip from her glass. "Anyway, Momma had some relatives in Mississippi, and one thing led to another, and we moved to Arbutus to live on someone's farm and take care of it."

"Clayton's place."

"Yes, yes, that was the name. Where Momma plowed the fields and did wash for the folks in Arbutus." She shook her head and chuckled. "The white folks said no one got things whiter than that black woman. Said it was witchcraft the way she could 'disappear a stain.' Their vernacular, not mine."

"I remember," Grady said.

"But Momma drummed Daddy's mantra into us. We were going to college, we were going to make something of ourselves, we were going to stand up and be counted." She turned to Grady and held him in a soft gaze. "That boy they hanged that night was going to be something." Her voice trailed off.

Grady cleared his throat. "He was a man, that's all that mattered, and it was wrong, wrong, wrong what happened to him, regardless of who he was going to be, because we never let that happen."

"Well, drop that burden right here in my trash," Charlotta replied, "You've carried it long enough." Then she took another sip and smacked her lips. "This stuff starts tasting like soda pop after a while, doesn't it?"

"Gets better, that's for sure," Grady said. "You know, it wasn't until that night that I really started doubting everything I had been taught to believe about right and wrong. And it was very, very hard to reconcile what was in my veins from birth, with what was in my mind. Do you know what I mean?"

Charlotta looked again at the sky, ablaze now with stars. "Oh, baby, do I know. I spent the first thirty-five years of my life just wanting to be able to sit at the same lunch counter, and go to the same schools, get real jobs, vote, see black doctors and lawyers and politicians, rise up, like Dr. King said. Rise up!" She sang the last words vigorously. "And throw off the shackles of slavery and denigration." She leaned forward in the swing and looked sideways at Charlie. "Do you know about these things, Charlie?"

"I've read about them. Saw the films," he answered.

"Well, boy, look into my face, get up and get over here and look into the face of history. Not the words in a book, but the face of history!"

Charlie stood and sauntered over. She took his cheek in her free hand and held him tenderly. "This is the face of truth. I marched with Dr. King in Selma, linked arm in arm with an old granny white woman and my sister-in-law. We felt the power, the spirit, in the air. We feared nothing and no one." She caressed him, sliding her hand down his cheek, but Charlie grabbed it and kissed the palm.

"Thank you, ma'am," he said. "I gotta get my camera."

"There is goodness here," she answered, moving her glance from Charlie to Grady. "But a restlessness, I see, too." Charlotta caught Charlie's finger as he pulled away. "Be yourself, boy," she said. Charlie leapt down the three steps of the porch and jogged to the Mustang.

Charlotta took another swallow of whiskey and regrouped, picking up her story where it had left off. "In a matter of months it all had changed, and I slid into a new world where I was accepted, respected, even admired, you might say, by people who once wouldn't deign to look in my eyes as I walked down the street. Can you imagine how that made me feel? Where once I couldn't sit at the same lunch counter as white folk, now I was between the president of the university and the Vice President of the United States, Hubert Humphrey to be exact, at a banquet. I had friends of all colors, friends from countries I'd never heard of. I saw affirmative action make lawyers and doctors and teachers out of ghetto kids who, without it, would have had no future, none. I saw the walls of Jericho come tumbling down, Grady. All in such a short time, after such a long, long time." She paused and stared out into the darkness of her front yard. "It took me years to fully realize that, with all we had gained, we had not come nearly as far as it appeared."

"What do you mean?" Grady asked.

"It dawned on me that I was the respectable Negro that the university could trot out whenever it needed to prove its enlightenment." She put up a hand. "Well-meaning people, don't get me wrong, fundamentally good people who truly believed they were doing the right thing. I have no argument or qualms with them or their motives; it's just that for all the good they were doing me, I was doing them ten times the benefit. Even when President Reagan appointed me judge," she swiped at the air with her hand. "Made him look good as much as it made me."

Charlie was back now, and the dark night was being punctuated with blue flashes from the camera.

"What you must understand is that we got the outer trappings of freedom, like some kind of fancy clothes you wear to cover up and hide what's underneath, like a corset, cinched up tight so you can't even breathe," Charlotta continued, oblivious to Charlie's activities. "We – at least I – thought it was what we wanted, that it would be enough, just give us that, lordy, just that. But it wasn't enough."

209

"Why is that? Why is it not enough?" Grady asked.

"Do you have any idea what it's like to be black, Grady?" She waited a beat. "Of course, you don't. You can't."

"No, I'm certain of that."

"How many times a day does the color of your skin come to your mind?"

"Never, I'd say."

"When you're a black person in America, I venture to say that there is not a day goes by that something doesn't bring to your attention the fact that you are colored. Not loud stuff necessarily, though it happens now and again, but subtle things. When you walk into a store, the way the clerk just looks at you. When you stop to pump your gas, the other people around you, reminding you by the way they look or don't look or say hello or don't say hello, that whatever they're doing, they're doing because of your skin. It doesn't matter what their intentions are. They may be deferential to you; they may be hateful toward you. But your color, your blackness, hits them one way or the other. That awareness – it's not easy to live with, day in and day out."

"Man," Grady sighed, "I never . . ."

"And no matter how far we come, how much progress we achieve, there is still that reality blowing in the wind, sometimes a breeze, sometimes a storm." She threw back her head and drained the last few drops of her drink. "Whew, what a night, huh?" she chortled, bringing the empty glass down.

"What a night," Grady replied.

Charlotta stood up and grasped the chain of the swing to steady herself. Grady rose and took her by the crook of the arm. "You okay?" he asked.

"I'm hammered," she replied, laughing loudly. "But at least it's Black Jack and he doesn't leave any scars in the morning!" She sauntered toward the front door, laughing more, throwing back her head. "Boy, you bring in those glasses and the bottle, okay?" she said to Charlie. "You can crash on the couch. Your granddaddy can use the guest bedroom."

Grady stopped and tugged on her arm. "Charlotta, we can't . . ."

She turned to him, her eyes bright and alive. "Look, we just polished off – the three of us – half a bottle of Jack Daniels. I'm not letting anyone drive out of here tonight."

"But Charlotta, you don't have to . . ."

"Besides, we got things to do tomorrow."

"Things to do?"

"Yup, right after breakfast." she turned to Grady and tapped him on the chest with her index finger. "I make the best, the world's greatest, buttermilk flapjacks."

"But what are we doing after that?" Grady asked, immediately acquiescing to her invitation, knowing full well neither he nor Charlie could drive.

"Well, we're gonna go let you say hello to Momma."

"Momma?"

"Mizz Principia Montcrief, to be precise," she answered, sliding through the door.

Principia! Alive! It wasn't possible. "Wait, please. Are you saying your mother is still alive? My God, she must be . . ."

"Ninety-five, blind as a bat, mean as a rattler, but her mind is still on fire like a twenty year-old."

Grady held the door for Charlie, who staggered through, almost knocking him over. "Oh, lord, do I have to go through this again?" the old man grumbled, mostly to himself.

Charlotta was in the hallway now, mingling with the shadows, becoming vapor. She looked over her shoulder again. "You won't be satisfied until you do," she explained. "Plus, you never know, may even be a surprise waiting for you."

"What kind of a surprise?" Grady asked as she disappeared into her room. "What kind of surprise?

"Aren't you jus the little boy at Christmas? Can y'all turn off the lights and lock up? I'm too smashed," came the answer through the crack in the closing door.

Gol'dang. Principia. Still alive. And then another scene came to him, full-fledged, instantaneous and real. The last time he had seen Rudy's mother. It was the day after.

36

It had not rained that night, although the sky had growled and exploded until dawn. It was as if God had decided to vent his anger in wave after wave of heat lightning and thunder, but held back the cooling, cleansing rains that may have washed away the dirt that now settled over Arbutus. The same storm raged inside of Grady Hagen, who lay in his own bed and listened, rubbing where his arm had been broken. He had run home the entire way, more than two miles, in the hot darkness, watching the trees light up, seeing houses and barns erupt in color for an instant before fading again. He had left Billie Rae and the other boys to the remains of Rudy Montcrief without warning, simply pulling himself up without so much as a goodbye and following his legs home, where he didn't even undress, just fell onto his bed and tried to sleep. But what was behind his closed eyes was more frightening than the lightning and the dry thunder, so he stayed awake and tried to think of nothing.

The next morning he walked back to town for no apparent reason, still just following the pull of the strings of whatever gods now controlled his life. The town still hadn't fully awakened. Stores were still locked, shades drawn. The street was devoid of cars and carriages. Grady figured that it must not yet be six o'clock. He didn't look over his right shoulder to the spot where the thing had happened last night, and he wondered for a second if it had all been a bad dream. Yes, perhaps that was it, a bad dream, goddamned bad dream, but, of course, it wasn't.

He knew it, and that's why he would not look. Head down, hands scrunched in his pockets, he thought of Cissy Moody. And just like that, his slurry steps became quick, and he jogged toward Dr. Max's office just as the little old man with the snow white hair was coming out the side door.

"Dr. Max, Dr. Max!" Grady shouted from a hundred or more feet away.

The doctor jumped, almost dropping the black kit he carried in his right hand. "Holy begonia, Graden, y'all liked to scared me t'death."

Grady ran to him, slowing as he arrived. "Sorry . . ."

"How's that arm of yours, boy?"

Grady offered it up for him to observe. "Still skinnier than my left and it doesn't work very well, I'm afraid. I can't throw very well, can't swing the bat."

"I told you it would take a good solid six months for you to build it back up to where it was before, but there's no reason why it shouldn't be fine if you give it time."

"How's Cissy?" Grady interrupted.

Dr. Max pursed his lips. "She was doin' 'bout what could be expected last night. I'm going up there now. You wanna tag along?"

"Yeah," Grady said, running to the passenger side of Dr. Max's black Buick and sliding into the front seat.

"No one else has been up to see her; I'm sure she'll like a visitor." Before Dr. Max started the car, he lit a cigarette, rolled down the window, tossed the match and took a drag, dangling his arm outside. "You know, the day is gonna come when they find out that these things," he held up the cigarette and examined it, "ain't very good for you. Heck, probably kill you sooner or later. They just can't be. Anything that insists you smoke 'em can't be very good for you." He took another swallow of the silky smoke and they were on their way.

The brightness of the room, the overwhelming whiteness of it, shocked Grady's eyes, knocked him back a few feet. But the frail and broken body shrouded in a transparent tent of some sort had an even stronger impact. Cissy Moody looked even worse than she had the day before. Her face was now entirely unrecognizable, a huge plum with slits and wrinkles where the eyes and mouth would be. Grady watched the sheets that swaddled her rise and fall with each deep breath she took. He found a slit in the oxygen tent and leaned in.

"Hey, Cissy, it's me, Grady," he whispered. "Just wanted to see how you're doin'."

An eye fluttered open from behind a yellowish purple mound. "My buddy," she croaked. Then her hand came from beneath the sheet and scrambled toward his. Her grip was strong.

"You look good, Ciss."

She made a noise and Grady thought for an instant she was choking, but he soon realized it was a feeble laugh. "I look like a wreck," she said. "But I'm gonna be okay, Grady, I swear I'm gonna be okay." Her other arm, sleek and white, came out from under the covers and stroked her abdomen.

"What the hell happened, Cissy?"

"Oh, Grady," she cried, taking his hand. "I've been so bad, so bad."

"Shush that talk now, Cissy."

"No, it's true. You know it's true."

"Don't worry about none of that right now," Grady whispered.

She tried to lean forward. "I'm gonna have a baby," she croaked.

Grady gripped the sheet to keep from falling backward. His head was about to collapse from yet another weight. He gasped, struggled for some shard of wisdom to venture forth. "My goodness," was all he could say.

"I had to tell my daddy, and when I did, he just exploded. And when I told him it was Rudy's, there was no stopping him."

"Jeez, Cissy. Jeez," Grady grimaced. He was emptied of words and wanted, simply, to run out of the room and not have to deal with what he was hearing.

"You knew it though, about me a Rudy, I mean," Cissy cried. "You saw us at the cave that day. I know you did."

"Don't talk about it right now, Ciss. Just relax and get better."

Cissy turned her head away. "He told me, when he was beating on me, that he ain't my daddy anymore."

"Well, I'm sure he's worked up . . ."

"Did they arrest him?" Cissy asked, still turned away, a thumbnail in her teeth.

214

"Fletcher?" Grady said reflexively, immediately realizing the absurdity of his response.

"Rudy," she choked.

Oh mother, Grady thought. How do I answer this? "Yeah, Ciss, LaGrone went and picked him up." That should be enough for now.

"Is he okay?"

Shit. He couldn't flat out lie. "Cissy, don't worry about him right now," Grady replied, smoothing her hair. "Take care of yourself and the baby."

Cissy croaked again, that weak laugh. "We'll see," she said, barely audible.

Silence hung between them for several seconds. Finally Grady leaned and kissed her on the forehead, the only part of her face that remained unblemished. "I'll see if I can get a ride from Doc Max again later in the week, come see you."

Cissy grabbed his arm and pulled him close. "Please, Grady," she whimpered

Grady leaned in and kissed her again. "You be good."

"I love you, Grady," she answered.

"I love you too, Ciss."

"Be my friend forever? No matter what?" It was both a question and a demand.

"I promise."

Back in town, two hours later, after Dr. Max had made his rounds, Grady noticed that a pall of normalcy had descended. The streets were, once again, alive with the mundane. Stores had opened; canopies had been unfurled. Nothing had happened last night; at least you couldn't see it reflected in the windows of the stores, in the shadows on the streets, in the air that lay hot and heavy.

"There you are!" a voice shouted from behind him as Grady emerged from Dr. Max's car. Billie Rae was coming at him, a dervish of agitated arms and elbows, eyes as bright as two stars. "Where the hell you been with Doc Max?"

"Went to see Cissy."

"You tell her we took care of that nigger for her?"

Grady could barely look him in the eye. "She's doing fine. Glad you asked."

215

"What the hell's eating you?" Billie Rae snarled, following as Grady turned back onto the sidewalk. "And where the hell did you go last night? I needed some help. Barbecued coon weighs a lot more than you think." Then he stopped and pulled Grady's arm. "Hey, lookit there."

Grady glanced up. "Goddamn," he whispered.

Principia Montcrief was trudging up Jefferson Street, each step an effort of mammoth and mythic proportions. She slogged in the middle of the road, the weight of her grief bending her at the waist, which she clutched with folded arms. All the air and life and soul had been drained from her, leaving behind nothing more than an assemblage of gray clothes in the shape of a body. Her eyes, red and throbbing in the sockets, stared hundreds of miles ahead, it seemed, at something only she knew or saw, but they did not move, did not blink.

"Now that is one goddamned good looking colored woman, I have to say," Billie Rae mused. "You ever wonder what it would be like to fuck a colored girl?"

"What in the hell is the matter with you?" Grady spat.

"What in the goddamned hell is the matter with me?" Billie Rae shouted back. "What the fuck is wrong with you?"

Grady pivoted away from him. "You're sick. You're sick," he grimaced, though he knew he was speaking to himself as much as to Billie Rae.

"Get the hell back here, goddamnit," Billie Rae said, pulling on Grady's shoulder and spinning him around.

"Get your fucking hands off me!" Grady shouted, pushing Billie Rae backward. He thrust one arm outward to keep from falling, grabbing the front of Grady's shirt with the other and pulling him down.

Grady wrenched his friend's hand free, but Billie Rae had sprung forward now and he buried his head in Grady's abdomen and drove him back into the brick wall of the drug store. At that instant Grady Hagen came out of himself. The obvious grief that poured off Principia Montcrief collided with his own guilt in the heat and ether of the moment, causing a chemical reaction of rage that exploded inside him. In one single motion, his shoulders turned and his left arm and fist came forward and up like a lightning strike. The knuckles of his fiercely

216

balled hand crashed into the cheek of Billie Rae Tolleston, lifting the boy from his feet and propelling him up, splayed like a spider. He seemed to hover for several seconds midair, floating down like a piece of paper on the wind. His body landed with a sickening thud in the street. On his back now, Billie Rae lifted his head and gazed at Grady, then let it fall onto the pavement.

Grady looked up at Principia Montcrief who staggered down the center of the street toward the police station, her back to him now. Then he walked away, leaving Billie Rae on one elbow, a rivulet of bloody spit strung from his mouth to the ground.

That same day, Grady Hagen bummed a ride from Gap Browne halfway to Jackson, hitchhiked the last fifty miles, and enlisted in the army. He was seventeen but looked much older, and the recruiter didn't ask any questions.

37

Charlotta Montcrief Endicott was right about one thing, her buttermilk pancakes were, indeed, the most spectacular Grady had ever eaten. She was also wrong about something. Black Jack did leave scars in the morning, if you weren't as accustomed to his face as she obviously was. His head throbbed in a rhythmic cycle, a pulse here, then on the other side, then at the back, then his forehead, then the base of his spine. Thump, thump, thump. Charlie didn't seem any the worse for wear, though. Must be that college constitution.

They sat in the kitchen, a yellow room, bright and warm. "How about some more, three more? That's all that's left." Charlotta said to Charlie. "You're just a boy, you need this calcium." She didn't wait for an answer, just reached across the table and dropped a new stack on his plate.

"Thanks," Charlie said. "These are good."

"Good! Good! Heck, boy, good is Denny's. These are great."

"That's what I meant," Charlie stammered. "These blow Denny's away."

"That's right. That's right."

"You said you had a surprise for me," Grady said.

"Hmmm?" Charlotta answered.

"Last night you said we were going to go see your momma and that maybe there was a surprise for me."

Charlotta seemed to be raking through the memories in her mind for several seconds. Then her eyes brightened. "Oh, yes! Lordy, this is

218

going to be quite a day for you. Hope your heart can hold out." She turned to Charlie, "You think his heart can hold out?"

Charlie stopped chewing. "It's worth a shot," he mumbled through a mouthful of pancakes.

Charlotta stood up, lifting her plate from the table. "C'mon Grady, help me with these dishes real quick and I'll tell you what's going on."

"Charlotta, I have to tell you, I don't know if I can go through the story again," Grady said, rising and sweeping his plate from the table. "I appreciate your hospitality and kindness, but I think Charlie and I should . . ."

"Momma told me you were coming," she interrupted, turning on the faucet in the sink.

"What? How? How could she know I was coming?"

She took the plate and cup from him and slid them into the sudsy water. "Now, let me first of all say that I am a pragmatic woman, a logical woman, a reasonable woman. Not one to open up and swallow crazy explanations for things, and, believe me, as a judge I heard every cock and bull story you could conjure in your mind for why people do and think certain things; enough hot air to make you fall over laughing." She was wiping the dish now, holding it under the faucet to rinse and handing it to him. "Towel's over there," she said, motioning with her head. "Anyway, Momma said on the night Rudy died, an angel came to her clear as day right at the foot of her bed!"

"Really?" Grady said, drying the dish and placing it in the open cabinet above his head.

"You don't believe it?"

"I didn't say that," he answered. How could he? He was, after all, the guy who carried on dialogues with his dead wife.

"Now, it may just have been Momma's unrelenting faith in mankind that someone would come forth eventually and ease her mind. She might have made up the story about the angel and all. But who knows? After last night, it didn't make much difference."

"I see."

"It hit me like a whap on side of the head with a two-by-four. Nearly knocked me over." She handed him another clean wet plate. "Bet you thought it was the Jack Daniels, huh?" She delivered a radiant smile from a row of still perfect teeth.

"That's what knocked me on my butt," Grady replied.

"Me, too," Charlie said, standing up now and bringing his plate to the sink.

"Well, Momma told me a hundred times, if she told me once, to watch and wait for a boy who was going to come to answer all her questions about what happened to her Rudy. That this boy was there and saw all that happened, and that he was going to come to her with love, not with hate, and that she should accept him the same as he came. I wasn't even remembering this when you came, and then when you told me about that, uh, night," she cleared her throat, "my first thought was hate, hate sour and blinding. My mind said to throw my glass of tea at you and choke you and chase you outta my home." She made a grand gesture with her arm, pointing at the front door.

"Actually, that's what I thought you'd do," Grady replied.

"Until my momma's voice came back to my mind, and I wondered, just wondered, if this point in time happened for a reason, and I do believe it did."

Grady dried the last dish and placed it in the cabinet. "God, Charlotta, I don't think I can do it again, tell her the story."

"She doesn't want to hear the story. There's just something she doesn't know that she needs to know."

"What is it?"

"You'll have to ask her. Play it by ear. See what she says. I'm not telling her a thing when we go in the room. Remember, the angel said to receive you the way you came, with love."

"But the angel said that a boy was coming. Look at me; I'm hardly a boy anymore."

Charlotta pulled the plug on the sink and the water rushed down with a grunt. "Oh, Grady," she said, tapping him on the chest with her index finger. "There's still a boy in here, isn't there?" Then she turned to Charlie. "Can we ride with the top down?" she asked.

"Sure," Charlie answered.

"Yeah!" Charlotta whooped. "I'm gonna sit in the back seat like the queen!"

The sour and mournful smell of old age jumped Grady's senses, like a cat on a mouse, the instant Charlotta led them through the front door of the nursing home. "Day like today, Momma is probably outside on the back veranda, but we still have to check in before we can go see her," she explained, not even stopping to adjust to the scent. They entered a bright and warm room sprawling with couches and card tables that were sporadically occupied by people. A cluster of four ladies argued over a pile of cards in one corner. A large woman in a pink smock leaned and whispered into the ear of a frail white-haired old man who stared straight ahead. Eight others sat on chairs in a semi-circle and lifted their arms in unison at the direction of the physical therapist.

"Good morning, Miss Charlotta," the receptionist said, looking at her wristwatch. "You're kind of early today."

"Yes, I have some old friends of Momma here. Mr. Grady Hagen and his grandson Charlie."

"How y'all?" the lady asked, smiling broadly.

"Momma on the veranda?" Charlotta asked.

"Actually, she wanted to go down to the garden by the pond in the way back. Said she could smell the flowers from her room and wanted to get closer to them. As you know, what Principia wants, she gets."

Charlotta thanked the woman and led Grady and Charlie through a maze of hallways and rooms, to a back door that opened to a broad lawn. The minute they emerged, Grady sucked in a big mouthful of clean outside air. Thank God, he thought. He could see the muscles on Charlie's face relaxing, as well, and the boy shook his head when his eyes met his grandfather's. Grady decided that if they went inside again, he would pack that gulp of fresh air in his lungs like a camel stores water in a hump, and use it to ease into the odor until he could adjust to it.

Charlotta walked to the sunny side of the huge nursing home complex, following a brick path into a labyrinth of hedges exploding with color and fragrance. It was as though someone had taken every kind of flower imaginable and tossed them at the greenery, letting them land where they would, so random and wonderful was their distribution. Charlie lifted his camera and snapped a few shots. And then they saw her, some one hundred feet ahead, sitting in a wheelchair, a beatific calmness on her face. Principia Montcrief, tiny, barely a handful it seemed, in a clean, vibrant pink dress. Her feather white hair was a stunning accent to her caramel skin.

While her visitors were still fifty or more feet away, her countenance suddenly changed and she lifted herself slightly, her head alert and sensing. "That's my lady coming, my girl!" she shouted, clapping her hands.

"Hello my Momma, my love," Charlotta sang, running the last few steps and taking her mother's face in her hands and kissing it again and again.

"You have someone with you, two men," Principia said. "They are strangers. Who are they?"

"I thought she was blind. She can see us?" Charlie asked Charlotta in a soft voice.

"In her own way, yes, oh yes," Charlotta answered. "When Momma went blind twenty-five years ago, she said she got another sight in return, a brighter one."

"Amen! Amen!" Principia said, reaching up and trying to find Charlie with her open hands. "Come, come here." Finally she contacted his arms and ran her fingers up and down them. "He's just a boy!" she said. Then she turned to Grady. He looked directly into her eyes, which were milky white and rigid. She let go of Charlie and reached out for Grady's hands. He stepped forward and took hers, squeezing them, and as he did his heart broke once more as his own knobby and ancient fingers wrapped around hers.

Principia explored his arms and chest, then pulled him closer and ran her hands over his face and into his thinning hair. "What is your name, boy?" she said. Her hands moved away from Grady's face, soft as a butterfly.

Grady looked to see if the word 'boy' meant she was directing this question to Charlie, but realized her attention was firmly riveted on him. "I'm Grady Hagen, Mizz Principia."

Her eyes closed for several breaths. "Oh, my," she whispered.

"Charlotta brought us here to see you," Grady stammered. "This is my grandson Charlie."

Principia raised her index finger and wagged it back and forth. "No, no. God brought you here. Charlotta just did the driving."

"Actually, Momma, Charlie did the driving, in a red Mustang convertible; you wouldn't believe it! With the top down and me riding in the back! Made my hair a mess, but oooo, was it fun!"

"Red?" Principia squealed. "Oh, that's fine, that's real fine." She turned her head in Charlie's direction. "Your daddy and momma buy that for you?"

"Yes, ma'am."

"You must be a good boy, or spoiled rotten," she laughed.

"Probably both," he answered.

"They rich, your momma and daddy?"

"Well, Dad's a lawyer and Mom's a doctor."

"Doctorin'. That's hard work, hard work for a man or woman," Principia intoned. "You give her big hugs and kisses every night?"

"Well, I . . ."

"You start doing it, right now, y'hear?"

"Yes, ma'am."

She reached up an angular thin hand and Charlie took it. "Nice to meet you, Charlie. I knew your granddaddy here, long, long time ago."

Grady was surprised. "I didn't think you would remember me."

She turned her face back to him. "I remember you," she said. "Knew your momma. She brung us a cake when my boy died. She was the only white person ever did anything for us in our time of grief."

"I didn't know that."

"She was a good woman."

"Yes, she was."

"Why you come to see this old lady now?" Principia asked, folding her hands in her lap. But there was a smirk on her face, as if she was testing him.

Oh, Jesus, Grady thought, turning toward Charlotta, whose nod urged him to continue.

"I come to talk about Rudy, Mizz Principia," he choked out the words.

Principia's face brightened. "You remember my boy Rudy?"

"Yes, I do. Very well."

"They hanged him up like a criminal, though he didn't make no crime on nobody!"

Charlotta rubbed Principia's shoulder. "That's why Grady came to see you, love."

Principia reached up and patted her daughter's hand. Then she smiled. "You always thought I was a crazy old woman, didn't you? You, the lawyer, the judge, who don't believe in the power of the spirit, of the angels?" The words were teasing, yet kind, free of any rancor or anger.

"You always said someone would come."

"Then why don't y'all just walk on down to the lake down yonder and let me talk to Mr. Grady by myself. Okay?"

"Sure, Momma," Charlotta replied, brushing a stray hair from her mother's forehead. She straightened herself. "You wanna see some catfish, Charlie? Come right up to you, they do!"

"Sure," Charlie answered, following Charlotta down the slope.

Grady wiped a bug of sweat from his forehead and prayed, once again, for the words. He wished he wasn't alone as he watched Charlotta and Charlie leave.

"You was there that night?" Principia said.

"I was."

"Hmmph."

Grady was disgusted with himself at that moment, not just for what he had done, but for his ineptitude with words. Like a drunk on cobblestones, he wobbled and stumbled over what to say. "I'm full out of misery, Mizz Principia. I've lived my whole life in shame. And I know that no matter what I felt, it can't compare with your sorrow. I am very sorry."

"You come here now an old man, the devil at your front door, with your hat in your hand, looking for redemption, thinking that you can just say you're sorry and I'll forgive you?" Principia's words, as harsh as they were, were wrapped in a cotton inflection and came out almost consoling, rather than scathing.

Grady choked, closed his eyes and pinched the bridge of his nose. "I don't expect forgiveness, don't deserve it. But would cherish it as the greatest gift I ever received if you were so kind to grant it." Grady turned away from her, his eyes welling, once again, with tears he thought he had used up.

"Don't turn away from me now, boy," Principia said in a near whisper. She sighed and cleared her throat. "Did he die brave, with his head high?"

"Yes, ma'am, he certainly did."

Principia lifted her chin and squared her shoulders, turning her head out toward the lake, a million miles away from him now, it seemed, buried in thoughts. "Hmmm mmm," she nodded. "I think he always knew he had a grander destination. He might coulda been a doctor like your chile did, but instead he got to be something bigger, more profound. He got to be an angel!" There was a deep sorrow in her eyes as she finished these words. "I had to give God an angel, and it hurt so deep and so long," she whispered, tapping her heart.

"I can understand how much you hate me and all I represent to you, ma'am," Grady said, hanging his hands at his side. "I will leave you now, but, for what it's worth, I want you to know, once again that at least one person from what happened there is profoundly and eternally sorry. I wish you peace."

Principia's eyebrows raised. "Hate? Oh, no, Mr. Grady, I don't hate you, and you might not believe it, but I don't hate no one who done this to my boy. Sure, I did for a time, but you can't live as long as I have with hate in you, not even one speck. It will eat up your insides."

Once again, Grady didn't know how to respond. He croaked out, "I'm sure it took a lot of courage to forgive . . ."

Principia waved both hands in the air. "Whoa, whoa, whoa, I didn't say I forgave nobody. There's a difference between releasing hate and forgiveness. Even the good Lord Almighty won't forgive you unless you come and ask it."

"I see."

"What about you? What about the hate inside you? I'm surprised it ain't consumed you like a fire."

"I didn't hate your son, ma'am."

Principia smiled and her entire face glowed. "Not Rudy, boy. I'm talking about the hate you been carrying forever for yourself. It's time to shed that once and for all."

"I wish I could, Mizz Principia."

"You can. Just let it go, like a bird, and it will fly away."

"You make it sound easy."

"No, it ain't easy, boy. You want easy, go get a box of cake mix," she retorted. He was a child again, being admonished by an adult for his foolish childishness, being shamed for his notions, but learning something profound in the process. Principia continued. "And when you let go of your hate, then, and only then, you get a favor back from God."

"I wish, I hope I can do that," Grady whispered. "But I don't think I can."

Principia took his arm. "Listen to me. When I decided many, many years ago to purge myself of all hate, all I asked back from God was that we could bury my boy and pray over his grave and let the people, our people, come forth and cry with me. Let them raise their hands to heaven and thank the lord, thank God, for the goodness of my boy's soul!" She let go of Grady's arm and raised her hands in the air, then dropped them to her lap, where her fingers threaded together in a prayer-like clutch.

Grady looked at Principia, his brow furrowing. "You didn't have a funeral for him?"

"They took away his body, and there was nothing for us to bury," she replied.

Principia twisted a fistful of dress in her hand. "I come into town the next day, walking from the farm just to come get my boy, and the policeman said he don't know, that somebody, but he didn't remember who – 'cause he was so upset and confused – was supposed to bring my baby back to me."

Grady staggered backward, the world around his head reeling, and he reached for something to keep him from falling. Oh, Jesus, to die now. He thrust his right hand toward the back of a bench, steadied himself and then sagged onto it.

"Are you okay, Mr. Grady?" Principia asked.

Grady took several deep breaths. "I'm fine." He wiped his face with both hands and then looked up at her. "It's been a long few days," he croaked.

Principia raised her head to the sky and closed her eyes. She began to sway ever so gently. "I dreamed of the day when I could walk him right down that street. How sweet it would be! To hear my people singing. To hand him off to God." Her head snapped forward and her eyes opened. Her voice grew hard. "And to walk him past the stores and let those people see what they done. Let them know they couldn't just waltz away from their sin. Let them see the pain they caused."

Her features softened. "And then take my boy up that dirty old road to the colored graveyard where the ground is holy and sanctified by the sufferin' that's been laid to rest there. And then my boy could be free." She stopped, closing her eyes once more.

From the moment Grady had set foot outside his home and took the first step of this journey, what he needed to do next was never clear. It was as if some angel or cosmic Puck was hiding it from him, keeping it in a pocket; teasing him with it; letting him know it was there, but never revealing it. Until now. Until these words from this old lady.

"But now, you see," Principia continued, opening her eyes again and locking him in them. "Everything is right on course."

"Yes," Grady said. "Yes, it is."

A commotion erupted somewhere behind all of them, like the sudden ascent of a flock of birds, and then a voice floated on the air. "Is my Great Gram-mama here? Is she here?"

"That's my baby! My baby!" Principia rose from her chair halfway and clapped her hands. "My baby, my baby!"

In an instant someone rounded the corner, all arms and legs akimbo, running toward Principia, and Grady fell back in the bench at the sight of her. She was young, about Charlie's age, and exquisite beyond words. She was, Grady thought, what God had intended for perfection. She was tall and liquid and drew all the colors of the sun into herself. Her skin was neither white nor black, but a soft cream-in-coffee color. An amazing cascade of hair that could only be described oxymoronically as bright black, trailed behind her as she came forward. And her eyes, Jesus, her eyes, the color of the sea on a perfect day, and nearly as deep. Grady couldn't take his own off her as she bent and hugged Principia, who buried her face in the girl's shoulder and sang, "My baby, my baby."

A few hundred yards away, Charlotta had taken Charlie's hand now and was running with him up the gentle slope. It was as if some signal had been given, some bugle blown, calling everyone to converge on this spot.

"There's my girl!" Charlotta cried, moving quickly into the young woman's arms.

"Auntie Char," she squealed.

"I didn't know you were coming along, honey child!" Charlotta exclaimed. "This is my grand niece," she said to Grady, as the girl pulled away from her embrace.

Principia interjected, "Name as beautiful as she is, Starling! Isn't that a beautiful name?"

"Indeed, it is," Grady replied. He glanced up at Charlie who had fallen backward as if from an explosion and now leaned into a jungle of flowers, as if wanting the whole bush to swallow him up. All the color was drained from his face.

"Free as a bird. Starling. Though she calls herself Star," Principia said through a blissful smile, shaking her head. She turned toward Grady. "Starling, baby, this is Mr. Hagen and Charlie who came all the way from Arbutus to see us," Principia said.

"Hi," Starling said, offering a hand to Grady, who audibly expelled air as he stood to shake it.

"This is Charlie," Grady said, turning toward his grandson.

In that moment the world, for an instant, stopped. Grady could sense it. God how sweet it tasted and felt, and the sheer beautiful magnitude of it raised him upward. He remembered that day a long, long time ago on the ball field when he ignited with Betsy Sue. Now that moment was being recreated in front of his eyes. Starling and Charlie drained all the sound and color out of the surroundings, standing face to face, not saying anything for several breaths; breaths that everyone there shared and let ride. Of all the flowers in the garden, no two were more beautiful than these. Charlie gulped visibly and looked toward her.

She went first, sticking out her hand and lilting, "Hi, I'm Star."

"There they are!" a voice rounded the corner just an instant before the body that followed, and Grady looked up to see another person entering the tiny and suddenly incomprehensible world in which he found himself. A woman, salt and pepper hair bouncing with each of her quick steps, was gasping as she came toward them in hurried strides. "My goodness, Starling, you're always in such a hurry!"

She was Caucasian, and even though her face was obscured behind large sunglasses, there was something vaguely familiar about her. She was out entirely out of breath as she addressed Charlotta, who was now behind the wheel chair. "Charlotta, I got your voicemail message and came as soon as possible. Is everything all right?" She took off her sunglasses, leaned in and kissed Principia. "Hello, Momma. God love you," she said, squeezing the old lady's frail hand. Then she stood up and turned around to face Grady. "So what's the big event? What's going on . . .?" She stopped, and her voice flew apart like dandelion dust in the wind. Her right hand went up to her mouth and she gasped. Then she opened both arms and ran to Grady.

"Oh, Grady," she said holding him, crying, shaking.

"Cissy, Cissy," Grady murmured incredulously. "Is it really you?"

They held each other then, letting all kinds of moments flow through one another; moments that didn't need words. They broke now and then only to take in one another's face.

"Surprise!" Charlotta roared.

"You are one mean woman, Charlotta," Principia said. Then she started cackling. "I love it! I just love it!"

"You didn't tell me! Why didn't you tell me?" Cissy cried, her face streaked with tears. She wiped her cheeks with her fingers.

Grady glared at Charlotta. "You asked if my heart could take it," he groused. "It can't."

"Look at you! Just look at you!" Cissy said, pulling away slightly, putting both hands on Grady's shoulders. "It's been so long."

"A lifetime," Grady replied.

Cissy drew away from him, but buried herself in the crook of his arm, her cheek on his shoulder, and turned him around. "You have met my granddaughter Starling, I presume?"

"Indeed," said Grady, his eyes glistening.

"My son's little girl, all grown up," Cissy sighed.

"Your son?" Grady said, his eyebrows rising.

"Yes, sir. The last time you saw me, he was in here," Cissy answered, patting her midsection. "Seems, in many ways like yesterday, and in others like a hundred years ago."

"Yes, yes, I remember," Grady replied.

She squeezed him again and then withdrew, and her face took on a puzzled look. "Why are you here?" she said, the odd and sudden appearance of her old friend obviously dawning on her as something more than a mere coincidence.

"Phew! Girl, you won't believe what's happened in the past two days," Charlotta interjected.

"Tell me, please, tell me," Cissy said.

Charlotta and Grady alternated with bits and pieces of the story, to which Cissy could only reply, again and again, "Oh, my."

When they had finished, Principia popped up. "Before this family reunion gets crazy, I got to ask Mr. Grady one question," she said. She turned her vacant eyes toward his, and Grady was certain she could see him clearly, see him for what he really was. She lifted her chin and said, "Now, I just need to know if you are the one."

"The one?" Grady asked.

"The one who can give me back my boy."

Grady cleared his throat. "I am."

"Praise God's holy name," Principia whispered.

Then Grady squatted down in front of Principia. He took her hands again. "Mizz Principia," he said. "I promise you I will do everything in my power to let you lay him to rest right and proper." He leaned forward and did something he never envisioned, never expected, never conceived himself ever doing. He kissed this ancient and miraculous lady on the forehead.

Principia reached up and caressed Grady's cheek. "I knew you when you was a boy. I knew you wasn't bad like the rest of them."

Grady squeezed her hand and let it loose. "I have to go back to Arbutus."

"Sounds good to me!" Principia said, pushing herself to her feet but holding on to both rails of the wheelchair. "Let's go."

Grady's head shifted from her to Charlotta to Cissy. "Are you – is she – kidding me?"

Cissy raised her eyebrows. "You can't stop her anymore than you could stop a tornado."

"I wanna ride in that red Mustang with the top down," Principia squealed.

38

Arbutus, Mississippi – August 8, 1942

Someone had flipped the crate back on its side and stood on it to cut the rope. The body fell, collapsing within itself on the ground, and the mob, still broiling with the sheer hysteria of the night, fell upon it. Grady watched as people emerged with souvenirs. Scraps of clothing, hunks of scalp, even fingers.

Jesus, God forgive us.

Then someone doused the corpse with gasoline and threw a match. It burst into flames with a wallop that reeled those standing closest.

An angry whack of lightning illuminated the scene, followed by a belch of thunder.

"Come on, gol'durn it, help me," Grady heard from behind him, just as Cecil LaGrone pushed through, grabbing his arm as he passed. With surprising speed, the policeman pulled Grady into the middle of a circle of people. "That's enough, that's enough!" he shouted, stomping futilely to quell the fire. Then he ripped off his uniform shirt and began beating at the flames. "Lord God a'mighty, what's the matter with you people? Somebody help me for the love of God!"

Instinctively, Grady pulled off his own shirt and joined in. Someone brought a blanket, and threw it over the flaming ruins, and the fire died fighting. When the blanket was removed, only a smoldering pile in the curlicue shape of a large fetus remained. Chief LaGrone stood up, the belly spilling over his belt as pink and large as a pig. His blackened shirt dangled in his hand. He looked up at the crowd and in a soft voice said, "Y'all go home now." When no one moved, the Chief balled his fists, shook both of them at the people and shouted, "Get home now, the all of you!"

Still no one moved. It was as if the shock of the event finally reached the faces that stared at the remains of what, only moments before, had been a breathing, living man. Silence emanated from the ashes, moving up and out in waves, roiling over these now frozen spectators. Face after face assumed the same shape – eyes wide, mouths agape. Chests heaved in unison, but the frantic intake of air was without form or substance. Even the distant thunder had paused. Not a bird chirped. The crickets did not stir. Finally, after perhaps ten minutes, the crowd just seemed to melt away. Although Grady sensed virtually no movement, people began to disperse, back to their homes, their beds, their children. People who would return to their jobs or their fields the next morning, who would be sitting Sunday in Parson Kincaid's church, singing their lungs out.

A few of the younger guys, boys from school, and some older fellows like Fletcher Moody's younger brother Parker, milled around, laughing. Billie Rae Tolleston was now standing at Grady's side. "Ain't that somethin'!" he howled. "I ain't never seen nothing like that!"

Cecil LaGrone pulled the Moody boy by the shirt until he was standing toe to toe with him. Then he grabbed Billie Rae by the arm and spun him around. He snarled at Tolleston first. "You go over to your daddy's store and get a gunny sack or something. And a broom and shovel," he said, pushing the boy away.

"Yes, sir!" Billie Rae exclaimed, turning and taking flight.

His fist still wrapped in Parker Moody's shirt, LaGrone pulled him closer. "When he gets back here, you help him sweep this up and take it – him – to his momma."

"Take him where?" Moody cried, his eyes widening. "Are you shitting me?"

"You heard me, damnit," LaGrone growled. He turned and looked at the trembling assemblage of charred bone. "Good Lord a'mighty, what have we done?" he whispered, grabbing a handful of sweat from his forehead and flinging it away where it glistened like jewels against the light from the streetlamp. "I promised her this wouldn't happen."

Then LaGrone turned to Grady. "You, get a bucket of water and make sure this is all cooled down so it don't burn up the gunny sack. Then help these boys get him to his momma."

Grady didn't answer; didn't even breathe.

A sheet of heat lightning painted the sky, and a low growl of thunder rolled over them. "Good Jesus, now it's going to rain," LaGrone whispered. "It's the Lord speakin', sure as death."

Grady took a few steps forward, sweat cutting rivulets through the grime on his bare skin. He knelt by the smoking pile that was part solid, but also wispy and soft and flying upward in tiny bits of ash. Thunder stirred again in darkness. Then he doubled at the waist, turned away from the smoldering bones and vomited. The stream he deposited splattered against the pavement and scurried toward the curb.

When he was empty, he pulled himself upright, using his filthy shirt to wipe the lines of puke from the corners of his mouth. Parker was stomping on embers that took flight from the charred debris. In the distance Grady could hear invisible voices, men laughing. A block away, a string of silhouettes appeared under the street lamp, four men, hats cocked. One of them lit a cigarette and exhaled a ghost of smoke that gleamed in a thin transparent mist against the backlight. He leaned forward, match in hand, and lit the other men's smokes as well. Soon a storm of wispy violet-tinged clouds swirled around them as they walked away, slapping one another on the back.

Grady Hagen came to full height, his arms heavy at his sides, dirty shirt balled up in his hand. He seemed to be lifted by the moment like a piece of paper on a noiseless wind, floating away and into the darkness. He began to run. The slapping of his feet against the brick road was the only sound he heard. He snaked first through the park, around trees, then bounded across the street and past the last building, running toward the darkness and the restless night.

39

"I had the baby three months later. He was nearly a month premature, probably from all the stress, looking back. But it was kind of a blessing, because he was still a good six-and-a-half pounds," Cissy said, walking with Grady, her fingers entwined in his. Like two old gray doves, they strolled along the edge of the lake behind the nursing home while Charlotta took Principia back to her room to pack for the trip back to Arbutus. "And when he came out like he did, colored, as the birth certificate said, well, they said they couldn't keep him there; I mean, heaven forbid they care for a colored baby in a white hospital. So they kicked us out."

"Of course they would," Grady grunted. "What did you do?"

"I was standing there on the steps of the hospital with a baby in my arms, legs like melted wax, sick and in pain, a long way from home, and nobody, nobody there."

"What about your daddy?"

Cissy smirked and pursed her lips. "Oh, Grady, there was no way he was going to take me back. Needless to say, I had disgraced my family and my race. I had run the Moody name into the dirt. He made that very clear to me when he was beating me half to death."

"I can only imagine."

"I always wondered that if my momma was still alive at that time, if she would have, maybe, still, you know, kept me." Cissy was crying now. But she reached up and wiped the tear away, and lifted her chin. "I didn't know what to do. And Dr. Max came out and asked me if

234

I needed a ride somewhere. There was no place to go, but I said yes anyway. I got in his car and figured it out on the way back."

"Good old Doc Max."

"He was one of the few saviors in my life. He continued to take care of the baby and me by sneaking out to see us at night, God bless him."

"Obviously you decided to go to Principia."

"The only place I had to turn was to Principia."

"Lord, Cissy. I wish I would have been there." Grady brushed a strand of her hair away from her forehead. "What happened when you went to her?"

She smiled. "I wasn't exactly the prize patrol showing up at their door with that baby in my arms." She chuckled and shrugged. "Well, you know what I mean."

"Not too thrilled, I take it?"

Her voice grew wispy, fragile. "There was so much pain in the house, like it had come and taken away the breathing air, and there I stood in the dark threshold, baby swaddled in an old blanket, and Principia stood and glared at me, one hand on the door." She shivered. "Cut through me like a knife."

"What did you do?"

"I handed her the baby."

"And that was it?"

Cissy raised her head and smiled. "That was it. You see, Principia may be a tiny little thing, but there is so much love, God, it's awesome, in her. She is truly a creation of astounding magnitude. Still to this day."

"But you didn't stay in Arbutus."

"Principia went to every home in that town looking for someone to tell her where Rudy was and not one, not one, Grady, would give this little woman that minuscule bit of comfort," Cissy answered, her eyes filling up with tears again. She blinked them back. "So, she said Arbutus wasn't worthy of her presence, spit on the ground, and we all came up to Georgia."

"And you and she raised the baby?"

"Charlotta, too. His name is John Moody."

"You gave him your name."

"That was the last name on the birth certificate. That's what he got," she replied. "My old man, by God, was none too happy. Even though he disowned me, he wasn't keen on having a so-called colored baby walking around town with his name. So, he was pleased to see me go." She coughed slightly to clear her throat. "I never saw him again. When he died, I got word somehow – I don't remember who told me – and I thought about going back for the funeral. But I decided it would cause too much of a ruckus. So, I said a prayer for him, and that was that."

Grady nodded. "I never understood you and Rudy, though. It never made sense."

Cissy sighed. "Oh Grady, I was always kind of boy crazy; you knew that. Heck, I had a crush on you for ten years. But Rudy wasn't like any other boy in Arbutus. He . . . did you know he wanted to be a doctor? He read books like other people eat potato chips. He could talk for hours about far away places he wanted to see. I had never met anyone like him before, and then the color just disappeared. Do you understand how shocked I was at that? That I didn't even think – or care – anymore what color he was?" She paused and wiped her eye again. "Only problem was, his color couldn't disappear from anyone else."

"Yeah," Grady answered.

Cissy started walking again. "I did it to him. He didn't do it to me. I chased him, followed him, seduced him. And it got him killed."

"I don't think you should blame yourself."

"Of course I do, Grady. Every day of my life from that moment on. I was wrong, wrong in every way. I was a fornicator, not to mention I had broken the most serious of taboos. But I never believed that the people of my town, my little town in the heart of Mississippi, could have so much rage and hate in them that they could make something like that happen. People I knew and loved. People I went to church with. Never believed it."

Grady changed the subject. "Did you ever marry?"

A beautiful smile spread across her face. "When Johnny was twelve. To a wonderful man," she paused, "a white man named Lee Blakely, although his race had nothing to do with it. I don't even know why I mention it now. Anyway, he took us all in, Principia, Johnny and me. Charlotta, in the beginning, then on and off as she ascended her rainbow."

"Where is he now?"

"He passed in 1996." She looked up at a cloud and smiled. "Went straight to heaven, that man did. Straight to heaven."

"What about John?"

"Oh, Johnny. He's a ball of fire. Owns twenty-nine McDonald's franchises in Virginia and North Carolina. He's been businessman of the year about twenty times." She motioned in the direction of Charlie and Starling. "That beautiful young thing over there tearing the heart out of your grandson is his daughter."

They came to a bench and Grady sat down. "Give me a minute," he said.

"You okay, Grady?"

"I'm just trying to take all this in. It's been a helluva week for me."

She sat down next to him and glanced away from the lake toward the garden. "Look at them, Grady."

Grady turned and saw Charlie and Starling sitting on a short brick wall, faces close together, talking. "My goodness," he said.

"Did you see the look on their faces when they met?"

"Took the air out of the garden," he replied.

"My granddaughter. All grown up." She wrapped her other arm in the crook of Grady's, laid her cheek on his shoulder and squeezed. "You ever think we'd get this old?"

"Nope."

"You know, I got hit like that once, so did you," she said, still looking at the two young people. "Problem was, for me it was fatal."

Grady pursed his lips and shook his head. "I think it's always fatal."

They sat for several minutes without speaking. Then a voice came from the top of the hill. Charlotta was standing on the veranda of the nursing home, Principia next to her in a bright yellow suit with a matching hat. "Momma says come on, we're burning daylight!" Charlotta repeated.

40

Somewhere from the very marrow of his ancient bones, Grady Hagen extracted what he believed would be the last drop of courage residing therein. He was certain there was nothing left there; that all the wringing and squeezing in the world would produce nothing, and that his glands and organs that would have – could have – produced the audacity to carry on were atrophied beyond repair. But he found one last fragment, and it had been enough to move his legs into the center of the place where he now stood. Light fell from the ceiling in bluish gray pyramids, creating a honeycomb of shadows and light that both highlighted and hid the seemingly random array of tools and cords and lawn mowers and aisles of boxes lined in perfect parallel, like the stitches on a hem, agape with shining silver and brass nuts and bolts.

Things were different, of course, in Tolleston's Hardware Store, but so much the same as well. Billie Rae Sr. had been a big game hunter, and every year would return with another trophy that he had stuffed and then hoisted with a winch to a large shelf high above the merchandise, where, with glass eyes, they looked down upon the shoppers and the merchandise. People would stop and stare at the white mountain goat from Canada with its curled horns, or the Montana grizzly standing seven feet tall, claws and teeth bared, or the assorted black bears and moose and majestic elk with gnarled antlers expanding wider than your arms. These sentinels still stood, dirty and fraying in spots now, but still fending off time and decay thanks to the taxidermist's art. Grady looked at the large bald eagle, glued or nailed to a perch, its wings wide with imaginary air.

"You buying or looking?" the voice came from behind. "This is a store, not a museum."

Grady turned to face the little man from which the raspy words emerged. Billie Rae Tolleston, Jr. was eyeing him up and down, one eye squinting through the trifocal glasses. He was, like everything in Arbutus, smaller, more dried out. His hair was gone, and a hearing aid engulfed one ear. "Well?" he said. "What you looking for?" Then he stopped, catching the last word in his throat. His face brightened with recognition, like a vessel filling with liquid. He yanked his glasses from his head. "I'll be goddamned to hell. The prodigal son returns," he said, his voice more wooden than pleased.

"Long time, Billie Rae. Didn't think you'd recognize me."

"Yeah, well, probably wouldn't have 'cept Truman said y'all was in town causing trouble."

"Truman. He talks a lot."

"Can't shut him up," Billie Rae said, replacing the glasses and adjusting them through a moment of silence as thick as pudding. He cleared his throat. "So, what can I help you with?" he reached down and lifted a hammer from the bin next to Grady. "This what you lookin' for?"

Grady reached back and scratched the base of his neck. "No, Billie Rae. In fact, what I need, you don't have in the store at all."

Billie Rae tossed the hammer back in the tray, then put both hands in the pockets of his pants and rocked back on his heels. "Yeah, well, then I probably ain't got it," he growled.

"It's just information I want, that's all."

Billie Rae came forward, moving his face to within a few inches of Grady's. He rasped in a voice slightly higher than a whisper. "I know what you want. Truman told me the whole thing. Come down here out of the goddamned blue yonder fixin' to fuck up our town. I got information for you, all right, skedaddle your ass back north and leave us alone. You ain't one of us no more, and we don't need the trouble you bring."

Grady stood his ground. "I just want to know what you did with Rudy Montcrief's remains, so that his momma can give him a proper burial."

Billie Rae's eyes opened wider. "That old broad is still kickin'? Ain't that something?" Then he stood on his tiptoes and looked around. "She here with you?"

"Up the road at the motel. She's resting after the trip."

"Yeah, well, God bless her."

"What did you do with him that night, Billie Rae?"

Billie Rae grunted and made a spitting sound. "If you'd a stayed with me, you'd know. Truth is, I forgot, myself."

Now Grady leaned closer, smelling his old friend's mothy breath. "You got nothing in you for the grief of that old woman?"

Billie Rae pushed away. "Oh, so that's what this is all about," he mocked. "Here I thought it was just you trying to atone for the wrong you done, when in fact, you was just trying to help that old woman find peace. Well, excuse me for misreading your fine Christian intentions." He held up both hands. "But, I gotta tell you, I can't help. I'm old and demented now, ask anyone around here who knows me. What you want to know is clean out of my head." He turned and started to walk away. "Front door is that way," he snapped over his shoulder.

Grady strode forward and grabbed his arm. Billie Rae wrenched himself free. "Get your hands off me," he said.

Grady pulled back. "Please, Billie Rae. Just tell us. We aren't here to cause trouble."

The old man leaned close again. "Yeah, maybe you don't want to cause trouble. But you know what? Trouble is all that can come of this. Nothing but trouble."

"I'm telling you, let his momma bury him."

He turned Grady slightly to the left. "See that man over there? That black man behind the counter? That there is Marcus Templeton, the best goddamned employee I have ever seen. That man can turn an apple into an orange with duct tape and a toggle switch. Now what do you think he's going to think of me, his boss, when word gets out that I was . . ." he let the words fall and pulled away from Grady. "Get out of here before I call the police," he spat.

Starling's face, ungodly beautiful, fuzzed out in the concentric crosshatching of the camera lens, as Charlie manipulated the focus ring. He held his breath as her countenance assembled in the ground glass, and, for an instant, he was startled by the mystic vision, as if seeing her for the first time. They were in the park across from the hardware store, waiting for Grady to emerge, and Star was sitting on the ground, leaning against a tree, twisting a piece of grass in her fingers. Charlie had already burned her image into two rolls of film, and now she was scrunching her features and sticking out her tongue. "Don't you have enough of me yet?" she mocked.

Never, Charlie thought, pushing the button on the camera. The shutter whirled and stopped time, somehow pulling the scene into its dark confines, and at that instant the phone on Charlie's belt rang. Again. He looked down at the display.

Lorene. For the tenth time that day. He let the trilling propel her into his voicemail where another message, this time angrier or sadder or more desperate, would be waiting for him. If she only knew how the events of the last few days had changed him, the way an earthquake changes a highway, bending it to a completely different direction – not to mention the nova that erupted in front of him this instant, making faces and noise – why, even Charlie found it hard to comprehend. How would Lorene ever understand?

"Better answer that. I bet it's your girlfriend," Star said.

"Who said I had a girlfriend?"

Starling laughed and pointed at the phone. "Honey, I know a girlfriend's ring when I hear one."

Charlie lowered the camera. "Yeah, well, things change," he said softly.

Starling walked toward him and purposely bumped him as she passed. "I hope so," she said, so close to his face he could feel her breath.

Star broke into a brisk run toward the opposite end of the park. Charlie followed, holding the camera with one hand to keep it from banging against his chest. By the time he caught her, she had stopped and was studying the trees. He could see each breath she drew give motion to her chest. "Do you think it was one of these?"

"One of these?" Charlie asked.

"Trees," she replied, the word floating like a feather. "But I don't think so. They aren't old enough or big enough."

Now Charlie understood what tree she meant. He turned back toward the town to get his bearings. "According to the picture, the tree would have been over there," he said, pointing to the spot.

"Picture?"

Oh shit. She didn't know about the picture. Why bring it up now? He unscrambled his thoughts. "I meant, the way I pictured it, it would have been maybe over there."

She looked at the spot. "But it's gone now."

"Pappy said it died of shame."

"Hmm mmm," she breathed. "That would be appropriate, but then again, the poor tree didn't have anything to do with it, did it?"

"Well, no."

"It couldn't get up and run away."

"No."

"I bet it was like that for some of the people, too," she said. "I can't believe there was ever a time when so many would have so much, so much hatred, so much anger, so much . . ." she let her thoughts go unspoken. She turned to Charlie and her eyes filled with tears. "I just can't comprehend that everyone could just do this and not know or believe how wrong it was." She put her face in her hands.

Charlie walked to her and, pulling his camera to his side, gathered her in his arms where she seemed to dissolve into him like rain, pouring through his shirt, his skin, his heart. She didn't shake or sob, just sighed rhythmically against him, nudging him with her head, gnawing a thumbnail. They stood like that for several moments. Charlie had had his share of intimate encounters with women, hell, it was the way it was these days. But never one like this, as subtle as a sunset, at the same time as thunderous as a sea storm.

"He was my grandpa," she said, wiping her eyes. "And it's your grandpa who's going to bring him back to my grandmother and great-grandmother. Momma says Great Gram-mama has been waiting for this her whole life. It's why she didn't die a long time ago. Unfinished business." Starling laughed and withdrew slightly from him. She shook her finger and spoke with Principia's voice, "Y'all got unfinished business here before you can go out and play. Wash them dishes, girly girl."

Charlie laughed, keeping his hand on her waist, and she reached up, turned his face to hers and kissed him. No warning. No second thought. Just came up to him like a snake striking, and like a snake, poisoned him with a nectar sweeter than he would have ever imagined. Her lips melted against his, as if a butterfly had landed there.

Jesus, he thought. "Don't do that unless you mean it," he heard the words coming out of his own mouth as it withdrew from hers. Star responded by kissing him again, harder this time, her own lips trembling.

"Charlie! Charlie! Where you at?" a voice rattled the leaves of the trees.

Charlie turned and saw Pappy standing at the Mustang, hands thrust into his pockets, head shaking. Something was wrong, very wrong. Charlie slid his arm from around Star and took her hand. The two of them ran in perfect unison toward the old man.

41

The heat finally broke, sneaking out of Arbutus under cover of night, and by the time the sun rose, a gauzy patina lay over the land, and a cool breeze ruffled the kitchen curtains where Grady Hagen stood. It was the only relief in the air, as he leaned on the stove with both hands, and watched spurts of coffee percolate in the glass globe atop the stained metal pot on the burner. His failure to bring closure to anyone connected with Rudy Montcrief – let alone rescue his own soul from the abyss of his long-ago actions – weighed on him, scrunching his bones.

Last night when he returned to the hotel where Cissy and Principia waited and told them of his conversation with Billie Rae, the ancient one somehow found him with her milky blind eyes and said, without a drop of rancor in her voice, "Oh, now, don't you worry none, boy. The good Lord didn't go and stir you up and then bring us all back here for nothing. It will all come out in the wash."

Grady had shaken his head and sighed. "I just wish he'd get a move on. Neither one of us is getting any younger."

Principia hooted back. "You can say that again! Just remember: the Lord is never too early and never too late."

Grady felt himself smiling as he reheard these words and poured coffee for himself. He pulled a chair away from the table, sat down and took a sip. The liquid scalded his lips and shook him with its overwhelmingly bitter flavor. Damn, too strong again, he thought, sucking cool air into his mouth to quell the pain on his tongue. He stood up and emptied half the cup, then filled it with cold water. Sitting down again, he dumped several spoonfuls of sugar into the still inky liquid and stirred. He thought again of Rachel, but not as if she were there. He had no sense of her presence, like in the park a few days ago, so he looked for her in the rustling of the curtains and the light floating in through the screen door.

"You here, darling'?" he said, just above a whisper.

"Yeah, but how many times do I have to ask you not to call me darling?" Charlie mocked from behind, yawning and scratching the back of his thigh.

Grady looked up. "I wasn't talking to you," he replied, "darling."

Charlie grabbed a cup from the dish strainer and poured some coffee. He took a sip and flinched backwards several inches. "This coffee or paint?"

"Either one," Grady answered.

Charlie sat down and emptied the sugar bowl into the cup. "So, what's the game plan?"

"That's what I'm trying to figure out."

"Talking to yourself?"

"Yep, at least I always understand what I'm saying."

Charlie took another sip. "Whew! This shit is lethal."

"Once you get used to it, it's worse."

"I believe it," he answered. He slid his chair back and, without getting out of it, reached the handle of the refrigerator and opened it, extracting a bottle of milk. "Here, put some of this in there," he said, sliding back to the table.

Grady raised a hand. "No thanks, it's starting to grow on me," he lied, taking a sip.

Charlie poured milk into his cup and stirred it into froth. Then he took a sip and shook his head. "Whew. What a trip, huh?"

"You bet."

"Thanks for letting me come along, Pap."

"Despite everything?" Grady asked.

Charlie grinned. "Shit, Pap, this has been the most interesting, enlightening, coolest thing I've ever done." He lifted the coffee/milk concoction to his mouth and scrunched his face again. Then he continued. "On the other hand, it has really screwed up my life. You know, the whole med school thing, photography . . ." his voice trailed off.

"Your situation . . ." Grady murmured, not looking up.

"My situation?"

Grady raised his eyebrows but didn't say a word.

"What?"

Grady replied, "Come on, boy, I may be dumb but I ain't stupid."

"Oh, you mean Star?"

"Yup."

"And Lorene?"

"Uh huh. You've got some explaining to do."

"What?"

"I got two eyes, boy, and I didn't fall off the turnip truck yesterday. Star has a strong hold on you, and I'll tell you something, you got her, too."

Charlie brightened. "You think so?" he asked.

Grady nodded. "Me, Charlotta, even blind Principia can see it."

"You're shitting me?"

"Nope.

Charlie fiddled with the spoon in the cup, tapping it on the side, dipping it back in. "On one hand, it seems like a no-brainer," he finally said. "I mean, I never in my life met anyone like her."

"She is something else, that's for sure."

Charlie brightened. "Yeah. She's just so, hell, I don't know."

"Beautiful?" Grady posited, a smile widening on his face.

"Yep."

"Enchanting?"

"Yeah."

"Can't think of anything but her?"

"Can't sleep, Pappy. Can't wait to wake up and see her again."

"Ka-boom."

Charlie took a sip of coffee and the color on his cheeks changed again. "Goddamn, this is camel piss," he grumbled. "On the other hand, if I go with my head and all the history I have with Lorene, I mean, she and I have two years together, and we're supposed to be getting married, and she has kids' names picked out, for chrissakes."

He dropped the spoon again and ran a hand through his hair. "I don't know what the hell is going on," he sighed, leaning back in his chair.

"Want to know what an old man thinks?" Grady answered, pushing his cup away.

"I think I'm going to whether I want to or not."

Grady cleared his throat and began. "As you know, Charlie, I'm not an educated man, not an intellectual like you or your momma, so I don't have all the fancy-assed big words or research to back up what I think. I just have eighty or so years of slogging through life and learning as I went along." He folded his hands on the table and looked out the window. "And I just know that if I had gone with my gut instincts throughout my entire life, rather than relying on my head," he tapped his temple, "I would have been right most of the time. The head, the brain, it's no good for anything but thinking up reasons to talk yourself into something, or out of something. Right here," he pointed to his stomach then to his heart, "or here; that's where wisdom lies."

Silence wafted between them and the air seemed to stop. Charlie came back first, "It's just so, so unreal, everything that has happened. So fast, too. Like I don't have any control over anything that's happening to me."

"That's a tough thing to cope with, I know, but you might as well get used to it, because it's going to happen to you more than you think."

"Not if I can help it," Charlie answered.

"Control? Over destiny? Good luck." Grady's hand moved to his chest and rubbed his shirt over the scar. "This here scar you were so fixated on the other morning? I think you know how I really got it. Young punk kid just comes out shooting. One shot. No more. Bullet could have gone into the side of a building, into a tree, a car on the street. It hits me. One little bullet and me, at the point of convergence."

"You were just in the wrong place at the wrong time, I guess."

"Maybe not. Maybe I was exactly where I was supposed to be. Because of what that bullet led to. That's the irony. It means I go to an army hospital and meet your grandmother. Now, if my chest and that little ball of lead aren't brought together at that moment, I don't ever meet her, we don't get married, and your mother never gets born, which means you're never born. It's like it was meant to be." He shook his head and smiled. "When I look at you, I just don't buy that you're some random accident."

"Fate, destiny," Charlie replied. "So you think there's such a thing?"

Grady thought about coincidence, how the lines and angles of his life had formed a montage of bizarre isosceles triangles that connected him to places, people, and events that would forever shape him and his life. Being in certain places at certain times that led to certain things, cataclysmic things, that quaked his foundation and threw him in directions he'd never anticipated. Betsy Sue, Cissy, Billie Rae, Bo, Momma, a teenaged Nazi, Rachel, Rudy Montcrief.

Rudy.

All knitted together.

Grady stared into the coffee. "The more I see, the more I'm beginning to believe that nothing that's happened here is accidental, that there is some kind of something going on out there," he waved a hand in the air, "that not a one of us can figure out or control," Grady said, pointing and tapping his index finger on the table. "Now, put your own situation up for scrutiny. A week ago, did you have any idea you'd be here?"

"Hell no," Charlie chuckled.

"Exactly. I didn't have any plans for you to be here, either. I didn't want you here. I only wanted to get on a bus and come here by myself and do what I had to do. But something, that something out there, intervened, and here you are, and because you're here you meet Star. Now, take it one step further. She was only visiting her grandma Cissy for a few days. If any number of events occur, if you drop me off at the bus station like I asked, or if I decided to go last week or next week and everything else happens exactly as it has, you don't meet Starling because she isn't visiting Cissy."

"That's the crazy part, isn't it?" Charlie exhaled. "I can't figure out if it's all a bunch of gobbledygook or something profound; whether it's coincidence or bullshit."

"It is what it is, and it's done what it's done. Call it destiny if you want, or call it bullshit, but don't call it coincidence because if it was, it would be just a story and not a life-changing event." Grady slapped the table and slid the chair back.

"So, I should go with Star because that's what fate or destiny or something demands?" Charlie wondered aloud.

"All I know is that if you don't, you'll wonder your whole life."

"I think you're right."

"But you have a responsibility," Grady answered, nodding at the phone on the boy's belt.

"Lorene. Yeah, I know."

"All the love and the way you're smitten right now for Star shouldn't blind you to the fact that there is someone else out there who's going to be hurt from this."

"Should I call her and tell her?"

"Wait till we get back. Don't do it on the phone. Be man enough to sit down with her and tell her what's happening. She'll hate you for it, of course, but later on she'll appreciate you took the time to do it right."

Charlie puffed out his cheeks and pushed the air out in an audible pop. "Damn, this isn't easy, is it?"

"Nobody said life was easy, boy."

Charlie reached across the table and took his grandfather's hand, squeezing it. "Thanks, Pappy. I bet I have the smartest granddaddy of any kid in the world."

"Most likely," Grady smiled, slapping his hand atop Charlie's.

"What about your problem?" Charlie asked, finally surrendering to the cup of steaming mud and shoving it away.

"Oh, brother," Grady exhaled.

"Is it possible that anyone other than Billie Rae knows where the bones are?"

Grady pursed his lips. "Sure, I just don't know how to find him or her, if they're still alive. If they are still breathing, would they tell me? I don't know. This town has buried that memory."

"Well, then, you only have one choice right now; take another run at Billie Rae."

"He's a stubborn old bastard, that one."

"What I mean is with a subpoena. I bet my dad could find a way to get one pulled together, even down here. I mean, you know he knows." Charlie leaned forward, enthused now as the idea formed in his mind.

"Imagine, putting him up there on the witness stand, watching him try to get out of it."

"I'm not here to cause trouble. You heard what that Chief said. Besides, I got no ax to grind against Billie Rae. He's no worse than me in terms of this situation."

"Yeah, but he has the answer you're looking for."

Grady nodded. "Maybe if I spoke with him one more time, try to appeal to his higher instincts."

Charlie stood up, walked to the sink and dumped the coffee down the drain. "Good plan. Let's go. Maybe between here and there we can find some coffee that doesn't taste like jet fuel."

Grady struggled to his feet. "You've got a point there, son."

42

What happened next was unexpected; then again, Grady thought, nothing about this quest, this trip, this sojourn that somehow stirred the past, present, and future into a single stew, had gone as anticipated, even considering that those expectations were nebulous at best. The scene was several blocks away, but bathed in a surrealistic waterfall of light that pierced the clouds and agitated the colors of the clothes of the people in the crowd in front of Tolleston's Hardware store.

"What's going on up there?" Charlie asked leaning forward against the steering wheel of the Mustang, as it crawled behind a stinking garbage truck.

Grady couldn't answer, except that he viscerally understood that it had something to do with him and what he had unleashed in tiny Arbutus, those demons or angels or guardians of history and memory.

Several dozen people had gathered around someone or something on the sidewalk there. All Grady could see was the rear of the crowd, heads with baseball hats bobbing, kids clutching legs and peering from behind them, all kinds of hair – silver, brown and blonde, teased and whirled into curls or buns, all moving to the uneven rhythm of tiptoed feet and swaying shoulders. An angular man in his early twenties broke from the mass and floated off down the street, shaking his head, chuckling, and letting fly a stream of tobacco juice. An old timer followed, dragging one weakened leg after the other, a strenuous activity that made him list and sway like a boat on a stormy sea. Whatever it was that got their attention, failed to hold it for long, but Grady's instincts made him anxious as the Mustang lurched behind the garbage truck.

"Get up, go around these guys when they hop off," Grady said, pointing at the two men in blue jump suits who rode on the back bumper of the truck, clinging to the framework.

"I can do that?" Charlie asked.

"It's not a school bus," Grady answered.

The two workers hopped down and scurried toward several plastic garbage containers on the side of the road, and Charlie whipped around the obstruction. As he did, two teenaged girls, hands cupped over their laughing mouths, as if to keep their giggles from falling onto the sidewalk, pulled away from the crowd, creating a seam to the center that closed almost immediately behind them. But it was open long enough for Grady to catch a glimpse of Principia Montcrief seated in her wheel chair in a bright lilac dress, a blue umbrella resting on her shoulder.

Charlie angled the car into a parking space, and Grady was out before it had stopped rolling. He pushed through the group and noticed that Charlotta and Cissy flanked Principia in matching chairs and held similar umbrellas to keep off the variegated shafts of sunlight that rippled through the clouds.

"Grady!" Cissy said, as he approached. "Won't you join us?"

"My good Lord, Cissy, what is going on?"

"We come to help," Principia replied.

"How did you get here?"

"Taxi. Cost six bucks for all of us," Charlotta answered.

"I told you I'd call you."

Charlie had pulled up next to Grady now, which prompted Starling to appear from out of nowhere. "Look at these old ladies," she laughed. "They're insane! I love them so much!" She clapped her hands together and laughed some more, then leaned up and kissed Charlie on the cheek. "What took you so long?" she whispered.

Charlie wrapped an arm around her and nestled her as close to himself as possible or decent, then jerked his thumb over his shoulder at the garbage truck. "Sanitation engineers," he said.

"We got ourselves a party here, Mr. Grady," Principia said. "And it ain't gonna be over until we meet the proprietor of this here establishment."

"Mizz Principia, I don't know . . ." Grady stammered.

"We came here first thing this morning, before the sun even opened one eye," Charlotta explained. "Momma was up and dressed and there was no stopping her."

"You can't stop her," Cissy interjected.

Charlotta continued, "When the store opened, Cissy and I went in and asked for your friend Mr. Tolleston . . ."

"And I thought his jaw was coming unhinged when he recognized me," Cissy added.

"But, like you said, he was having nothing to do with us," Charlotta continued. "He stomped away without a word and locked himself in the office. So we bought these folding chairs and decided to camp right here with Momma while he thinks it over."

"The nice man Mr. Marcus, in the store, come out a few minutes later and just give us these umbrellas so as to make us comfortable from the sun," Principia said. "I told him we'd give 'em back when we were finished."

The whole thing had become hers now, Grady mused. A force of nature of ninety-five years and pounds, Principia Montcrief was like gravity reaching out and grabbing you by the handful and pulling you in.

A loud voice broke through from within the crowd, "Excuse me, let me through, please." Again, a crevice opened and a woman bulled through, a spiral notebook in her hand. She was young, mid twenties, perhaps, dressed in khaki pants and a dark blue blouse that she smoothed as she approached Principia. "I'm Maggie Dyson from the *Daily Democrat* here in town," she said, extending her hand.

Principia couldn't see it, so Charlotta leaned over and lifted her mother's hand into the hand of the reporter. "Hello," Principia said.

"What's going on here? I mean, why are you sitting here?" Maggie asked, her voice rising.

"We just got some business to conduct with Mr. Billie Rae, is all."

"Who are you people? What kind of business? Why are you sitting here?"

These were the questions of a young and inexperienced reporter, Grady thought, as he watched Maggie Dyson flip through the pages of her notebook until one devoid of chicken scrawling emerged from the stack.

"Well, now, that's just private business between me and Mr. Billie Rae," Principia answered, adjusting her umbrella. "We didn't come here to cause no trouble."

"What kind of trouble?" Maggie asked.

"No trouble," Principia answered.

"Is this some kind of protest?" Maggie leaned in. Her face lit up. "You're not Rosa Parks or anybody like that, are you?"

Charlotta leaned her head back and laughed.

"Just waitin' for Mr. Billie Rae, that's all," Principia replied. "Soon as he comes out and talks to us, we leave."

Frustration and confusion poured into Maggie Dyson's face. She finally cobbled together some thoughts and words. "Can I have your name?"

"Why you need my name? You don't need my name," Principia replied, not unkindly.

Grady stepped forward and leaned down to the old woman. "I'm going to go inside and see what I can do," he said. "Why don't y'all get in the car and head on back to the hotel?"

Principia twirled her umbrella. "I'll wait. I'm getting me a sun tan!"

The people in the first layer of the crowd who heard the remark began to laugh and turn around and repeat it. In this way it rippled backward and soon the entire mass was bouncing with laughter.

"I'm going with you," Maggie Dyson said, sidling next to Grady.

"I don't think so," he replied, taking a step away. Then he thought better of this uncharacteristic response and turned to her. "Listen, Miss Dyson,"

"Ms.," she corrected.

"This is a private matter between these folks here. It has no value to you or the readers of the *Daily Democrat*. Okay?" Grady waited until he knew the girl understood, and then turned again and walked into the hardware store.

Marcus Templeton greeted him halfway between the counter and the entrance. "What's going on out there?" he asked, pointing through the gold leaf lettering on the window.

"Where's Billie Rae?" Grady asked.

"You're his friend from a long time ago," Marcus said. "He told me about you."

Grady began to walk through the store, between the old player piano and the aisle of plumbing fixtures. "Is he in the back office?"

"You'll see."

Grady wended his way past the stacks of silver conduit and electrical boxes toward the singular wooden door, scarred with gouges that even fifty or more years of shellac could not improve. At one time this place was billed as the largest hardware store in western Mississippi. When he was a boy, the place was a grand and astonishing palace, with ceilings so high no man could reach them, and aisles strategically threaded through endless fields of nuts and bolts and tools and pipes, so long that eight-year-old legs could damned near get up to full speed before running into something. But now, even his old and jittery legs could make it across the full prairie in a matter of seconds, and he was standing at the door to old man Tolleston's office – a threshold he was forbidden to pass when he was a kid. He immediately experienced the odor of cigarette smoke, faint and thin, squeezing through the crack in the bottom of the door. He took the knob with one hand and knocked with the other.

"That you, Marcus?" Grady heard, as he swung the door inward.

Billie Rae Tolleston was seated at the ancient wooden desk that his daddy had once used, the roll top still varnished tight into the slot. Piles of papers seemed to be strewn, with no rhyme or reason, on every flat surface in the room. He was leaning back in a wooden chair, one foot up on the desk, but his face belied the casualness of his sprawl. The skin had been drained of color and moisture, carving even greater riverbeds into the already parched landscape. God in heaven, he had grown even older in only a few days, Grady thought.

Between two fingers rested a smoldering cigarette that Billie Rae tapped in a desultory fashion against a small beanbag ashtray on the desk. His face registered no emotion as Grady entered. He caught and held Grady with his eyes and took a long drag on the cigarette,

255

expelling two streams of smoke from his nostrils. "You know, I haven't had one of these in twelve years," he said, holding the cigarette at eye level and turning it between his thumb and forefinger. "Now my old buddy comes back into my life after a hundred years and leads me straight back to a world of sin."

"That's kind of a reversal of roles, now, isn't it?" Grady replied.

"I thought we were done talking," Billie Rae growled. "In fact, I'm certain I was."

Grady eased himself into the room. "I thought it was worth another shot; before it got out of hand," he said.

"You're a real sonofabitch, you know that?"

The crowd of curious onlookers was in constant flux, yet remained the same, like waves on the sea. It seemed that everybody in Arbutus was fulfilling a duty to come look at the old women perched in front of the hardware store, and, when they had seen enough, peel away only to be replaced by the next row as new bodies were added to the back.

"Looks like Lois Lane is bound and determined to get a story," Charlie said, nodding toward Maggie Dyson, who was speaking, with her arms folded, to a woman in the throng.

"Who's Lois Lane?" Starling asked.

"Her. That reporter," Charlie answered.

"I don't think that's her name."

Charlie laughed. "Well, it's not. I was just making a joke."

Star looked up at him with a quizzical look in her eyes. "I don't get it."

"Lois Lane, you know, a reporter."

"I don't know who that is."

"Superman's girlfriend," Charlie insisted.

"Oh."

"You don't know about Lois Lane?"

"Uh, no. I was never into comic books."

Charlie put his arm around her. "Don't worry, I'll talk you through," he chuckled.

"Starling, honey child, come over here," Cissy said, motioning to her granddaughter. The sun had come out now, full of vinegar, and the three old ladies on the lawn chairs were beginning to wilt, like flowers in a dry vase. Star kept holding Charlie's hand as she came forward.

"Yes, Gramma," she said, squatting in front of Cissy.

"Can you get us something to drink, some water or something?"

"Get me a beer, and not one of them light ones," Principia croaked. "I ain't had a beer in fifty years."

"I don't ever remember you having a beer," Charlotta said, leaning up and sideways in the chair.

A wrinkled face, deep in thought. "You might be right," Principia said.

Cissy grinned. "Soda or water, whatever they have." She reached down for her purse.

"I have money," Charlie insisted. "I'll get it for them."

"He has money, Gramma," Star said, touching her arm.

"He's a good one, comes from good stock," Cissy said, winking at Charlie. "Thank you, Charlie."

He smiled, "You're welcome." He lifted Star's hand and squeezed it before letting it go. "I'll be right back with the drinks. I need to get my camera out of my car, too."

Charlie circumnavigated the crowd and bounded up the curb and onto the sidewalk. The grocery was a few doors down and he jogged to the door. In a few minutes he was outside, six bottles of cold water dangling from the plastic holder in his hand. Evaporation from the heat caused trickles of water to run up his hand. He darted across the street to where the Mustang was parked and was at it in a few strides. He popped the trunk with his electronic fob and ducked in for his camera bag. He loaded a roll of film into the Nikon in the semi-darkness of the bag, threaded the camera strap over his shoulder and made his way back to the crowd. He immediately sensed that, in the few minutes that he was gone, the tone and timbre had dramatically changed, as if a storm cloud had rolled in full of bluster and threats.

An old man, huge and pink as bubble gum had muscled his way through the crowd and was standing in front of Cissy. He was rippling out of a sleeveless tee shirt, full of sweat and stains, and his stomach tumbled over gray cotton pants held up by suspenders. He said nothing, just looked Cissy over with two pinprick eyes buried deep in the folds of his bulbous cheeks. He swiped a straw cowboy hat off his head in a single motion, revealing a muskmelon scalp. In the same combination of motions, he pulled a flag-sized red bandana from his back pocket and ran it across his forehead. Then he waddled a few steps to his left and inspected Principia in much the same way. Silence rang from the crowd like a church bell.

Charlie got to Star as fast as he could. "What's happening?"

Starling grabbed his arm with both of hers. He could feel her trembling. "This man just bulled his way through the crowd. I thought he was going to . . ."

Then the big man spoke. He pointed to Cissy. "I know you," he said in a voice high and thin as thread. Then he turned to the crowd and spread his arms. "I know who she is!" he shouted, a wicked glee overtaking his face.

"The whole goddamned world is one fucking lunatic asylum, and the instant someone goes nuts, every camera in America is there to record it," Billie Rae Tolleston grumbled. He made an "O" with his mouth and puffed out three perfect smoke rings. "Look at that," he exclaimed. "It's like riding a bike, I guess. You never forget how."

"So that's why you shut yourself in here and refuse to deal with what's happening outside your store?" Grady asked.

"Some punk robbin' a gas station or whatnot deserves to get his head tuned up a little bit by the cops, right? But some asshole across the street points a camera at it and gives the video to the news stations, and all hell breaks loose. Suddenly the cops are the bad guys, and this prick, with some other guy's money in his fucking fist, is a victim." Billie Rae took another drag. "And people wonder why this country is going to hell. It's because we can't take care of business ourselves, like we used to." He held Grady's eyes in his own and raised his eyebrows. "If you know what I mean."

"This has nothing to do with that. No one wants to make you the bad guy here. Just let that poor old woman out there have her peace," Grady pleaded.

Billie Rae began to laugh, and the spasms caused him to spit out several bullets of smoke. "And it'll all go away? Is that what you think? You just gonna tell all those people to go home, and they're going to believe you? Gimme a break."

Grady scratched his ear, pulling on the lobe. "I don't really know what they're going to do, but the toothpaste is out of the tube now, isn't it?"

"I didn't squeeze it," Billie Rae snarled.

"Oh, yeah, we both did. Years ago."

"I already cleaned it up, least as far as I'm concerned."

Grady was exasperated, getting angrier by the second. "You know, Billie Rae, we're both old men now, and I would have thought you would have learned by this age that, sooner or later, it's not just about you. The whole world isn't about you. That sometimes, most of the time, other people and their feelings are more important than what you want or what makes you feel good."

Billie Rae started laughing, coughing, sputtering smoke out of his nose and mouth. His eyes welled up. "Oh, shit, that's good, Reverend Moonbeam," he said, catching his breath.

Grady backed away, feeling as he did that early morning many years ago when he and Billie Rae tussled in the street. He held himself back from grabbing his old friend and shaking the information out of him.

Billie Rae plowed forward. "Y'all found Jesus, and, hey, that's okay with me, I don't give a shit. But draggin' me out to a motherfucking crowd," he pounded his fist on the desk, "so that I can beat my chest and rend my garments, is something I ain't gonna do." He tapped a long ash off the end of the cigarette and into the ashtray. "You know, Grady, problem with you is you have no concept of betrayal, no idea in your head. Never did. You never understood that when you just up and disappeared from Arbutus without a breath of word to me, you left me standing alone with this in my heart; just tossed this pile of shit into my lap and washed your hands of it. And you goddamn well know that you were as responsible for what happened as any of us." He threw an ash off the cigarette. "As any of us."

Silence blew into the room, mingling with the smoke. Grady saw now, for the first time, the fissures in Billie Rae's spirit, filled with the same dirt as his own.

Billie Rae took another drag. "You never knew, you bastard, that you were my hero, and not just mine, but every kid in town. They – we – wanted to be you, wondered what it was like to be inside that body and be able to do the things you could do." He exhaled noisily and spit some shards from his tongue. "But I couldn't, and I knew it. But I could do the next best thing." He looked up with imploring eyes. "I could be your friend, your best friend. And then, poof, you was gone."

Grady sighed, "I didn't know . . ."

Billie Rae looked up with searing eyes. "I would have taken a bullet for you. Even tried to. Tried to go and join up in the army, but they wouldn't take me. I was 4F." He pointed a finger at his chest. "Bad heart, they said, them doctors." He took another swallow of smoke. "Those bastards are probably all long dead now and here I am, still ticking." He choked out a laugh.

The air had been taken out of Grady now. "Gol'dang," he whispered, shaking his head and looking at the floor. "You know, you're right." He turned and glanced out into the almost empty store. Marcus leaned on the counter at the far end, hands out front, eavesdropping on the conversation, transfixed.

Grady Hagen had come to believe, at this late stage of his life, that he instinctively and experientially understood his own nature, his few strengths, his myriad weaknesses. But Billie Rae Tolleston had taken Grady's consciousness to another place, a colder corner of his being that was virtually obscured by the clouds of ignorance. Of course he looked different to the people of Arbutus many, many years ago because he represented to them the unfathomable – a talent and charisma astonishingly unique to their small town; a gift from the gods that afforded him the luxury of choice. Grady Hagen, the king of Arbutus, could abdicate his throne and become king anywhere he wanted by sheer force of his ability and presence. He represented to the fifth and sixth generation shopkeepers and farmers and lumber yard owners whose great-granddaddies had fought in gray in the Civil War, a simple, yet profound and foreign concept that none of them, none, would ever realize. Freedom. Freedom from history and ancestry and the paralysis of spirit that swooped down on each new baby born here and ensured its permanence in this little southern town. Of course, Billie Rae – cocksure, swaggering, omniscient, opinionated, loud, occasionally obnoxious, wearing his cackling voice and his borderline insanity like a tailored suit – would feel like everyone else.

"Christ, Billie Rae," Grady stammered. "I'm sorry."

Billie Rae jumped slightly in his chair. "By God, that's all I needed to hear you say. Now everything's just fine and dandy." The sarcasm reverberated after the last word had faded.

"I never meant to . . ."

"Yeah, you said that before. Now go look out my window, see what your fucking guilty conscience done left me with. Just like you left me with that bag of bones all by myself. Just like you left me laying against the curb in the street without a single word of nothing."

"I'm sorry about all that, but what's going on out there could have been avoided."

Billie Rae slid his foot off the desk and leaned forward in his chair. "Bullshit! You've been up north so long, breathing that dirty air, that your mind has gone all scrambled. The minute you set foot in this town you put into motion things that are gonna ramify through every house and person in Arbutus." He took a quick and noisy hit off the diminishing butt of the cigarette. "What you don't seem to grasp is that it was all over. All over for sixty motherfucking years. People have changed, Grady, and we don't need that shit being stirred up."

Grady spoke quietly. "Just because you shove it back further and further into history doesn't mean it didn't happen or that our responsibility as human beings has been somehow forgiven, simply because of time."

"Our responsibility as human beings? Give me a break!"

Grady waited for several seconds, watching his friend's face wax and wane and scrunch and relax as he pondered something. "So, what are we going to do?" Grady asked.

Billie Rae looked up. "I ain't doing shit." He stubbed out the cigarette and coughed into his fist.

"What did you do with Rudy Montcrief?"

"I hanged him up for raping and beating a white woman which was what he deserved, and if you don't remember it, let me remind you that you was there, too," he answered through clenched teeth, pointing a finger at Grady.

"Just tell me and I'll leave, and so will they," Grady said, motioning with his head toward the front of the store.

"Fuck you." He slid open the desk drawer and removed a pack of Camels. Then he threw it back in and slammed the drawer.

"Please," Grady pleaded. "I'm asking you please."

Billie Rae leaned back in the chair, bending his head backwards and closing his eyes. "The last thing in the world I was going to do was to show up at that woman's house with a bag of her boy's bones and ashes."

"That's understandable."

He tilted his head upwards and looked at Grady. "I might have, if my friend would have come with me."

"I was a coward! A piece of shit coward! Is that what you want me to admit?" Grady cried, his arms out stretched. "I couldn't face it."

"I did face it, goddamnit," Billie Rae hissed. "And now I'm done. Your problem is your problem, not mine."

"So, what did you do with them?"

The head went back again and the eyes closed. Billie Rae held the position for a few beats. Then he leaned forward. "Get the hell out of here," he said, springing from his chair and pushing Grady through the threshold. Then Tolleston slammed the door. Grady felt the whoosh of wind as it closed. He stood there for several seconds.

"Heaven help you," he heard his old friend mutter from within the room.

The big man had swirled up like a sudden avalanche, rolling in front of the crowd, a revivalist preacher in full fury. He paced before the three women, stopped, leaned both hands on his knees and bent forward for a better look. He up righted himself and turned back to the crowd. "I know who they are!" he wheezed. "Question is, what are they doing here?" He looked over his shoulder at the hardware store. "Indeed, indeed."

"Where's my beer?" Principia shouted. A rumble of laughter from the crowd.

"This woman," the big man said, pointing at Cissy, "many years ago took up with the coloreds, forsaking her own white family in the eyes of God almighty!"

Cissy braced both arms on the chair and staggered to her feet.

Star dug her nails into Charlie's arm. "Charlie!"

Charlie Garrett stepped forward and inserted himself between the man and Cissy. "C'mon, sir, let's cool it," he said, a soft hand on the man's chest.

"Is that my boy, Charlie?" Principia said, sliding forward in her chair. "You got my beer?" Another ripple of laughter from the crowd.

Charlie pulled a bottle from the plastic holder and opened it for her, keeping his eyes on the old man as he slid toward Principia. He put the bottle in her hand, and she snatched it like a cat catching a mouse. She took a hard swallow.

"That's the sorriest excuse for beer I ever tasted!" she growled, followed by another swig.

The fat man rose up again, flourishing his red bandana. "Y'all want to hear the whole story, don't you?" he said. The crowd whooped and clapped.

Charlie distributed the other bottles to Charlotta and Cissy, and then moved to the old man. "I said that's enough, pops," he grimaced, grabbing the old man by the arm and turning him around.

"What you gonna do, Yankee boy, knock this old man on his cracker butt?" he sneered.

Charlie glared at him. "If that's what I have to do."

"Wait a minute." A voice coming over Charlie's right shoulder. He turned. Maggie Dyson was now inserted virtually between Charlie and the old man. "I want to hear your story, sir," she said. "What's your name?"

The fat man scrunched his face in a grin that left only a razor thin line of lips and a mass of wrinkles where the eyes would be. He was looking at Cissy. "Ask her," he said, revealing a brief flash of eye white that disappeared back into the folds of his skin.

Maggie Dyson turned to Cissy who was standing now. "Man's name is Parker Moody. Last time I saw him, he was twenty-three, twenty-four, years old. He's my daddy's baby brother. That makes him my uncle."

The young reporter's countenance changed, as if she suddenly discovered that the pencil in her hand had turned to a worm.

Cissy reached back and grabbed her chair, folding it. She walked the few steps to Moody and placed her face a few inches from his. "Yeah, he and I weren't but six years apart in age, and he liked that;

liked that a lot. He made sure he took a handful of whatever I had every time I walked by him. Didn't you Parker?"

"Crazy old woman," he snarled. "I wouldn't touch you . . ." He caught his words and then turned back to the crowd. "You wanna hear the sad, sad tale?" he shouted.

"You think I'm afraid of you or what you have to say?" she asked. "I've been to hell already, Parker, and I came out of it. There's nothing you can do or say that will give my heart a single extra beat."

Parker Moody seemed to deflate, reflexively taking a step backward. Maggie Dyson wedged into the gap. "Mr. Moody, can you tell me what this is all about?"

The crowd began to buzz like a high tension tower, sliding forward, drawn by the incendiary potential of the incident. The movement created a circle now that barely contained the primary players in the drama.

"What's going on here?" Grady Hagen shouted, pushing his way forward. When he got to the center he didn't hesitate. "Come on, time to go," he said, taking the folded chair from Cissy's hand.

"You get what you were looking for?" Charlotta asked, rising.

Grady said nothing.

"Good!" Principia intuited. "Let's go."

Parker Moody opened both arms. "Wait, don't you want to stay and make sure I get the story right?"

Charlie clasped his large hand on the old man's forearm and squeezed, buckling Moody at the knees. "Why don't you just go home and shut the fuck up," he hissed into a tiny pink ear.

"Hey, leave him alone," a man shouted from the crowd, eliciting a palpitation of assent and causing the crowd to surge more precipitously forward.

A loud whoop-whoop-whoop fractured the rumble and rattle of tension, and the crowd fell away, as a police car nudged forward. It stopped. The driver's side door immediately opened and Chief Mitchell got out, nightstick hanging from his belt and clacking on his hip. "Get back," he said, motioning people aside to give him a swath much wider than he needed. "Y'all go on home. Get back to work."

Grady took a deep breath.

"What the heck's the problem here?" Mitchell said, arriving at the center now. He caught Grady's glance and frowned. He turned to Moody. "Parker, what you all worked up about? You're so red, looks like your head's about to explode." He cupped the old man on the shoulder and turned him around. "Git, now. You git back to your checkers game. Percy Hall wants to win his money back." Moody threw a look to Cissy that said this ain't over yet, turned and pushed through the thinning crowd. He mockingly waved his red bandanna over his shoulder as he departed.

"Ms. Dyson, how are you today?" Mitchell said, nodding at the reporter. "You get all you need here?"

"No, Chief, I did not," came the reply.

Mitchell sighed and looked up at Grady. "Mr. Hagen, I thought you said you were leaving town."

"As soon as I finished my business," Grady answered, throwing his head back.

"Thought we had an understanding."

"We did, Chief. But what you understood and what I understood were obviously different."

"I see," Mitchell said, his face frosting over.

"You the policeman?" Principia croaked, waving her near empty bottle of water in his direction and dispersing drops of condensation across her lilac dress.

Mitchell nodded. "Yes, ma'am."

"Hope you're better than the one I knew from here," she said. Then she wiped her hand across her dress to dry it and thrust it forward in the Chief's direction. "My name is Mizz Principia Montcrief," she said.

Mitchell released an audible sigh and glared at Grady. He reached down and took the woman's hand. "Ma'am, it is an honor to meet you."

"So, you heard of me?" Principia asked.

"Indeed I have," Mitchell replied.

"And you're going to help us?" the old lady asked.

"As much as I can."

"Good! Then go inside and whup Billie Rae Tolleston upside the head with your nightstick."

Mitchell laughed. "I'm not sure that will have any affect on that hard of a head." He moved his eyes, catching Charlie in his gaze. "You still driving?"

"Yes, sir," Charlie replied.

"How about you take these ladies somewhere cool?"

"Amen," Principia replied, folding her umbrella. "Somebody go give this back to that nice Mr. Marcus in the hardware store."

Chief Mitchell squinted as he addressed Grady. "Why don't you and I go to my office, have a little chat?"

As Charlie wheeled her to the Mustang, Principia Montcrief listed sideways, as if all the air and life had been sucked out of her. Her right arm was thrown like a doll's raggedy appendage over the armrest. Starling held her tiny hand. "You okay, Great Gram-mama" she whispered.

"I'm so tired, baby. So tired."

As he drove away, Charlie noticed that while the crowd had thinned, stringing through the town now, several people clustered in a corner. The center of their attention was Parker Moody, whose hands flapped like the wings of a huge eagle as he spoke with Maggie Dyson.

Grady Hagen was alone now, awaiting Chief Mitchell in the tiny interview room he had occupied only a few days before. Was that even possible? That he had been here so recently, when the short time that had passed seemed to have happened years ago or perhaps not even at all, but rather were the embellished memory of some strange dream?

"Got myself a handful of tiger," he said to the shower of white light that poured in through the milky window. He thought he heard Rachel's voice.

"It can't hurt you," she said.

"You say something?" Chief Mitchell said, opening the door and sliding a can of Coke across the table to him. A stream of water bubbled in its wake.

"Uh, just talking to myself," Grady answered, snatching the can.

Mitchell flipped a chair around and sat down, leaning his elbows on the back. "I bet you don't have to guess that I am not a very happy camper right now."

"I suppose not," Grady said, pulling the tab on the can.

266

"Looks like you had a pretty successful little trip."

"Not what I thought it would be."

"With what I saw going on out there, it's shaping up exactly like I thought it would," Mitchell groused. "And that's precisely what I was trying to avoid."

Grady rolled the cold can in his hand. "Some things can't be avoided." He glanced up at the policeman. "And some things shouldn't be avoided."

"Which category does this fit into?"

"Both."

Mitchell rustled in the chair and looked out the window. "I suppose that's true. Anyway, it's too late now." He paused, then turned back to Grady. "So, why don't you fill me in on exactly what's going on out there."

Grady provided a quick overview of his last several days, ending with his conversation with Billie Rae.

"I suppose I could go talk to him," Mitchell sighed.

"I'm not optimistic," Grady replied. "That old coot isn't afraid of anything. Never was. I suppose torture is out of the question."

Chief Mitchell didn't smile, just ground his teeth and squeezed his lips together. "Aw, cripes," he exhaled. "What now?"

43

He sat in a shawl of melancholy dusk on the front step of the old farmhouse and waited, his head cradled in his hands. What next? It was a good question posited by the Chief, and Grady had no answer for it. Truman rocked behind him, sipping from a mason jar and exhaling a guttural shudder, followed by a boisterous "hoo-we" after every swallow. Grady had to continually talk himself out of his cousin's offer of the toxic homemade spirits. On one hand, it would blunt the crackling tension that raged through him. On the other, he would probably croak in a fit of foam and agony after one sip, like Goering at Nuremburg. Still, the offer was tempting.

"Nice night," Truman said. "Cooler than usual." Then he took a swig. "Hrumph, urgle, hoo-we."

Starling sat on the hood of the Mustang, draped on Charlie who leaned against the door. They were looking at pictures. Charlie had taken a dozen rolls of film into a camera shop on Jefferson, and the proprietor assured him he could develop everything perfectly. "Kodak, pure Kodak," the old timer had said, leaning on an antique eight-by-ten box camera with a fraying hood. From what Grady had seen, the shots had come out splendidly.

"That's my Great Gram-mama!" Starling squealed. "My God, she looks like, like. . ."

"She looks like an angel," Charlie interjected. "That's why I shot it that way. See how the sun halos around her?"

"Wow, these are really nice," Star whispered. She grabbed Charlie by the chin and turned his head to hers. She kissed him. "You are a very, very talented photographer."

"Thanks," he mumbled.

Starling shuffled through several more shots. "And who is this? Is this Lorene?" She pulled out the last word.

Charlie took the snapshot and tilted it. "No, no." He pulled off the Mustang and walked to Grady. "Pap, remember this girl in the gas station?"

Grady took the picture. "Tiffany," he said. How did he remember her name?

"Ooooo, Tiffany," Starling cooed, rolling her eyes.

Charlie stammered. "Look, look at this other shot of her. This is what I was trying to get." He leafed through several similar shots and handed one to her. She took it and he pointed across the surface. "See, in this one, the light coming in from the side? She's the same height and color of these pumps in the foreground. It's a distorted perspective, but because of the light, she looks like a human gas pump, as if she's been, I don't know, almost absorbed into the whole environment, captured by it, as if it was a prison or something."

"Wow," Starling said. "You knew it would come out like this?"

"I hoped it would. I hoped I could hold focus with the change in light."

"It's amazing."

"I want to scan it at home and then strip out all the color. I think in black and white it would be really something."

Starling nuzzled him. "You're really something. You know that?"

He pulled her close. "For the first time in my life, I feel like it."

Grady saw it through the trees. A ball of yellow dust, moving up the long driveway. It was a vehicle of some sort, lunging forward, spilling a soft cloud behind it. The Chief? Maybe he had throttled something out of Billie Rae.

No.

A pick-up truck. Dark blue, almost black. Grady braced himself with both hands against the wooden step and stood up.

"Somebody comin'," Truman growled. "Nobody never comes here." Then he took another pull. "Hrumph, urgle, hoo-we."

Letters on the side of the truck. I'll be gol'darned, Grady thought. Tolleston's Hardware. Damn, was it Billie Rae? Does he have a conscience after all? Grady was moving toward the truck as it circled in front of the barn rubble. Charlie and Star had detached themselves from each other and the Mustang. Even Truman wobbled down the porch step, his oxygen canister clattering behind.

The truck stuttered to a stop, and it took time for the froth of dust to settle, but Grady could see through it. The driver wasn't Billie Rae at all. Just by the way he was sitting, Grady could tell it wasn't his old friend. Then who the heck was it?

The door moaned as it opened, and closed with a thunk. Marcus, the man from the store, slid around the hood and came forward. He was wearing a Tolleston Hardware cap. He took it off as he moved forward. "Evening," he said, bowing slightly. "Name is Marcus Templeton. I don't think we formally met." He moved smoothly to Grady and extended his hand.

"Hello, I'm Graden Hagen." He took the man's hand and felt the firm grip. They stood in silence, hands interlocked for several seconds. Grady came back first. "Uh, I'm sorry," he said, releasing the man's hand. "This is my cousin Truman, my grandson Charlie, and his, uh, friend Starling."

"Nice to meet y'all," Marcus said, bowing slightly again, kneading the cap with both hands. His eyes locked on Starling's and you could almost hear them connect on some subliminal, surrealistic level. Something in the blood. Had to be.

Silence came down again. Truman broke it. "Y'all come on up to the porch, Mr. Marcus. We'll git y'all a nice chair." Truman turned and moved back toward the sagging porch, dragging his canister across the grass. He motioned to Charlie to go in front of him and pointed at the door. "Charlie, go get Mr. Marcus here a chair."

"Sure," Charlie bounded up the stairs in two long strides.

"May I offer you a libation?" Truman said, raising his jar. "My own cousin won't imbibe with me."

"Now, Mr. Truman, I'm a good God-fearing Baptist boy," Marcus replied. "Wouldn't want to get caught with the devil's brew." He flashed a conspiratorial grin.

"God ain't been out to this place in a coon's age," Truman answered. "Meanin' raccoon, of course, no offense intended."

"As long as God ain't looking, sure. I think I'm going to need it."

In a few minutes the entire group was assembled on the front porch in various stages of relaxation. Grady sat on what was left of the railing. Star and Charlie sprawled on the steps. Truman had handed Marcus a drink, in a fancier glass with red and yellow flowers on it, and the visitor sat down on the wooden chair Charlie had brought from the dining room. Grady watched as Marcus lifted the glass to his lips and took a sip. The man barely winced. Grady had expected him to instantly internally combust.

Good Baptist tea-totaller my ass, Grady thought.

"I appreciate it," Marcus replied, taking another sip. He looked at Grady. "I wasn't too sure whether to come out here or not and talk to y'all. For one thing, I'm not too sure that what I know is going to do you any good at all. Which makes the second thing even worse. If Mr. Tolleston finds out I'm here, I'm in a heap of trouble."

"He never has to know," Grady said.

Marcus raised an eyebrow. "Y'all don't know Mr. T. too well, then. He knows whose cat dies and when."

"He hasn't changed a bit," Grady sighed. Then he looked up at the man. "What do you know?"

Marcus cleared his throat. "I'm pretty good at putting things together, mechanical things, mostly. But when it comes to people, it takes me a while," he began. "Today when y'all was out front of the store and them two nice black old ladies and the white one, too, was there in the hot sun, I didn't know what you was up to. Didn't know such a ruckus would be agitated up." He took another sip. He coughed slightly. "Never gave no mind to what it might be, neither. Just thought it was maybe somebody didn't like the lawn mower or bathroom fixture they bought from old Mr. Tolleston. Maybe it was broke or something. So, I thought that if I brung out some umbrellas and showed we was pretty good people, maybe everybody would simmer down and when Mr. Tolleston come, everything would be all right."

"You had no way of knowing why we were there. It's understandable," Grady replied.

Marcus continued. "Like I said, it took me a while to put two and two together. Wasn't till I heard you arguing with Mr. T and then seeing Parker Moody carrying on like a fool that it all come to me in a blinding flash, and I knew you was there about something terrible. And then he said your name, Mr. T did, and," he pointed to his temple with a finger, "it all come together right here."

"You figured out why we were there?" Grady asked.

Truman rocked more frantically now.

"Never would've dreamed it was what it was," Marcus answered. He took another sip of the moonshine and then gazed out across the field. "Something so awful, so long ago."

"You from these parts, Mr. Templeton?" Grady asked.

The man raised hand. "Please, call me Marcus. My daddy is the only mister in our family."

"Sure, Marcus. Did you know the story? I mean, why we were out there?"

His eyes drifted away from them, turning inward, it seemed. Then he closed them and spoke. "Sure," he sighed, shaking his head. "Everybody knows the story, especially the black citizens. We don't talk about it too much. Maybe 'cause it was so long ago. Heck and shoot, I wasn't even born until twenty years after that, so it didn't take place in my reality. But like everybody else, I seen the pictures, and it was still being whispered about among the African-American folks. But every now and then you could hear a white folk talking about it, too." He set the glass down on the floorboard next to his chair. Then he leaned forward and folded his hands. "That's why I come out here tonight."

"Go ahead," Grady said, shifting his weight.

"Like I said, probably get me fired, and maybe for no good reason," Marcus replied, reaching up and squeezing his temples. "But you know, comes a time in a man's life, he has to choose between what is right and what is easy. Well, I can tell you, this ain't easy." He released his head and locked stares again with Starling. "But it's right."

"You know something that can help us, don't you?" Grady said.

Templeton pursed his lips, blew out and immediately inhaled. "I ain't sure. I do know something, and maybe it will make sense to you. Maybe not, too. I don't likely know for sure. But first, I got to see if my arithmetic is right or not. Y'all come down here from wherever to find the body of Rudy Montcrief and give him the proper Christian burial. Am I right about that?"

"Yes," came the reply from four mouths at the same time.

Marcus nodded and took a deep breath, steeling himself. Then he began. "Like I said, people talk now and again. Especially when they drink this kind of stuff," he reached and picked up the glass. "Don't know loud from soft anymore when this gets into your head." He took a sip. "Helps the tongue, though," he mused, finishing his swallow. "Anyway, I'm delivering sheet rock out to the O'Malley farm where they was doing some remodeling. Then I was to take the truck to Mr. T's house 'cause he needed to use it for something or other, don't matter what. I get there and there's a few cars lined up against the curb in front of Mr. T's house. I pull up and park behind a big old fancy black sedan part ways down the block. I got the keys in my hand and am walking up the sidewalk. 'Bout four or five of them are in the living room. Parker Moody was there, along with Clyde Peach and Freddy Dobis, somebody else, too, but I don't recollect who. They was playing cards, but talking and laughing and going at it the way men do. All the windows was open to the screens, it being a nice warm night and all. You could tell by the way the words was flying around the room, the boys were feeling no pain, if you know what I mean." He raised the glass and toasted Truman.

"We've all been there," Grady said.

"Amen," replied Marcus. "But what stopped me was when the noise, all of a sudden, come drifting down, like a feather." He flattened the palm of his free hand and fluttered it downward. "Mr. Tolleston was saying something."

"What?" Starling gasped, leaning forward.

"About it," Marcus softly replied.

"About what?" she said.

"That hangin' that took place."

"What did he say?" Grady asked.

"Lord have mercy," Marcus sighed, raising the glass to his lips, then shaking his head and setting it back down. "One of the men, don't recollect which one, says, 'You ain't never said what you done with that nigger.' And Mr. T said, 'There wasn't much left but mud and bones.'

Then he says, 'Can you believe that fat bastard LaGrone tells me and Parker to take the mess back to his momma? Well, I can tell you for sure, I wasn't about to walk up to no Negro homestead with a bag of shit and hand it to some woman and say, here's your boy.'"

"Sounds like Billie Rae, all right," Truman grunted, rocking.

"Did he say what he did with him?" Grady asked, his heart racing.

"I'm getting there. Old Mr. T, he just opened one eye wider than the other and said he decided to put 'em where no one would ever find them – the bones and whatnot. Then Parker Moody says, why the hell don't you just tell them? And Tolleston says shut the f – well, you know – up, Parker and start dealing."

"Then what?" Grady asked.

"Well, Parker shuffled the cards and began to deal and says something like, who gives a poop after so many years, and Mr. T says shut the f up and deal." Marcus picked up the glass and swirled the liquid, then took a small sip. He turned to Starling. "Sorry about the crude language, miss, but that's what they were saying."

Star smiled and patted the top of the man's shoe which was close to her hand as she sat on the step. "That's okay. Keep going."

Marcus cleared his throat once more. "This went back and forth a few times. Then Moody fans out his cards and says something like what the hell difference does it make anymore, anyway." He swirled the glass several more times.

"What did Billie Rae do?" Grady said.

"He wasn't none too happy. He slammed his cards on the table and screamed at old Parker that they had taken a blood oath and all." Marcus set the glass down once again without drinking. "Then he said, 'If I'da took Grady Hagen with me instead of you, you wouldn't even know about the place, and I wouldn't have to shut your trap with the back of my hand.'" Marcus looked up at Grady and nudged his head forward. "Does that make any sense to y'all, Mr. Grady?"

Grady could hear the rumble of comprehension on a distant horizon in his brain, knew that he knew what Billie Rae had been talking about. He raked through the fragmented sands of his consciousness trying to figure it out. "Somewhere in there," he whispered to himself.

Marcus continued. "Then Mr. T. says maybe he shoulda just took care of it himself, but it wasn't easy, you know, dragging the bag 'cross that creek in the dark. Fucking things weren't light." He caught himself and turned to Starling. "I'm sorry, Miss Starling, it's the moonshine. I couldn't stop the word from coming out."

Boom! An explosion in Grady's mind. "Of course!" He flew off the banister. "Of course! My God! I was an idiot! So obvious, so damned obvious!"

"What, Pap?" Charlie asked, standing up and taking his grandfather by the arm.

"I have to call the Chief."

"You know what Marcus is talking about?" Charlie asked.

"Glad somebody does," Truman interjected.

"Me, too," Marcus answered.

44

The chain saw whirred, spitting clouds of wood onto the operator, and the particles clung to the sweat on the arms and face of the man like shards of metal on a magnet. The obstacle to be removed was a scrub oak, now almost a foot in diameter, with a frantic explosion of branches that had become tangled in the other vines and weeds and bristles that had grown over what Grady was finally certain was the entrance to the cave. The trek in had taken longer than he anticipated, so turned around was he by the evolution of the forest. Entire geological masses, it seemed, had shifted, bending the stream farther south than he had recalled it being. The teeth of decay had chewed away the tree he had once used to bridge the water, turning its pulp, he was certain, into silt for the bottom of the stream. He spent the first hour in the woods lost, though he wouldn't admit it to anyone in the crew. Thankfully, Chief Mitchell was prescient enough to bring along two deputies and two volunteers with various combinations of power and hand tools. Charlie was there, too, camera around his neck. And when, after foraging this way and that into frenzies of anarchic vegetation that sliced his hands and arms, through sizzling heat that had soaked his shirt to a laundry degree of wetness, he literally stepped on the round blue "bald man" stone. It, too, like everything else in his memory, had shrunk. The surface protruding from the grass was now the size of a basketball, although, in this case, the incessant gnawing of the earth had probably more to do with its shrinkage than Grady's memory. So, Grady put a foot on the stone and pointed at what had to be the entrance to the cave. Then the work began.

The air was vibrating with the hysterical screaming of the chain saw, and then Grady saw the scrub move to its left and collapse gracefully to the earth. The operator shut down the saw, and the silence that ensued fell as softly as snow. He turned to Chief Caleb and raised his goggles. His grimy face was seasoned with tiny speckles of wood, except where the goggles had been. "It sure don't look like there's nothing behind here to me," he said.

Grady strode forward and reached into the tangle with both hands, pulling limbs and handfuls of plants that had become woven together with vines and stickers. "It's here, it's here, I know it is," he cried. He slid his hand behind an angular rock, and with a grunt and all the strength he could muster, he shook it back and forth. "Here, let me help you with that," Charlie said, squatting next to him and grabbing an edge.

This wasn't here before. Somebody put it here to hide the entrance.

The old man and the boy rocked the stone, back and forth, like a craggy tooth in a socket.

Billie Rae, most likely. Maybe that very night. Maybe later. Who knew? He had closed the cave for good, that much was obvious.

The stone was rocking freely now, and Grady could feel its resistance ebbing. But he still hadn't braced for the moment when it released its grip, and the sudden loss of resistance sent him straight onto his ass sliding down the embankment. He stopped in a pile against another thorny hedge, but from his seated position, he could see the entrance, a gaping hole yawning darkness.

"Oh, God, oh no. You okay, Pappy?" Charlie asked, scurrying down the hill.

Grady patted himself, looking for parts that may have come dislodged. "I'm fine, boy. But look, lookee there. I told you it was there!"

"I'll be dipped," the chain saw man said. "There is a cave here! How come nobody ever knew about it?"

"It was a secret," Grady explained as Charlie helped him to his feet. He staggered up the hill, brushing mud and the gristle of vegetation from his clothes.

Caleb Mitchell reached out and grasped the old man's hand, pulling him close to the entrance. "Let's go in," he said, nodding toward the opening.

Grady steadied himself. "Can I go first?"

Mitchell stepped aside and gestured him past. "Be my guest."

First thing was the smell. Why was it always the smell? Musty and damp and cool and forceful enough to turn him back into a little boy who stood in this darkness for the first time, with his old friend, and realized they had found a treasure. The insistent darkness that filled the space from floor to ceiling embraced him, swallowed him up in a single bite. It took a while for the void to filter through Grady's eyes where it morphed into a grayness and then into shape and form from which detail emerged. The cave, and all the emotions and memories it clasped in its walls, became clear.

Lord. Where all the rest of Arbutus had shifted and painted itself and evolved, this place, this secret domain, had remained the same. A ring of stones sat like a bulls eye in the center of the room, framing a pile of cold ash that somehow had not been claimed by the hard floor. The blankets that he and Billie Rae kept here for camping had been rendered into strips of disintegrating rags, held together by random strands of feeble thread. The walls still bled moisture in a thin film.

"Damnation, look at this place!" Charlie gasped, his head swiveling. "You knew about this when you were a boy?" The cave was now filling with large men and tools.

"Yeah."

Charlie exhaled a loud, "Wow." Then he moved farther in and ran his hands over the walls. "How cool it must have been to have a place like this."

Grady heard a click and saw a sheath of blue light cut into the walls of the cavern, giving it even more shape and texture. The other workers followed suit, firing up their flashlights and swinging them in random directions, where they crisscrossed like sword blades.

Caleb Mitchell sidled up to Grady. "Well, so far you're right," he said.

"At least it's a lot cooler in here," the chainsaw man said.

Grady walked across the room to the hole. "In here," he pointed.

One of the workers knelt down and shined his flashlight into the hole, craning and twisting his head to get a view. "Can't see much," he grumbled. He withdrew his head. "Any idea how deep it is?"

"We used to toss rocks down there and listen to them hit bottom. I'd guess eight or ten feet," Grady answered.

"Who's got the gaffing hook?" Caleb Mitchell asked.

"Right here, boss," a deputy said, dropping a coil of rope off his shoulder and unwinding it to reveal a black metal hook.

"Lucky for us old Jesse's pap used to run deep sea fishing boats out of Biloxi," one of the other deputies said. "Them there gaffing hooks ain't just hanging around anyone's garage."

"Will it fit?" Mitchell said. The deputy knelt down and slid the hook into the crevice. "Slide it in slowly and let's see how deep it drops. Soon as it hits, stop the rope," Mitchell ordered.

The drop proved to be almost fifteen feet, and, like blind fishermen in the night, the volunteers who had followed Grady Hagen through snarling woods began the arduous task of dropping and dragging the hook, relying on sheer luck that it might snag a corner of burlap. Only one man could work at a time, and the others leaned against the wall and smoked.

"You sure those bones didn't just get dumped down there?" Mitchell said, his stomach flat against the stone as he swept the floor with the hook.

"I don't know," Grady sighed, holding his head in both hands.

The activity went on for some time. Then Mitchell turned rigid. "Wait, shit!" he cried, shifting his body.

The workers all stood in unison and leaned in. "What?" came from them over and over.

"I think I got a . . ." Mitchell shifted again, fumbling with his foot to find a place to brace it. When he had a solid grip, he reached around and grabbed the rope with two hands. "C'mon, baby."

The cluster of men was as tight as fist now. The only sound was their rhythmic breathing, hard and harsh in the silence. Except for . . .

. . . except for a scraping sound, faint and distant and below them – something swooshing against stone.

Mitchell turned away from the hole and tossed some rope behind him. "Heavier than I thought it would be," he said, pulling now with both hands. "Don't fall off the hook, damn it." For a full minute he cajoled the catch upward. Grady and the others began reaching forward, trying to help. "Careful, guys, I don't have much room to work with," Mitchell said.

And then it peered over the lip of the hole, firmly skewered by the hook. The tattered corner of a burlap sack. Charlie reached out and grabbed a fistful of bag from beneath the hook and pulled. "Damned thing *is* heavy," he said. Several other hands reached in, and the bag swung out, groaning with its contents that rounded the bottom. Four different men had hold of it now, and they gently set it down in the middle of the floor.

Chief Caleb Mitchell leaned against the stone wall, a coiled cobra of rope at his feet. His chest heaved, and sweat seeped through his uniform. "Be respectful, men," he whispered.

The workers stood around the sack now, which glowed gray in the trapezoidal beams of the flashlights. "We gonna open it?" one of the men asked.

Mitchell pushed himself to his feet and slid over to the bag. Kneeling down, he fiddled for several minutes with the knot at the top, an indistinguishable tangle of merged and coalesced fabric. One of the men reached and withdrew a knife from his belt, flicked it open, and handed it to the policeman. The viciously sharp blade moved through the old fabric like a needle. Mitchell handed the knife back and pulled the hole open a bit further. One of the deputies moved closer with his flashlight and shined it into the bag. Grady was at Mitchell's shoulder, kneeling now, peering in.

At first the contents appeared formless, a pile of dust and dirt, like the insides of a vacuum cleaner bag. Blue and gray and odorless. Mitchell reached in with a finger and pushed some of the debris aside, grasping something delicately and dislodging it. He pulled it out and held it into the light.

It was the lower jawbone of a man, teeth still in place like tombstones.

Recognition seeped slowly, like a mist, into the men, and one by one they removed their hats. Silence as complete and awesome as any Grady had ever heard filled the cavern. Even breathing seemed to stop, as everyone stood motionless. Charlie placed a soft hand on his grandfather's shoulder. Then the chain saw operator knelt onto the hard floor and kneaded his cap as he intoned, "Our Father, who art in heaven . . ."

Ninety minutes later Grady traversed a long beige hallway that smelled of new paint and carpet toward the door of Charlotta and Principia's room. His legs protested every step, and Charlie steadied him as he trudged forward.

"Why don't I check us in, and you get cleaned up before seeing them?" Charlie asked. "I can get the luggage out of the trunk." Grady's shirt was sopped entirely through and clung to his thin body, adhering to the contours of his rib cage. Mud and sawdust peppered his arms, and his hair was a nest of tangled twigs and grass. Tiny cockleburs clung to his pants. Charlie hadn't fared much better. His tee shirt and shorts were gory with mud and sweat, and his face was streaked with black dirt except around his eyes which had been partially protected by his sunglasses and which now were framed in two white circles.

"I'm afraid I won't hold up, boy," Grady explained. "It's been one sumbitch of a day."

They had emerged from the cave into a descending dusk that had begun to fill the cracks and crevices of the woods like syrup, meandering between the trees and settling on the ground. Charlie and three of the volunteers carried a blanket pulled tight as wood upon which rested the burlap bag. Someone, Grady didn't notice who, had picked a wild flower and placed it on the sack, setting a stone on the end of the stem so that it would not blow off. Not a word was spoken as the procession moved through the rapidly darkening topography. Two of the volunteers led the way, their flashlights plowing a road of light.

Grady Hagen had to push himself to keep up with these younger, stronger men, holding onto branches and leveraging tree trunks to urge his frail body forward. He would not, gol'dangit, relent to the screaming weariness of his bones and allow them to sit down, not even for a minute. He was a soldier. He was a man.

Like a glutton at a gourmet feast, Grady Hagen had tasted every conceivable emotion in the last week and stuffed his stomach with each one until there was no room for more. But now, as the hallway air conditioner blew a cool artificial wind onto his skin, he had no idea what feelings were pulsing through his being. In one sense, the discovery and recovery of Rudy Montcrief's remains would fulfill the belief and dream and faith that had sustained Principia for most of her life and bring closure to the rest of the family. On the other hand, a palpable sadness also intruded on his thoughts.

"We're here, Pappy, this is the room," Charlie said. "Do you know what you're going to say?"

Grady smiled. "Boy, you should have figured out by now, I have no idea what I'm ever going to say until after I say it." He knocked on the door. "Problem is, it's often too late, then."

The door swung open, throwing yellow light into the hall and silhouetting a shape that caused Grady to flinch. Wrong room? He wondered as his eyes focused. Standing before him was a tall man wearing a bright white shirt with a loosened tie and open collar. From behind the man came voices, familiar. And yet . . .

"Who are you?" Grady blurted.

"Who are you?" the man retorted, leaning on the partially opened door.

"Grady, Grady, is that you?" Cissy's voice, hurrying forward. Then her arm reached around the man and she grasped Grady's arm with both hands and pulled him into the room. "Oh Lord, oh my Lord, where have you been?" she cried. "Get in here and tell me everything!" The man at the door flattened himself against it to avoid contact with the filthy assembly of rags that swept in.

"My God, look at you," Cissy said, pulling a long piece of grass from under his collar. Then she wiped his face with her thumbs. "Starling, honey, get me a washcloth, cold water." Cissy looked up at Charlie, "And look at you, Charlie! You boys look like you have been through a sewer!"

Grady caught a glimpse of himself in the mirror behind Cissy. He did resemble an underfed outhouse rat. He also saw Starling blow a quick and tiny kiss to his grandson.

Cissy took his arm and eased him to the vinyl chair next to the reading lamp. "Sit, sit, please, you're exhausted." Starling handed her a washcloth and she caressed his cheeks with it. The cool water revived him, and he let her indulge him for several seconds. "Where have you been? Where did you go?" she whispered.

Grady reached up and let his fingers brush against her hand. "Shhhh, it's a secret, sealed in blood."

She stopped her wiping motion. "Oh, my God," she sighed. "Is it what, where, I'm thinking?"

Grady nodded.

"Holy God in heaven. I don't believe I could even find . . ." Cissy said. "You wander far from home, but when you come back, you come all the way back. Don't you?" she said, wiping his eyes carefully one more time and pulling the cloth from his skin. She nudged him by the shoulders to face the tall man who had closed the door, and was fully back in the room and sitting on the foot of the bed. "Grady Hagen, this is my son. This is John Moody."

"So, you're the old friend of Mother's who has gotten us into this mess," he said. Then a brilliant and welcoming smile overtook his face and he extended his hand. "I'm very, very pleased to meet you." He turned his head and faced Charlie, who was now standing next to Starling, who rested a single finger in his dangling hand. "And this is the famous Charlie, who Starling can't stop telling me about."

"Daddy!" she cried, rolling her eyes.

The two men shook hands.

At that moment a tall, dark woman entered the room from the doorway that separated one room from another. "Grandma-ma is snoring like a . . ." she stopped when she saw the two dirty and ragged men. "What have we here?" she asked.

"Gentlemen, this is my wife, Yvonne," John Moody said. "Darling, this is Graden Hagen."

Grady stood up and offered a hand. "I am pleased to meet you," he said.

Yvonne raised an eyebrow as she glanced at his hand with a look that said, you don't want me to touch that do you?

Grady caught the gist, took the washcloth from Cissy and cleaned his hand, running the cotton ends between his fingers. Then he offered the hand again.

Yvonne smiled and grasped it firmly. "Mr. Hagen," she said.

"Grady," he insisted.

"And this is Charlie," John said, motioning toward the young man.

Yvonne let go of Grady's hand and took Charlie's. Eyeing the torn and wet shirt and filth on his face, she turned to Starling and mused, "He's not exactly what I expected."

"Mommy!" Star answered, rolling her eyes again.

"So, Grady, I guess you have some news for us," John Moody said.

Grady took him in. His skin was, frankly, no darker than Grady's own, but he was clearly of color nonetheless. The thought flashed in Grady's consciousness that sixty years ago – hell, maybe still today – he would be relegated to an entirely different status simply because, despite his almost Caucasian coloring, there was something about him that was unmistakably black, even if that word was an entirely inappropriate description of anything about him. Certainly there were features. His graying hair was tight and short. His eyes were widely set. But that wasn't it. It was less his looks and more an aura, perhaps. At the same time, however, the image of Cissy was all over him. Her angular, younger face. Those same violet eyes. He was leaning back, his arms folded, but he comported himself with a palpable dignity that clearly indicated that he was a man of substance. A man to be heard.

"Yes, well," Grady answered. Then he realized that someone was missing. "Where are Charlotta, Principia?"

Cissy motioned with her head to the partially opened door next to the dresser. "Sleeping. Principia goes out like a light at eight o'clock and wouldn't move till morning if you set her bed on fire. Charlotta was so upset with everything that happened today, she slugged down two shots of Jack Daniels and crashed. Maybe I should wake her, though. What happened out there?" She clutched his hand in both of hers. "No, don't tell me. I can't take it."

"It's okay," Grady answered, squeezing back. "Rudy's free, and he's coming home."

45

"Last time I rode in a Mercedes, I was hammered drunk on schnapps," Grady said as John Moody maneuvered his huge silver S55 AMG down a two-lane highway outside of Arbutus. "It wasn't anything like this, though," he said, running his hand across the leather dashboard. "Nothing like this."

"Only two good reasons to get a car like this," John replied, keeping his eyes focused on the road. "One, 'cause it doesn't give you any trouble. Busy as I am, I don't need a car in the shop for some piddly-assed problem."

"And the second reason?"

"Because you can afford it!" he roared, slapping the steering wheel.

"Damned good logic," Grady replied, turning the baffles so that the cool air hit him more directly.

They were returning to Arbutus after visiting Cole Brothers Funeral Home some thirty miles away where Grady insisted on purchasing an exquisite rosewood casket to hold the remains of Rudy Montcrief. John had agreed to the expensive gesture on the critical condition that the coffin be transported on a decaying and ruined sharecropper's wagon he saw leaning against a barn a few blocks from the funeral home. He bought the wagon from the stunned farmer and instructed the Cole Brothers to do whatever it took to make it work. The contrast would be dramatic – the magnificent and costly casket on the back of a dilapidated wagon.

"You said you drove a Benz blitzed on schnapps?" John asked.

"Hell no! I rode in it. Didn't know how to drive, frankly." Grady glanced out the window. "We, uh, borrowed it from a garage next to a mansion in Germany; borrowed the schnapps, too, come to think of it."

"Ah! World War Two, I bet."

Grady nodded. "Almost got me killed. I went practically straight from the car to the hospital. That's where I met my wife."

John Moody raised his eyebrows and turned toward Grady. "Sounds like quite a story."

"Well, it certainly is."

They were heading east, early morning, into an anemic sun, the mud sucking at their boots, each soldier encased in a cloud of his own breath. A sea of fog clung to the ground, and it was hard to make out exactly where you were going. What you saw most clearly was the man in front of you. When he stopped, you stopped. The platoon slogged to a rest and slowly collapsed upon itself, the soldiers moving closer together, craning their necks to see what obstacle blocked their path. It was a faltering fence of barbed wire, its poles listing. Someone was cutting the wire so that they could pass through. A few of the others followed the meandering, twisted wire to see if it terminated at a gate of some sort.

Grady stayed and helped cut. He was one of the first ones through the hole, using his forearm to push the sharp barbs away from his face. Through the swirling gray mist, he saw something rolling toward him. It seemed to moan as it swept forward like a wave. Then it took shape. Human shape. But humans unlike any he had ever encountered, even here, even in this godforsaken hysteria of humankind that had left bodies and pieces and parts strewn in ruts of anger and hatred. These were humans, certainly, but ones reaching across a threshold. Barefoot, eyes gaping, skin as gray as the striped rags that hung on them. Ghostly in the shroud of mist. Here are the Jews, he suddenly realized, the ones everyone had talked about; the people Bo Hagen had warned him about. One of them came up to him and fell at his feet and hugged his legs and wept. Grady froze. Should he pull this man off? This, this stinking, rotting specter whose arms, despite their emaciation, clung to him with surprising strength? What would the old man think, his son being embraced by a Jew? Grady reached down and stroked the back of the man's head as if he were a baby.

The soldiers were ordered to go into the town – Weimar was the name, they discovered –where they kicked open doors and pulled out citizens and marched them up the road and into the camp. For the next two days Grady and the others pushed the German civilians with the butts of their rifles to keep them at the grim task of burying the corpses. At night the soldiers went back into the town and tried to drink away the faces that screamed through their brains. Anything they purloined was consumed with fury, with no concern for the consequences. Schnapps, brandy, champagne – contraband booze found in cabinets and hidden in the attics of the homes that lined the square. They unfurled a Nazi flag on the sidewalk and watched the Germans walk around it, their heads hanging.

Grady and four others had taken the big black Mercedes touring sedan and raced it around the town, hanging out the windows with bottles in their hands and cursing the German citizens hiding behind their locked doors. They ran the car until it sputtered out of gas not far from the big house they had commandeered as barracks. As they approached a blown-out barn, someone burst through the open door, nothing more, at first, than a shadow in the murky night. It ran toward them, screaming and waving, and Grady swayed as he squinted to make out who, or what, it was. Then he saw that it was a boy, not more than fourteen-fifteen years old. A sliver of light, a mixture of moon and incandescence from a nearby house, slashed across the face, illuminating a stream of tears. The boy shouted something in German, stumbled in a circle, turning completely around, and raised his hand toward the soldiers. In that fraction of a second, Grady realized the kid was holding a pistol.

What happened first was the blow, like a fist – no, more like a hammer – to the solar plexus that literally lifted Grady off his feet, sending his bottle of schnapps propelling through the air. Then, an instant behind, came the noise, a telltale pop, the repeat of a weapon, sound catching up with the bullet. The ground disappeared from beneath him and Grady was face down in the soft earth, a puddle of muddy water running into his eyes and mouth. He instinctively rolled onto his back. A river of flame coursed through him and he tore open his jacket. Blood spurted from a hole in his shirt. Spurted. Arcing up like water from a hose. At that moment Grady Hagen knew he was dying, could feel breath and vision and memory flying out of him. Dying, for chrissakes, when only minutes before he was giddy drunk on his own survival. With the fleeing blood went warmth, and he began to shiver.

With one hand he tried to fight back the tide of blood while with the other – where was his rifle? Blown clean out of his hands, gone somewhere in the high weeds that engulfed him. No wait, not a rifle, a bottle. How could he fight with a bottle? The darkness was getting darker. Someone's hands were on him now.

He reached into his pants pocket and frantically searched for the chain. Wrapping it around his index finger he pulled it and it flowed out like a snake. He held up the silver medal hanging from the end of it, watched it sway in the crescendo of memories that engulfed him. The miraculous medal, Betsy Sue McDonough had called it. And he transferred it to his other hand and held it against the wound.

And the bleeding stopped.

Grady had never told anyone the story and was a bit curious as to why he felt compelled to tell it to John Moody now. Perhaps it was to prove to him that this old man sitting in the passenger seat hadn't been a coward about everything his whole life. Maybe it would quell some of the animosity Moody had to feel – just had to feel – about Grady's complicity in what had transpired in Arbutus in 1942. But there was no hint of disdain in John's voice.

"Your whole life has been quite a story, hasn't it?" he said.

Grady replied, "Isn't everyone's? Isn't yours?"

Moody laughed. "Oh, my God yes. Carrying around in my heart the story of my father. Trying to figure out where I fit into the picture."

"Where you fit in? What do you mean?" Grady asked.

John reached his arm across the console and laid it against Grady's. "Here, look at this."

"What am I looking at?"

"Skin color. Whose is darker? Yours or mine?"

The fact was, the hot Arbutus sun had painted a reddish brown hue onto Grady's arms and, if anything, he might have been darker than Moody.

John didn't wait for an answer. He laughed. "I love doing that to people. You see, there's not much difference there, is there? And yet, every morning the face I saw looking back at me in the mirror was the face of a black man. I wasn't a gnat's ass darker than anyone else, including my parents, but I was still black to the rest of the world. Every school function, there I was with my two white parents, and you could feel people looking at them and me and trying to figure it out." He raised his arm off the console and returned his hand to the steering wheel. "Not that I'm complaining. Not at all. I am who I am, and I'm damn proud of who I've become and what I have accomplished. I am extremely fortunate to have the family I have and to own the perspective on life they've given me. But I was neither fish nor fowl. Not dark enough for the black fraternity, too dark for the white one."

Grady didn't know what to say.

"Made my life interesting," John exhaled.

"I can only imagine," Grady replied.

"Oh, for chrissakes!" John suddenly grumbled. "What the hell is this?" He was gazing up to the rearview mirror.

Grady turned and looked out the back window. A police car, lights whirling atop, was on the Mercedes bumper. Moody pulled over and immediately reached into his back pocket, extracting his wallet. His driver's license was in his hand before the officer was at the window.

"Afternoon," the cop grumbled, taking the license.

"How fast was I going?" John asked.

"Didn't say you were speeding. You got a registration goes with this car here?" the policeman lifted his sunglasses to read the license, "Uh, Mr. Moody."

John reached across Grady's chest and opened the glove compartment. "For the love of Christ," he muttered.

"What's that?" the policeman growled.

"I'm getting you the fucking registration," John spat, turning and locking eyes with the cop.

The policeman smirked. "For a minute I thought you was getting a little uppity with me. You weren't, were you?"

Grady saw Moody's fingers strangle the registration paper, and the old man reached out and stilled John's hand. "Hold on minute," he whispered. He turned to the cop. "Are you with the Arbutus force?"

"Just gimme the registration please."

"Why don't you radio in and tell Chief Mitchell who you've pulled over here?" Grady suggested.

The cop removed his sunglasses and leaned into the car. "Who the hell are you?"

"My name is Grady Hagen, and I'm just saying, before you go any further, you might want to call into your boss. Trust me. You might save yourself a whole shitload of heartache."

The cop looked at the two men, eyes shifting from one face to the other. Then he pushed away from the window and sauntered back to his cruiser.

"Just another nigger with a Benz," John Moody spat. "Let's pick him up, make sure it isn't stolen; at least hassle the boy a bit."

The word – *that word* – reverberated through the air like an aspen in the wind, and ignited Grady's core. The old man looked for words, but couldn't find any, not a single one that was appropriate to what was happening.

A few minutes later, the policeman was back at the window, his hat off. He handed the license back to John Moody. "You can go," he said, turning and walking back to the patrol car.

Moody put the license in his wallet, wrenched the car into gear and pulled away. "That's what I mean," he grumbled.

46

He was home, a place he once believed he would never see again, would never be again. Walking up the sidewalk, he felt like air, alive with anticipation; like right before a storm, full of ozone and mist. At the same time, he felt as if he wasn't really there. Everything around him fuzzed out, except for the front door. Bright red – she had made him paint it to accent the brick trim on the lower half of the house. Now, this door, with the brass knocker in the middle just below the arched windows, reached out and pulled him in. Home. His home. God almighty, his home.

Grady was half way to it when he heard the sound.

"Woof." A single, deep, friendly noise.

He turned in the direction of the sound and jumped backward in surprise and delight and with a feeling that took his breath away. A big and familiar ball of gold, like the sun, romped to him. "Oh, God, Sammy, Sammy!" Grady cried as the glorious dog, the only dog he had ever owned, pounced to him, spinning around, running between his legs, rubbing fur and love all over him. Grady squatted and reached out, pulling the dog in. "Sammy, Sammy, where have you been?" Sammy responded by leaping forward and putting both paws on his master's shoulders and licking his face.

"My good boy, my good, good boy," Grady cried, tears streaming down his face. His heart was like a kite that had broken its string, caught up in gusts of sheer joy. Sammy panted in his ear, crying, too. Then they were moving together toward the front door.

Grady ascended the stoop and patted his pockets.

No key.

Where the hell is the key? He opened his sport coat, reached inside the breast pocket. Nothing. Gol'dangit, where was the key? Not in his pants. Not in his coat. Wait! They always kept a spare on a hook under the flower box. He leaned to his right across a rose bush.

Inside the house the phone rang.

He stretched, but couldn't reach the key. Where the hell was it?

The phone rang again.

Shit! Panic overtook his joy. He had to get into that house! He had to get that telephone!

Ring.

Where's the goddamn key?

Riiiinnnnggg!

He couldn't breathe.

Grady sat bare-legged, his feet on the floor of a room that was spinning, as if the air had been let out of it, frantic and fast, then slowing down, taking form. It was dark, but light was approaching, filling the space, leaking in. He blinked, teetered, caught himself with his hand. His flesh goosebumped, the hair standing straight up in the cold. He heard a word drip out of his mouth.

"Sammy."

Sammy. But Sammy was gone, of course. The old dog had died ten, maybe twelve, years ago. Sammy had adopted Grady, not the other way around. He was a little ball of fur who tumbled out of a box in front of the Callaway's house, knocking over the "Free Puppies" sign and following Grady, yapping and jumping the whole way. In the three short blocks it took to get home, a bond had developed, and Sammy became Grady's constant companion, going fishing and riding and Frisbee catching with him; always smiling and barking and licking when he came home. But then, as time does, it wore the dog out until – some fourteen years later – he couldn't get up on his hind legs anymore, and they had to put him to sleep to get the sorrow and pain out of his eyes.

No Sammy. My best pal, Sammy. And Grady's heart broke again.

Charlie was a tangle of flesh and linen, facing him, his eyes closed. He pressed a phone to his ear. "H'llo," he mumbled. Then his eyes opened and he sat up. "Hello, Babe," he said, running his hands through his hair and yawning.

Grady heard a nibbling of noise through the receiver.

"You're shitting me!" Charlie said, standing up and sliding things around on the nightstand that separated the two beds. He pulled the phone below his chin. "Pap, where's the remote control?" he said.

Grady reached behind the lamp and found it. "Here."

"Turn it on, turn on the television," Charlie said, pointing toward the TV. "What channel did you say?" he said into the phone.

Grady pushed the power button and the television sputtered alive.

"Channel seven," Charlie said.

Grady, his hands still tingling from the abrupt awakening, fumbled with the tiny buttons, finally hitting the seven.

Chief Caleb Mitchell's face filled the screen. He was in the middle of a sentence. ". . . the remains are being examined and we should have a, uh, identification within ten days to two weeks."

"Sumbitch," Grady grunted.

"Do you fucking believe this?" Charlie cried. Then back into the phone, "Sorry, Star."

The news reporter, an attractive blonde woman, honed in. "Is there any doubt in your mind, Chief, that these are the remains of Rudy Montcrief, the black man who was lynched in Arbutus many years ago?"

"We can't speculate on that at this time; we're going to have to let the identification process run its course."

"But aren't you fairly confident, based on the nature of how and where you found them that you have Mr. Montcrief's remains?"

Chief Mitchell was walking away now, and the reporter had to jog to keep pace. "Can you tell us about the man who led you to these remains?"

Mitchell didn't turn his head. "I have no comment to make on that at this time," he said, ducking into the squad car.

The reporter turned to the camera. "That was Police Chief Caleb Mitchell, commenting on a breaking story here in Arbutus regarding a man, reportedly a former resident of the town, named, uh," she glanced down at a small notepad in her hand, "Graden Hagen or perhaps Hayden, who just suddenly showed up a few days ago to, our sources tell us, turn himself in for the lynching of a black man way back somewhere circa nineteen forty-one or two."

The scene cut to a newsroom. The field reporter's face stayed in a box in the corner. The silver-haired anchor man spoke. "Is this some sort of guilt trip this man took, coming back after all these years?"

"We don't know, Frank. We're trying to locate him now to ask him that very question."

"Can he be prosecuted for this crime, Melinda?"

"Certainly, there is no statute of limitations on murder, but earlier today Chief Mitchell said they don't have enough evidence showing that this Hagen or Hayden had a direct hand in the lynching. We're looking into the facts and will have things sorted out by the noon broadcast."

"Melinda, thanks," the anchorman said.

Charlie turned his attention back to the telephone. "What do we do now?" he whispered. Then he listened for several seconds. "Okay, talk to him. I'll talk to Pap. We have to figure something out." Charlie clicked off the television. "Oh, boy," he said.

Grady rested his arms on his knees and braced his head. "I think the words you're looking for are, 'Oh, fuck' or something on that order."

"See, it is a very useful word now and then," Charlie deadpanned.

"Yeah," Grady sighed.

The telephone rang. Charlie picked it up and quickly snarled. "Oh, shit." He dropped the phone into the cradle.

"Who was it?"

"Hotel manager," Charlie said, standing up and walking toward the window, scratching his ass and yawning. "I think we're in for an interesting day," he said, peeking through the heavy plastic curtain. "Holy shit," he repeated. "Take a look at this."

Grady teetered to his feet and shuffled to the window. He glanced through the crack. A crowd of people stood in the parking lot. Camera operators, reporters, gapers. Four vans with satellite dishes were scattered among the other vehicles. "Oh, fuck," Grady said.

"Nice language," Charlie replied, letting the curtain go.

Fifteen minutes later he and Charlie were in John Moody's room with all the players in the drama. Principia sat in the vinyl chair under the lamp. Charlotta was perched on the armrest, holding the old woman's hand. Yvonne leaned against the bureau with her arms folded, and Cissy and Starling sat on the edge of the bed. The telephone was off the hook.

"You have, indeed, opened up a can of worms, Mr. Hagen," John Moody said, tossing a newspaper onto the bed.

The front page of the *Arbutus Daily Democrat* contained a single photo that bled from edge to edge. The limp body of Rudy Montcrief seemed to sway, and you could hear the shouts of the crowd that surrounded him, even though the reproduction of the hideous picture card was as frozen as it had been in the millisecond it was created. This confluence of light and shadow and chemistry, this miracle that stopped time forever, still had a power to breathe, it seemed, especially when exploded to such a large size. And there, sure enough, taking the air out of Grady's lungs was the boy he used to be. He turned his head in shame. It was like an electric jolt, restarting a heart.

Above the photo and bearing Maggie's Dyson's byline was the headline: "A Man's Soul - Free at Last."

How she had gotten it, Grady could only surmise. Most likely Parker Moody, perhaps someone else. Hundreds, maybe thousands, had been printed, after all.

Starling lifted the broadsheet and stared not at, it seemed, but *into* the photograph. "That's my granddaddy there," she whispered, a silver tear rolling down her cheek.

"My daddy," John replied. "Just a boy. Just a boy."

"I'm glad I'm blind," Principia spat, "Don't have to look upon that trash."

"I'm very sorry. For cripes sakes, I've said that so much lately it doesn't even sound true to me anymore," Grady said. "Frankly, I don't know what to say."

John opened the palms of his hands and waved the words away. "Don't need to apologize to us. This isn't a bad thing. Not at all."

"But, God, John, have you seen what's outside? The media, a million questions, the invasion of privacy," Grady stammered.

"Maybe America needs to be jolted back to reality every now and again," John answered. "Get a wake up call."

"Johnny!" Cissy said.

"It's true, Momma. My daddy, my birth daddy, died before I was even born for no reason. No reason under the sun. Until now."

"Until now!" Principia echoed.

"Oh, Johnny," Cissy whispered.

"Now he has come alive again," John Moody said, making a fist and looking up to the ceiling. "To show people, to speak to people . . ."

"Speak to people!" Principia repeated.

". . . remind folks that hatred is ugly and sinful and destructive to mankind."

"Destructive!" Principia shouted.

"To maybe make men get down on their knees and ask God to take it out of them, all that hate and prejudice," John said, opening his hand and holding it above his head.

"God, take it!" Principia cried.

"To give my daddy a purpose for his living, and his dying," he said, closing his hand and dropping it. "To maybe change one man's heart. Wouldn't that be something? To change one man's heart?"

"One heart!" Principia intoned.

Silence strained to escape the room. Settling on everything. John Moody coughed and stuck his hands in his pockets. "I'm sorry," he croaked, "to get so worked up."

"But you're right," Grady said, walking toward him. "You're right." He took the man in his arms and they embraced. "If they want the story, they're going to get it."

"Praise God for Grady Hagen!" Principia wept, raising her hands and looking to the heavens.

Pulling away from John Moody, Grady moved toward the door.

"Pappy, what are you doing?" Charlie asked, moving toward him and taking his arm.

"They're out there for me," he said. "And they won't stop until they get me. Let's cut to the chase."

"You're not facing them alone," Charlie said.

Charlotta stood up. "I'm going with him."

Cissy was already at his side. "You took the words right outta my mouth!"

Principia tried to stand. "Get my chariot. They gonna have to deal with me, too!"

Yvonne Moody pulled away from the bureau and situated herself in front of the door. "Whoa, whoa, settle down, everyone. Just settle down," she said, holding both hands out. "If we're going to deal with this, we have to do it correctly. That means having a plan and not running off half-cocked, not thinking about what you might want to say." She turned her head and looked straight at John, raising an eyebrow in the process.

John Moody sat down on the edge of the bed. "Okay, what do we do?"

"Momma's in public relations," Starling whispered to Charlie.

"First we think about what the questions are going to be and exactly how we're going to answer them."

Cissy pulled a notepad and pen out of the desk drawer. "Okay, let's go," she said.

Yvonne continued. "Then I think we should call the manager of this hotel and have them prepare their largest meeting room," Yvonne interjected. "We're not letting Grandma-ma out in that hot sun."

John Moody smiled. "What a family we have here! What a family!"

47

How must they have looked, this family, this amalgamated family of black and white, young, middle-aged, old and ancient, lined shoulder to shoulder on chairs behind two eight-foot tables? Principia Montcrief dazzled like the sun in a bright yellow dress and matching floppy hat. "This is not a day for black," she'd said. "That's for when we take my boy to Jesus."

They told their tale from the angle and view of it that each of them had occupied. This simple act of truth had stripped from all of them the anonymity they had worn their entire lives, tearing it to rags. And their images and their stories were digitized and propelled into the skies and burned onto printing plates and transferred to paper in millions of tiny dots, and like water from a broken dam, poured into homes throughout the world. And when they had finished, when more than two hours of questions from the frantic, huddled, screeching, reaching, shouting crowd of reporters had been answered, Grady, drained of color and air, believed it was, at last, over. But, of course, he was wrong. It had just begun.

The personal, private journey upon which Grady Hagen had embarked little more than a week ago, had become a story for all humanity to hear, and the media could not get enough of it. Hordes of people besieged the tiny hamlet. Reporters and television crews continued to arrive from everywhere, of course, as did politicians, civil rights activists, lawyers, analysts, and people on the periphery of political opinion. They dangled on tree branches and clambered atop satellite vans, staked out squares of territory with their lights, thrust microphones into the faces of citizens, and drained the grocery store of bottled water. It seemed that the residents of the town had virtually abdicated the street to these frantic invaders, moving up and into the windows of the storefronts. By the day of the funeral, more than 15,000 people, one of the newspapers estimated, had gathered in Arbutus to be a part of Rudy Montcrief's final journey. It was as if someone had emptied a jar of ants onto a picnic blanket. Their presence rang through the streets in a rambunctious clatter of indecipherable sounds. In the crowd were faces of many colors, and Grady, dressed in his dark suit and holding his mother's Bible as the State Police led him through the sea, could see in those with which he connected extraordinarily disparate expressions, fueled by what had to be the internal combustion of thought and emotion, as different in each as the color of skin, or age, or origin.

Hands reached out to him, like branches in a windstorm, pounding, patting, waving copies of the newspaper with the post card image, begging him to autograph the grisly scene. Words flew at him:

"Murderer."

"Nigger lover."

"Look what you've done to us."

"Autograph, please, please!"

"You are a hero."

"Are you sorry, now?"

"Can you sign my paper?"

"What took so long?"

"Why'd you stop with just one?"

"You're a fool."

"We admire your courage."

A person was elbowing through the crowd, her hair nailed in place even in this hot weather, a white blazer with Channel 15 on the pocket. "Mr. Hagen, sir, Jessica Bell from News 15 in Jackson. Can you tell me what you're feeling here this morning?"

"No, thank you, ma'am," Grady replied.

"I see you have a Bible in your hands, sir. Can you tell us why?" Jessica Bell said, pulling the cord on her microphone and trying to keep up.

"I'm on my way to a funeral."

"Are you planning to read some scripture during the services?"

"No."

"Does it make you feel," she yanked the cord free from beneath the foot of one of the people in the crowd as the cameraman struggled to keep up. "Are you proud of what you have done here today? Does it make up for . . ." she glanced at a spiral notebook she carried in her other hand, "uh, what happened on this very spot in nineteen forty, uh, two?"

Grady stopped and flicked a bead of sweat from beneath his eye. His shirt underneath his suit coat was being sucked against his skin by the heat. He turned to Jessica Bell. "One thing I've learned in the past few days," he said, barely above a murmur, "is that no man can redeem himself. Redemption is a road you can't travel alone. Mercy is granted, a gift that comes from the kindness of others."

Jessica Bell hesitated, thinking of another question, and Grady tried to push past her, his fingers clutching the blue shirt of the trooper who cleared a path. But in a few strides, the microphone was once again in his face. "Mr. Hagen, what kind of a man *are* you?" The question poured over him like acid.

He stopped. Through all the thousands of questions he'd answered, here was one that had not been asked in a dozen ways, and Grady wondered what she meant by it. Was it some veiled insult, or a sincere attempt to try to package him in some way so that somehow the world would understand? "I am a man. That's all I am. I'm not a particularly good man, not particularly bad, either, at least I don't think so, deep down inside," he said. Then he pushed forward.

Somehow through the cacophony and anarchy, he heard Principia's voice. "We ain't goin' without Mr. Grady," she cried. "Where is Mr. Grady?"

"Here he comes, Momma love," Charlotta said.

He could see them now, in the center of a wide hole in the crowd. John Moody first, tall and proud, holding the hand of his beautiful wife, Yvonne. Charlotta and Cissy and Starling, strung together next to them, wearing matching black dresses. And, of course, the regal Principia. She was seated in her wheelchair, shoulders thrown back, head high. She wore black, too, but atop her head was a flowered hat of explosive burgundy, wrapped in a mauve ribbon that flowed onto her shoulders.

Starling caught his eye, and Grady mouthed the words, "Where's Charlie?" She pantomimed taking a picture and opened both hands upward, looking out at the crowd. Photography had gone from a hobby to a profession for the young man in one single moment when a reporter for *Time* magazine learned that Charlie had been taking pictures from the first day of the journey. The publisher bought the rights to the photos and hired him to chronicle the funeral.

Grady was clear now of the masses, moving toward the family, when he saw something else. It wasn't, of course, unexpected. But the reality of it being here now, the magnitude of his history, and the journey it represented, took his breath away.

The rosewood casket, setting in the back of the old sharecropper's wagon which had been hammered back together and greased up, but not painted ("Oh, no not painted. That would ruin it now, wouldn't it?" John Moody had insisted). A mule, gray and fat, was harnessed to the front, and he kept swishing his tail and looking back, wondering when he should begin. Grady closed his eyes and bowed his head.

It was the second time Rudy Montcrief had been brought to this square, borne on the shoulders of a crowd.

When he reopened his eyes everything had disappeared. The crowd. The noises. The rustling of trees. All that remained was a single person, standing on the curb, angelic in a cameo of mist, like when a window frosts up, except for the spot you scrape off with the heel of your hand to see out.

Rachel.

Radiant and beautiful. Mystical. Ethereal.

"Hello, baby," she said to him.

He said hello with his heart, and she heard him.

"Everything is okay now," she said, blowing him a kiss and then dissipating.

The scene converged inward on him again, like a building in collapse. He heard Principia's voice.

"Mr. Grady, is that you, at last?" the old lady sang.

Grady saw her there, resplendent, and moved to her. He twisted the Bible in his hand as he approached. "Mizz Principia, I got no right to walk with you," he said.

301

She reached out, her hands scurrying down his forearm, finding his own. "You gonna walk with me!" she said. "Walk straight, boy. Walk proud."

Then the crowd immediately to Grady's left ripped open and five men emerged, coming toward the family. Dressed in black suits, shoes impeccably shined, they were followed by several camera crews. Grady recognized the man in the center. Reverend Eli Grant, civil rights activist, presidential candidate, friend of Martin Luther King, Jr., strode toward Principia, stopped and leaned to her.

"Who's that?" she said. "Who's coming to me?"

"Mizz Montcrief," he said, lifting her free hand and shaking it. "I am Eli Grant."

Principia's eyes widened. "Pleased to meet you, Reverend. Thank you for coming to my boy's funeral." She dropped his hand and rattled Grady's. "Let's go."

"Mizz Montcrief," Reverend Grant bored in. "I just want to extend to you my sympathy and prayers on this momentous day."

"Thank you. Now let's go."

"I would like your permission to offer a short eulogy at the graveside, if I may."

Principia looked forward. "That's a very kind offer comin', from a man of your stature, but you didn't know my boy, Reverend."

"I knew him as a brother in our struggle. We are all united in that way, ma'am."

She turned and looked up at him. Her face softened. "I'm sure your words would be elegant, but it just don't seem appropriate to me."

Reverend Grant plastered his finest smile on his face. "Mizz Montcrief, the whole world is watching you today. We have here a momentous opportunity to reach our people with an important message."

By now the television cameras and microphones had tightened into a knot around the scene. Principia motioned with her free hand. "Come closer. I need to tell you something."

Reverend Eli Grant, knelt on one knee and lowered his head next to hers. She placed her mouth a few inches from his ear. "You know,

Reverend, all due respect, I been listening to you now for forty years. And you know what I hear?"

"Please tell me," Reverend Grant replied, smiling.

"Nothin' but words."

"Uh . . ."

"Know what I see? I see my people going backwards. Families deteriorating. I see blacks killing blacks. I see drugs and despair and no hope. I see no daddies at home and kids who don't even care to learn to read. I see grammas raising the babies of their drug addicted daughters."

Reverend Grant expectorated a nervous laugh. "Our struggle is far from over . . ."

Principia interrupted, "Racism? Sure, it's out there everywhere. I ain't no fool woman. But we ain't never gonna conquer it until we deal with what we're doing to ourselves."

"The effects of a racist society."

Principia put a finger up. "Try this, Reverend. Tell our children to stay in school. Tell our brothers that if they make a baby they take care of that baby. Tell them that at some time in their lives, they need to rise up and take responsibility for who they are and who they gonna be, regardless of what happened in the past." She grabbed Grady's hand in both of hers. "Talk to them about courage instead of hate. Give them pride, not false pride because they belong to the red gang or the blue gang, but pride in their minds and in their accomplishments."

Reverend Grant rose, forcing a smile. "We do, Mizz Principia," he muttered.

"Very nice to meet you Reverend Grant. We're honored that you come to help us lay our boy to rest." She slapped a hand on her thigh. "Now, let me take my boy home. Who's pushing me?"

"I am, ma'am," said a young black man with "Cole Brothers Funeral Home" embroidered on his black suit coat.

"What's your name?" Principia asked.

"I'm Anthony, ma'am."

"Well, then, Anthony, let's go," she said. Her voice cracked. "Let's take Rudy home."

And so they marched down Jefferson, pulling the crowd with them. Silence descended as the procession swept by. The wagon groaned and swayed. They passed the jailhouse. Chief Mitchell stood out front with his entire troop; white men and black men at attention, dressed in clean and pressed uniforms. At Mitchell's orders and in unison, they raised their right hands to their temples and saluted. The marchers moved past the Civil War statue, around the corner and directly in front of the spot where the tree once stood. Principia's hand stayed entwined with Grady's own. Her smile never faltered as her wheelchair rambled over the cracks and bumps in the street. Grady didn't even try to stop the tears from running down his cheeks.

They walked to the far end of town, and the colored graveyard where a few stones stood, but most of the graves were marked with simple numbers imbedded in small concrete inserts. Three black men leaned on shovels, in the shade away from the canopy that hovered over the hole in the ground. The associates from the funeral home helped Cissy and John and Starling and Yvonne and Charlotta carry the coffin to the graveside. When the remains of Rudy Montcrief were at last lowered into a consecrated, hallowed place, the family, as was the custom, grabbed handfuls of dirt which they trickled and tossed into the hole. When Grady approached, he reached into his jacket pocket and pulled out the shredded remnants of the picture card. He squeezed the pieces tightly for a second or two and then released them. A few caught the wind and blew away, but most just fluttered down into the grave, like flakes of snow.

48

"Why are you stopping here?" Grady asked, as Charlie pulled the Mustang into the parking lot of the old baseball field just outside Arbutus.

"'Cause I think you're full of shit," Charlie answered, laughing.

Starling reached up from the back seat and squeezed Grady's shoulders. "He means, full of beans."

"Oh, that's better," Grady snapped.

"C'mon, get out," Charlie ordered, throwing the car into park, shutting off the engine, and opening the door in one motion. He was outside the car now, moving toward the trunk.

What the hell was this kid doing now? Grady grunted as he used the open door to pull himself to his feet. Starling slid out like an egg on Teflon. "C'mon, Pappy, let's go," Charlie said, head in the trunk.

Grady came around to where he was standing. "What are you up to?"

"Here," Charlie replied, tossing Grady his old baseball cap.

"What the . . ." he choked out before the next object came sailing at him. His hand shot up to catch it. His old mitt. "What's all this?"

"It's your stuff from Truman's house. You didn't think I was going to leave it there, did you? Hell, this stuff is history." Charlie turned and dove back into the trunk. Grady could hear the rattle of wood. "Ta da!" Charlie said, turning and holding up a bat and ball.

"Where'd you get that?"

"I always carry my softball gear with me."

305

"That ain't a softball, I hate to tell you," Grady said, pointing to the shiny white sphere in Charlie's hand.

"It's the one you bought from that kid on the street."

"What you gonna do with it?"

"What the heck were you planning to do with this ball anyway?" Charlie answered, flipping it up and catching it. "Hell, you paid twenty bucks for it. Let's get going."

"For what possible purpose?"

"C'mon, hit the field, old man," Charlie said, turning Grady toward the open gate. "Put your hat on."

"What the hell you doing?" Grady asked.

By now Star had reached into the trunk and extracted a baseball cap and Charlie's softball mitt. "Play ball!" she said.

"I'm going to find out if what you and everyone else in this town says is true," Charlie answered, pushing open the gate. "That that there mitt was where line drives went to die."

"You're kidding?" Grady chuckled.

"I'm saying, all you could ever do was knock a ball down with that dead possum. You couldn't get a wad of moist glue to stick in that thing. Now, if I'm wrong about that, prove it."

"Knock down, my ass," Grady growled, tugging the hat over his hairline and slipping the mitt on his left hand. He pounded it into a cup shape. Then he held it up. "Just like that! Ain't nothing ever got through it alive."

"Put your money where your mouth is."

Grady ambled out to centerfield, the grass soft under his shoes. He could see Charlie with the bat on his shoulder, standing at home plate. "You ready?" the boy shouted.

Grady pounded a fist into the mitt again. "Hey batter, no batter, hey batter, no batter," he chanted.

Charlie tossed the ball in the air and pulled the bat back in a single motion. Grady saw it, the ball, coming off the bat, followed by the sound. It flew toward him, no, too far left. Shit. It whooshed like a jet plane over his head. Gol'dangit. Starling ran to it in the grass and threw it back.

"You have to move at least a little bit," Charlie shouted. "Try this." He tossed the ball up again and swung.

306

This time it landed twenty feet in front of him. Grady pounded his fist in the mitt and gritted his teeth. Go where it's going, not where it is, he thought. The key, he had always understood, was creating a point of convergence. He crouched, leaned both hands on his knees, and watched Charlie toss the ball into the air.

This time Grady was moving with the crack of the bat. The ball soared, again to his left, but he was already going that way, like it was 1940 and he was a kid, and his legs were swift and strong, and there was no more beautiful feeling in all of God and man's creation than the arc of a baseball against a pure blue sky. He was running now, actually running, and all time melted away. The ball accelerated, and Grady could hear it sizzling in the air.

He thrust his left arm out, opened the fingers on the flat and dry leather and the ball fell into it. He instinctively squeezed at the exact point of impact and pulled the mitt and glove toward his body. His momentum carried him a few more steps and he stopped. Gasping. Laughing. He held the ball over his head.

"I'll be damned!" Charlie said.

"Whoo, whoo, whoo!" Starling squealed, rolling her fist in the air.

Grady threw the ball toward the infield. It didn't make it all the way, of course. "Hit me another one," the boy inside him shouted.

About The Author

In a writing career that spans more than three decades, Michael J. Griffin has won more than 100 national and international awards for his work. As a journalist, advertising executive, public speaker, consultant and director he has written fiction, articles, top-level corporate communications, films, speeches, brochures, advertising campaigns, marketing plans, music, lyrics, and training programs for some of the most well-known names in business and industry.